Praise for

BUDDHA'S ORPHANS

"This absorbing novel is as rich in its quiet moments of loneliness and tea making as it is powerful in its presentation of an ancient culture . . . Upadhyay's masterful prose shows increasing sophistication and a grasp of the sublime, and he is surprisingly effective in conveying the horrors and wonders of motherhood . . . Beautifully told."

—*Publishers Weekly* (starred review)

"[Upadhyay] is a marvelous storyteller, literate and engaging, lyrical and sensitive . . . Samrat Upadhyay puts us in a world we know little about and makes us feel at home. Who could ask for more?"

—Bookreporter.com

"A success . . . Upadhyay offers us a narrative which calls attention to a country often overlooked with the pan-ethnic rubric that situates the field."

—*Feminist Review*

"Upadhyay has masterfully blended history, tragedy, politics, and romance to create the arresting story of a family that is at once unique and universal, set against the backdrop of a vibrant, complicated, modern Nepal that will fascinate readers."

—Chitra Divakaruni, author of
One Amazing Thing and *The Palace of Illusions*

"Literature strives to provide an authentic glimpse into the inner life of another being, a momentary insight into the human truth of suffering, impermanence, and liberation. At the same time, fiction can offer a tempting . . . respite from the difficult work of finding those truths within ourselves. Upadhyay's skillful telling of Raja and Nilu's losses and loves, their politics and their passions, gives us some of each."

—*Tricycle*

Praise for
SAMRAT UPADHYAY

"Upadhyay is among the smoothest and most noiseless of contemporary writers."

—*Los Angeles Times*

"Upadhyay strips down even further Lahiri's and Sharma's most un-American style—a plain prose that skillfully accentuates the emptiness and tension of each character. It is a style as fresh as the coconut oil one of Upadhyay's women might comb into her hair."

—*Newsday*

"Stories with an exceptional sense of place . . . The primary attraction, however, is Upadhyay's sharp eye for human psychology, his ability to write with clarity about emotions common in the everyday."

—*Cleveland Plain Dealer*

"[Upadhyay] writes about his middle-class Nepalese characters with humor and compassion."

—*New York Times*

"Upadhyay's writing is complex and delicate."

—*Baltimore Sun*

"Without flinching, Upadhyay burrows deeply into his native culture and emerges without pat endings. But we are wiser for what he illuminates: a culture struggling to modernize, and the conflicts that loom large in the traditionalist's psyche."

—*Philadelphia Inquirer*

"Upadhyay writes unflinchingly about displacement and deprivation in the Nepalese capital of Kathmandu."

—*Bloomsbury Review*

"[Upadhyay's] delicate realism helps us recognize, with compassion and awareness, the stories and feelings of which our own lives are composed. Fiction doesn't get much better than this."

—Kate Wheeler, author of
When Mountains Walked

BUDDHA'S ORPHANS

BOOKS BY SAMRAT UPADHYAY

Arresting God in Kathmandu

The Guru of Love

The Royal Ghosts

Buddha's Orphans

Buddha's Orphans

Samrat Upadhyay

MARINER BOOKS
HOUGHTON MIFFLIN HARCOURT
BOSTON   NEW YORK

First Mariner Books edition 2011

Copyright © 2010 by Samrat Upadhyay

www.hmhbooks.com

Library of Congress Cataloging-in-Publication Data
Upadhyay, Samrat.
Buddha's Orphans / Samrat Upadhyay.
p. cm.
ISBN 978-0-618-51750-3
ISBN 978-0-547-46990-4 (pbk.)
1. Orphans — Fiction. 2. Nepal — Politics and government
— Fiction. 3. Nepal — Fiction. I. Title.
PR9570.N43Q84 2010
823'.92 — dc22   2009014019

Book design by Melissa Lotfy

Printed in the United States of America

DOC 10 9 8 7 6 5 4 3 2 1

Quotations on page xi are translated by Jeffrey Hopkins,
Geshe Michael Roach, and Bradford Hatcher, respectively.

To the women in my family:
Ammi, Sangeeta, Babita,
and my "snow leopard" Shahzadi

While you see that those close to you are drowning in the ocean
    of cyclic existence,
And are as if fallen into a whirlwind of fire,
There is nothing more awful than to work for your own liberation,
Neglecting those whom you do not recognize due to the process
    of death and rebirth.

— Chandragomin, "Letter to a Student"

Learn to see that everything
Brought about by causes
Is like a star,
A problem in your eye,
A lamp, an illusion,
The dew, or a bubble;
A dream, or lightning,
Or else a cloud.

— from The Diamond Cutter Sutra

Even the shortest of moments might be at least six days wide.

— Gua 57, The Book of Changes

Book One

Part I

Orphan

R AJA'S MOTHER HAD abandoned him on the parade ground of Tundikhel on a misty morning before Kathmandu had awakened, then drowned herself in Rani Pokhari, half a kilometer north. No one connected the cries of the baby to the bloated body of the woman that would float to the surface of the pond later that week. The School Leaving Certificate exam results had just been published in *Gorkhapatra,* so everyone deduced that the woman, like a few others already that year, 1962, had killed herself over her poor performance.

That morning Kaki was at Rani Pokhari, getting ready to sell her corn on the sidewalk, when she saw Bokey Ba approach from the parade ground area, carrying something on his palms, as if balancing a tray.

"After ages, Bokey Ba is coming to visit me," Kaki said to the woman who was sweeping the sidewalk in front of the shoe shop, where Kaki sold her corn. Bokey Ba, so called because of the goat-like beard hanging from his chin, was a derelict who'd made the parade ground his home for no one knew how long.

He knelt in front of Kaki. In his arms was a baby swaddled in a woman's dirty shawl. Kaki let out a gasp. "Whose baby did you steal? Look, Vaishali, come here."

Vaishali ambled over. Her hand flew to her mouth. "Let's fetch the police," she said to Kaki. "What did this nut case do?"

"Whose baby is this?" Kaki spoke loudly, even though Bokey Ba wasn't hard of hearing. "Tell me, where did you get it?" She gingerly reached over and lifted the shawl. "It's a boy," she whispered. "And barely a few months old. Bokey Ba, what are you doing with this baby?"

Bokey Ba tried to form the words, but they didn't come. It had literally been months since he'd talked to anyone. He pointed behind him, toward Tundikhel.

"Where's the baby's mother?"

Bokey Ba shrugged, cleared his throat, and managed to hoarsely say, "Don't know."

"So why bring him here?" Vaishali said. "Take him back. What can we do?"

"Wait," Kaki told her. "Let me look."

Bokey Ba handed her the baby, and thinking that his job was done, he stood and was about to leave when Kaki yelled at him, "Where are you going? Sit!"

Bokey Ba sat on his haunches. Kaki inspected the baby's face, running her fingers over it. "He seems healthy enough." The baby began to cry again, and she said, "Maybe he's hungry." Her maternal instinct made her want to open her blouse and let the baby feed on her breasts, but she realized how foolish that was: a dry woman past middle age in a crowded street, feeding a baby she didn't know. So she requested that Vaishali mind her corn station as she and Bokey Ba looked for the baby's mother.

For the rest of the morning, Kaki and Bokey Ba roamed the area in search of someone who'd claim the baby. Kaki walked in front, clutching the baby to her chest, already feeling protective. She puckered her lips in kisses at him whenever he cried. They circled Rani Pokhari, where the mother's body now rested at the bottom of the pond. The pond was said to be haunted at night by ghosts of those who'd committed suicide in its waters and those who had been repeatedly dunked, as state punishment, until they could no longer breathe.

But for restless students at Tri-Chandra College, the sight of the pond had a calming effect as they skipped classes and spent hours on the roof, smoking, discussing politics. It had been more than two years since King M's coup, and he showed no sign of returning power to the elected officials.

Bokey Ba and Kaki entered the grounds of Tri-Chandra College, both of them looking out of place among the college students loitering on the lawn and drinking tea; then the two continued on to the premises of the Ghantaghar clock tower and finally returned to the khari tree on the parade ground, where Bokey Ba slept at night. The baby hadn't stopped crying all morning, so Kaki handed him to Bokey Ba and went to fetch some milk. Bokey Ba sat on the platform surrounding the tree, holding the infant, afraid to look at his face, and the baby's cry rang out across the field, attracting the attention of some of the regulars. A small crowd formed around Bokey Ba, hazarding guesses as to what had transpired: the old man had stolen the baby from a rich merchant; the baby was Bokey Ba's own child, born from the womb of an old prostitute. Stoically, Bokey Ba waited in silence for Kaki, who arrived after some delay. She'd had to appeal to a neighbor of hers to lend her a bottle and some warm milk.

Kaki shooed the crowd away. "Here, feed him," she said, handing the bottle to the old man, who shook his head. "You found him," she insisted. "You feed him." He took the warm bottle from her and inserted the nipple into the baby's mouth, and he sucked hungrily. His eyes explored Bokey Ba's face as he drank. Soon the bottle was empty, and the baby began to bawl once more. When Bokey Ba looked helplessly at Kaki, she laughed. "Rock him, sing to him. He's yours now."

And before Bokey Ba could say anything, she traversed the field to her corn station, where Vaishali was battling the coal embers and complaining that the smoke was stinging her eyes. "This is not easy work," she told Kaki, who took over.

Kaki grilled corncobs on the sidewalk and sold them at one suka apiece. Early in the morning she'd remove, one by one, the outer husks from corn she had purchased from a farmer. Around eight o'clock, once the area began to thicken with people, she'd light her earthenware stove, a makal, which was filled with pieces of coal. She'd first grill the corn over an open fire, then cook it further in coal embers, letting the heat perform its magic and using her fingers, which were callused and thick, to turn the cobs occasionally. This was a good spot to do business. The bus stop stood across the street, at the entrance to Tundikhel. The marketplace of Asan was only a furlong away, to the right, and the girls' college, Padma Kanya, was up the street, to the east. The girls from Padma Kanya College especially loved Kaki's corn, which she dabbed with a special paste of green chutney that teased, tickled, then shot flames in the mouth, making her customers go "Shooooo" and "Shaaaaaa." The two other corn sellers in the area, one stationed at the mouth of Asan and the other close to the Muslim enclave near the Ghantaghar clock tower, didn't command as large a clientele as Kaki did. Her advantage was that chutney, and though the two other corn sellers had tried to pry the recipe from her, Kaki kept it a secret and made her chutney at home.

The following week, Kaki and Bokey Ba took the baby to the Bal Ashram orphanage in Naxal. The lady who ran it told them that no space was available and that the government had decreed that only those orphans who had absolutely no one to take care of them could be accepted. The woman insinuated that she didn't believe Kaki's story, that perhaps the baby was a product of her illegitimate union with the homeless man with the goatee.

Bokey Ba held the baby in his arms as he and Kaki walked all the way back to Tundikhel in the afternoon sun. They passed the back of the old royal palace in Tangal. Nearby, in the field where the washer people, the dhobis, worked, clothes hung from ropes and fluttered in the wind. Bokey Ba suddenly stopped. Before Kaki knew what was happening, he tightened his grip on the baby with his right arm, and with his left hand he clawed at the wall, feeling for a crack he could grasp to hoist himself up. But the royal wall was covered with moss, and his fingers kept slipping. The baby slid from his grip. Had Kaki's arm not shot out and caught the baby's leg, the young thing would have crashed headfirst to the ground, maybe broken his neck. "Have you gone insane? What do you think—this orphan is really a king?" She scolded the old man and held the baby close to her chest as they resumed their walk.

Dark, monstrous clouds had gathered in the sky. Kaki knew that the monsoon season was terribly difficult for Bokey Ba. The branches of the khari tree didn't block the lashes of rain, which slanted in under it; throughout the night the poor man clasped his knees, wet and shivering. Sometimes he slipped in through the hole in the gate of Bir Hospital nearby and waited out the downpour under the awning of its main entrance, in the company of several street dogs. But the baby couldn't survive that; he needed better shelter against the monsoons.

As though sensing Kaki's thoughts, Bokey Ba left her with the baby once they reached Rani Pokhari; he hurried to cross the street. She ran after him, the baby held tight against her chest. "Bokey Ba, you can't do this!" Bokey Ba stopped at the edge of Tundikhel, faced her, and pointed to the sky. Rain began to fall, slowly at first, then in a torrent. They ran into Tundikhel and sought shelter under a tree. "This baby isn't mine," Kaki said, and Bokey Ba angrily gestured, pointing to her chest, then his, possibly to indicate that he wasn't a woman and wasn't properly equipped. Kaki laughed. By this time she'd learned to grasp at least some of the meaning of his strange, at times wild, hand gestures. "My chest is all shriveled up and useless," she told him. "There's no milk."

Bokey Ba repeatedly jabbed his finger toward the Mahabouddha area.

"I can't take him home," Kaki said. "I'm lucky my son and daughter-in-law let me live with them at all. Look, I have to prepare my own food, on a separate stove, with money earned from selling corn. I have to sleep in the chhindi under the stairs. If I take this baby there, my son will simply kick me out — all he needs is an excuse. Then where will I be? Where will the baby be?"

Bokey Ba hung his head. Kaki looked at the old man: his nose was running, and small drops fell on his beard; he could hardly appear more defeated. She looked at the baby, who was moving his mouth as he waved his small arm at her. A surge of maternal love rose in her chest, and her eyes filled with tears. This baby needed her more than she needed her son and his wife. Kaki placed her free hand on Bokey Ba's arm. "Look, even though I can't keep the baby, I'll help you in any way I can. First, we'll have to build a shelter. Otherwise this baby will die in the rain. I'll do whatever I can for him during the day, even while I'm selling my corn, and between you and me, we can take care of him."

Kaki thought that the baby needed a name, not just "bachcha," kid, as she and Vaishali called him now. But she couldn't think of any, except the most generic ones: Ram, Shyam, Bharat, Hari. Then she remembered Bokey Ba's failed attempt at dumping the baby inside the royal palace, and she laughed. The boy's name would be Raja, the king.

Before long, Raja and Bokey Ba slept under a blue tarp that Kaki helped set up on the northern edge of Tundikhel, across the street from her corn station. The police knew the two slept there, but they didn't do anything about it. To pursue the matter would involve taking the old man to the station in Hanuman Dhoka and writing a report, which was just too much work.

More than a year passed, and under the blue tarp Raja began to grow. Bokey Ba wiped the child's bottom with strips of cloth that Kaki had torn from an old dhoti and fed him milk from the bottle that Kaki replenished. Throughout the day Kaki crossed the street to make sure that everything was all right, and when Raja climbed onto her lap and began to play with her nose, she found it hard to leave. "If I stay here to play with you, how will I earn my living?" she chided the boy, who had begun to call her "Ka Ka Ka." Once, for a whole week Raja was sick with a hacking, barking cough, and Kaki had to steal cold syrup and tablets from her son's drawer, to give to the boy. Kaki also took the child to Shanta Bhawan, to the elderly foreign couple who ran a hospital there, for his dose of worm medicine. She held Raja straddled on her hip as a young nurse, in a startling white cap, poured the medicine down the boy's throat.

Kaki and Bokey Ba frequently had to chase Raja as he crawled rapidly across the parade ground to play with the people who relaxed nearby. "What's his name?" young girls asked, cooing to him. "When is his birthday?" And on this last question Bokey Ba and Kaki were stumped. Kaki surmised that he was nearly two years old, but, growing tired of answering that she didn't know the exact birth date, she asked Vaishali's husband, Dindayal, to consult the religious calendar. She then settled on a date in October, the auspicious day on which the great Dashain festival started. And, two weeks later, to commemorate Raja's second birthday, Kaki performed a puja in the Guheswori Temple; to everyone's amazement, she offered the goddess a baby goat in sacrifice, asking her to bless her Raja. She joked that the baby goat, had he been allowed to live, would have sported a goatee like Bokey Ba's.

One morning soon after, Kaki's son kicked her out of the house, accusing her of stealing money from under his mattress, which she had done — to pay for the goat. For the rest of the day Kaki roamed the city, carrying all that remained of her belongings. Too weak to gather her bedding in her arms, she'd left it in the courtyard where her son had thrown it. All she had now was a box filled with jewelry and trinkets; a black-and-white photo of her son as a boy, taken by the street photographer in Baghbazar; and a bag crammed with two petticoats, three blouses, and an extra dhoti. She thought about the people she might go to: a friend who'd recently married the brother of her dead husband; a widowed aunt who lived in Bhaktapur, sweeping the streets and begging from tourists; a man she disliked who'd wanted to marry her, repeatedly claiming that he was moneyed and would give her a good life. But she kept on walking into the bustle of the Juddha Sadak Gate. People swarmed around her: a man walking in front of a medicine shop paused to pick his teeth, a young boy on his bicycle zoomed through the crowd on the sidewalk, and people called to one another back and forth across the street, laughing. Movie lovers exited Ranjana Cinema and flooded the streets, squinting as their eyes adjusted to the sunlight; a bawling baby crawled up its mother's emaciated chest as she held out her dark, skinny hand for alms.

Kaki could go straight to Rani Pokhari, pick up her makal from Vaishali, who kept it for her overnight, and get to work, pretending that nothing had happened. But something had happened: she no longer had a home.

In Basantapur, Kaki stood in the middle of the vast courtyard, surrounded by temples. Small statues of Lord Shiva and his consort, Parvati, leaned out from a window. Directly in front of Kaki stood the enormous Maju Deval Temple, its many steps leading up to the phallus in the shrine. A government vehicle slowly passed by, its loudspeaker exhorting citizens to come together as one community for nation building.

A few drops fell on Kaki, and she looked up and saw dark clouds swelling in the sky. She put down her things and hesitantly stuck out her tongue, tasting the rain. As people scurried about looking for cover, she stood, exhilaration rising within her; her situation no longer seemed that bad at all. For tonight, and perhaps subsequent nights (until the police chased her away), she could find a nook somewhere among these temples to sleep in, an awning under which she could take shelter once darkness claimed the land. She would still sell her corn near Rani Pokhari, but now she wouldn't have to return home to her family's constant criticism and condescension. And she could give her undivided attention to Raja. She was meant to take care of the boy, and this jolt of fate she accepted with an ache in her heart.

• • •

When he was three years old, Raja sat under the tarp, watching the rain. Lightning streaked the sky. The thunder was so loud that it threatened to crack open the earth. The rain hit hard, and some of it dribbled under the edges of the tarp, wetting the ground beneath it. Bokey Ba was lying in the corner, coughing, with saliva oozing down his chin. "Ba, pani," said Raja, pointing at the sky. Bokey Ba's chest heaved; phlegm shot out of his mouth and landed on his shirt. He lifted his head, looked at his spit in the semi-dark of the shelter, and saw streaks of blood. Just then, Kaki appeared, holding a black, beat-up umbrella. "Here, Bokey Ba, drink this," she said, and handed him a bottle of cough medicine. The old man sat up, lifted his chin, and drank. Kaki noticed the blood and said, "I think we need to take you to the doctor."

Bokey Ba shook his head, said something Kaki didn't understand.

"You will die here, Bokey Ba," she said. "Let's go." The old man didn't move, but Kaki was adamant, and soon she had him standing, leaning against her, and the three walked out into the rain, crossed the street, and entered the office building where Vaishali and her husband, Dindayal, lived.

Kaki had been staying here too since her son kicked her out the year before. The building's ground floor had housed a printing press, now closed; a legal battle prevented the space from being occupied by another business, though the location, in the heart of the city, was indeed desirable. So Vaishali and Dindayal, with the building owner's express permission, had been living there comfortably for months, and in return Vaishali acted as custodian for the entire three stories. A restaurant and bar took up the second floor; a tailor's shop was situated on the third. When she learned that Kaki had been turned out of her son's house and had been sleeping in the temples, Vaishali had invited her to live there. But now, when Kaki, Raja, and Bokey Ba entered the building together, Vaishali grew alarmed. "I can't possibly let all three of you sleep here," she said to Kaki, who found a towel among her belongings and began to wipe Raja's head and face. Coughing fiercely, Bokey Ba had slumped to the floor against the wall. "The owner will kick all of us out," Vaishali said. "Then where will Dindayal and I go?"

Kaki told her that the old man would die if he slept outside that night. Finally, after some persuasion, Vaishali relented.

The rainstorm raged, and for a long time none of the group could sleep. The wind howled like a pack of wolves, and now and then a loud rattle or clatter sounded from the street as gusts hurled and banged things about. Raja clung to Kaki as he snored. Finally, at around three or four in the morning, the storm subsided, and everyone drifted off.

In the morning when they awoke, Bokey Ba's spot in the corner was empty.

"I'll keep an eye out for him," Dindayal said as he got ready for work. Employed as a peon for a merchant who owned several spice and sweets shops in the city, Dindayal rode his boss's bicycle all day, transferring packets of goods and cash between shops.

Throughout the day, as Kaki sold corn dabbed with her irresistible green chutney, she remained alert for signs of Bokey Ba. Many young people, especially students, stopped to buy her corn that day. They were on their way to the Supreme Court to listen to a former prime minister, known for his bellicose and eccentric ways, who was expected to defend himself against accusations of treason and sedition. Meanwhile, in his undershirt and underpants, Raja played in the dirt next to Kaki, sometimes crawling at breakneck speed toward other vendors along the street.

Briefly, Kaki became distracted by a couple of fussy customers; when she looked up, Raja was at the edge of the sidewalk, headed toward a small truck, its engine revving, alongside the street. Kaki shouted Vaishali's name and, ignoring the money the customers had thrust at her, she rushed toward the boy. Vaishali followed instantly. But Raja was fast, and by the time Kaki reached the three-wheeler truck, the child was in the middle of the street. A few Padma Kanya College girls across the way spotted him and screamed. A small truck swerved to avoid Raja, a Bajaj scooter nearly rammed into him, and Kaki, her heart thudding, hurled herself into the heavy traffic after him.

One college girl ran and tried to grab the boy. He slipped out of her grasp and soon was at the entrance of Tundikhel. Kaki ran at full speed after him, the object of honks and drivers' curses as she crossed the street. But the boy was already inside, near the shelter where he'd been living for the past few months. There he stopped, staring wide-eyed at the tarp. It had been ripped by the storm; the poles had buckled under the strong winds. "Ba, Ba?" he asked.

Kaki stopped to breathe, her chest heaving. "You'll be the death of me," she told him.

"Where is Ba?" he asked.

His clear speech startled her, and she responded as if he were an adult. "I don't know. Maybe he ran away. Let's go." She lifted him. He felt heavier, and his face now seemed more solemn. As she approached the sidewalk, Kaki's eyes fell upon an object glistening on the ground. She bent to pick it up. It was a button; it featured a photo of a balding man with small eyes, a foreigner. "Here," she said, handing it to Raja. The Padma Kanya girls who'd been alarmed over Raja now congregated around him, touching him, reprimanding him. One of them spotted the button in his palm and said, "Where did you get this Mao button? Thinking about becoming a communist?" The girls laughed. Later in the day, Kaki noticed a student sporting the same button, with the balding man's broad face. The word *communist* came to her, and although she didn't know what kind of people were communists, something about the way the Padma Kanya girl had uttered the term made Kaki uncomfortable. Maybe Mao was a rabble-rouser, connected to the conspiracy against the king.

During the night when Raja slept, Kaki stole the Mao button from under his pillow and threw it out the door. It rolled down the sidewalk, then clanked into a gutter, where it vanished.

· · · ·

Bokey Ba didn't return to the building that night, or the next night, or the next week. Kaki cursed the old man. He couldn't wait to leave, she fumed to herself, as she fanned the coals in her makal. But as weeks passed and it became obvious that Bokey Ba was gone forever, Kaki's resentment was replaced by a slow, sweet happiness, which enveloped her whenever she looked at Raja.

Off to Ganga Da's

R AJA GREW TO BOYHOOD by Rani Pokhari, close to where his mother had committed suicide. At about the same time, the city built a park across the street, at the northern edge of the parade ground, and named it Ratna Park, after the queen. Suddenly fishponds appeared, and large stone umbrellas, which shaded people as they sat and shelled peanuts and took long afternoon naps. Bright flowers sprung up from the ground. In the evenings families flocked to the park and took leisurely strolls; parents used their new cameras to snap black-and-white pictures of their children.

Although by the age of six he did not remember the tarp shelter where he and Bokey Ba had slept during the monsoons, Raja learned about it from Kaki, and sometimes when he crossed Ratna Park to that spot near the Juddha Sadak Gate, he was certain he could see his baby footprints in the mud. At age six, his imagination ran wild, and at night, when he saw wide-mouthed ghosts salivating near his feet, he curled his toes under the blanket and clasped Kaki so tightly that she pushed him away, saying, "Let me breathe!" Raja often said he dreamt of a young woman with a gaunt face. When Kaki asked him if the woman spoke, Raja said no, that she only looked at him sadly. The boy acted out the dream, mimicking the woman's expressions; his eyes became large and misty, and his serious performance left Kaki stifling her laughter. "It must be your mother's spirit missing you," she told him, even though privately she wondered whether a mother who'd abandon her baby was capable of such an emotion.

Raja often pestered Kaki with questions. One day he demanded to know whether Bokey Ba, whom he didn't actually remember, could tell him where his mother was and whether she'd come back to play with him.

"You mean in your dreams?" Kaki asked.

Raja said, "No, in real life."

When Kaki said no, he petulantly asked why, and Kaki slapped him lightly on the head and said that no one, not even his real mother, would play with him if he continued his bratty ways. Then she kissed Raja on his forehead and coaxed him to sleep. After he finally closed his eyes, she sang a lullaby he liked when he was younger, one that she hadn't sung in a while: *Aijaa chari kataun kaan, laijaa chari Gosainthan.* Soon he slept, snoring a little with each exhalation. Watching him, Kaki realized that she hadn't thought of her own son for quite some time — so completely had she given her attention to Raja. What would happen tomorrow if suddenly Raja's mother were to appear and demand that Kaki return her son? The unlikelihood of this, especially after six years, made her smile. Yet she couldn't sleep; her mind was engaged in an imaginary argument with Raja's mother, telling her the boy was hers now. She saw herself pleading with the woman, who then left, only to reappear with a couple of policemen. The mother's face was stern, unrelenting, and Kaki saw herself crumpling to the ground as the police pulled Raja from her arms.

During the day her eyes lingered over the faces of certain women who came to buy corn: those who looked unhappy, or emaciated, or troubled in some way. At those moments Kaki made sure that Raja remained within her sight, and she watched the suspected woman carefully to make sure that she didn't make any moves toward the boy.

Once, as Kaki returned from the Asan market after buying some vegetables, she spotted a woman holding Raja's hand and bending down to talk to him at the edge of the park. Kaki's heartbeat quickened, and she rushed toward them. "Who are you?" she asked fiercely as she pulled Raja away from the woman. "Why are you bothering the boy?"

Startled, the woman said, "I was just asking what his name was, where he lived."

"What business is it of yours?"

"I was only talking because I thought the boy was cute. What kind of a person are you?"

"You want to talk to cute boys, why don't you go and give birth to your own son?"

Out of the woman's earshot, she admonished Raja not to talk to strangers, particularly women.

"Why?" Raja asked.

"Some women are really bad," Kaki said. "They know hocus-pocus and will lure you away with their magic."

Raja pondered this for a while, then asked, "Was my mother bad too?"

"Yes."

Now making a living was becoming more difficult for Kaki. Every year more and more people migrated to the city. They cited hardships in the village — farmlands gone dry and unyielding, back-breaking work from dawn to dusk — and they swarmed to the capital. Consequently, every month or so, some poor villager opened a tiny portable shop in the Rani Pokhari area. Nothing much: just a nanglo, a basket, filled with Bahadur cigarettes; or titaura, or candy. The more entrepreneurial offered pencils and thin, poorly made notebooks for schoolchildren. Two more corn sellers had also appeared, and though everyone agreed that their corn was not nearly as delicious as Kaki's, these competitors still diverted customers from her.

On rainy days, when people didn't venture out, Kaki barely made a few paisa, and she then had to borrow rice and dal, and sometimes even oil, from Vaishali. Raja loved meat, and Kaki wished they could afford it once a week, or at least once a fortnight. Every Saturday, folks went to the meat shops and haggled with the butchers for choice pieces of goat, or chicken, or buffalo. Dindayal was also very fond of meat, and Vaishali managed to cook for him a few pieces of meat every weekend, even though they were more bone than flesh, bargained from the butcher at a nominal price. As Dindayal sucked out the marrow of a bone or chewed a piece of fat, Raja watched him, salivating. Occasionally, taking pity, Dindayal gave him a piece. Raja would hide it under the heap of boiled rice on his plate. This way the meat would be the last item he would eat, and the aftertaste lingered for hours.

Despite Kaki's injunctions to avoid talking to strangers, six-year-old Raja roamed the Ratna Park area on the lookout for a woman with a sad face, like the one in his dream, and since plenty of sad women lived in the city, he couldn't settle on a single one. He'd find a woman sitting by herself on the grass, doodling on the ground with a stick, and he'd perch a few yards away. He'd wait for the woman to look up and perhaps recognize him; then, as he imagined it, with tears filling her eyes, she'd run to him and claim him. But before that woman looked up, another would glide past, gesticulating with her fingers as she carried on a silent conversation with herself. Then Raja would abandon the first woman and follow the second. And during this pursuit, he'd spot one or two other women who didn't look any less sad, and he'd feel confused and go to a bush and pee.

When this search for the dream woman overwhelmed him, Raja looked instead for an old man with a pointed beard who could direct Raja to his mother. So he hunted for a man who matched Kaki's description of Bokey Ba. Because of Kaki's strict instructions not to venture too far, his pursuit of a promising-looking candidate stopped at the periphery of the park, where he watched the prospective Bokey Ba disappear into the crowds headed for Baghbazar, or Mahabouddha, or Kantipath.

Once he spotted a middle-aged man wearing the official national dress, daura suruwal, with a black Nepali cap on his head; he was peeling an orange in a corner of the park. The man had a small, closely cropped beard, and although it was not pointed, it gave Raja hope. The man looked up and saw Raja, and he ate a slice of the orange. Raja's mouth watered. The man smiled, motioned him over. Thinking that the man might tell him something about his mother, Raja went to him. But the man merely offered him two slices of orange. Raja gazed at the ground and shook his head. "Take it, take it," the man said. "Don't be so bashful." Raja took the slices from him. "Sit," the man said, and Raja sat down next to him but didn't eat.

"Where are your parents?" the man asked.

"I don't have parents," Raja said.

The man, about to eat another slice, stopped. "No parents? Who looks after you?"

"Kaki."

"Your aunt?"

"She's not my aunt."

"Well, Kaki means 'aunt.' If she's not your aunt, who is she then?"

The boy shrugged. "Everyone calls her Kaki."

After a moment the man asked, "Where is she now?"

Raja pointed behind him. "She sells grilled corn. Do you want to buy a cob?"

"No," the man said. "I have to get back to my office." Then he appeared to change his mind and asked, "Is her corn tasty?"

"It's famous," Raja said. "Everyone calls it Kaki's corn."

"I'll buy her corn if you eat my orange slices."

Raja inserted a slice into his mouth. The man stood up, smoothed his tie, and offered Raja his index finger. Raja took it and led him to the park's exit. "Do you know a man named Bokey Ba?" Raja asked.

"Bokey Ba? Is that his real name? Like a goat?"

"He has a pointed beard."

They crossed the street and approached Kaki. She was balanced on her haunches in front of her makal, chatting with a customer. To keep up with her competitors, she now also sold cigarettes and toffees and titaura, all neatly arranged on a nanglo beside her. Vaishali had also set up a small tea stand next to her.

21

When Kaki spotted Raja with the man, she asked, "Eh, badmash. Who did you bring?"

"He wants to buy our corn."

Kaki lathered some chutney on a corncob and handed it to the man.

"Quite a clever boy you have here," the man said as he paid her.

"Too clever for his own good," Kaki said.

As he munched Kaki's corn, the man asked where they lived and what had happened to Raja's parents. He listened thoughtfully while Raja fidgeted by his side, craning his neck to watch the man's face, then looking around at the pedestrians, his eyes especially drawn to children in bright clothes, out with their parents.

"Do you make enough to survive by selling corn?" the man asked.

"It's never enough," Kaki said. "But life's always like that for us around here."

"If you keep saying it's not enough, it's never enough," Vaishali said, pouring tea for a laborer whose callused hands resembled the bark of a tree. "If you say it's enough, then it's enough."

"Does he go to school?" the man asked, placing his hand on Raja's shoulder.

"Where would I get the money for his uniform and his books and pens?"

"I can work," Raja said. "But no one gives me a job."

Kaki and Vaishali tittered.

The man bent down to face him. "I'll give you a job. But to do my job, you'll have to live in my home." He turned to Kaki. "I'm serious. We've been looking for some household help for a while now, and I'm thinking that you look like a decent type. Only me and my wife in the house, so the work is easy. This boy is also smart and needs to go to school, and he can attend the one near my house."

Kaki's fingers deftly turned the cobs over the hot coals. "I've never worked as a servant in anyone's home, unless you count how I lived with my own son and daughter-in-law. I don't know whether I can even do the job."

22

The man gnawed through the last bit of the corn and threw the cob to the gutter. "I'm saying it more for the sake of the boy than anyone else. It's up to you. If you want to come and see what the job entails, we live in Lainchour, right behind the school. Everyone knows me as Ganga Da."

Kaki put her palms together in namaste. Ganga Da tousled Raja's hair and bid him goodbye. Raja followed him until the man crossed the street and disappeared into Mahabouddha.

That night Kaki tossed and turned in bed, waking Raja, who became annoyed and thrust his face into his pillow. Their bedding lay in a corner of the first floor of the building that, miraculously, Vaishali and Dindayal still occupied, after seven years. The legal battle over this particular space dragged on.

Once though, two years ago, these first-floor occupants had experienced a turn of bad luck that shook Kaki badly. The police rapped on the door early one morning, tossed their belongings onto the sidewalk, and announced that all of them were evicted. Vaishali and Dindayal and Kaki hurried to collect their possessions before pedestrians absconded with them. Raja wrapped his arm around the rusted tricycle that Dindayal had fetched for him from somewhere, even though it was now broken; a policeman had lifted it high above his head and then smashed it on the sidewalk. The officers padlocked the door and left the evicted stunned on the street. Two hours later, the owner of the building, his jaw set in a grimace, arrived with a different group of policemen and broke open the padlock with a hammer and a screwdriver. "Don't worry," he told Vaishali. "As long as I'm alive, these motherfuckers will never get this floor. I have this. See?" From his pocket he extracted a paper stamped by a number of officials, and he waved it at them. For close to a year he'd known that Kaki and Raja were staying with his "esteemed guests," as he jokingly called Vaishali and Dindayal, and he'd not objected. The paper he brandished was the legal document declaring the floor to be his property, but apparently his opponents possessed something similar. The eviction had terrified and humiliated Kaki. She'd clasped Raja to her chest and avoided looking at the passersby who'd stopped to observe their sorry-looking bedding and pots and pans and stoves scattered on the sidewalk. Raja asked her whether the police would imprison them.

In bed, restless, Kaki continued to disturb Raja, who said, "You blame me when I squirm in bed. Now you're not letting me sleep!"

"Go to sleep," she commanded.

"But I can't!"

She put her hand on his forehead and stroked it in the dark, sighing. "God will never forgive me if I let this chance go by," she said.

"What chance?" he asked drowsily.

"To have you attend school. You already forgot that gentleman?"

"Oh, Ganga Da," Raja said, in the tone of someone who'd known the man for years. "His beard is almost like Bokey Ba's."

Instead of lighting her coals the next morning, Kaki headed toward Lainchour with Raja. As they passed Rani Pokhari, they noticed people pointing to something on the water, something that resembled the head of a fish, or another sea creature — it was hard to tell. People said it was the monster that lived underneath, now surfacing for fresh air. "Probably just a log," someone commented dryly, and Kaki pushed Raja forward.

"I want to see," he complained. "I dream about the pond too. I see the sad woman walking across it."

Firmly clasping Raja's hand, Kaki continued north. They walked toward the Dairy, then crossed the Lainchour field. Inside the Jagadamba School, children from the morning shift shouted and screamed; a few stood on the balcony.

As the two skirted the school, a pebble flew through the air and bounced off Kaki's head, making her cry out in sharp, stinging pain. Above, on a side balcony, several boys were attempting to hide behind a pillar. Raja wrenched his hand from Kaki's and lunged toward the small gate that led up to the balcony. Before she could make sense of what was happening, Raja had clambered up to the second floor. The boys began laughing at the six-year-old who dared confront them. Her chest tightening, Kaki rapidly climbed the stairs, and heard a scuffle as she reached the balcony. On the dusty floor, Raja lay, pinned down by a boy twice his size. His lower arm pressed against Raja's throat, choking him; Raja's fists pummeled the air, occasionally hitting the boy. The other boys were egging their friend on. Kaki grabbed hold of the older boy's hair from behind and yanked back his head so hard that she thought she heard the neck snap. The boy lost his grip and fell back on the floor. Raja sat up, coughing and heaving, his hand on his throat. Kaki repeatedly kicked the older boy.

A teacher ran toward Kaki, flailing his arms and commanding her to stop; the boys scrammed. Kaki pulled Raja to his feet. The teacher was asking her why she was hitting his student, and Kaki angrily told him, "You need to control your boys." She dragged Raja down to the street, where she inspected him. He had a bruise on his throat where the boy had pressed with his elbow, as well as a reddish splotch on his forehead. "Why did you go nuts like that? Who asked you to run up there?"

"The boy threw a stone at you."

"At me, not at you. Why did it bother you so much?" A bunch of schoolboys watched them from the balcony now, and Kaki worried that this could be the school that Raja would attend if she was to work for Ganga Da. No doubt these boys would bully Raja. She recalled stories of school fights during which eyes had been gouged out. "We're returning home," she told Raja, and pulled him in that direction.

"But I don't want to go back," Raja replied, twisting his hand in hers, almost crying. "I want to go to Ganga Da's house."

"This is not a good place," she said, but Raja wrenched his hand free and plopped down on the ground; no matter how much she tried, she couldn't budge him. The schoolboys were jeering from above, and eventually Kaki saw that she had no choice but to agree to Raja's demand. But in the past few minutes she'd already made up her mind not to work at Ganga Da's — she'd just go there now to mollify Raja. She wetted her fingers with her tongue, rubbed them on Raja's bruises, and told him that his present appearance would make Ganga Da think he was a bad, undisciplined boy.

The two began searching for the house. After about ten minutes, they heard a shout: "Over here!" Ganga Da was standing on the roof of a house, a lungi wrapped around his waist; he was holding a toothbrush. "Come, come," he said, and waved them over.

He met them at the gate, his lips still crusted with toothpaste. They took off their slippers at the door and entered the house. Ganga Da ushered them straight into a room where the curtains were still drawn, blocking the morning sunlight. On the bed in the corner a woman was sleeping, her back to them. "Jamuna, oh Jamuna," Ganga Da called. The woman didn't budge. Scores of bottles and tablets sat arrayed by the bedside. A rancid odor emanated from the woman. Ganga Da called her name a couple more times, then sat next to her and placed his hand on her shoulder.

Abruptly the woman turned and hissed at him. "What? Not one moment of peace for me in this house? Don't you have better things to do?" The woman was slim and pretty, but her eyes were fierce, burning. Raja hid behind Kaki. Without glancing at the visitors, the woman turned to the wall again.

"Jamuna," Ganga Da said gently. "There's someone here who might work for us, for you."

"I don't need anyone," Jamuna said.

"We've been talking about it for days," Ganga Da said. "Don't do this when I've finally found someone."

Kaki thought this was a good opportunity to get away from this disturbing place, so she said, "If she doesn't need help, maybe we should go."

Ganga Da lifted his palm, asking for patience. He motioned to Kaki and Raja to sit on the floor, which they did. "Our lives will be a bit easier," he told his wife.

The woman finally turned, slowly, and a current of air carried an awful smell toward Raja, who put his hand to his nose. The woman's eyes fell on Kaki, and she turned to her husband. "Is it becoming hard for you to live with me? Is that why you've brought this witch here?"

Kaki abruptly stood and pulled Raja with her. "We didn't come here to listen to this."

Ganga Da too got up and said, "Don't go by her words. She means nothing. Please."

Kaki remained standing, her expression dark. Jamuna finally addressed her in a conciliatory voice. "My tongue is rotting these days. Worms are eating it. That's why my words are dirty."

The rest of the conversation was a blur to Kaki. As if puffs of cotton were drifting from his mouth, Ganga Da spoke soft words to his wife, who responded mostly with incoherent talk, punctuated by lucid comments or questions. She asked Kaki how much she'd expect to be paid as a household help, and when Kaki looked questioningly at Ganga Da, Jamuna said, sternly, that it was she, not her husband, who made financial decisions. "We'll settle that later," Ganga Da told Kaki.

Then Jamuna's gaze fell upon Raja. He was hiding behind Kaki again, peeking at the strange woman. "Who is this now?" Jamuna said. "Do you like flying kites?"

Kaki intervened. "Let's talk about my work first. Where will we sleep? What kind of work would I do?"

To Kaki's surprise, Raja emerged from behind her and went to Jamuna, who put her hand to her mouth when she saw his bruises. "What happened to you? Who did this to you?"

"The boys over there," Raja said shyly, pointing out the window. Jamuna pulled him toward her. "Let's look." She touched the bruise on his face, and Raja flinched. "Let me get some iodine." And she left the room to fetch it.

Kaki leaned toward Ganga Da. "Is she not right in the head?"

Ganga Da hesitated. "She's harmless. Once in a while I need someone to handle her, but mostly she just talks nonsense."

"I don't think I can do this work," Kaki said. "No telling what she might do to my boy."

Ganga Da stared at her, his eyes getting moist. "Don't say that.

She loves young children, and she'll never do anything to harm them. Please. I'll send the boy to a good school. You'll be happy here."

Jamuna returned, carrying a bottle and a wad of cotton. She knelt before Raja, who, to Kaki's surprise, didn't shrink from her. Jamuna dabbed a piece of cotton with iodine and applied it to his face. "You're a brave boy, son," Jamuna said. "A bahadur." She took Raja to the bed and made him sit next to her. "You two go out and talk about the wages. He will stay with me. Go!"

"No, no, I want to talk in this room," Kaki said, but Ganga Da signaled to her that it was okay. Reluctantly, she left Raja with the woman and went out. Ganga Da took her to the kitchen, where dishes were piled in the sink, flies buzzing around them. "Cook and clean, that's all you have to do," Ganga Da said. "Our clothes are washed by a dhobi nearby, and he can also clean Raja's clothes and yours. The work here is very light. I'll give both of you new clothes during Dashain. Sometimes if you want to go visit your family, in the village or elsewhere, that too can be arranged."

"I have no family," Kaki said. She wondered what her own son would think of her working as a servant. He probably wouldn't care, she concluded sadly. "Good riddance," she could hear him say to his wife. But, a part of her mind argued, surely he thought about her sometimes, wondered what she was up to?

"What do you think?" Ganga Da asked. The toothpaste had dried on his lips.

"We haven't talked about my wages."

"I was going to ask you. How much do you want? Now remember—I'll pay for the boy's school too."

Kaki mulled it over. What she really wanted was to tear Raja from that woman and return to Ratna Park. "Fifty rupees a month," she said, confident that Ganga Da would balk at the amount. A couple of women she knew who worked as servants received only slightly more than twenty rupees monthly, and others were paid only the food they ate and new clothes during the annual festival; in rare instances, bus fares for visits home were included. Kaki waited for Ganga Da to laugh at the audacity of her request and dismiss it, which would give her an excuse to walk out. Ganga Da turned away momentarily, his back to her; then, facing her again, he said, "It's higher than what I expected, but I'll give you what you want. Once you start here, however, you have to stay with us. Leaving after two days because the work is too hard — if you do that, no one will be a nastier person than me. I want you to understand that."

Kaki's breath stuck in her throat. Fifty rupees! Within two months she'd be able to return to her son and throw his fifty rupees in his face and float another fifty in the direction of his wife. But this line of thinking made her ashamed. She couldn't take this job to satisfy a feeling of vengeance.

"And remember, the boy will be educated, lead a good life. We'll raise him like he's our son."

Ganga Da's voice jolted her out of her thoughts. Telling him that she needed to check on Raja, she hurried to the other room. Raja was lying on Jamuna's lap, his eyes closed, and the woman was gently blowing on the bruises on his cheeks, where she'd applied iodine. Between her breaths, she hummed a lullaby: *Chimichimi nani chimichini, makkhan roti chimichini.* Raja's face was so serene, so content, Kaki could only watch, speechless.

"Let the poor boy sleep for a while," Ganga Da whispered from behind Kaki. "Come, I'll show you something else."

He took her to an empty, narrow room next to the kitchen, explaining that this was where she'd sleep once she began working. "And you can use this bathroom." He led her into the back yard, where an outhouse stood near a water tap. Ganga Da turned the tap on, and water rushed out in a torrent. "And water flows here twenty-four hours a day, so you won't have to go elsewhere to fetch it," he said. He came to her and said, "What do you think?"

"Everything is fine, but your wife . . . I'm just a bit scared. What if she gets ideas in the middle of the night?"

Ganga Da laughed. "Is that what you think she'll do? She's tortured more by her own voices than anything else. Sometimes when I'm at work she'll try to leave the house because she gets paranoid

that someone will come in and abduct her. That's why I need you."
He became quiet, then said, "I talked to you only because you look
like a decent woman, and I feel for this boy. Think about it. Do you
really want him to grow up on the streets? Here, he'll eat well, I'll
clothe him, provide for all of his expenses."

Kaki found her will weakening as she considered Ganga Da's argument. If you really thought about the good of the boy, she told
herself, you'd take this job. You can always leave if the woman turns
dangerous, or too much to handle. This man is right: compare this
to Raja's life alongside Rani Pokhari. Finally she asked, "When do
you want me to start?"

"We can go to your place and get your belongings right now."
He looked at his watch. "I can go to work a little late today. At least
I'll be happy that there's someone in the house with Jamuna. Maybe
you and I can go to Ratna Park and leave the boy here for now?"

"No, no," Kaki said. "I want to take him with me."

Inside, Raja was still sleeping on Jamuna's lap, and she too had
propped herself against a pillow and closed her eyes.

"Why wake them?" Ganga Da whispered. "Look how comfortably they're sleeping. Like a mother and son."

There was something touching about the way the two were napping, with the sunlight streaming through the curtains, accompanied by the distant low chorus of children's cries from the Jagadamba School.

When Kaki announced that she was leaving to work for Ganga Da,
Vaishali appeared relieved, but then she wept. "I'll miss you, didi,"
she said. "And I'll miss Raja."

"I'll miss you too, but it's not like I'm moving to a foreign country. Whenever you feel like it, come to visit." She looked at Ganga
Da, who was standing by, eyeing his watch. "I think we'd better go."
She left her makal with Vaishali, thinking that if things didn't work
out with Ganga Da, she'd have to return to sell corn.

Ganga Da carried Kaki's rolled mattress under his arm and
grabbed two of her bags, one of which contained Raja's clothes.

Outside, Ganga Da headed toward an idling taxi. The two had come to Ratna Park on a bus, so Kaki had thought they'd return the same way. She didn't get to ride in cars too often. The last time she'd taken a taxi was during her son's wedding festivities.

Kaki's first car ride — well, it was actually a truck ride — took place shortly after her own wedding, when, dressed in a bright red bridal sari, she'd accompanied her husband to receive blessings from some relatives. The truck ride had been a grand gesture on his part. He'd gone out of his way to procure the vehicle, which, he proudly told her, had been used only a few years before in the construction of Juddha Sadak, the road that linked the old city with the new; now it formed the commercial heart of Kathmandu, overflowing with foreign goods.

"Did you have to pay to get it?" she asked her new husband.

"Don't you worry your pretty head about it," he said. At that time, the Tribhuvan Rajpath highway had yet to be built, and porters had to carry cars into the city all the way from Bhimphedi. One of Kaki's nephews had enlisted as a porter, and he'd told her how they collected hay as they trundled along the two-week route so they could make sandals for their bruised and battered feet.

In keeping with the modesty of a new bride, Kaki had softly complained that they couldn't afford the expense of renting a truck. Waving his smoldering cigarette about as the truck rattled to their destination, her husband had declared, "You can't have fun after you're dead — *hoki hoina?*" Despite herself, she'd turned her face to the window, away from him, and smiled. It had only been two weeks since she'd gingerly entered his house as a bride, and she was getting to know his habits, his gestures. *"Hoki hoina?"* he asked, thrusting forward his chin, after commenting on myriad subjects: the weather, the rude shopkeepers, the pestering beggars, the irresponsible cousin. "True or not?"

"True, true," she whispered to herself while he was alive, and after he died, only three years after their wedding, from, according to the doctors, excessive smoking. *Hoki hoina?* she chanted to her son as he grew up without a father.

31

"Raja must be crying," she told Ganga Da in the taxi.

"Jamuna is caring for him."

Outside Tri-Chandra College, traffic had slowed. The police were chasing some students onto the campus grounds. "What's happening here?" she mused aloud.

Without much emotion, Ganga Da watched as a policeman whacked a young man repeatedly on the back with his baton. "Rabble-rousers all," Ganga Da said. "That's exactly what they deserve."

"This king is turning out to be quite stern, isn't he?" Kaki said. It was something she'd heard people whisper in Ratna Park. She herself didn't understand much of what was going on, but she'd suddenly begun to notice buttons, with King M's photo, on the lapels of government officials who stopped by to munch on her corn; those buttons resembled the one with the Chinese Mao that Kaki had found a couple of years ago and given to Raja. The boy had asked one such official, "Dai, do you have a king's button you can give me?"

"Het!" The official, a short, plump man with a protruding belly, clad in daura suruwal and wearing dark glasses as King M always did, had scolded Raja. "You think this button is something cheap? To be worn by every vagrant on the street? See here." The official pointed his pudgy fingers at the king's profile. "This is our king, understand? They say he's an incarnation of Lord Vishnu himself. You can't touch our king with your filthy hands."

The man's words had stung Kaki, and she could see how crestfallen Raja looked; she had half a mind to not give the man his corn, which she'd just spread with her special chutney. But all she did, as she handed him the food, was say, "Dai, why do you say such a thing to a young boy? Haven't you heard? *Raja sabko sajha.* The king belongs to everyone." After the officials left, she pulled Raja close and said, "Don't worry. I'll get you that button. Somehow." But she didn't know where to look, or even whether such a button was sold in shops. But the next day, after Dindayal returned from work, he called Raja, asked him to open his palm, placed something in it, and closed it. When Raja uncurled his fingers, there it was, the button. Kaki exclaimed and asked Dindayal where he got it, but Dindayal merely smiled.

For days Raja wore the button on his shirt, thrusting his chest forward so that Kaki's customers would notice it. *"Raja sabko sajha,"* he chanted as he ran circles around Kaki's corncob station, rapidly wheeling a discarded bicycle tire borrowed from another boy whose mother sold knickknacks on another corner. Then one day Kaki discovered Raja chewing on the king's button in their room. "Eh, eh, mula," she shouted. "What are you doing? You can't do that to the king."

But Raja, ignoring her, kept chewing.

Kaki grabbed him by his arms and shook him. "What's wrong with you? Dindayal Mama goes through so much trouble to get you that button and you disrespect him like that? Apologize to him right now."

"I don't want the button anymore," he said, and hurled it into the corner.

"A few days ago you were crying for it, and today you don't want it?"

"That king's helper said I was a bad boy. I don't want it."

"Which man?" Then it dawned on her that he was referring to the plump government official. "What does it matter what he said?"

Dindayal went to the corner, picked up the button, and looked at Raja forlornly. "Look what he made of our king. Look." He brought it over and showed it to Kaki. The king's face was crushed, one of his eyes distorted.

"You rascal, they're going to lock you away if they see this," Kaki said.

Dindayal laughed. "Look, the king looks like he had a pretty bad accident."

Vaishali, who was cooking in the corner, came over, and she laughed with her husband. "Appears that someone took a hammer and smashed his face in."

"Yes, you keep talking like that and they'll take both of you, along with this boy, to the slammer."

But Raja wasn't laughing. He was sitting with his head down, looking bereft. Kaki watched him for a while, her anger gradually melting away. That night after supper — Raja ate little — she held him close and asked, "What's wrong with my son?" But Raja wouldn't answer. His chin sagged liked an old man's, and his eyes had gone misty. She rocked him in her arms and spoke to him gently.

Finally he said, "Where is my mother?"

"I am your mother."

"My real mother. When is she coming back to get me?"

Kaki was stumped. Finally she said, "She'll come, Raja, she'll come. I am here for you. What you need, you tell me. I'll give it to you."

"I want my mother."

She rocked him, and for a long time he kept his eyes open, not saying anything. Then he fell asleep.

The next day she bought for him, from a toy store in Asan, a rubber duck, which he squeaked delightedly all around Rani Pokhari.

The taxi had pulled away from Tri-Chandra College and was now speeding toward Lainchour. Ganga Da seemed lost in his own thoughts.

"How long have you been married?" Kaki asked.

For a moment, Ganga Da didn't answer, as if the topic was hard for him. "Four years."

"And no children?"

He shook his head.

"Maybe giving birth to a child would cure her."

"You sound like my Bala Maiju from Tangal," he said. "That's what she keeps telling me." He went on for a while about Bala Maiju, his maternal uncle's widow. She was his closest relative in the city. He missed her but hadn't been able to visit her lately. "I need to go see her soon," he said.

As soon as the taxi halted outside Ganga Da's door, Kaki hurried inside and found that Raja was sitting on Jamuna's lap on the living room floor, a magazine open before him. "A man on a horse, see?" Jamuna was saying. A half-eaten packet of arrowroot biscuits lay next to them. "I'll teach him how to read," she said to Kaki, smiling, and Raja too smiled.

"Jamuna Mummy says she'll buy me ice cream every day," he said.

For Kaki, the problem at Ganga Da's was not the work, which was as easy as he'd promised. Early in the morning Kaki made tea with milk, which the milkman delivered in the dark. "Give the boy two or three glasses of milk every day," Ganga Da had advised, and so she did, astounded that only a few days ago they'd have been lucky to afford one glass of milk every other day. After the morning tea, Kaki headed to the Thamel vegetable market, bills and coins bound tightly in a knot of her dhoti. Sometimes Raja accompanied her, but often he'd just be waking up, so she let him be.

But as she shopped in the Thamel market she began to grow anxious. Who knew what Jamuna could be doing to her boy? She could twist Raja's arm roughly enough to break it or pinch his nose so hard it'd bleed. With her shopping only partially done, Kaki rushed home, only to often find Raja in the woman's lap; she was reading him a children's book that Ganga Da had purchased for him. "Say it: *Kapoori ka.*" Jamuna was urging him to learn the alphabet. He'd pronounce the letter, then pick a colored pencil and attempt to draw the word.

Ganga Da, sitting on his bed, remarked, "Yes, yes, that's the way, now loop it into a big, fat belly."

Then Ganga Da laughed, which made Jamuna laugh, and Raja looked embarrassed and said, "What? What?" He turned to Jamuna and said, "Jamuna Mummy, why are you laughing?"

The first time Raja called the woman Mummy, Kaki had objected. "Don't call her Mummy," she said on that first day, when

Raja beamed at the possibility of a daily ice cream treat. She'd heard some rich children call their mother that, and it seemed that this single word distanced Raja from Kaki.

"You are Kaki," Jamuna said. "I am Mummy, and he is Ganga Da. We're all happy, aren't we all?"

Ganga Da took Kaki by her elbow to her room. "Let him call her whatever she wants," he whispered to her. "You and I know the truth."

"I don't want her to get ideas."

"It's just a word. You're still his mother. If Jamuna is happy, it'll make your work easy."

"What if Raja really believes she's his mother?"

"Look, the boy is very clever. He knows he's an orphan, that even you aren't his real aunt."

Ganga Da was right. Raja was too aware of his own history to fall into the trap of mistaking Jamuna for his real mother. It was also true that Raja's presence soothed the craziness inside Jamuna. Mummy. It's only a word, Kaki told herself. It doesn't mean anything.

Kaki's Jealousy

R AJA CLUNG TO JAMUNA from early morning to night, and
within weeks he began treating Kaki as if she was indeed only
a servant in his house. He didn't even bother Kaki when he wanted
to eat; he went straight to Jamuna, who in turn asked Kaki to cook
him kheer or give him buttered Krishnapauroti bread. When Kaki
implored him to come to her, he ignored her or walked away. The
only time she could hold him tight was at night, and only after he
fell asleep, because while he remained awake in bed he pushed her
away and cried out for his Jamuna Mummy, who then came running
from her room and embraced him. Jamuna stroked his forehead and
consoled him with her gibberish. Once, Jamuna took him to her
own bed, where he spent half the night before Kaki went to fetch
him. "Let him sleep here," Jamuna whispered, looking pleadingly
at Kaki. "If he sleeps with you, the snakes will come." Nonetheless,
Kaki reached over and pulled him away from her in the darkness.

In bits and pieces, Kaki was learning from Ganga Da how he'd
ended up marrying Jamuna and how he'd first learned of her mental disease. At the time of his marriage, he'd just started his job at
the National Planning Commission, where he was now a second-
class officer. In the years since his father's death, his mother, clad
in the white dhoti of the widow, had turned to scriptures and pra-
bachans. The proposal for Jamuna had come through a distant relative who'd known Jamuna's family for years. "Ganga's and Jamuna's

names refer to two of the holiest rivers of India," the man had said with a smile, "whose confluence is a sacred spot; thus this marriage is dictated by the heavens."

Within days of Ganga Da's wedding, his mother left for Banaras to live in an ashram, something she'd wanted to do since her husband's death. The next morning Ganga Da was reading the newspaper in the bedroom, the glass of tea Jamuna had brought steaming beside him, when he heard a loud clatter in the kitchen. "Jamuna?" he called. There was no answer. He assumed she'd gone to the toilet outside and resumed his reading. Soon he heard what sounded like a child whimpering. Could be the neighborhood cat, he wondered, but then there was the distinct sound of a human chuckle. A tingle scurried up Ganga Da's spine. He looked out. The toilet door was open, swinging a bit in the morning breeze. He went to the kitchen. Pans scattered all around her, Jamuna was seated on the floor against the wall, her eyes raised toward the ceiling.

"What are you doing?"

She didn't look at him. "May Lord Pashupatinath protect us all," she said.

"Stand up," he said as he went to her and lifted her by the arm. She began to chant a hymn. Kicking a pot out of the way, he took her to their bed. Helping her lie down, he asked, "What happened? Are you not feeling well?" He felt her forehead, but her temperature seemed normal.

With her lips slightly twisted, she stared at him. Something about her eyes — she wasn't really looking at him. He felt disoriented. "How long have you been like this?" he asked, his voice shaking.

She turned away from him to face the wall. She lay on the bed like a statue, her back to her husband. After a while, he sat down. He hoped this was a joke and that in a few minutes, or perhaps by the time he returned from work, she'd punch him on the arm and say, "Did you think that you were shackled to a madwoman for life?"

But when he returned from work, she was lying in bed, staring at the ceiling. He called her name, and she gave him that empty look.

As time passed, Ganga Da learned that he couldn't, and neither could she, predict when her illness would flare up or when it would subside. At night he'd wake to discover that she'd locked herself in the storage room next to the kitchen. Fearing that she'd harm herself, use a knife on her wrist or swallow rat poison, he pounded on the door. It would take her a while to finally open it, and by that time he'd be exhausted, with a tightness in his throat and chest that lasted through the day at work. Then there were days when she'd stay in one spot for hours, motionless, her face blank. She wouldn't brush her teeth or bathe, and sometimes she even urinated where she sat.

When her disease, her rog, as she liked to call it, subsided, her face became transformed. She laughed more, hummed as she cooked, and pleaded with Ganga Da to take her on outings, perhaps to Budhanilkantha or Gokarna or to the movies. In the darkened cinema hall she'd slip her hand into his, especially when a romantic scene appeared on the screen. Watching the Indian movie *Sangam*, she'd pinched his palm when Raj Kapoor, perched in a tree, played bagpipes and teased Vyjantimala, who was swimming sensuously below him in a pond, asking her when the Ganga of his heart would be united with the Jamuna of hers. At home that afternoon, as Jamuna made rice pudding, she hummed and sang, *"Mere man ki ganga or tere man ki jamuna ka, bol Radha, bol sangam hoga ki nahi."* When she brought Ganga Da the pudding he pulled her into bed, even though it was still daylight outside.

He took her to doctors who explained that they were not psychiatrists, and since there were none in the city he'd have to take his wife to India, to the well-known mental hospital in Ranchi. As soon as Jamuna heard Ranchi mentioned, she balked. "I'm not going to that loony bin. You go," she told her husband, and her behavior became worse than ever, to the point that Ganga Da had had to tie her wrists for an hour or so until she calmed down.

Although he didn't take her to Ranchi, Ganga Da tried other treatments. He took Jamuna to people known for their miracle cures: a healer at the base of the Swayambhunath hill; the college girl in Thamel who became possessed by a powerful Newar goddess at the chanting of a few mantras; Patan's Ama, who was reputed to heal patients declared untreatable by the doctors at Shanta Bhawan Hospital nearby. But Jamuna's condition, instead of getting better, got worse. Toward the end of their second year of marriage, it became further exacerbated by her failure to get pregnant.

Ganga Da's mother visited, unannounced. She told him that she had come to Kathmandu to transfer all their property to his name — the house and nearly one lakh rupees that Ganga Da's father had left for her — as she now wanted to renounce all earthly matters and devote herself to God under Swami Nityananda's tutelage. She asked Ganga Da and Jamuna why they hadn't yet given her a grandchild. The next day Jamuna entered the living room carrying something cradled in her arms. It turned out to be a doll with a bald head and a big hole in its chest, which Ganga Da recognized as belonging to the neighbor's daughter. Jamuna unbuttoned her blouse, reached inside, and pulled out her breast. She pressed the doll's face against her nipple.

The next week, after completing the documents for transfer of property, his mother left for Banaras, and she never returned.

Even Ganga Da was surprised by how quickly the boy and his wife had taken to each other. Since Raja's arrival in their home, Jamuna had begun taking care of her appearance — keeping her hair combed and even applying light makeup to her face in the morning. She spent all day with Raja, and when the boy went out to the neighborhood to play with his newfound friends, she paced the yard, went to the gate to peer out, sighed, then scolded herself. Or she simply sat near the gate, waiting for him, her eyes impassive. Most days when he returned home, his face coated with dust, she took him to the bathroom, where she helped him undress and take a bath. "No, Jamuna Mummy, no," he cried when she rubbed soap on his hair and face, which made his eyes burn.

"Just one more round, then we're done." She coaxed the boy through it. Watching her, Ganga Da often wondered if this was the same wife who'd recently cried uncontrollably over a mangled doll.

Out of the corner of his eye he could also sense that Kaki, who'd be chopping vegetables on the kitchen floor, was listening to the two in the bathroom. After Raja's bath, Jamuna would make the boy lie on the carpet in their bedroom and massage him. She'd rub her palms with oil and draw circles on his belly with her fingers, making his shriveled penis jiggle. He'd ask her to tickle him more, and she'd oblige, running her fingers up to his armpits.

One day, as Jamuna tickled him, Raja said, "Tickle Ganga Da."

Unable to bear this, Kaki came to the bedroom door and shouted, "Badmash! Watch what you say." She glared at Jamuna.

Raja shouted again, "Tickle Ganga Da!" Her hands smeared with oil, Jamuna chased her husband. Simultaneously laughing and getting angry, Ganga Da ran around the house. Raja, on his stomach now, rested his chin on his palms and watched them. Jamuna, as quick as a cat, pounced on Ganga Da in the hall, tackling him like a wrestler. She then lifted his shirt and tickled him, her fingers plunging down into his pants.

Kaki spun out into the yard. Ganga Da, feeling ashamed but also aroused by his wife's touch, poured his anger on her. She giggled and smirked, then slid closer to him, touching him through his pants. "But you like this, don't you?" she whispered.

"Go to her and apologize," Ganga Da whispered to his wife. Out in the yard Kaki was sitting by the water pump. Sulking, Jamuna went out and talked with Kaki. Ganga Da couldn't hear what she said, but finally Kaki came back in and, without meeting anyone's eyes, resumed her work.

Ganga Da tried to get Raja enrolled in boarding school. He, Kaki, and Raja visited two possible choices, but they were turned away. One school was simply too full, and the principal there bragged that the movers and shakers of the city had placed their children's names on his waiting list. At the other school, after learning Raja was an orphan, the principal said that he needed the names of the boy's parents in order to enroll him. Ganga Da argued that as long as the fees were paid, it ought to make no difference to the school who the student's parents were. Kaki, naturally, didn't have any documents

41

concerning Raja's birth. "He's more than my own blood," she told the principal. But the principal pursed his lips and shook his head.

Disappointed, the three turned toward home. On the way back, on the city bus, Kaki said that if Raja couldn't go to a good school, as Ganga Da had promised, she'd rather return to Ratna Park. He snapped at her, making other passengers swivel their heads with interest. "You're thinking only of yourself, not the boy," he said loudly, and she sulked for the rest of the trip. When they got off at Ratna Park to change buses, Kaki told them that she needed to talk to Vaishali, that Ganga Da and Raja should go home by themselves.

After Kaki returned to Lainchour from her private visit with Vaishali, she didn't say anything but quietly went to the kitchen and began to prepare dinner. She'd gone to Vaishali to see if the woman would take Kaki and Raja back, but Vaishali had said that since the two left, the building owner had come by and said explicitly that she was not to have guests or relatives staying with her.

Kaki watched Vaishali to detect whether she could be lying, but Vaishali met her gaze. "Just for a few days, until I find a place for the two of us?" Kaki pleaded. "That crazy Jamuna is sucking my blood."

"If I let you stay here," Vaishali said, "the owner will kick all of us out. Is that what you want?"

Kaki wiped her eyes and said that she wouldn't want such a fate to befall her friends.

With great reluctance Ganga Da took Raja to enroll him in the Jagadamba School, which was not Ganga Da's first choice, as it was merely a government school, not a private boarding school. But since the moment Kaki had stopped by Vaishali's place, Ganga Da suspected that she was scheming. He felt he needed to begin Raja's education immediately to discourage Kaki from leaving.

In front of the Jagadamba School stretched the expansive field where the students gathered during breaks and where, in the evening, local boys played soccer or people practiced riding bicycles and motorcycles and, occasionally, driving cars. Facing the school to the south was Ascol College, whose politically minded students frequently agitated for change; in response helmeted police often were brought in to squelch the disturbance. The Jagadamba School was a government school, which meant that many poor students attended it, wearing ill-tailored uniforms and slippers instead of shoes. Disruptions at Ascol College frequently spilled over to the school, and some days it was simply impossible to teach; then the students were let go, and the teachers headed to the nearby tea shops.

The principal of the school, Singh Sir, was a longtime acquaintance of Ganga Da, and earlier that morning Ganga Da had called him at home and explained the situation. "Bring him over," Singh Sir had said. "Let's see what we can do."

Jamuna had dressed Raja in blue half-pants and a sky-blue shirt — the school's uniform — and for added effect had even strung a tie around his neck. Raja protested that the tie was too constricting, but Kaki emerged from the kitchen and rebuked him. "If you don't look good, which school will take you? And then what will you be, huh? An ignoramus?"

Raja sneered at her and said, "If I'm an ignoramus, then you're . . . full of goo."

Singh Sir was amenable to accepting Raja, but, squirming in his chair, he said, "I am not supposed to do this, I mean, take a student in the middle of the year. If the superintendent finds out, I could get into trouble."

"I don't want you to . . ."

It turned out that Singh Sir wanted what he called "a small donation" to deflect any possible criticism. Ganga Da understood, and he quickly went home to fetch some money. Raja's teacher was then called to the office, and she led him through an open hallway to the first-grade classroom, which was crammed with kids; the air smelled of sweat and rancid breath. A hole in the wall the size of a soccer ball provided a glimpse of the college across the street, and another in the next wall revealed students in the classroom next door. The children's high-pitched voices fell silent as soon as Raja walked in, accompanied by his teacher. Without speaking they watched the new boy, until someone from the back said, "Hero!" probably referring to Raja's tie, and the rest burst into laughter. This prompted the teacher to raise the stick that had been leaning against the blackboard and slam it repeatedly against her desk. *Chup! Chup!* Raja watched the stick, and suddenly his knees became wobbly; shivers ran up his spine, and he wanted to cry.

During the tiffin break, Raja stayed in the classroom, lingering at the hole in the wall that gave him a view of the college students across the street; he felt impatient to grow big like them. He wondered what Jamuna Mummy was doing right now, whether Ganga Da would come to see how he was faring, and whether once he got back home Kaki would scold him for no reason, as she often did these days.

During the hours when Raja was in school, Kaki performed her household chores but felt as if something was pressing against the crown of her head. Once in a while her eyes would drift toward the gate, and she'd realize that only an hour or so had passed since Raja had left, that he wouldn't come home until late afternoon. Jamuna, she knew, was also pining for Raja, but Kaki felt no sympathy for the crazy woman. For her, Raja was only a distraction from the voices in her head. She had bought his affection with toys and bright clothes. The more she dwelt on Jamuna, the more Kaki's chest smoldered with rage. Her Raja had already begun to forget his street days in Rani Pokhari. In fact he was beginning to lord it over Kaki, treating her as though she'd crawled into the house from the street. Just the other day, when she'd put her arm around him after he got dressed for school, he flung it away and said, "You smell! Do you ever take a bath?" She had just been cooking in the kitchen, and she knew he probably smelled garlic and onions on her. It was a child speaking, but it didn't prevent her from feeling crushed. He'd also taken to calling her pakhi, a village dolt. She didn't know where he'd learned the word, but the first time he said it, Jamuna had put her palm to her mouth and tittered; emboldened, he'd repeated the slur. "You're a pakhi, aren't you, Kaki?" Fighting back tears, she'd asked him to stop calling her that, but he wouldn't. He approached her in the kitchen as she sat skinning some potatoes and, mouth against her ear, shouted, "Pakhi Kaki!" making her head ring. Then he ran to Jamuna.

And even after Raja returned from school, he hurried straight to Jamuna, shouting, "Jamuna Mummy, Jamuna Mummy," and ignoring Kaki. It was in Jamuna's arms that he babbled on about his school. It was to Jamuna that he waved his notebook, showing her what he'd accomplished that day, which wasn't much — mostly incoherent drawings, as he still had to learn how to write and string letters together to form words as he read. Kaki knew that she ought not to mind that he shunned her, that he disregarded her feelings. She reminded herself that he was only a young boy, that he'd come around one day; that, if she really cared for him, she ought to be grateful that two strangers with some financial means were showering their love on him; that he was able to attend school, unlike thousands of children in the country who labored on farms or began working as servants at an early age; that one day he was going to be a fine, intelligent young man with a job at an important office. But every day, as Kaki watched Raja becoming more attached to Jamuna, feelings of despondency preyed on her. She saw Raja repeat, in some sense, the treatment her own son had bestowed upon her. Every time Raja's arms reached for Jamuna and not for Kaki, she couldn't help but feel that she'd lost him, that he was never coming back to her. What is it in me, she asked herself, that has made both my sons reject me?

Once, she contemplated leaving Ganga Da's house, thereby freeing Raja altogether from his past on the streets, leaving him unencumbered by his history as an orphan. But she couldn't bear the thought of going back to Ratna Park without him, of surrendering him to Jamuna. How Kaki loathed the way Jamuna called him, her voice dripping with affection: "Raja! Chora! Babu!" But then, within a few weeks of Raja's enrollment at the Jagadamba School, Jamuna's symptoms resurfaced. One afternoon while Ganga Da was at work and Kaki was in the kitchen, she heard Jamuna muttering in the yard. When Kaki glanced out the window, she saw that Jamuna had bent down to draw something with a piece of coal on the rectangular patch of brick next to the porch. Jamuna was focusing intensely on her work, talking to herself, shaking her head vigorously when her drawing displeased her and smiling when she approved what she saw.

Kaki returned to cleaning and rearranging the cupboard, but later, when she went to the yard to dust a mat in the sun, she saw what Jamuna had drawn: badly sketched figures of a child and a woman. A looped line ascended from the head of each. It took a split second for Kaki to realize what they were: nooses.

That afternoon Kaki abandoned her work and sat on the cold kitchen floor. Jamuna napped in her bedroom. Thunder rumbled at around two o'clock, and a sudden shower poured down from the sky, washing away Jamuna's drawing. Raja arrived home from school and as usual ran to Jamuna's arms. Kaki quickly placed a glass of milk and a boiled egg, its shell peeled off, in Jamuna's room for the boy. Telling Jamuna that she'd be back in an hour, she headed out. She wound through the back alleys of Thamel, then through Jyatha, and she emerged at Kantipath, where she crossed the street and entered another alley next to a hotel painted yellow. Kaki knocked on one door after another until she was directed to the house she was looking for. For a moment, she stood in front of its big brown iron gate. Then she banged on it and when a servant of about her own age appeared, Kaki identified herself and entered.

Every day, for an hour or so after Raja left for school, Jamuna paced the yard or stood next to the guava tree and rocked back and forth. Then she went inside and sat on her bed, which was next to the window, and kept a watch on the gate, even though Raja wouldn't arrive home until the afternoon. After an hour or two, she'd fall asleep, her head on the windowsill, as the lunch that Kaki had prepared for her got cold.

Today, at around eleven o'clock, Kaki peeked into the bedroom and saw Jamuna stretched out on the bed. "Are you sleeping? Do you not want to eat?" she called out softly. When Jamuna didn't answer, Kaki went to her own room. There she slung two bags, which she'd packed the night before, over her shoulders, and left the house. Rapidly she made her way to the Jagadamba School and entered its gates. She asked a man where she could find her son. "Class One is in the corner there." The man pointed to it. Kaki went and stood by the door. Immediately she spotted him, in the back of the class, sandwiched between six or seven other boys on a bench. The teacher, who was writing on the blackboard, noticed her and came to the door. Kaki told her that something had come up and that she needed to take Raja away for the day. The teacher asked her who she was.

"I am a servant. His mother sent me."

"Raja!" the teacher called. "Your servant from home has come to fetch you."

Carrying his bag and looking surprised, Raja came. Kaki took his hand and led him out of the school.

"Where are we going, Kaki?"

"You want some ice cream?" she asked. These days it was so rare, she realized, to be alone with him like this.

"Is Jamuna Mummy with you? Where is she?"

"Forget about Jamuna Mummy. I'll buy you ice cream."

They took the same route Kaki had taken the other day. "The ice cream shop is around the corner," she said, to reassure Raja as they navigated the alleys on the way to Kantipath, where she bought him a khuwa ice cream next to the yellow hotel. Thoroughly engaged with his treat, Raja didn't ask where they were as Kaki banged on the large brown gate. The same servant opened it.

"We're here," Kaki said. "Show us our room."

Nilu Nikunj

At NILU NIKUNJ in Jamal, six-year-old Raja cried for Jamuna Mummy, and his wails echoed throughout the halls and rooms so plaintively that the other servant, Ramkrishan, came to the kitchen, where Kaki was frying some potatoes. He said, "Isn't there a way you can quiet him? Muwa will have a fit."

Kaki turned to Raja, who was sitting on the kitchen floor, throwing his legs about, his cheeks damp with tears. She said, "If you don't stop crying, I'll beat you with nettles."

"I'll throw you in Rani Pokhari," Raja replied.

"You and your Jamuna Mummy," Kaki said. With a spatula she scooped some potatoes into a bowl and gave them to Raja. He took the food and began eating, whining that he needed his Jamuna Mummy, that he wanted to go to school.

Ramkrishan said that his nephew attended a school nearby, and Raja could also go there. Just then Muwa appeared in the doorway. She wore the white dhoti of a widow and a white shawl. Her face was stern, her eyes were narrow, and her arms were folded at her chest. Kaki glanced at her and said, "The aloo is nearly done, Muwa."

Muwa's eyes fell upon Raja as he munched the potatoes. He stopped chewing and stared at her. She'd never smiled at him, nor asked him his name, and instinct told him that the best thing to do in her presence was to sit still.

"Is he ever going to shut up — what's his name — this boy?" Muwa asked.

"Raja," Ramkrishan, who had just finished chopping some squash, said.

"Name is Raja," Muwa said, barely moving her thin lips, "but cries like a beggar."

Kaki flinched, even though Ramkrishan had warned her that Muwa's tongue was rough. The fries were done, and she scooped them onto a plate and gave them to Ramkrishan. "Does Nilu Nani also like them salted?"

"No," said Muwa. "And the next time, don't feed your boy before my daughter eats, all right? I don't want him to get the wrong idea."

Kaki nodded. It was going to be different here for the two of them, especially for Raja, than at Ganga Da's house. But here, Raja was hers, and she didn't have to writhe as she watched that madwoman stake her claim on him. It was through Vaishali that Kaki had heard about the widow who lived near the yellow hotel, that she was looking for a second servant to help around the house. Nilu Nikunj, the house was called, Vaishali informed Kaki. Nilu's Dwelling. The widow's husband, now dead, had named the house after their only child, a daughter. Kaki had visited here two days earlier, and she'd poured her heart out to the widow about raising Raja on the streets, about how frustrating it was to live with a madwoman. Muwa had listened impassively, her back stiff as she sat on the couch, a cigarette between her fingers. She finally said, "You and your son will live well here." She would pay Kaki twenty rupees a month and provide new clothes during Dashain, and of course their meals would be free.

"I have nowhere to go," Kaki said, and Muwa nodded slightly, as if that fact satisfied her.

Kaki and Raja would sleep in the shack in the garden, formerly used to store garden tools and old furniture. Ramkrishan had emptied the shack and cleaned it for them. "It took me three whole days to do this," Ramkrishan said. "That's why you've been hired — I can't do all the work in this large house. My back hurts. Now that you're here, life will be a bit easier for me." He leaned closer to her. "Her husband's death has done something to Muwa," he whispered. "You'll find out."

Muwa's husband had died in a car accident when their daughter, Nilu, was four years old, Ramkrishan told Kaki. He owned one of the city's first travel agencies, housed in an office with large glass windows in Basantapur. He also owned pieces of land and shares in jute and sugar cane factories throughout the country. That unfortunate morning he had parked his car in front of his travel agency and was locking the door when an out-of-control truck slammed into him and crushed his head to pulp. Muwa sold the agency to a cousin at a hefty price. The income from her other properties and investments was enough to last for generations, Ramkrishan said, but Muwa hadn't yet recovered from her husband's death. While he lived, Muwa and her husband used to lead an active social life; now she stayed home most of the time. "She likes to . . ." Ramkrishan pointed his thumb at his mouth.

Kaki knew this already. Muwa's mouth smelled of alcohol, and Kaki had seen bottles in her room. "All the time?" she asked Ramkrishan, who replied that she usually drank in the evening, but sometimes started in the morning.

"For weeks after saab was killed, Muwa simply lay in bed, drinking. It's hard on Nilu Nani. She's still so young."

Kaki's new life began to take shape. She and Ramkrishan talked as they washed the dishes, cut and sliced vegetables, swept the floor, tasted the food from ladles, and planted flowers and vegetables in the garden. Raja wandered around the house, and now and then Kaki called him to make sure he wasn't bothering Muwa. When not drinking, Muwa napped in her room on the second floor or read Indian magazines detailing illicit romances, murders, and decapitations. The room was lit by a bedside lamp, since she kept her curtains drawn.

Nilu's room was next to Muwa's. Large dolls surrounded her bed, their eyes clear and blue, their hair yellow, unlike the sorry-looking handmade dolls Kaki remembered from her own childhood. Her mother had fashioned them out of old pieces of cloth, just like the dolls poor children in the city still played with. Nilu's dolls wore colorful, frilly dresses, and a hint of a smile played on their pink lips. The girl's room too was dark, its curtains closed, as though she were a miniature version of her mother. When Kaki went up to Nilu's room, the girl was often in bed like her mother, her fingers stroking a doll's hair. She looked at Kaki with interest whenever the woman came in to sweep the floor or collect empty glasses and dishes. One day she asked Kaki where Raja was.

"Downstairs, Nilu Nani."

The girl was flipping through the pages of a picture book, and she asked, "Does he know how to read stories?"

"He had just started school when we came here. Barely knows his alphabet."

"Is he not smart?"

"No, no, that's not it," Kaki said. She was folding Nilu's freshly laundered silk frocks and arranging them in the cupboard. "He's a tuhuro, and we're poor, so he got a late start."

Nilu kept turning the pages, then said, "What does it mean to be a tuhuro?"

"It means you don't have parents."

Nilu put down her book. "What happened to them?"

"I don't know. Someone found Raja in Tundikhel."

"I've been to Tundikhel, but only once. Muwa said that the riff-raff hang out there, so we never went back."

Kaki wiped the headboard of Nilu's bed with the end of her dhoti.

Nilu propped herself against a pillow, her arm behind her neck, and asked, "How did you find him?"

Just then Muwa walked in, and, seeing the two of them, said to Kaki, "After you finish your work, make me some tea, okay?"

"I was about to tell Nilu how Raja was found in Tundikhel."

"Call her Nilu Nani. All of our servants have called her nani."

"Muwa, Raja was born in Tundikhel," Nilu said to her mother.

Muwa's face showed a trace of a smile. "He wasn't born there. He was found there." She turned to Kaki. "Well, are you just going to stand there? What did I tell you a moment ago?"

"Muwa, she says Raja doesn't go to school," Nilu said.

Muwa sat next to her daughter, caressed her chin, and said, "Isn't my Nilu baby hungry? Do you want to drink a glass of warm milk?"

Nilu shook her head and told Kaki, who was about to leave, "Raja could come to my school, but it's a girls' school."

Nilu and Raja hadn't yet talked, although they'd run into each other around the house. Once, just back from school, Nilu had come into the kitchen and found Raja on the floor, lying on his stomach, crawling like a snake. Both Kaki and Ramkrishan were out in the garden, uprooting weeds. Nilu watched the boy from the doorway. He was snarling and growling, clawing the air in front of him as he slithered forward. When he became aware of her presence, he stopped, his arms frozen in the air. She turned and walked upstairs to her room, from where she shouted at Kaki to fetch her a glass of water. Kaki in turn called to Raja to get Nilu Nani some water. Raja poured a glass from the container in the kitchen and took it to her room upstairs.

She was sitting on her bed, still in her blue-and-white school uniform, twirling a long stick she'd picked up on the way home from the school bus, which dropped her off around the corner from the opening of the alley. Raja's eyes widened at the sight of the dolls. As he approached Nilu, she scrunched her eyebrows, made her face stern to look like her mother's, and said, "Why are you so slow?"

Raja didn't answer. He offered her the glass, but instead of taking it, she lightly tapped the stick on her palm, like a schoolteacher. "Put it there," she said, indicating the bedside table. She watched him as he obeyed, and when he was about to leave, she said, "Wait." She tapped the stick on the floor at the foot of the bed and said, "Sit!"

Raja abruptly sat down and crossed his legs. Nilu stared at him, and she took a few gulps of air as if she was about to make an important announcement; but in the end all that came out of her mouth was "Are you a tuhuro?"

Raja nodded, expecting her to say something bad about it.

But Nilu only tapped the stick on her palm while gazing at him. They looked at each other like this for a while. Then Nilu's eyes softened. "Do you remember your mother?" she asked.

He shook his head.

"Do you remember your father?"

He shook his head again.

She sighed. "Is there anyone you remember?"

"I remember Jamuna Mummy."

"I remember my father a bit, sometimes."

"But you are not an orphan, like me," Raja said grudgingly. He then stared at Nilu's dolls, clearly admiring them.

"Do you want to play with my dolls?" she asked.

He shook his head, a bit afraid that Muwa would learn about it if he did such a thing.

"Don't worry," she said. "No one will know."

He hesitantly went to the dolls and picked one up. He stroked its hair. Nilu demonstrated how to hold the doll properly in the crook of the arm, like a baby. "And this is how you talk to it," she said, and cooed to the doll.

He smiled shyly. They passed the doll back and forth for a while; then Kaki called Raja and he left the room. Nilu drank her glass of water and lay down in bed, wondering what it might be like to not know one's own mother.

Every day Raja waited for Nilu to return from her school, which was called St. Augustine's, and as soon as she wolfed down some bread and eggs and drank a glass of milk, they'd run into the yard. They played hopscotch, erected mud castles in the garden, and once a week, when Muwa was not home (she had an aunt in Kupondole whom she visited every week), the two went up to Nilu's room, where Nilu dressed Raja in one of her frilly frocks and applied lipstick and rouge to his face; then together they danced or enacted silly, childish skits.

Raja abided by her rules, for Nilu had made it clear that she made the decisions. "No, not like that," she chided him when his feet didn't move correctly to the dance steps she'd learned at school. She changed her mind frequently, without notifying him, so that the routines he'd learned yesterday she'd deem wrong today. But there was no questioning her; she didn't like to be challenged. But he didn't mind this because he himself couldn't come up with ideas for play as quickly and creatively as she could, so he happily followed her lead. She didn't smile much when they played together, but her eyes were gentle and soft when they fell upon him. Even after she reprimanded him for a flub or a blunder, she'd put her arm around him and say, "Come, let's try it again."

One day they stole sand from the yard of a neighbor whose house was under construction. The laborers had left early that afternoon, and Nilu decided that they too would build a house. They found a couple of buckets and began to haul the sand to a corner behind the shack where Kaki and Raja slept. Ramkrishan and Kaki were resting in the kitchen, and Muwa was up in her room, so the children carried on their task uninterrupted until they had piled up a fairly large mound of sand. By mid-afternoon they had stolen a number of bricks from next door as well, and they stacked them into a cubicle that they could slide into. They dumped the sand along the base for a foundation, and they found a cardboard plank to serve as the roof. Only after they were done did they realize that they had neglected to make a door for their house.

Nilu scolded Raja: "The man of the house is supposed to think of such things." Glumly, he accepted the blame. "No matter," she said. "You're still my husband. I won't leave you." The two then took a few bricks from one side of their cubicle, stepped in, and stacked the bricks behind them, so it became dark inside. It was cramped too, but Nilu pronounced it a good home. She gave it an English name: Private Palace. "I'm tired after a hard day's work," she declared, and suggested that the two go to bed. They both tried to lie down, but the space was too narrow. "We'll sleep while sitting," Nilu said, and she and Raja sat with their backs against each other. Raja kept giggling, and Nilu had to hush him. "Be quiet, so we can make a baby," she told him.

They were still inside Private Palace as the sun went down, and the small amount of light that seeped in began to wane. Raja whimpered. "I am scared," he said.

"Lie down on my lap," Nilu suggested, so he rested his head on her lap and she sang a lullaby to him. Like a baby, he fell asleep in that position, and when, a few minutes later, Kaki called them for dinner, Nilu didn't respond. After half an hour, both Kaki and Ramkrishan stepped out of the house, shouting their names. Kaki's voice became frantic as she and Ramkrishan roamed the yard and the gate area. Kaki went to see if the two had gone up the alley to Kancha's shop. Ramkrishan checked the back of the house. Through gaps between the bricks, Nilu saw that the light in Muwa's room was on, and soon the woman opened the window and asked Ramkrishan what the matter was. When he told her that the children were missing, she didn't say anything. Will she come down? Nilu wondered. She waited. Muwa stayed on the balcony; then, as Kaki's calls grew hysterical, Muwa emerged at the front door.

Muwa was the one who discovered Nilu and Raja. She lifted the cardboard and laughed at Nilu. All the clamor never woke Raja. "Chee!" Muwa said. "Sleeping with a servant boy. You are a dirty girl." She must have liked the sound of her own words, for she laughed; then she picked up the bricks one by one and, tottering, threw them into the neighbor's yard. Once Muwa went back upstairs, Kaki pulled Raja to his feet, conked him on the head, and twisted his ears. She threatened to strike him with nettles the next time he did anything like this. Then she embraced him and cried.

Nilu dismissively referred to all her friends at school, with the exception of a girl called Prateema, as girls with "no brains." Raja loved hearing her say that phrase, and he started silently repeating it to himself at night, like a chant. He expected that at some point she'd call him the same, and he mentally braced himself for it, but she never spoke those words to him, even when she was dissatisfied with his performance at play. "That Smita has no brains," she announced abruptly as they dug a hole in the garden to bury worms that they'd held as prisoners. Nilu talked to Raja frequently about school: the strict teachers versus the easy ones, the blind woman who sat by the school gate and begged for coins, and the new playground, which featured a large swing and a tunnel shaped like an alligator that you entered through its toothy, cavernous mouth and exited by squeezing yourself out its narrow arsehole. Raja listened attentively and marveled at this wonderful, strange world of Nilu's. The school building, he imagined, was a magnificent castle with thick pillars and long, quiet corridors; the teachers were old women wearing somber gowns; and students gathered daily for something called morning assembly during which they sang a song praising the king and the principal offered bits of wisdom about God, hard work, and good morals. St. Augustine's was nothing like the Jagadamba School, and at times Raja felt ashamed that he had nothing exciting to report about his experience there, which was already becoming fuzzy in his mind. Kaki, fearful that he'd go back to Jamuna, had stopped his schooling altogether.

One day, drinking a glass of milk in the kitchen, Nilu asked Raja, "Why don't you go to school?" Kaki was cleaning the bathroom upstairs.

He shrugged and said that Kaki wouldn't let him.

"Well, why not?" she asked.

He had no answer for her.

"Do you know how to read?" she asked him.

He'd heard her read from her English books, stories about the hare and the tortoise, about the poor servant girl who stole the heart of a prince. Embarrassed about his illiteracy, he nodded, avoiding her eyes.

"Okay then, read me a story," Nilu said. "Come." She led Raja by his hand up to her room, where they sat on the floor. From her bag she withdrew a book, and he became anxious when he saw that it was in English. She placed it in front of him and said, "Read."

He gazed at the marks on the page and said, "I don't know English."

She looked at him in disbelief, her face stern. Then she took out another book, in Nepali, and flipped to a page. "Read this," she said. And he labored over the words, his tongue becoming thicker as he moved his finger across the first line. "That's wrong!" she shouted, and he feared that she might pick up her stick and ask for his palm, to strike it. That's what the teachers at her school did, she'd informed him, to punish unruly girls. Raja tried again, but every time he pronounced a word, Nilu shook her head. Tears formed in her eyes. She stood, then threw herself on the bed, turning away from him. She muttered something under her breath, and his heart seemed to stop with dread as he waited for her to indict him as a boy with "no brains." But she turned to him, her cheeks damp, and said, "Don't you know how important it is to read? Mother Stevens says if we don't know how to read, then we'll be fools for the rest of our lives. We'll have no brains. Don't you know that?"

He shook his head. She'd mentioned Mother Stevens before, and he now pictured her as a woman with an unyielding, judgmental face.

"What are you going to do?" she asked.

He stood by her bed, his palms pressed against his sides, at attention. "I don't know."

She shook her head sadly. "You will be a servant until you die."

Raja wished he could comfort her. With Kaki cooking and cleaning all day, and their living in the small shack in the garden, he was beginning to understand that his status in this house was that of a servant. But he was incapable of extending that idea all the way to the moment of his death or connecting it to his lack of reading skills.

He was baffled, but not for long. Nilu soon said words that came from deep inside her. "You have to learn how to read. I'll teach you."

From then on, once she returned from school in the late afternoon, Nilu pulled Raja from the kitchen, ignoring Kaki's warning that

Muwa would get angry. The two sat on the porch or in Nilu's room, and the girl flipped open her old Nepali *Barnamala* with a drawing of the goddess Saraswati on its cover. She read aloud the big letters in the book, enunciating carefully, then asked him to repeat them. Kaki brought Nilu her snacks, a boiled egg or a buttered toast along with a glass of milk, and after Kaki left, Nilu asked Raja to share her food, or she simply pushed her egg or toast toward him, saying she'd eaten some candies from the shop at school.

By late afternoon Muwa was in a booze-induced stupor in her room, and if the children were loud in their recitations, they disturbed her; she'd call Nilu, sounding as though she had a rock under her tongue. On occasion Nilu simply ignored her mother. But Muwa's voice made Raja stumble over his words. He worried that Nilu would be punished for spending time with him, although he'd never seen her disciplined for anything. Once Muwa, after Nilu ignored her calls, appeared at the door, surprising them. With a crumb of egg yolk on his lips, Raja froze. Nilu kept her eyes on the book. "What, you're a big man now?" Muwa said to Raja. "Go down." He jumped to his feet and stumbled down the stairs. Normally, however, Muwa didn't emerge from her room until late in the evening, after her afternoon daze had worn off; then she ate dinner with Nilu and later sat in the living room, listening to Radio Nepal, with a glass of whiskey by her side.

Whenever Raja saw Muwa, with her dry, sunken cheeks and her harsh words, his throat turned dry, and he felt that he became stupid, a boy with no brains. Since he and Kaki had arrived at Nilu Nikunj, he'd understood that the best way to deal with Muwa was to avoid her gaze, lower the head, and nod yes or no to her questions, which were often sharp when directed at him. When Muwa spoke to Nilu, however, her voice acquired a lilting, loving quality that reminded Raja of Jamuna Mummy, making a lump rise in his throat.

He missed Jamuna Mummy's caresses, missed sitting in her soft lap and being fed sweets, missed her lullabies and the funny words she made up as she went along. Every few days he asked

Kaki whether they'd ever visit Jamuna Mummy or perhaps even chance upon her on the streets, although Kaki hadn't let him venture beyond the opening of the alley since they moved. Each time, Kaki crushed his hopes, telling him he ought to consider his Jamuna Mummy as good as dead. Then, realizing that she was being too cruel with the boy, she ruffled his hair and said, "You have me, Raja. You don't need anyone else." She stroked his chin, but he winced because her palms were callused and rough, unlike Jamuna Mummy's.

For her intrusion, and her banishment of Raja from her daughter's room that day, Muwa received a sound tongue-lashing. Nilu threatened to report the incident to Mother Stevens, the principal at St. Augustine's, who would be clearly unhappy with Muwa's efforts to snuff an orphan's education. "Mother Stevens says education uplifts mankind," Nilu informed her mother tearfully. The sisters ran another school near Patan that served village children at virtually no cost, didn't Muwa know?

Muwa told her daughter to shut up, that she wasn't going to raise her child to befriend servants. So Nilu didn't speak to her mother, or anyone, for days, and stayed shut in her room before and after school, refusing to eat, until Kaki and Ramkrishan appealed to Muwa to talk to her child, to compromise.

Muwa, who'd begun drinking more since Nilu's tantrum, finally relented and made her way to her daughter's room. Nilu was lying in bed, reading, the radio softly playing near her head. She didn't glance at her mother, who sat down on her bed, her loud exhalations filling the room with the stench of alcohol. Nilu kept her eyes glued to her book. Muwa gazed at her for a while.

"Why aren't you eating?" she asked.

Nilu didn't answer.

"How long are you going to remain like this?"

Nilu didn't answer.

"So you want to spend your life cavorting with a low-class boy?"

Nilu's eyes, fiery with anger, fell upon her mother briefly; then she turned to face the wall.

"What do you lack in this house, huh?" Muwa said. "Ever since your father died, I've fulfilled each of your demands. What have I not given you?"

Nilu didn't answer. The soft chatter of the radio floated gently across the room. Muwa sighed, then lay down next to her daughter, making the bed creak. "All right, if what you want is to teach that stupid boy how to read, who am I to stop you? Just don't come crying to me if he doesn't learn anything. You don't know these people — there's only so far that they can go."

It took him a few weeks, but finally Raja was able to falteringly navigate the pages of the big-lettered Nepali *Barnamala*, recognize words, and sometimes even read passages from Nilu's schoolbooks. He ran to Kaki, shouting out the words from the book he held in his hands. Kaki, who was sitting on the kitchen floor, skinning zucchinis, looked pleased, but when he said that now he wanted to go back to the Jagadamba School, her face tightened and she said, "You're not going back there."

"Why not?"

"Because I say so. Don't answer me back; if you do, I'll tear your mouth open."

"Who are you to tell me not to go to school?" he said, throwing the book at her. It struck her face and fell to the floor. "Are you my mother? Are you my father?"

"I raised you," she said, tossing the book aside. She placed the zucchinis in a bowl of water, wiped her fingers on her dhoti, and stood.

"I'm going to run away from here," Raja said.

Fear gripped Kaki. She wanted to embrace the boy tightly and tell him never to utter those words again. But she didn't want him to think she was giving in, so she said calmly, "Who's stopping you? Leave. Take off this very minute."

Raja crossed his arms at this chest. "You think I won't do it? Once you discover that I'm missing, then you'll know."

Kaki began pumping up the kerosene stove. It was about five

o'clock, time to prepare dinner. Ramkrishan had gone to his village to visit his family, so for the past three days Kaki had to do all the housework by herself. Muwa would soon return from the weekly visit to her aunt's house, and although she barely ate, sometimes she demanded that Kaki bring the food to the dining room, a chilly, soulless room next to the kitchen, so that she and Nilu could have a proper family meal. Muwa drank only a peg or two in the morning before visiting her aunt; this change in habit made her complain of headache and fatigue as she left the house. But she abstained in deference to her aunt. Sometimes this self-control proved so difficult that Muwa couldn't help but curse her aunt, wishing she was dead so this weekly charade could end. And Muwa's dinnertime attempt at family togetherness with Nilu often failed, for she'd begin to drink in earnest as the food was being served, and halfway through their meal, she was toppling glasses and dropping food on her sari.

Kaki nonetheless carefully prepared their meal. Because of the din of the stove, she didn't hear Raja challenge her: "You think I won't run away from here?"

Raja glowered at her, then left the kitchen to go to the yard. He looked up to see if Nilu had come to the balcony next to her room, but she hadn't, and he thought about calling her to come down to play. But he was still mad at Kaki, and he remembered his threat. He opened the gate and walked into the alley. In the distance, he could see people walking, cars rushing by. Things moved quickly there, so he headed in that direction, kicking the dust under his feet. He needed to teach Kaki a lesson.

At the opening to the alley, he peeked into the door of Kancha's soda shop, a space so cramped that Kancha had to crouch inside. The man sold candy, spicy titaura, cigarettes, and other knickknacks from the window, which opened onto the sidewalk. A few times Nilu and Raja had run to the shop during breaks from their play, despite Kaki's injunctions not to venture out of Nilu Nikunj compound, to buy candy and drinks. Their favorite was fizzy soda, which tickled their noses as they drank.

Now, as Raja walked by, Kancha said, "Eh, badmash! Eh, idiot! You need to pay me for that soda I gave you the other day." Ignoring him, Raja walked on. Traffic zoomed by. People hurried along the sidewalk. From a shop across the street loud radio music blared. Raja and Nilu had stood at this spot before, licking their titaura, and Nilu had pointed out her school bus stop to the left, across the street from Rani Pokhari. Raja didn't know whether Lainchour was in the direction of Nilu's bus stop or the opposite way, to his right. He nearly asked Kancha where it was, then stopped, because Kancha would surely tell Kaki, who would come, irate, to fetch him in Lainchour. So he took a left toward Rani Pokhari, attracted by the crowd, hoping that he'd spot the Jagadamba School around the corner.

A few hundred yards away, he waited to cross the street. Scooters, tiger-striped taxis, and bicycles whizzed by. His eyes followed a man riding a gleaming new Hero bicycle, a woman on the carrier seat behind him. Raja wondered when he'd be able to ride a bicycle like that. Nilu had a small, pink tricycle, which she never rode; it sat in a corner of the yard. Once, at his request, Nilu had let him ride it in the yard. He went around in circles, loving how fast it went, but within minutes Kaki stepped outside and, glancing up at Muwa's bedroom, snatched the tricycle from him.

An old woman was standing next to him, waiting to cross the street. At a break in traffic, the woman shuffled across, and Raja stuck close to her. She frowned and continued walking. Once they reached the other side, she vanished into the crowd. He didn't know where to go. Traffic swirled about him. Everyone seemed to be in a hurry, except the street vendors, whose wares included newspapers, roasted peanuts, clothes, and small toys. A dark man selling cotton candy slowly went by. Raja's mouth watered.

He approached the black fence surrounding Rani Pokhari. As he walked alongside it, he slapped the metal bars with his left palm. Soon he was in the Ratna Park area, and he circled the small Ganesh shrine, even recognizing the old white-bearded priest who doled out prasad from the inner sanctum. Excitement clamped his throat: this had been his neighborhood until a few months ago. Pushing past people, he ran to the area where Kaki used to sell her corn. A shoeshine man sat there, rapidly rubbing a piece of cloth on a customer's black boots. Raja watched. The customer had a heavy jaw and a curly mustache, and he snarled at Raja. The shoeshine man glanced at Raja's feet, noted the slippers, and asked him to move on.

Raja crossed the street and entered the market of Asan, once again dimly recalling having come here in the past, perhaps with Kaki. As he moved farther into the market, then on to Indrachowk, the crowd swallowed him. There was no expansive field here, as in Lainchour, only narrow alleys lined with shops displaying their wares on the ledges of doors and windows: hats and caps, wool sweaters, colorful blankets and cushions, religious prints. The constant chatter of the people around him, the *tring-tring* of bicycle bells, and the *vroom* of the occasional scooter—it all became too much for him, and he began to weep. A pedestrian or two stopped and asked him if he was lost, but he feared that these strangers would lure him to their own homes, so he shook his head and continued.

He traversed the city all afternoon, becoming hungrier by the hour, but he had no money to buy food, not even cheap candy. At some point he made a turn, and suddenly the streets were wider, and the shops had large, clean windows. He then remembered that Lainchour was not too far off, and neither was Nilu Nikunj. If he stopped and oriented himself carefully, he could probably find his way back to Nilu Nikunj. But he really didn't want to return to Kaki. He kept moving, then actually gathered the nerve to approach a stranger, to ask him where Lainchour was. The stranger pointed in the direction that Raja had taken.

By this time the sun was already beginning to set, and he grew anxious, his heart hammering at the thought that, once night fell, it might be hard to recognize Jamuna Mummy's house. As darkness wrapped Raja in its cloak, the road seemed to stretch for miles, and the boy trudged along; the shadows that wove in and out of the trees that lined the sidewalk seemed ominous. His mouth moved automatically to a prayer he'd heard Kaki utter as she worked around the house: "O God, your miracles are beyond compare." To avoid looking directly at the shadows, Raja studied the ground and listened to the slap of his slippers. "O God, your miracles are beyond compare."

Then he saw it: the flat, long building of the Dairy in the dimming evening light, and then the field in front of the Jagadamba School. He picked up his pace and began to run. He crossed the field, watching as his old school came nearer; then he entered the alley behind it and finally found the gate to Jamuna Mummy's house.

He unlatched it and entered the yard. Light shone from Jamuna Mummy's bedroom, and he saw the figure of Ganga Da sitting on the bed. "Ganga Da," Raja shouted, running through the front door, which was slightly ajar, then into the room.

Ganga Da's face lit up; then he put his finger to his lips. Jamuna Mummy was lying in bed, her eyes closed, a wet handkerchief on her forehead. "She just fell asleep," Ganga Da said. "How did you get here?" he whispered, pulling Raja out to the yard. "Where's Kaki?"

When Raja told him that he came by himself, Ganga Da stared at him in disbelief. "You shouldn't have done such a thing," he finally said.

"What's wrong with Jamuna Mummy?"

"She's gotten worse since Kaki took you away. How long has it been now? Four months? She stayed in the mental hospital for a whole week. Now she has a high fever."

"I want to go to her."

"I don't know, Raja. Maybe it's better if she doesn't see you." Ganga Da didn't tell Raja that soon after he and Kaki left, he'd found out through Vaishali that they were working in Nilu Nikunj. He had considered visiting them to persuade Kaki to allow Jamuna to see Raja once in a while. But it wasn't such a good idea, he decided, for it would unnecessarily excite his wife, give her false hope. "You must go home," he told Raja now. "Come, I'll take you to Kaki." He went to the gate and called to the next-door neighbor in a soft voice. A young man appeared, and Ganga Da, after explaining to him what had happened, asked him to keep an eye on Jamuna while he took

Raja back to Nilu Nikunj. Over the past few weeks Ganga Da had had to enlist the help of all of his neighbors to keep watch over his wife.

The young man wondered if the boy shouldn't eat something before he left.

"You're right. He must be hungry. I'll feed him something in the Mahan Restaurant up the street," Ganga Da said.

Raja sat in the yard, overwhelmed by the day's journey.

"Raja?"

It was Jamuna on the porch; the wet handkerchief was stuck to her forehead.

"You're too sick to come out," Ganga Da said.

"Raja?" Jamuna rushed toward the boy, stumbling.

Raja too stood up and went to her, mashing his face against her hip, tears suddenly streaming down his cheeks. She clasped him tightly. Wobbling, she knelt before him and wiped his tears, her hands shaking. "Where were you all these days? Where did she take you?" Her voice was barely audible, as if she'd not eaten or drunk anything for days.

"Nilu Nikunj."

"Nilu Nikunj?"

"That's where Nilu and Muwa live."

She frowned. "Where is Kaki?"

"She's a servant there."

"Has she kept you in a cage there? Huh? Tell me, don't lie. Did she keep you bound and gagged there?"

He shook his head. "But she hasn't let me go to school."

"That witch," Jamuna said. "I knew she was a witch when she first came here. You're not going back." She stood. Pulling Raja close to her, she faced Ganga Da defiantly. "Raja is home now."

"Jamuna, he can't stay here. Kaki is probably worried sick about him. Let me —"

Jamuna's grip almost suffocated Raja. "Who are you to decide that? I've been sick for days without him, and now you care about that witch more than me?"

The young neighbor also tried to persuade Jamuna, saying that keeping someone else's child was criminal. Jamuna accused the man of peeking through the window while she undressed. "You are a spy for the government," she said. "Where are your dark glasses, huh? Didn't His Majesty give you any?"

Ganga Da signaled to the young man to leave. After he closed the gate, Ganga Da turned to Jamuna. "Okay, it's already dark, so we'll let him sleep here tonight. But we have to send . . . talk about this tomorrow morning."

Remarkably, the wet handkerchief still adhered to Jamuna's forehead, and Raja pointed to it and began to laugh. "Let's go inside," she said, smiling, as Ganga Da went to the Mahan Restaurant to fetch some food.

When he returned with a plate of dal-bhat and chicken, Raja was displaying for Jamuna the bruises on his legs he'd acquired from playing. She was touching the bruises, commiserating, and also asking him questions about Nilu Nikunj, what Nilu and Muwa were like. Ganga Da scooped some chicken and rice onto a plate and brought it to Raja, who ate ravenously, his mouth bulging as he answered Jamuna's questions. Ganga Da touched Jamuna's forehead to gauge her temperature; her fever had come down. Once in a while, Raja, who was sitting on Jamuna's lap, would hold a piece of chicken to her lips, and she'd open her mouth and take it, saying, "Mmmm." Watching them, Ganga Da wondered where their intimacy came from. He worried that by now Kaki must know that Raja had run away to Lainchour, and she'd come barging in soon, accusing them of stealing him from her.

That night Ganga Da slept on bedding on the floor, while Jamuna and Raja slept on the bed. The boy's head was buried deep in Jamuna's bosom, and he was squirming like a newborn puppy. Now and then Jamuna ran her hand through his hair, her expression blissful.

The day Kaki had abducted Raja from school, Jamuna had run around the neighborhood, asking people if they'd seen her son. Helplessly Ganga Da had tagged along, making hand signals to people behind her back to tell them to humor her. "Raja will come back, I promise," he told her repeatedly as he led her home late that night, after a fruitless search in the neighborhood and the Ratna Park area.

All night she sat in bed, looking out the window, cursing Kaki or chuckling and saying, "Coming! He's coming!" The moonlight made her face look ashen, and Ganga Da wondered if this was the moment when her mind would completely and utterly lose its grip on reality. Tired, she let her head fall to her chest.

"Come lie down here," he said, but she remained in that position for the rest of the night.

The morning after Raja left, as Ganga Da was cooking in the kitchen, Jamuna walked into the yard and took her clothes off. He managed to drag her back into the house, but that night he awoke to find her side of the bed empty. He located her in the kitchen, with her back against the wall; she was holding a little knife used for peeling potatoes. She struck at him, missed, and ran into the darkness outside. Minutes later he found her by following the incessant barking of the neighborhood dogs. They had cornered her outside the closed shutters of the Mahan Restaurant. Half a dozen of the mangy creatures, who in daylight went slinking about, tail between their legs, now growled at Jamuna, baring their teeth as they closed in. Jamuna was wildly waving the peeling knife at them under the streetlamp. That night, with the help of the owner of the Mahan Restaurant, Ganga Da took her to the mental hospital in Patan, where she stayed for three days on a cot with stained sheets. The whole ward, consisting only of nine beds, with several patients sleeping on the floor, smelled awful — of antiseptic, body odor, even urine — and Ganga Da had to cover his nose with his handkerchief. He managed to arrange a proper bed, instead of the cot, for Jamuna only after he pushed twenty rupees into the hands of the head nurse. A doctor gave Jamuna several injections, which made her drowsy.

The days in the hospital were a blur to Ganga Da. A girl in the bed next to Jamuna laughed hysterically at the ceiling fan every few minutes, pointing to something only she saw; an old woman clawed the air, and a man in tattered clothes hovered around Jamuna's bed, contorting his eyebrows until a nurse took him away. On the seventh day, Ganga Da asked Jamuna, whose eyes had begun to sink into their sockets from the electroconvulsive therapy, whether she wanted to go home, and dumbly, she nodded. The doctor advised Ganga Da against it, but the hospital atmosphere had become too much for him. Every time the girl on the next bed cackled, he wanted to leap up and clamp his hand over her mouth. Toward late afternoon, when the doctor and the nurses were away, he enlisted the relative of a patient to help him walk Jamuna out of the hospital and into a taxi, to go home.

Now Raja had somehow escaped Kaki and ended up back with them. Who would be blamed for thinking that this boy, sleeping so contentedly on Jamuna's lap, was indeed born from her womb? Watching the two turned Ganga Da's thoughts toward his own mother, how soft and inviting her lap had been when he was a child, how comforting the feel of her hands as she cupped his chin with her palms. His mother was now lost among the ghats of Banaras, captivated by a smooth-tongued swami who was promising her liberation from this samsaric world. Ganga Da missed her and tried hard not to begrudge her this last-minute salvation, but now, watching Jamuna and Raja, he felt in his own bones his mother's absence, with a pang of resentment at her for vanishing from his life. Tomorrow he'd have to wrench Raja away from Jamuna because he was not her child, and tonight the woman, Kaki, who'd wiped the boy's bottom and helped him learn how to walk, was tossing and turning, worried about where he was—a woman who had more of a claim on this boy than anyone else did.

Or did she?

Ganga Da's eyes fell upon his wife's face. How calm she had become since she'd been able to hold Raja in her arms. Raja was her cure, and God knew, she needed a cure. It was incredible to Ganga Da that despite all that Jamuna had put him through, when he looked at her in sleep, a feeling of intolerable compassion rose in

68

him. Nothing mattered, not what others said, not the unpredictability of his wife's behavior, not the fitful nights he'd spent worrying she'd harm herself, or him, in one of her episodes. Despite everything, this was the woman whose hand he was meant to hold on his deathbed.

An idea pushed itself into the forefront of Ganga Da's mind. Throughout the night, as he drifted in and out of sleep, he pondered it, and by dawn he knew what he needed to do. He quietly changed his clothes, opened his small steel safe inside the cupboard, extracted eight hundred rupees, and left the house. His destination was only a short distance away, a house near the incline that opened onto the Thamel market.

He spotted the house owner, Bhimnidhi, in his garden, taking a bath, with a lungi wrapped around his waist. Bhimnidhi worked as a midlevel administrator in Prasuti Griha, the maternity hospital in Thapathali. "Ganga Da, what an honor," he shouted as he splashed water on his chest. Ganga Da waited until the man was done bathing, then they both went inside.

Bhimnidhi's wife brought them tea. Ganga Da shut the door behind her and told Bhimnidhi what he wanted.

"But that's impossible," Bhimnidhi said. "This early in the morning, you come to talk about such a difficult matter. It'll be a paap to do such a thing."

"The boy will have a better life with us. You'll be performing a dharma, not a sin."

"I'm a Brahmin's son, Ganga Da. Even contemplating such a thing is a sin for me."

Ganga Da reached for his wallet, took out five hundred-rupee notes, placed them on the mat in front of him one by one, and smoothed them. "Everyone will benefit. My wife will get a son, I'll have peace of mind at home, and you . . ." He extended his lower lip toward the notes. Just a few weeks ago, Ganga Da had heard Bhimnidhi complain about his two teenage sons, whose extravagant tastes he couldn't fulfill with his modest salary. Five hundred rupees nearly matched Bhimnidhi's monthly salary, Ganga Da knew.

Bhimnidhi warily observed the bills. After a moment he cleared his throat and said, "You put me in a bind."

Five minutes later, Bhimnidhi had pocketed the money and was writing down the specific date and time that Ganga Da dictated to him. After he finished writing, Bhimnidhi said, "I'll try my best, all right, Ganga Da? Sometimes matters like these are a bit delicate. You never know who is your enemy, who is waiting for you to make a move like this so they can pounce on you."

Ganga Da pulled out two more hundred-rupee bills, waved them in the air, and said, "There's more here if other mouths need to be gagged, but first I'll need the document in hand."

Bhimnidhi spread his palms. "It's in God's hands."

"When will it be done?"

"Come to Prasuti Griha this afternoon."

"Today?"

"Yes, today. If it needs to be done, why delay?"

"But whatever happened to our famous Nepali way of putting off until tomorrow what can be accomplished today?" Ganga Da joked.

Bhimnidhi laughed heartily, and the two men departed in a jovial mood. Before he left the gate, Bhimnidhi asked that he bring the additional two hundred rupees to the hospital, as "more hungry mouths might need to be fed." This elicited even more laughter from both men.

At home, Jamuna and Raja were still sleeping. Ganga Da woke them and asked them to quickly get ready, as they had to leave.

"Where? Raja hasn't eaten anything," Jamuna said, rubbing sleep from her eyes.

"Right now it's more important that you two go before Kaki comes."

At the mention of Kaki's name, Jamuna promptly stood, picked up Raja, and carried him to the bathroom, where she washed the half-asleep boy's face; offering him water from her palm, she made him gargle. After Jamuna and Raja dressed, the three of them left the house. They walked toward Tangal, and Ganga Da's heart jumped to his throat every time he saw a woman's figure that remotely resembled Kaki. They made their way behind the royal palace, past the moss-covered walls that Bokey Ba had attempted to climb with baby Raja in his arms.

The three moved speedily; Raja sometimes walked on his own, sometimes was carried by Ganga Da or Jamuna, until they reached an old house in Tangal with a large unkempt yard. They opened the gate and went inside. A woman in the white dhoti of a widow, her hair graying, came out to the porch. Her face brightened at seeing Ganga Da, and she gave a curt nod to Jamuna. Before she could ask who the boy was, Ganga Da raised his palm and spoke quickly. "Bala Maiju, you'll need to house Jamuna and the boy for a few days here."

Bala Maiju looked shocked. "What's wrong? Is this the boy whose mother worked—"

"She's not his mother," Jamuna said testily. "I'm—"

"That's not important right now," Ganga Da said. "When the time comes, Bala Maiju, I'll explain everything."

"This doesn't look right to me. What is going on?"

Ganga Da went to her, put his arms around her, and said, "You think your nephew will do anything untoward and get you involved? What would Gaurav Uncle think of you if he were alive today?" Invoking Gaurav Uncle, Ganga Da's maternal uncle, always worked with Bala Maiju, whose eyes teared up at the memory of her dead husband; he had doted on Ganga Da.

"That's not what I'm saying," Bala Maiju said. "But keeping someone else's child without their knowledge . . . I assume the mother doesn't—"

"It's just a legal matter," Ganga Da said. "It'll get resolved in a few days, and I'll bring them back home."

"You know that you're welcome here for as long as you want," Bala Maiju said, looking directly at Ganga Da, not Jamuna.

"Of course I know that. In fact, you shouldn't bear the sole burden of these two extra mouths to feed, so . . ." He took out the two hundred rupees he'd waved in front of Bhimnidhi. A certain type of madness had come over him.

Bala Maiju slapped his hand and said, "Don't insult me like this. What would your Gaurav Uncle think of such a shameful gesture?"

Smiling, Ganga Da put the money back into his pocket and raised his arms in surrender. The three of them went inside, where Bala Maiju once again tried to pry from Ganga Da why they couldn't stay in their own house. But Ganga Da kept shaking his head, saying he'd reveal everything at the proper time.

After drinking some tea and eating a leftover roti, Ganga Da left, heading straight to his office, as it was nearly ten. Once there, he signed in, then sat at his desk for about an hour, taking care of some paperwork. He yawned, scratched his throat, then went to the corridor, which looked out on the lane that led to his office building, to see if Kaki had appeared. Every hour or so, Ganga Da wandered back to check again. The colleague who shared his desk remarked gently that it seemed as if Ganga Da was impatient for a lover to arrive. "Doesn't he look like a restless Romeo?" the man said, addressing everyone in the room. The others nearby murmured their assent and either went back to work or kept sipping their tea. Around noon, Ganga Da purchased tea and samosas from the canteen. As he ate, he eyed the manager's office, which was right across the corridor. The sliding sign outside the manager's office had been stuck on OUT for years now. The perpetually unreachable manager, thought Ganga Da. He carefully pulled out a long piece of hair that was stuck between the peas inside the samosa, threw it away, and plopped the rest of the samosa into his mouth. The manager emerged, wiped his hands on his door curtain, stretched, then ambled off to the canteen, which was in the adjacent building. Ganga Da gulped his tea and, turning to his colleague, said that he'd be back within an hour. The colleague raised his eyebrows, but Ganga Da quickly made his exit.

The Prasuti Griha Hospital was about a twenty-minute walk from where he worked. It was located right next to the Bagmati

River, and the sweet smell of the water followed him as he went into the building. A baby cried ferociously somewhere inside, and a quick glance through an open door revealed a young woman moaning in her bed. He found Bhimnidhi in a room with another man, who looked at Ganga Da as though he already knew his secret. Bhimnidhi closed the door and asked Ganga Da, "Did you bring it?"

Ganga Da patted his pocket.

"Give it to me."

"Where is the paper I asked for?"

"That will happen," Bhimnidhi said impatiently. Gone was his earlier cheerfulness; now he looked serious, almost rude. He spread out his palm to Ganga Da, who reluctantly placed the two hundred rupees in front of him. A nurse's muted shout sounded outside the doorway. Bhimnidhi passed the money to the other man, who silently opened the door and left.

Bhimnidhi didn't say a word to Ganga Da as they waited, standing. The man returned within two minutes and handed Ganga Da a yellow sheet of paper. He studied it and said, "This is it? This small paper?"

"That's it."

Ganga Da's next stop was an astrologer's dim room in Hanuman Dhoka. He handed the bearded man the yellow paper and told him what he wanted.

It didn't surprise Ganga Da when he saw Kaki stationed outside his gate in Lainchour, her hands on her hips, her face dark. "Raja is missing since yesterday," she said, cutting right through his pleasantries. "Where is he?"

He told her he didn't know.

Her eyes probed his face, half in contempt. "This is the only place Raja could come to. He couldn't have gone anywhere else."

Ganga Da opened the gate and went in. "Did you inform the police?" He didn't know how long he could keep up the façade.

She followed him and said, "No, I was hoping that he'd return to me or that I'd find him. Here." Her eyes scanned the house, the yard. Then she noticed the big lock on his door, and said, "Where's your wife?"

"She's gone to her mother's."

Suspicion marked Kaki's face. A wave of guilt washed over Ganga Da. But he couldn't let her presence weaken him, so he mentally evoked, and amplified, the resentment he'd felt toward her for violating her promise, for leaving. He said testily to her, "You didn't think twice when you took him with you, and now you have the nerve to come here. Even if he was here, why would I tell you?"

"You've hidden him somewhere, haven't you?" Kaki hissed. "Where is he? Tell me before I fetch the police."

Ganga Da folded his arms on his chest.

Kaki shouted Raja's name. She ambled to the back of the house and peered in through the window, then came to the front and banged on the door, all the while shouting the boy's name. Then she sat down on the veranda and began to weep. Ganga Da remained with his arms crossed. Neighbors appeared at their windows, and Kaki appealed to them, asking if they'd seen Raja in this house. They quickly withdrew their heads, then peeked through gaps in the curtains. Kaki turned to Ganga Da. "You've stolen him from me," she said. "You've conspired with that wife of yours to rob me of my boy." She placed her head against the pillar on the veranda and closed her eyes, apparently weakened by the ordeal.

His throat tight, Ganga Da sat next to her, took her hand in his, and said, "Come, I'll take you home." He was acutely aware of the yellow sheet of paper in his shirt pocket. It felt hot, as though it were ready to burn a hole in his chest.

She shoved away his hand and stood, saying, "Don't touch me. I spit on people like you. I'm going to the police."

For the next hour, Ganga Da sat on the veranda, watching the sun set behind the Nagarjun hill. Some of his neighbors were still at their windows, whispering among themselves. He didn't know what would happen next. He knew he ought to go to Bala Maiju's house, tell Jamuna that Kaki had come to look for Raja, that the police might be involved. But the tussle with Kaki had exhausted him. Raja belonged to Kaki. She had raised him, had taken care of him when the rest of the world hadn't. And now he and Jamuna were yanking him away from her. It was wrong.

He felt a bit dazed at the thought that the police might come knocking on his door in the middle of the night. They could ask for Jamuna's whereabouts, and he'd just have to keep saying that she had left town, gone to a relative's place somewhere. But in truth, he just couldn't see why the police would take the complaint of a servant woman seriously, unless Kaki managed to involve her current employer. But he'd deal with events as they happened.

He had promised Jamuna that he'd go to Bala Maiju for the night, but now he became suspicious that Kaki might be lurking in the shadows nearby, waiting for him to go to his wife and Raja so she could then follow. It was a silly thought, but it made him scrutinize the yard and the surrounding walls as darkness began to slowly spread and the crickets started to chirp. He sat still, his heart hammering, and out of the corner of his eye, he saw something move in the tulsi bushes. "Who?" He stood up, and two birds — swallows? — swooped through the air and disappeared into the darkening sky.

Part II

The Document

NORMALLY SISTER ROSE combed through each piece of writing before Nilu, who was now in the tenth grade and the editor of the school magazine, took them all to the printer to be typeset. Sister Rose scoured the articles for innuendo criticizing the school or its policies, parodies of teachers, or love poems containing hidden sexual messages, especially from one girl to another. This year Sister Rose had already forced Nilu to remove improper lines from several articles.

During the winter, in one of these "proofreading meetings" held informally on the bed in Sister Rose's narrow room next to the library, the two reviewed the pieces for the next issue; the early afternoon sun warmed their faces and legs. Sixteen-year-old Nilu's back leaned against the wall, while Sister Rose lay on her side, head propped by an arm, knees pulled in, her shoes on the floor. A faint odor emanating from Sister Rose, like a mixture of men's aftershave and the potatoes she'd eaten for lunch, was making Nilu slightly nauseated. As far as Nilu was concerned, the pieces they were reviewing were fine, and she wanted to be done quickly so she could go and finish her homework for her next class.

"What is this girl trying to say here?" Sister Rose asked, holding a Nepali poem up to the sunlight. "What does she mean by *tyo saririk nashako sugandh*? Let me see, that means 'that smell . . .' no, 'fragrance of . . . physical drunkenness,' right? Or intoxication. What does this girl, Prateema Ganguly, mean by that, pray tell me?"

"She's just marveling at her own body there, Sister, almost in a spiritual way."

"But doesn't *tyo* refer to the body of the man she's just talked about? In the previous line?"

"No, no," Nilu said, although she knew that to be precisely the case. She even knew the man that Prateema Ganguly, her best friend at school, was writing about. Prateema claimed to have fallen in love with the teacher who tutored her at home in Nepali, her weakest subject. He was a poor man who taught at a local school, but something was happening during these tutorial sessions, Prateema told Nilu with dreamy eyes, and suddenly she'd begun writing poems of longing in Nepali, a language that had always troubled her, as her family was originally from Calcutta and they spoke Bengali and English at home. "I'll teach him English, he'll teach me Nepali, and our children will write poetry in both languages, no?" Prateema had once said to Nilu, who liked her friend enough to forgive her this romantic crush, which she thought was awfully silly and likely to be short-lived. Probably the tutor had a wife and child back in his village, Nilu thought. She herself had never lost her head over a boy, let alone a man. Strangely, she still thought of Raja, her childhood friend, and she wondered what he was like now. She dreamt about him, still: the two would be playing in the yard, jumping into a mountain of sand, or they'd be strolling in a foreign country amid beautiful pillared monuments. She didn't know why, after all these years, Raja still haunted her, why she wasn't interested in the boys around her, as her friends were. In fact, when a boy made romantic overtures to her, she rejected him outright, calling him an "idiot" or "nincompoop" to his face, so that even the most aggressive boys were slightly afraid of her. The boys she liked were those who, even if they harbored secret feelings for her, never revealed them and treated her like a friend. Nilu had a calm, solitary energy about her that attracted people; they were often impressed by her composure. She was bookish, and to fit the stereotype she wore big glasses that enlarged her eyes, making her look even more somber.

"Prateema and I have been reading the poetry of Rumi." Nilu lied to Sister Rose. "Have you read Rumi's poems, Sister? He talks about how spiritual our bodies are."

"Really?" Sister Rose said. She looked up at Nilu, her eyes registering a sudden interest. "Tell me more. What does Rumi say about physical intoxication?"

"Oh, he talks about how God can . . ."

Sister Rose placed her right hand on Nilu's thigh, which was exposed because her skirt had slid up. "Go on," Sister Rose said, and yawned.

Nilu squirmed and shifted her leg, so Sister Rose's hand would slip away, but it remained on her thigh. "Rumi . . . well . . . he suggests that physical desire can be channeled for union with . . . God."

There was no mistake now: Sister Rose's fingers had traveled farther up Nilu's thigh, closer to her crotch, and with a jerk Nilu bolted out of the bed and stood up. Her breath stuck in her throat, and when the words came, they tumbled out rapidly. "I have to go."

Sister Rose's pale face turned crimson. "Already? We haven't discussed the piece."

"There's nothing wrong with it," Nilu said.

"Sit down, Nilu. What's the hurry? Would you like a piece of Swiss chocolate?"

But Nilu grabbed her bag. "I have things to do."

Sister Rose's skin color had returned to normal, and now she once again frowned at Prateema's poem. "This poem can't go in the magazine. We'll start getting calls from parents."

"I don't care. I have to go." Nilu tugged at the doorknob, but the door didn't open. It was latched. Nilu felt her body grow hot: Sister Rose had must have fastened the latch when they entered the room. She clanked it open and strode out, running to the nearby bathroom, where she locked herself in a stall, breathing hard. She swallowed a few times, and the nausea subsided. She contemplated going to the principal, Mother Mann, and telling her what had happened, but even as she rehearsed what she'd say to her, she found herself fumbling with the words. The sisters at the school often put their arms around the girls, pinched their cheeks, or rubbed their backs in gestures of affection, so Mother Mann would most likely brush aside Nilu's version of the event, saying that she had imagined it, that Sister Rose's touch was innocent, a gesture of fondness from a teacher to a student with whom she was working on the school magazine. Mother Mann might even yell — she liked to yell, provoking a vein on her throat to throb viciously — at Nilu for casting aspersions on Sister Rose. Nilu thought about going to Sister O'Malley, her favorite teacher, an iconoclast who favored jeans and a flowery kurta to her nun's robe and frequently fought with the other sisters about draconian school rules. Among the students Sister O'Malley was popular, and a flock of girls were always hovering around her in the hallways, or on the playground, or in the canteen, which irked the other sisters. For her part, Sister O'Malley mocked her own colleagues, mimicking their speech patterns and facial expressions and making the girls hysterical with laughter. Sister O'Malley would most likely believe Nilu and curse Sister Rose under her breath (she didn't shy away from words that made the girls giggle and blush), but what more could she do? She was already treated like a pariah by the other sisters, and rumors were circulating about her possible transfer to a small Jesuit school in a village in southern India.

For another hour or so Nilu sat on the commode, hoping that the teacher wouldn't notice her absence from class. The opening words of Jonathan Swift's "A Modest Proposal," which she'd read in English class, taught by none other than Sister Rose, floated into her mind, and her own words began to mimic the style of Swift's: "For Preventing the Schoolgirls of St. Augustine's from Becoming Independent Thinkers." The words kept coming, so she took her notebook from her bag, tore a piece of paper from it, and wrote them down. In a cacophony of chatter, girls entered and exited the bathroom. Stall doors opened and slammed shut. Finally Nilu left and walked toward her classroom. As she turned the corner in the hallway, she saw Miss Aryal leave the classroom, her sari dragging behind her.

"Where were you?" Prateema Ganguly whispered to Nilu as she took her seat. "Miss Aryal was asking about you."

"I'll tell you later," Nilu said.

Sister Rose entered the room. She asked the students to take out the brief essay she'd assigned as homework. Nilu crossed her arms. Sister Rose glanced at her, then sat at her desk. "Okay, you girls in the first two rows, come up here and read your essays." One by one they went to the front of the class and read, after which Sister Rose assigned each one a grade. "One hundred," she said, or "Poor quality. Thirty." When Prateema returned after her essay was graded, it was Nilu's turn. She didn't move. Sister Rose was scrutinizing a paper, and finally she looked up. "Who's next?"

"Nilu," someone said.

Nilu stared defiantly at Sister Rose, who blushed slightly.

"Come up here and read your essay," Sister Rose said.

"No."

"You don't have it?"

Nilu looked steadily at her without answering.

A brief staring match ensued; the other students looked at Nilu, then back at Sister Rose. Nilu could sense that Prateema was holding her breath. Nilu's eyes burned but she kept them focused on the sister, who finally looked away and muttered something under her breath. Looking out the window, Sister Rose said, "If you girls want to act so hoity-toity, then I can't teach you." She picked up her books and left the classroom.

Fortunately, only a few more articles remained to be vetted and delivered to the printer, and one day after school Nilu and Sister Rose stiffly went over them in the staff room. The math teacher with the military mustache was reading an old newspaper nearby and sipping tea. Every now and then a teacher or a janitor came in. Sometimes a girl would burst in, breathless, asking in a singsongy voice whether a certain sister was there.

The two reviewed the articles in silence, with Nilu making a correction here and there and Sister Rose nodding gravely after she finished reading a piece. The sister didn't mention Prateema's poem, and Nilu didn't bring it up. After they were done, Sister Rose left silently, her back a bit stooped. She's afraid, thought Nilu, and from her bag she took out the essay she'd started. Late afternoon today was the printer's deadline, so she began to reread the beginning of her own handwritten piece, made a couple of corrections, but then folded the paper and put it in her bag. She just didn't have the motivation. She looked at her watch again: it was time to go to the printer.

The boarding students were in the field behind the school, playing soccer, hockey, and basketball. Nilu could hear their cries as she exited the school premises and headed toward the Patan bus station. Normally she'd go home by bus, taking one that dropped her off at Ratna Park, and she only had to walk past Rani Pokhari to reach her house in Jamal. Every day she looked at the pond and thought of Raja. On some days the memories were clouded, but on others they emerged with the clarity of events that took place only yesterday. She specifically remembered young Raja talking about this one dream that he kept having, about a woman rising out of the waters. "Feel this," Raja had told her as he took her small palm and placed it on his chest; Nilu could feel his heart skipping madly. "I wake up with my heart like that." She remembered a few other things: her attempt to teach him how to read, Muwa's displeasure when she saw them together, Raja's gleeful face as he rode her tricycle in the yard, and Kaki's eyes — how they went dead after the judge delivered the verdict, handing Raja to Ganga Da forever.

Kaki. Nilu didn't know all the details about the case involving Raja, but she remembered Kaki's return to Nilu Nikunj; the woman was exhausted from pounding on people's doors, appealing for help. Nilu remembered one particular afternoon clearly because it took place in the year that King M had a heart attack. She'd been sitting on the lap of Muwa's aunt, who was visiting that day. They were all lounging on the veranda, soaking up the March sun. Muwa sipped a glass of whiskey. "As soon as he fired the shot, he fell," said Muwa's aunt, who possessed a small fraction of the royal blood — her grandmother's cousin was related to King M's sister — and liked to pretend that she knew everything that went on inside the palace. Nilu felt thirsty, wiggled out of her great-aunt's lap, and went into the kitchen, where Kaki was splitting some beans.

"What do you need, Nilu Nani?" Kaki said, looking up. Her cheeks were soaked in tears.

"Nothing," Nilu said, and turned to the wall, pretending she had spotted a lizard there.

Outside, Muwa's aunt continued. "Imagine, having a heart attack while hunting, seated on the platform amidst the treetops. And right after he fires the shot, King M falls smack on top of that minister, that big-nosed one, what's his name?"

"Kirti Nidhi Bista," said Muwa, burping. "I already heard."

Sometimes when Nilu was alone, she brooded over the events of those days after Raja, angry at Kaki, ventured out of Nilu Nikunj to find Jamuna Mummy, and Ganga Da hid him in his aunt's house. Over the years, through snippets of what Kaki revealed and what Ramkrishan told her, Nilu had formed pictures in her mind about what had happened. Kaki had somehow managed to find Bala Maiju's house in Tangal, and after staking it out for an afternoon and seeing glimpses of her Raja in an upstairs window, had returned the next day with two young men — Dindayal's relatives — in tow. The young men carried large bamboo sticks, but they were soon cowed by a giant of a man, Bala Maiju's neighbor. This man had a lungi wrapped around him; his stomach bulged and heaved as he planted himself in front of them. Kaki attempted to sneak past him, but the giant moved to block her each time, as in a children's game.

The young men finally gave up and left, and Kaki sat on the ground next to the gate, taking a meditative posture, legs crossed lotus style, palms at her knees, eyes staring straight ahead, at the level of the giant's shins. Passersby lingered to watch, then wandered off. The day crept toward afternoon, then evening. The giant went home to eat. When darkness began to fall, Ganga Da came to the gate. "Raja is not here," he told Kaki, who didn't blink. He knelt in front of her as if he'd been enlisted to make her face reality. "Go home. You've tortured yourself enough." He lost patience and shouted at her, "What do you think you are doing?" Then he strode back into the house and slammed the door shut.

All night Kaki stayed outside Bala Maiju's house. Early in the morning the police came and took her away in a van. Her lips had turned blue from the cold; she was also running a fever. When she didn't speak, even after repeated requests, the police decided to let her out near the Martyr's Gate. She wandered around Tundikhel. The sun was bright, the sky intensely blue, and she lay down on the grass, where she fell asleep.

The rest of Kaki's battle with Ganga Da to win back Raja involved the courts—this much Nilu knew. Though she didn't know the details, Nilu remembered that, surprisingly, the only person with a degree of power whom Kaki could rely on was Muwa, who secured a lawyer for her. Nilu imagined a courtroom scene wherein the lawyers argued, then suddenly Ganga Da's lawyer flourished a piece of paper that he said proved conclusively whom the boy belonged to. He handed the paper to the judge, who scrutinized it and said, "It's the boy's birth report, issued by the Prasuti Griha Hospital. It's dated and stamped." He thrust the document toward Kaki, who snatched it from his hand and inspected it. But Kaki didn't know how to read, and she flung the paper away. It floated to the floor.

Ganga Da's lawyer handed over two other documents to the judge, who said, "And here's more proof." He lifted the smaller piece of paper. "Here's a tippani stating the boy's birth." The other document was a scroll, with paintings of Lord Ganesh and tables of planetary positions at birth. "This here is a chinha, the boy's astrological chart. It states clearly who the parents of the child are."

Jonathan Swift

WHENEVER SHE WAS OUT, Nilu scanned the streets for Raja, thinking—foolishly, she knew—that she'd recognize him if she saw him. Would he have a pencil mustache by now, as most boys his age did? Would he also be a loudmouth, like them? She pictured him as soft-spoken, with an errant lock of hair falling onto his forehead. Nilu didn't know why she thought about him at all—it had been so many years. Probably he wouldn't remember her. If she ran into him, would she have to prod his memory, and then would he feign remembering her, just so her feelings wouldn't be hurt?

As she got off the bus at Dharahara and made her way to the printer's shop, she observed the shop-window displays, but even in the reflections in the glass she saw Raja, saw Kaki. She also thought she discerned the man called Ganga Da, who stole Raja from Kaki, even though Nilu hadn't ever seen the man himself. Whenever she thought of Ganga Da, she likened his face to that of Sumit, the young man who now spent hours in Nilu Nikunj and lounged with Muwa in her bedroom in the afternoon. As Nilu muscled her way through the dense crowd, loneliness engulfed her, and the evening buzz of New Road, which she usually enjoyed, became tinged with melancholy. She wanted to go somewhere and lie down, but not at home, where Muwa and Sumit would be, where the sight of Kaki would add to her gloom.

Behind her, the door to the Crystal Hotel opened, and aromas wafted from its restaurant, The Other Room. A couple sauntered out, chewing fennel seeds, their eyes bright and laughing. The man said something to the woman, and she pinched him on the arm and giggled. Nilu caught a glimpse of the restaurant inside, with its comfortable-looking seats right next to the lobby, and on a whim she entered. The printer would be waiting for her, but right now she wanted to get away from the crowd.

She'd never gone to a restaurant alone, without her friends, and certainly not one situated in a well-known hotel. When Nilu was about four or five, even right after her father died, Muwa used to take her to restaurants for kulfi ice cream, for fat lalmohans that dripped with sweet juice. But those days were long gone. Now Muwa called Nilu only when she wanted to make sure that her daughter still lived in the house, or was still alive. Lately Muwa had started taking pills, which she claimed were prescribed by a doctor, some unnamed physician who kept plying her with cures in the form of colorful tablets. The "doctor," Nilu knew, was Sumit, who visited Muwa almost daily, often carrying a bag to transport drugs.

Sumit was often leaving the house just as Nilu returned from school, and he'd smile at her, revealing a gold tooth. "You doing well, Nilu Nani?" he'd ask. The first couple of times she smiled back at him, but when he began staying in Muwa's room behind closed doors for whole afternoons or evenings, Nilu stopped acknowledging him.

When Nilu asked Muwa about him, Muwa said, "Oh, Sumit? He's all right. He's the son of an old friend of mine." When Nilu pressed her mother about which old friend, Muwa simply said, "You don't know her. She died when you were young. Poor Sumit. He has no one. That's why he comes to see me."

But one afternoon when Nilu went up to her mother's room to look for a book—it was long overdue from her school library and probably lost—she found the door locked. When she knocked, Sumit opened it, only halfway, and asked her what she wanted. "Could you move, please?" she said, not masking her annoyance. "I need to get something in there." He replied that Muwa had a headache and didn't want to be disturbed. Nilu simply pushed him aside and walked in, her eyes on her mother's bed, where the woman seemed to stay all day, reeking of alcohol, surrounded by pills. Today another smell permeated the room, but Nilu couldn't identify it. The curtains, as always, were closed, and in the semi-dark, she failed to spot her book.

Muwa, whose back was turned, moaned. "Who is it, Sumit? Come back to bed." In the doorway, Sumit's face was shadowed.

"Muwa," Nilu called softly.

But Muwa didn't turn at the sound of her voice. Instead, she said, "The light is hurting my eyes, Sumit." Nilu headed toward the door, where for a moment it seemed as if Sumit wouldn't let her pass. Then he stepped aside, and as she exited, he lightly touched her back.

The Other Room was empty. Nilu removed the piece of paper from her bag, placed it on the table, and began to write. The waiter came and handed her the menu. Everything was pricey here. One samosa cost five rupees, whereas in streetside stalls you could get them for fifty paisa. Tea here was four rupees. But Nilu always carried crumpled ten-rupee bills, sometimes even hundred-rupee bills, in her school bag, in the pockets of her skirt, or even between the pages of a book. At school, it was she who treated her friends to snacks and Coca-Cola. When she ran out of cash, all she had to do was go to Muwa's room, open the drawer, and take whatever she wanted.

Nilu ordered one samosa and a cup of tea and reread the essay she had written. The last word seemed to be frozen on the page, blocking everything else. She stared at it as the waiter delivered her order. Some commotion was stirring outside: people shouting, the clatter of footsteps. One waiter peeked out of the door, then reported back to the other waiter: "A julus. A rally is coming our way." Then a group of middle-aged men wearing daura suruwal entered the restaurant. A waiter deferentially escorted them to a table, where they ordered some lassi to drink. Their conversation soon revealed that they had sneaked away from the rally, which they were required to attend. "On such a hot day," one of them, a thin man with a dark face, said loudly as they took their seats close to Nilu's table, "how long can we shout the praises of the Panchayat and the king? My throat is parched." The others hushed him, but the man obviously was irked, for he continued. "What is anyone going to do to me? Take me to jail? Let them. If they can jail great men like B.P. and Ganesh Man, what do I matter?"

"If you don't shut up, we'll all end up behind bars," another whispered urgently.

"And what would you rather have me do?" the thin, dark man said. "Extol the virtues of this government?"

"Without a strong king, India will gobble up Nepal, as it did Sikkim," his friend said. "That's why you need to shut up. Come, drink a lassi quickly to cool off. Then we can rejoin the rally."

"It's all that witch Indira Gandhi's doing," the dark man said. "If she hadn't put India under emergency rule, our king wouldn't be so emboldened. Now India has become a convenient role model for him as he lashes out against his enemies."

"Actually," another tall official said, "I am going to return to the julus. If the others notice that we're not there, it's not going to be good. I'm going back." With that, he hurriedly exited the restaurant. The rest glanced at one another anxiously, then they too, shouting to the waiter to cancel their order, bolted out the door, except for the dark man. When the last departing official turned at the door to summon him, he waved his hand in the air and said, "I'm not moving an inch until I finish my lassi."

The chanting outside got louder. The thin, dark man, looking miserable and increasingly worried, waited for his lassi. His eyes briefly met Nilu's, and she thought she saw a semblance of a smile, but she looked away at the wall, where a photo hung showing King B during his coronation ceremony the previous year. Wearing a fountainlike crown, the king rode an elaborately decorated elephant. Nilu had actually witnessed that parade last year, as it passed a few hundred yards from her house. A string of elephants — "More than twenty!"

someone had exclaimed — carrying maharajahs, presidents, prime ministers, and first ladies from around the globe had followed the king's elephant as it circled the city. Nilu hadn't watched the coronation itself; she'd left the house to escape Sumit and Muwa, and got stuck in the crowd.

Nilu returned to her essay. The voices from the rally were now fading, as the crowd moved in the direction of Indrachowk. Gradually, her words tumbled out, and she wrote, then wrote some more. From the corner of her eye, she saw that the thin, dark man's lassi had at last been delivered; he drank it in one gulp, then rushed out, nearly tripping at the door.

By the time Nilu was done writing, she was the only person remaining in the restaurant. The waiters were still murmuring about the rally, saying that it was probably making its way down the wide-avenued Durbar Marg by now, approaching the Narayanhiti Royal Palace to pay homage to the king. But Nilu was barely paying attention to their words. What she held in her fingers now, next to the half-eaten, oily samosa and the dregs of the tea, was — it amused her to affirm it — a masterpiece, and there was no reason why it shouldn't be published in the magazine.

Two months later, the new issue of the magazine was distributed to the students, and soon after that, the principal herself grilled Nilu about her shocking and outrageous essay; she then suspended the girl for a week. At the morning assembly two days after students received their copies, Principal Mann proclaimed, "All the sisters agree that a particular essay doesn't belong in the magazine you just received. The editor, who is also the author, is being punished for this transgression. We request that all of you bring the magazine from home tomorrow. Those who do not return it to the school will be fined a sum of one hundred rupees." The next day the magazines piled up in the principal's office, where a grim-faced Sister Krishnan ripped the criminal page from each one.

"The Maddest Proposal" argued that the girls at St. Augustine's should be enlisted as slaves to the sisters, "seventy-five girls per sister," and perform a long list of tasks: sewing, mopping floors, washing smelly robes for the "Grand Madames," and caring for all their needs, including scrubbing their big behinds with a wet towel every morning and "comforting" them at night, in bed. Mimicking Swift's prose, Nilu wrote, "A very worthy sister, a true *lover* of this school, was lately pleased when she sampled the kind of comfort that an enslaved St. Augustine girl could provide, in the privacy of her own bedroom."

The sisters carried hundreds of copies of "The Maddest Proposal" out behind the school building, where presently all the students gathered. Mother Mann asked Sister Rose to strike the match. Soon the pages burst into flames, and threads of smoke twirled up to the sky.

During the week of her suspension, Nilu expected Mother Mann to call her at home and tell her she'd been expelled. She didn't know what she'd do if she could no longer attend St. Augustine's; she supposed she'd start going to that local school a stone's throw away from Nilu Nikunj, the one tucked in an alley next to the exercise gym. But there were others. Didn't Raja attend the Jagadamba School? Nilu wondered. If she was expelled from St. Augustine's, she could attend that school, she thought.

On the evening after she was suspended, after making sure that Sumit had left, Nilu pushed open her mother's door. "Muwa?" she whispered. Muwa was lying in bed, eyes closed, mouth slightly open, a smoldering cigarette in her right hand. A nearly empty vodka bottle lay by the bed stand. She appeared to be dozing as the cigarette burned, the ash lengthening at the tip. "Muwa? Did you eat?" Nilu asked, sitting on the bed. More and more often, Ramkrishan brought Muwa's meals to her bedroom, and she and Sumit ate together. On occasion Muwa was too drunk to eat, and the next morning Nilu found the food, barely touched, in the hall outside Muwa's door.

Muwa opened her eyes. "Right now I'm not hungry, Nilu." She sat up, leaning against the headboard. She flicked the ash to the floor and took a long drag of her cigarette, gazing at the ceiling. She asked Nilu if she'd eaten, and Nilu said that she was about to go down to the kitchen. But even before she'd finished that sentence, Muwa sighed and mumbled, already distracted.

"Something happened at school today," Nilu said.

"Hmmmm," Muwa said, then took her last drag and crushed the cigarette in the ashtray. The nail on her index finger was yellow from nicotine. "Did you fight with anyone?" She motioned with her finger for Nilu to pass her a small bottle of pills from the bedside table.

"Mother Mann wants you to talk to her tomorrow," Nilu said as she handed her the bottle.

Muwa popped a pill into her mouth. Nilu poured a glass of water from the jug for her.

"Mother Mann?"

"The principal."

"Oh, yes," Muwa said, and leaned back against her pillow. "What for?"

"It's about something I wrote. I'm in trouble at school."

"What did you write? You're a good writer. You've always been a good writer."

As Nilu began to explain why the sisters were angry at her, Muwa asked, "Nilu, what do you think of Sumit?"

"Why?"

Muwa looked at her thoughtfully. "Study well, okay?" Then, she said, "Sumit and I . . . Sumit thinks that he and I . . ." Then she closed her eyes.

Nilu waited, but Muwa remained silent. Still, Nilu thought to ask, "Will you go tomorrow to see Mother Mann?"

Muwa nodded, then whispered something Nilu couldn't fully grasp. It sounded like a reference to her father. She arranged Muwa's blanket and, turning off the light, went downstairs. Ramkrishan was finishing up in the kitchen. Kaki was seated on the floor in a corner, leaning against the wall.

Nilu poured herself a glass of water from the filter and drank it. Most likely Muwa would forget about her errand by tomorrow, she thought, and, without anyone to speak on her behalf, she'd get kicked out of St. Augustine's.

"Nilu Nani, is that you?" Kaki asked now from her corner.

Nilu sat on the floor beside her and took the crinkly hand in her own.

Kaki peered at the girl. Kaki's sunken eyes seemed to swim in water. She asked Nilu, "Why do you look so cheerless? What happened? Muwa . . . ?"

"Just something small at school, Kaki."

Ramkrishan, who was washing the pots at the sink, turned around. "What happened?"

Kaki reached, with her shaking hand, to pat Nilu's face. "Did someone say something to you, Nilu Nani?"

"I might have to quit that school."

"What for?" Kaki asked, her voice rising.

"It's okay," Nilu assured her. "Muwa is going to the school tomorrow to talk to the sisters. Let's hope everything will be all right."

"Is she going to go? She hasn't been to your school in how many years?"

"I think she will."

"Is that Sumit still in her room?" Kaki whispered.

"No, he left a while ago."

"I don't know what that man is up to," Kaki said. "I don't like the way he sticks to her."

"You eat her bread, so you don't have a right to say such things." Ramkrishan rebuked Kaki as he worked at the sink. "Don't say whatever comes to your mind."

Kaki kept her mouth shut for a while, then told Nilu, "Make sure Muwa goes to your school. If she doesn't, I'll go for you."

Nilu squeezed her hand. After Kaki lost Raja, she had turned into an old woman overnight. When she'd first started working at Nilu Nikunj, Nilu remembered, Kaki would get up in the dark before the birds started chirping and work steadily until she went to bed, complaining only once in a while about an ache in her back or a

94

swollen ankle. Now in the morning Ramkrishan had to go to her shack and knock on her door with his shaky fingers. On occasion Nilu heard Ramkrishan scolding her. "Why are you torturing yourself like this? Raja is better off there, where he's a master. Here he'd have been a servant." Kaki nodded dumbly, as if she needed to be reminded of the true state of things. Over the past couple of years, Kaki's eyesight had also gotten worse. Now she recognized people only if they stood very close to her. Her face had amassed wrinkles, and there was no question of her doing any housework—she could barely move from one spot to another without Ramkrishan's or Nilu's help.

"This old body should die!" Nilu sometimes heard Kaki curse herself with these words.

Every day that week, Nilu expected Mother Mann to call to ask why Muwa hadn't come to talk to her, before delivering the news that Nilu had been expelled. On the seventh evening, a Saturday, Nilu sat on the balcony that extended from the guest room next to her room, still expecting the phone to ring and Ramkrishan to announce that it was for her. Her one-week suspension would end today. Did it mean that she could return to school tomorrow? She disliked her deep attachment to St. Augustine's; it wasn't the only school in town. But St. Augustine's had been an integral part of her life for ten years, and it seemed unthinkable to relinquish the many things she loved about it—her friends, especially Prateema; Sister O'Malley and her funny impressions of other sisters; the well-stocked school library where she spent many lunch periods poring over magazines and books.

Nilu didn't sense Sumit's presence until he was right behind her. Then she heard the shuffle of his footsteps and his labored breathing. She'd left her door unlocked, and he'd entered without knocking. She closed her eyes, hoping he'd think she was napping and go away. But he remained, waiting even after a long minute passed. She felt something crawl on her back, so she opened her eyes and stretched.

"You shouldn't doze in the evening like this," he said. "It'll disturb your sleep at night."

She turned around to look at him. He hovered close to her, his hips almost touching her chair.

"I can do what I want in my house," she said, and stood up.

"Sit, sit," he said, and pulled another chair close to hers. "You don't have to run every time you see me."

"I have homework to do," she said, and tried to slip around him, but his chair was blocking the doorway.

"Just a few minutes," he said, not budging. "Don't treat me like a stranger. After all, I've been coming to this house for months now."

She remained standing, her arms crossed at the chest.

"Nilu," he said, and she cringed at the slippery way he said her name. It reeked of suggestiveness.

"What do you need to talk to me about?"

"Don't look so annoyed. Am I not like your uncle?" When she didn't respond, he said gently, "What if I were to come and live in this house permanently? How would I feel if you were always like this?"

She eyed him. "What do you mean?"

"No, I'm just making conversation. Why can't you think of me as your uncle? If I were your uncle, wouldn't you be treating me more nicely?"

She once again tried to leave the balcony, but he didn't get out of her way; he even stretched out his arm to block the door. "Sit down, please. This will only take a couple of moments."

Muwa appeared behind him. "What's going on?" She tottered in the doorway. She too was smiling.

"Oh, nothing," Sumit said. "I was just telling Nilu that I'm like her uncle. Come, come. Let's all sit down together."

"I waited for you to come back from the bathroom," Muwa said to Sumit. Reaching out to him, she stepped onto the balcony, and he put his arm around her waist. His youthful face contrasted with her aging skin. They could be mother and son, Nilu thought.

Nilu went to the balcony railing. Only a trace of light remained in the sky, and below, Ramkrishan was shutting the gate. Did that mean that Sumit was staying here for the night? He and Muwa were engaged in a whispering argument. The doorway was free, so Nilu took the opportunity to slip past them and went to her room. She heard Muwa call after her, asking her to stay, but she softly shut her door behind her.

She bolted her door and stayed inside. A few minutes later Ramkrishan knocked to call her for dinner, and she told him she wasn't hungry. Muwa knocked too, and she told Muwa she had a headache. Sumit called, and she simply didn't respond. She lay in bed, looking at the ceiling; then, in a while, with some anxiety she began to arrange her books for school, for the next day. She visualized Mother Mann shaking her head, explaining to Nilu that she could not return. But then Nilu imagined herself fighting the expulsion, arguing, knocking on the door of the rector, Sister Moore, whom she didn't know but whose calm countenance and fine posture she had always admired. Maybe Sister Moore ought to know what Sister Rose had done. But whenever Nilu considered telling any of the sisters about what had happened in Sister Rose's room, she foresaw their disbelief: their eyes narrowed with suspicion, their faces stiffened in denial.

Nilu learned the next day that during her one-week suspension, Sister O'Malley had barged into the principal's office and demanded to know why a student — moreover, one who had distinguished herself as the school magazine editor — was being punished for what, by any standard, was "a top-rate essay," one that even Jonathan Swift would have been proud to call his own. Apparently an altercation had ensued, and the two sisters, red-faced, had continued their shouting match into the hallway.

The girls reported this to Nilu first thing in the morning, as they were lining up for morning assembly. All morning Nilu expected Mother Mann to summon her to her office, but hour by hour, nothing happened. During the morning recess, then during the lunch break, girls kept approaching Nilu, in the hallway, in the yard, asking her questions, about the essay, about what she meant by a particular line in it, whether it was true that she had composed the piece under Sister O'Malley's guidance, and whether she was going to submit it to *The Rising Nepal*.

Over the next few days, Nilu found herself in a remarkable new situation. The girls' admiration for her was overflowing. Even junior girls from the lower grades, who still couldn't control a runny nose and needed a handkerchief fastened to the front of their blouse, followed her around shyly, wanting to be seen with her. Other girls brought autograph books for her to sign and peered over her shoulder as she wrote their names, drew hearts, and penned words of encouragement and praise. When Mother Mann discovered Nilu's newfound stardom, she gave a lecture during Thursday morning's assembly, exhorting students to find correct role models and shun improper influences, especially during the impressionable years of youth.

All that day Nilu remained quiet, prompting a scolding from Prateema, who had thus far basked in her friend's popularity. When the bell rang for afternoon recess, Nilu silently put her books in her bag and told her friends that she was going home because she wasn't feeling well. "Make sure you get permission from Mother Mann," Prateema advised her, and Nilu said she would, but when she reached the principal's office, she kept walking. The guard at the main gate normally asked to see a permission slip from girls who left early, but he was dozing inside his guardhouse, and Nilu simply slipped past him.

At the Patan bus stop, she boarded a bus headed toward town, planning to go home and lie in bed for the rest of the day. The bus dropped her off at Ratna Park, and she walked past Rani Pokhari, where, right across the street from the entrance to Durbar High School, a small crowd clustered at the black bars surrounding the pond, watching people in a boat as they poked long bamboo sticks into the water. The talk was that someone had dived into the pond. A young man claimed it was a woman. "I spotted her climbing the bars from there." He pointed a bit to the side, toward the Ganesh shrine. "She had a baby with her, and she left the baby at the steps of the shrine."

Another man swore that he saw the baby too but didn't know what had happened to it. "Maybe the police took it away." Another man said that he saw a baby on the lap of the white-bearded priest who sat in the Ganesh shrine and dabbed red tikas on the foreheads of devotees.

As Nilu headed home, she remembered Raja, how he too had been abandoned across the street in Tundikhel, near the famous khari tree, Kaki had said — although that tree had been felled within a few short years of Bokey Ba's discovering the boy. In front of the alley leading to Nilu Nikunj, Nilu lingered. Muwa most likely was in bed, drugged or drunk, or both. Sumit could be sitting next to her, or perhaps even lying alongside her, his palm casually placed on her stomach. If Nilu went home now and Sumit heard her footsteps, he'd rush to meet her at the door.

Instead of turning down her alley, Nilu moved on toward Keshar Mahal. She kept walking, even past the palace — the bats in the tall trees above her made an uproar — until she reached Lainchour. It wasn't often she came to this part of the city, but it was hard to miss the school, which sat right at the end of the large field. Judging from the noisy chants coming from inside and her occasional glimpse of students in blue uniforms on the balcony, the school was still in session. Was Raja inside? Did Ganga Da and his crazy wife still live in the same house, which Nilu knew to be in the vicinity?

She entered a lane by the side of the school and stopped at the Mahan Restaurant, where a man was frying fritters in an enormous vat. She mentioned Ganga Da's name and asked him if he knew where his home was. "Just a few houses down," the restaurant owner said, and, pointing down the alley, described the house for her. Within a minute she was at Ganga Da's gate but didn't have the nerve to go in. Peeking through the narrow gap between the gate and the walls surrounding the house, she saw a woman sitting on a mat in the yard, squinting at the sky. Her lips were moving, and although Nilu hadn't seen Ganga Da's wife before, she deduced this to be her. Abruptly the woman looked toward the gate, startling Nilu, who flattened herself against the wall. Blushing because passersby looked at her curiously, she walked away. The Jagadamba School bell rang shrilly above the roofs of the neighboring houses, and the air erupted with cries of children. Nilu hesitated, then stopped. Now that she was so close, she had to see him. A few yards away from Ganga Da's house was a store. She entered it, bought a lollipop there, and, sucking on it, sat on the store steps. Soon the students from the Jagadamba School, in their dark blue pants and light blue shirts, began to drift by her in clusters, the very young ones first, then the older ones. She kept a watchful eye on the boys of her own age as they walked by, jostling, joking, on their way home. She made sure not to stare, as that would invite attention; she pretended to gaze at a poster on the side of the shop and darted glances at the boys to see who would break from his group and lift the latch on Ganga Da's gate. But all the boys kept passing the house, moving down the alley, deeper into Samakhusi.

Nilu's lollipop was nearly finished, and the student traffic had stopped. She was about to head home when she noted the lone figure of a uniformed boy, one who was long-haired, tall, and gangly. He sauntered down the alley. His hands were thrust in the pockets of his bell-bottom pants, and he was looking down, whistling as he walked, kicking pebbles. When he was a few yards away, he looked directly at Nilu. Color drained from her face, and she quickly looked away and sucked on the last bit of her lollipop. Something about his eyes, dark and probing, told her he was Raja. Or was she making it up? At once she became exasperated with herself for this foolish venture. Raja most likely didn't remember her, and here she was, far from home, waiting for him, stalking him even.

The boy stopped in front of her, and she searched his face. He had barely visible sideburns, and small hairs grew on his chin. His nose was long and thin. He was looking at her expectantly, and hope grew within her. Then she realized that he simply wanted to get to the shop counter; since the rest of the steps were stacked with boxes, she needed to let him pass. She scuttled against the wall, flattening her body. He climbed the two steps and sat on a small stool next to the shopkeeper, who asked him how school went. The boy said it was dull, that his classes were so mind-numbingly boring that he simply wondered what he was doing there.

Nilu wished she could turn around and look for signs of that earlier Raja, perhaps the cleft in the chin, a certain mannerism. But she didn't remember any features that would definitely identify him.

The boy and the shopkeeper talked on, and their unhurried, relaxed conversation indicated that they spoke like this regularly, perhaps every day. Their talk was punctuated with easy silences, during which the shopkeeper hummed, and the boy — Nilu had turned just a bit so that she could watch both of them out of the corner of her eye — gazed at the ceiling, lost in thought. During one such silence, the shopkeeper asked, "So, what's going through your mind, boy? What are you thinking?"

"Absolutely nothing."

"Nothing?"

The boy smiled.

"Impossible," the shopkeeper said. "There's always a thought inside our head, whether we realize it or not."

"Sometimes I think it's good to not have any thoughts. Life is simpler that way."

"I understand already. Your mother has entered your head; that's why you're giving me this talk about no thoughts and all that."

Nilu's heart began to hammer. His mother?

The shopkeeper picked up a notebook and began to jot down some calculations.

"Today in our history class," the boy said slowly, as though talking to himself, "we had to memorize the names of our past kings, you know, the entire lineup. Shree Panch Maharajdhiraj Girvan Bir Bikram Shah Dev, Shree Panch Maharajdhiraj Rajendra Bir Bikram Shah Dev, Shree Panch Maharajdhiraj Tribhuvan Bir Bikram Shah Dev."

"There you go again. No wonder you two, father and son, are always butting heads."

"Shree Panch Maharajdhiraj Birey Dai the Shopkeeper Bir Bikram Shah Dev," the boy said.

Birey Dai laughed, then told the boy to hush up, as someone might hear him.

The boy put his palm on his crotch and said, "You know this is what I care about people hearing."

Nilu felt her neck get hot, and suddenly the boy, seemingly aware that a girl had been there all along, straightened up. She thought his face had turned slightly red in embarrassment, but she couldn't be sure.

An old woman came to the shop. She stood between Nilu and the boy as Birey Dai poured lentils onto a piece of newspaper and weighed them on his handheld scale. Nilu sneaked a glance at the boy. With his head against the wall, he was observing the street. Nilu fought back the urge to reach out and touch him, ask him if he could guess who she was. After the old woman left, Birey Dai said, "Don't speak whatever gibberish comes to your mind. I know you don't mean it, but" — he lowered his voice — "there are spies all over the city these days. C.I.D.'s. They're keeping their ears open for any slander against the king." He looked at Nilu, as though he were seeing her with different eyes. "Who knows, our sister here could be a spy for the government, a C.I.D.," he said, half-joking, his voice now almost a whisper. "She could tell on you, and tomorrow our poor friend here would be hauled to the deep recesses of the palace where —" Birey Dai held an imaginary khukuri in his hands and brought it down as though he was decapitating someone.

The boy smiled wanly, as if he'd already contemplated the idea and was already prepared for such an event. Nilu experienced a rush of pleasure and fear at the boldness of the conversation. She'd never heard anyone talk about the king that way. At home, well, Muwa was too drunk to say anything coherent. At school, the sisters practically slobbered over royalty. On the rare occasion when the queen mother, wearing large dark glasses as her husband did when he was alive, graced hockey matches or debate competitions, the sisters tripped over one another in their genuflections and eagerness to answer the queen mother's questions. St. Augustine's was filled with girls from the aristocratic Rana and Shah families, some of whom still lived in the European-style mini-palaces scattered throughout the city. They spoke of silver cutlery in their houses. They described family trips to Hong Kong, or London, or Kashmir, where they were driven around in luxury cars as they shopped. During tiffin breaks, their nannies brought them aromatic lamb and special chutneys and fanned the girls as they ate — or didn't eat, if they found the food smelly or if their delicate tummies were upset. Some of these girls, knowing that Nilu too came from a well-to-do family, tried to befriend her and entice her into their circle. But Nilu rejected them and stuck to her friend Prateema, whose dark skin and Bengali origins automatically excluded her from the hoity-toity bunch.

Just then, a girl of about eleven, wearing a dirty frock, appeared with two glasses of tea and, squeezing past Nilu, handed them to the boy and the shopkeeper. "Raja Dai, how was school?" the girl asked.

Nilu felt heat rapidly rise to her face. Raja. It was him! Her hunch had been correct all along. Instinctively she wanted to get up and leave, so fast was her heart beating, but oddly enough, she instead heard herself ask Birey Dai if she too could get a glass of tea. She avoided eye contact with Raja, but she could see from the corner of her eye that he was observing her. Though he said nothing, Nilu could feel the presence of his restless spirit, a kind of yearning that spread from his body to the air around him.

"There's a restaurant up the alley where this girl works," Birey Dai said. "You can go there."

"It's so nice here," Nilu said. "Such an interesting conversation, I don't feel like moving." She asked the girl, "Can you bring me a glass too, bahini?"

The girl nodded and left.

Nilu knew that her request had alerted Birey Dai and Raja to her presence, and her words had even seemed to suggest that King B's Pancheys had indeed begun recruiting schoolgirls as spies. She could feel their gaze on her back but kept sucking on the lollipop stick, pretending it was normal for a girl in a convent school uniform to sit on the steps of a shop in an unfamiliar neighborhood.

"Is bahini's home in this vicinity?" Birey Dai finally asked her. "I don't recall seeing you here before."

Nilu turned, her heart skipping a beat, and she looked at Raja before addressing the shopkeeper. "My aunt lives nearby. I am visiting her."

"Who?" the shopkeeper asked. "Which house?"

Raja had turned his entire attention to her, the way a wild animal responds to the presence of something foreign in its territory. She felt herself blush, not so much at Raja's alertness to her but rather at her own stupidity in pursuing this ruse. But she was already ensnared in it, so she vaguely waved in the direction of Samakhusi. "Down there."

"What's your aunt's name?"

"Bhadra Kumari."

Birey Dai looked puzzled. "Never heard that name, and there's not a single house in this locality I can't identify." He turned to Raja. "You know a Bhadra Kumari?"

The boy shook his head.

"What's the last name?" Birey Dai asked.

"Singh."

"Did she move here recently?"

"Yes."

The shopkeeper laughed. "No wonder. And I thought something was amiss."

The girl from the Mahan Restaurant arrived with Nilu's tea, and Nilu asked her how much it cost and handed her the money. The tea was dark and tasted horrible, but now that she had found Raja, she could survive the most vile tea in the world. Raja's glass was empty, but he was still holding it between his palms. Their silence was broken by small talk—Mohan Bagan versus the RCT soccer team at Dashrath Stadium, the recently opened table tennis center by the Dairy, and the neighborhood library that some energetic youth had recently opened and filled with steamy Nepali detective novels.

104

Nilu was considering what to do next when the gate to Ganga Da's house opened. The woman Nilu had seen squinting in the sun thrust her head out and shouted, "Raja, isn't it time to come home?"

Raja made a face, said goodbye to the shopkeeper, and stepped out. "I'm coming," he told the woman.

"Why don't you come straight home after school, huh?" the woman said. "Every day you have to chat with Birey Dai?"

Birey Dai shouted from inside, "Jamuna Bahini, if Raja doesn't stop here, my dinner doesn't go down my throat."

After Raja slipped through the gate, the woman closed it with a loud clang.

Birey Dai smiled at Nilu. "Sometimes I think she doesn't like me," he said. "But I don't take it personally."

"Looks like you and the boy are very close," Nilu said.

"He's like a younger brother to me."

"Does he go to this school?" she asked, pointing toward the Jagadamba School.

Birey Dai nodded.

Trying very hard to make it sound like small talk, she asked, "What class?"

"He's starting tenth now, I think. He's a very good boy, but what to do. He was an orphan before our Ganga Da took him under his wing. The boy suffers at the thought that his real mother abandoned him — I know it, even though he doesn't talk about it much."

"After all these years?"

"It's a strange thing, bahini," Birey Dai said, "this blood connection we have with our parents. It never goes away, and I think it becomes even more pronounced in our Raja as he gets older. I can detect it in his eyes. But the boy doesn't want anyone to see it."

"Did this house's owner adopt him?" Nilu asked, even though she knew the story.

"Something like that," Birey Dai said. "Although there was something shady about it, from what I've heard. The woman who used to take care of Raja wasn't willing to let him go. Or something like that. Ganga Da had to hide the boy somewhere, then fought the woman in court. It's been so long now — it feels like it happened in another life. I'm not sure Raja even remembers that woman. This is his family now. But, what to do — you saw what the mother is like." Birey Dai made a cuckoo gesture with his hand, then, perhaps realizing that he was revealing too much to a stranger, he abruptly went silent. Nilu shifted the conversation to other matters, frequently addressed the man sweetly as Birey Dai, and, before leaving, bought a loaf of Krishnapauroti so he'd see that she wasn't merely a gabber.

She walked down the hill instead of up, to corroborate her lie about the location of her aunt's house, then she circled up toward Thamel.

By the time Nilu left the Lainchour area, it was already dark. She moved briskly, still holding the loaf of bread in her hand. Something was about to change for her. The events at St. Augustine's, this bizarre quest to find Raja, and her actual discovery of him in a shop next to his house — a momentum, a reshaping was under way. She could feel it.

Nilu Nikunj was dark, silent. Nilu turned on the kitchen light and saw Kaki's figure in the corner, propped against the wall, sleeping. Your Raja is fine, Kaki, Nilu said to her silently. He's a tall, long-haired, handsome boy. There's sadness in his eyes, you can see it, Kaki; his jaw is tight with anger. But he also likes to laugh. He's a practical joker, your Raja, I can tell.

She left the bread by Kaki's side and went up the stairs without switching on the stairway light. Muwa's door was slightly open, and on an impulse Nilu peeked in. It was empty. She was about to go to her room when the main door of the house creaked open. She went to the balcony railing and saw Ramkrishan enter, wiping his feet on the doormat. "Where's Muwa?" she asked him.

He looked up and said that she and Sumit had left earlier that evening for a party. "What do you want for dinner, Nilu Nani?" he asked. She responded that she already ate at a friend's house, and went to her room and threw herself on the bed. She had hoped to talk to Muwa about switching schools. She had wished, foolishly, that Muwa would infer that something had happened with one of the nuns and would encourage her to let the matter rest so she could at least finish her schooling there. Nilu had hoped that she could rest her head against Muwa's shoulder while Muwa stroked her face.

In the night she awoke to the sound of footsteps in the hallway and the murmurs and laughter of Muwa and Sumit. Nilu glanced at the clock: it was half past twelve. "No, no," Muwa said slowly, in a drunken voice. There seemed to be a small scuffle, accompanied by much tittering and whispering. Muwa's door creaked open, and it slammed shut.

Nilu's sadness over Muwa lingered at school all the next day, and although in the morning when she put on her uniform she had resolved that she would not go back to Lainchour, that whatever was propelling her toward renewed contact with Raja would only lead to embarrassment and rejection, by the time the afternoon rolled around and Sister Rose entered the classroom for her English lesson, the only thing that mattered was seeing Raja again. If Nilu didn't leave during recess, which was right after Sister Rose's class, she would most likely not make it to Lainchour on time. She wanted to be in Birey Dai's shop first, to await Raja's arrival, so that she could pretend that she had her own schedule, that she wasn't following him.

While Sister Rose was writing on the blackboard, Nilu nudged Prateema, who sat next to her. With whispers and gestures, she signaled to her friend that she was going to leave after this class. Prateema's eyes grew large. What for? — she mouthed the words silently. But Nilu couldn't tell Prateema; it would sound too silly, so she leaned close to Prateema and told her that she had some things to take care of. Right then Sister Rose turned toward the class. Her eyes bore into Nilu. She stared, and Nilu stared back. Noticing this new tension, the rest of the class looked at Nilu, then at Sister Rose, who finally spoke. "Do you two have a secret I should know about?" Then, perhaps remembering that the secret might be something that could damage her reputation and position, the sister blushed and said, "You two, Nilu and Prateema, out! Finish your conversation, then grace us with your presence again." Prateema protested, but Nilu picked up her bag and left the room. Once outside, she glanced back to see Prateema pleading with Sister Rose. Briefly, Nilu waited, then walked quickly down the hallway and toward the gate. The guard asked her for the permission slip, but she cold-shouldered him and left the school premises.

Did You Know the King?

Nilu pursued raja. She enrolled herself in the Jagadamba School by bribing the principal, Singh Sir, and by forging Muwa's signature on the admission forms.

When she arrived at his office, Singh Sir looked askance at the young girl. "Where are your parents? This is an impossible request. I can't allow any admission without a guardian's consent."

But Nilu was well prepared. She took an envelope from her purse and slid it across the table toward Singh Sir. "Sir, I am a very good student. My mother is very ill—that's the only reason she can't come."

Singh Sir gazed at the envelope. "Are these your school records?" he asked, then peeked at the contents, lifting the envelope's flap with his thumb and forefinger. He patted the envelope but didn't pick it up. "Has your mother been to see a doctor?"

"I'm taking care of her," Nilu said. "There's no one else in my family."

"It must be very difficult for you."

"I'll manage. But I can't afford St. Augustine's anymore."

Singh Sir's fingers played with the envelope. "Normally, I don't allow any breach of admission rules. But you have unique problems, so I'm forced to make an exception." He asked her to bring her records from St. Augustine's and told her she could start attending classes the next day.

Nilu didn't tell anyone at Nilu Nikunj that she'd switched schools. Kaki was too weak in the eyes and too ailing in general to sense what Nilu had done. Ramkrishan, even if he knew or suspected, as Nilu had a feeling he did, wouldn't know what to do about it. And Muwa, well, Muwa lived in a world of her own.

Every morning Nilu put on the uniform of St. Augustine's, a dark blue skirt and a sky-blue shirt, and left for the Jagadamba School. The two schools had the same uniform, except that Jagadamba didn't require a tie. The one person who noted that something seemed amiss was Kancha, who wondered, as he sat in his cramped shop, why the girl with the drunkard mother, instead of turning left at the opening of the alley, took a right and walked toward the palace until she disappeared. But Kancha was only a shopkeeper, so he didn't say anything.

At the Jagadamba School, it didn't take Nilu long to locate Raja's classroom, which was two rooms down from hers. During recess she saw him in the school courtyard; his hands in his pockets, he stood amid his friends but didn't really take part in their conversations. He'd be worrying something on the ground with his toe or looking around as though searching for someone who was yet to arrive. Nilu half-hid behind pillars, her eyes occasionally straying toward him. She took pains to avoid him inside the school compound so that he wouldn't think that she was pursuing him. Then, as soon as the school bell rang to signal the end of the day, she was the first one out of her class and quickly proceeded to Birey Dai's shop, so she would be sitting nonchalantly on her stool when Raja got there. If anything, she thought with a laugh, she could accuse him of chasing her, not the other way around.

A few days later, she did bump into Raja at school, outside Singh Sir's office, where she had gone to deliver her St. Augustine's records; there he was, sitting on a bench, looking bored. He glanced at her, recognized her as the girl from Birey Dai's shop, and gave her a slight smile. She asked coolly, "Is he in?"

"I think he is."

"Do you need to see him?"

He nodded.

Even though there was space on the bench next to him, Nilu leaned against the wall and waited. Raja was tapping his feet, as if he could hear music. Finally something seemed to occur to him, and he turned to her and said, "What do you need to see him for?" He spoke slowly, in the manner of someone who had all the time in the world, and she realized that she loved this about him.

His eyes fell on the St. Augustine's emblem on the documents in her hand. She placed them behind her. "Oh, nothing. What about you?"

"What are you hiding?"

"What? This? Just some papers."

But he'd already seen the school's name and its distinct symbol, a book with an arrow slicing it, and he asked, "You went to St. Augustine's?"

She cursed herself for her carelessness. "Yes."

"And now you go here?"

"Yes."

"Why?" His tone was challenging, nearly hostile.

A wave of irritation passed through her, but there was something endearing about his forthright questions. "I am living with my aunt now," she said. She stopped herself from reaching to run her fingers over his sideburn.

Singh Sir's door opened, and he called Nilu in. She handed the papers to Singh Sir, who smiled at her and asked her how her classes were going. She said they were fine. "Let me know if everything is all right," Singh Sir said. "Just come to me." Singh Sir had been very warm toward her since he'd accepted the three hundred rupees in that envelope.

When she came out, Raja was still sitting on the bench. His eyes followed her as she walked past, then he said, to her back, "When you're a St. Augustine's product, you get treated like a V.I.P. I was here before you, wasn't I? Maybe you come from the raja-maharaja stock."

She turned to face him. "But how sad that you're the one who's named Raja, the king." Reciprocating his confrontational tone, she hadn't smiled, and she wondered if what she said sounded condescending, a convent-educated girl making fun of a locally schooled boy. But to her relief a smile flickered on his face: he liked it that she knew his name.

"I'm the type of king who has to wait for an audience with his subjects," he said, tilting his head toward Singh Sir's door.

He didn't ask Nilu's name in return, as she'd hoped he would, but that afternoon at Birey Dai's shop he glanced toward her frequently and spoke in a more animated way than he had thus far. The next afternoon, when she told him her name, he showed no sign of recognition, and although she was disappointed, she also felt relieved. Gradually, over the next few days, he addressed her more than he did Birey Dai, and soon it was Raja and Nilu seated on stools next to each other, sometimes with their knees colliding, as they talked, while Birey Dai chimed in, like an outsider, from behind his counter.

One day Raja shyly showed Nilu the poems he had attempted in English. They were filled with melancholy. His language was stilted, the expressions at times ordinary, but a presence hovered over them, a feminine one, which she took to be his missing mother. This woman moved between the lines, weaving herself through the words. Nilu found herself shivering as she read the poems. "They're moving," she said.

"I'm trying to improve my English."

"Your English is already good," she said.

"English is like international currency," Birey Dai said. "You know English, you'll make money."

"Is that why you want to improve your English?" Nilu asked Raja.

"No," he said. "I just don't want you boarding school types looking down on me."

"When did I look down on you?"

He gazed into her eyes, then looked away.

"No, tell me, Raja, when did I look down upon you? What have I said that has given you that impression?"

When he didn't meet her eyes, she grabbed his arm and said, "Raja, look at me and tell me, please."

When he did look at her, she was slightly taken aback by how cloudy his eyes had become, swirling with some new influence, how suddenly his face had acquired lines of sadness. "Maybe not you," he finally said.

"Then who?"

He waved his hand at the lane outside the shop, at the sky beyond the telephone wires. "The world." Then he straightened himself. "But I'm not the type to be cowed by anyone. Let anyone even try. I'll . . ."

She understood that he was merely venting an argument that went on in his head.

The shop was silent; then Birey Dai coughed dramatically and said, "Before anyone can even speak, you know what our Raja will do?" Birey Dai rose from his seat, adopted an aggressive stance like a kung fu warrior, and spoke in an exaggerated American accent: "Fwat are u tahking abhout, machhikney? Me Rajah! Me big man. Me speak Angrezi!"

"Don't use such words in front of a girl, Birey Dai," Raja said.

"But you don't need to prove anything to anyone," Nilu said to Raja.

"Who said I'm trying to prove anything?"

"You're good the way you are."

He studied her intently, as though trying to understand her. "How do you know that? How do you know I'm good?"

"He's good," Birey Dai said.

"Keep quiet, Birey Dai. How do you know I'm good?"

Her heart beat wildly. She hoped she was not about to be discovered. "I just know. I am good at knowing people."

"She's good," Birey Dai said. "And her English is very good."

"This Birey Dai," Raja said, but he had begun to smile, and she was struck by how much even that tiny smile lit up his face. In that moment she saw him as he was when they were children together in Nilu Nikunj. She remembered that smile from when the two had sat on the floor of her room and gone over the alphabet, when he rode her pink tricycle in the yard, pedaling furiously to gain as much speed as he could.

He was watching her, and she wondered if he could read her thoughts, see the pictures of earlier times that ran through her head. But he was obviously thinking of something else, for he said, "I bet you my Nepali is better than yours."

"It probably is."

"Probably?" he questioned. "It is. It is. Here, look at my poems in Nepali."

She read them. His writing in Nepali didn't display the awkwardness of his English. Still, to chide him, she suggested some improvements. He observed her carefully, then asked her why, for someone who'd studied at an English-medium school, her Nepali was as good as her English. "I am a Nepali girl, am I not?" she replied. Birey Dai laughed and told Raja that he was no match for this girl, who, if he didn't watch out, would sell him at the market for two paisa.

Raja kept his eyes on her, but she, suddenly guilty about concealing their shared history at Nilu Nikunj, couldn't meet them.

The gate to Ganga Da's house opened, and there stood Jamuna Mummy, staring at them. Nilu became self-conscious and, bidding goodbye to Raja and Birey Dai, went down the lane. She passed Jamuna Mummy on the way, and the woman said, "Are you an avatar of the goddess Kali? Have you come here to suck our blood?"

Nilu kept her identity hidden from Raja for weeks as they spent more time together. At first Birey Dai's shop was their meeting place. At her insistence Raja showed her some short English essays that he'd composed during his free time, for himself. These pieces were a mishmash of slapdash humor, long soliloquies on the meaning of life, and short skits featuring a man in the official daura suruwal uniform, often a bureaucrat in a government office, arguing vehemently with a young boy. The official and the boy mocked each other, often in scatological terms, and they inevitably exploded into vociferous accusations and counter-accusations. Raja watched Nilu expectantly as she read, and it dawned on her that, despite his bravado, she was most likely the first person with whom he had opened up enough to share his writing. He had problems with grammar and punctuation and syntax, but what did it matter? She hesitated to tell him about any flaws in them, but he wouldn't let her off so easily; he told her that as a friend she had to be honest with him. So she was.

"And you are my friend, aren't you?" he said, half in jest, and she clasped his hand and assured him that yes, of course she was his friend.

"Are you my mitini?" he asked.

"Yes, I am your mitini." Friend for life.

She wondered if he remembered the strict, schoolmarmish ways of the Nilu whom he knew in Nilu Nikunj, and she marveled at the fact that here they were, thrust together again in a situation where she was, in a sense, giving him English lessons. At moments she became anxious that he was beginning to suspect who she was, and that any day now he was going to accost her, ask her to confess her real identity, demand to know why she hadn't revealed herself. But apparently her name hadn't jogged any memories. She felt sad, and foolish, when she contemplated the possibility that he might not remember her at all.

Birey Dai also offered his opinions as Nilu commented on Raja's English, although, he admitted laughingly, he didn't know English from a monkey's ass. After a few weeks, Birey Dai's presence interfered with their chats, and they stopped meeting at the shop. "It's all right," Birey Dai told them with a sigh when they stopped by after several days' absence. "I'll have to entertain myself by thinking about my own romantic teenage years, when my heart used to flutter so badly at the sight of beautiful girls that I thought I'd collapse. And look what has happened to me: I'm stuck with a woman I can't stand." Everyone knew of Birey Dai's domestic troubles; Nilu and Raja smiled.

It was in Biswojyoti Cinema, as they watched a movie starring Ji-tendra, that Nilu told Raja who she was. The slim, handsome Jiten-dra was dancing on the screen, wrapping himself around trees, the lock of hair on his forehead shaking as he shimmied his hips. Nilu leaned over and spoke in Raja's ear. Grinning, Jitendra danced in circles around Asha Parekh. All Raja did after she stopped speaking was squeeze her hand, then rest his head on her shoulder. The song was followed by a comedy scene involving Jitendra and Mukri.

Nilu did wonder, in the days that followed, if it hadn't mattered to him that she was a childhood friend, for he didn't raise the topic again. At the same time, something had shifted in him. She found him gazing at her at unexpected moments, and his eyes appeared even softer. Only after a fortnight or so did he approach the subject; he teased her a bit, in that quiet manner of his, that she was a cheat for not revealing to him right away who she was. He tried to recall some events from the days in Nilu Nikunj, but he couldn't come up with much, except that he was aware, without conjuring any spe-cific details, that he had lived there as a servant boy.

"Kaki." He said the name two or three times. "Ganga Da had mentioned her name."

Nilu watched his face carefully to see if she could discern how much he knew about the woman who had once cared for him and the tactics Ganga had used against her. But clearly he was in the dark, so finally Nilu asked, "Do you remember anything about her?"

He seemed on the verge of saying something, then stopped, then started again, and finally shook his head, clearly disappointed with himself, and a bit worried that Nilu would be disappointed in him.

And to tell the truth, she was crushed, for she'd hoped — she re-alized how foolish it was — that something would awaken inside him when he heard Kaki's name — perhaps a long-lost memory that would then spur others, culminating in a strong sense of connection to Kaki, and a strong desire to see her.

"She must be old by now" was all Raja said, and more as an at-tempt to console Nilu than as evidence of any real feeling for Kaki.

Nilu nodded, said that Kaki was in fact elderly, then changed the topic. Perhaps it was better this way, she thought. Even before she'd revealed her identity to Raja, she'd contemplated how and when to inform Kaki that she'd found her much-loved son. She'd been tormented over what that might do to Kaki. But now, since Raja appeared to have no memory of the woman who'd turned old and useless overnight because of grief over losing him, Nilu didn't have the heart to tell Kaki anything.

One day after school Raja took Nilu to his home. "We spend so much time together. Might as well let my parents know about you," he said. It was clear that he couldn't be bothered with what they thought, or if they approved of her. This dismissal of the world's opinion was an essential part of his personality. There was an air of defiance about him: the way he sometimes looked insolently at people on the street, the way he held his shoulders tight, as if he was waiting for the moment when he'd be asked to prove himself.

Over the past few weeks, Nilu had glimpsed the yard in front of Raja's house numerous times as they sat in Birey Dai's shop, especially when Jamuna Mummy opened the gate and asked Raja to come home. Nilu had never seen Ganga Da, and she was anxious about how he'd react to her. It was Ganga Da's, and not Jamuna's, approval or disapproval of her that would matter, if it mattered at all, Nilu surmised. When she expressed her anxiety about what Ganga Da might think of her, Raja looked at her in puzzlement, then pulled her to him and kissed her hard on the lips, so hard that she struggled for breath.

Nilu wondered if he was unhappy with his home life, if somehow his adoptive parents had turned neglectful. Nilu frequently compared her own home life to that of her friends. Whenever the other students at school spoke of something that had happened at home, Nilu listened intently; she imagined a family led by loving, doting parents. Even arguments or punishments seemed like evidence that those parents were at least involved in their children's lives, whereas when she reached home after school, no one called out her name, asked her about the events of her day at school. When she trudged upstairs to her room, Muwa's door was always shut. That the large house — with its empty hallways, its aging servants on the ground floor, and its mistress upstairs with her lover in a room reeking of alcohol and cigarette smoke — was named after Nilu felt like a terrible joke. I too am an orphan, she thought at such moments. Like Raja.

But judging from the way Jamuna Mummy clanked open the gate every afternoon to call Raja from Birey Dai's shop, and from the way Raja spoke of, and derided, Ganga Da's concern about him, Nilu knew that Raja's angst had nothing to do with lack of love at home.

Ganga Da didn't appear a bit surprised to see her. "I have been hearing about you," he told her in the living room. She and Raja sat together on the long sofa. In front of her on the wall hung a black-and-white photograph of Ganga Da, his palms together, his head bowed, in front of King M, whose palm was delicately raised in blessing. The king's eyes were hidden behind dark glasses. Ganga Da noticed Nilu's gaze and said, "That was not too long before King M passed away. Go near and look."

Raja sighed.

Nilu went to the wall and scrutinized the photo. Not knowing what to say, she foolishly asked, "Did you know the king?"

Raja said something that neither of them could fully hear, but Ganga Da gave him a look before he smiled at Nilu. "How can a common citizen like me know him? But I was lucky enough to receive a commendation letter from him for my work at the National Planning Commission." He paused. "He was a really visionary man, our King M. Looks like he has passed on his leadership skills to his son."

"A visionary leader," Raja muttered.

"What do you know about the real world?" Ganga Da asked him. "You weren't even born when King M had to take over the helm of this country, save it from bickering politicians. Do you have any idea how hard it might be to bring a country out of the stone age?"

"I have no idea. My mind is blank. Nothing up here."

Ganga Da looked at Nilu, as if to say, See?

Other photos of royalty were displayed on the wall: King M in full regalia, his small face and black glasses contrasting with the absurdly long gown flowing from his body onto the floor; the preserved head of a tiger, its jaws open as if the beast was roaring, had been placed next to the king's feet; in his right hand he held a rajdanda with a bulbous end, resembling those carried by the gods as they clashed in heaven. Another photograph, right above Raja's head, showed young King B and Queen A at their wedding, when the king was still the crown prince. Seated in separate chairs, they looked straight ahead. The king appeared slightly astonished in his black spectacles, his Nepali cap, with his hands clasped in his lap. Behind the queen's elaborate gauze veil, her large, beautiful eyes were visible.

After Nilu sat down beside Raja, an awkward silence ensued. Nilu imagined that the father and the son butted heads like this frequently, and today too they'd have likely continued their standoff, had it not been for her presence. Just as Raja seemed on the verge of speaking to Ganga Da, whose jaw was clenched, they all noticed, simultaneously, what Jamuna Mummy was doing in the yard. Earlier, when Nilu and Raja had entered the gate, they'd seen her at the side of the house, her back turned. Now she was signaling with her hands toward the sky, at the sun, repetitively raising her arms, joining her hands, then separating them again. She twisted her fingers into various shapes, like the mudras in religious textbooks. Then she'd observe the ground, as though expecting to see the fruits of her actions.

The three of them watched for a few moments, the father and the son as engrossed as Nilu was; it relieved the tension that had accumulated in the room. Finally, Ganga Da sighed. "Her sun salute," he said, then asked Raja, "How many times have I taken her to the hospital now, just this year?" Raja shrugged, as if to say he hadn't kept track. Ganga Da watched Raja briefly, gauging his mood, then turned to Nilu. "This is my life here, Nilu. These two, my dear wife and my dear son, keep my head spinning. Whatever anyone may say about my life, no one can call it boring."

Nilu worried that the comment was meant to irritate Raja, but Raja seemed not to have heard it, for he changed the subject. Pointing at Nilu, he asked Ganga Da, "Do you know who she is?"

Nilu and Raja hadn't discussed beforehand whether they would reveal this information to Ganga Da. She had assumed that for this first visit, she and Ganga Da would just be introduced, exchange the common courtesies. Before the two arrived at the house, she'd asked Raja, "What are you going to tell him? That I'm your girlfriend?"

"Isn't that a cow-eating Western term, *girlfriend*? Maybe I should introduce you as my premika. Lover. It's a much more beautiful word."

"Wait," Ganga Da said. "This is the first time Nilu has come to our house, and we haven't even offered her anything to drink. Let me bring some tea and biscuits." He went to the kitchen.

Nilu elbowed Raja and whispered, "Do you have to tell him today who I am? Couldn't it wait?"

He seemed not to share her worry. "Why not get it out in the open?"

"He might not like who I am."

Raja's arms were stretched out over the back of the sofa. With his right hand he began to stroke her face just as Ganga Da entered with a tray of tea and biscuits. Raja's fingers moved away and began drumming the sofa.

"Nilu," Ganga Da said. "Forgive me. We don't have a servant in this house, so I have to do everything. The tea might not be to your liking."

"I'm sure it's tasty," Nilu said, then braced herself for Raja's revelation.

"Take the tea, please," Ganga Da said, handing her a cup. "And tell me about your family."

Nilu mumbled a few vague statements, expecting Raja to interrupt and reveal who she was, but he didn't. He had decided to comply with her urge to wait.

"Oh, I'm sorry to hear that your father passed away while you were young," Ganga Da said. "In that case you must have a close relationship with your mother."

Nilu didn't bother to illuminate him. Instead, she asked where Ganga Da worked.

"I worked for the National Planning Commission for years, but now I work at Nepal Rashtra Bank."

Jamuna Mummy entered the room.

"Come, drink some tea," Ganga Da said to his wife.

Staring at Nilu, Jamuna came to the sofa, sat next to her husband, and picked up a cup of tea. She sniffed at it, then peered into the cup. She said something that sounded like "jadumantarfufufu," and out of nervousness Nilu softly giggled.

"What? You think we're going to poison you, Jamuna Mummy?" Raja asked.

Jamuna Mummy slammed down her cup, sloshing some tea onto the coffee table. She said something about day and night.

"Don't say such things, Raja," Ganga Da said. "Don't further inflame her paranoid mind."

Jamuna Mummy pointed her index finger at father and son, back and forth, until Raja reached over and grabbed her finger. But Jamuna Mummy didn't pay attention to Raja. She fixed her eyes on Nilu, then said, "What about this Kali Mata here? Why is she in my house? I'm watching you, Kali. I know you. You've come here to suck my blood."

"The only things that'll suck your blood are the leeches from our garden, understand?" Ganga Da said. "Eh, Jamuna, why don't you do that little twist dance that you like? Show our guest here what a good dancer you are."

"I'm not going to dance in front of Kali," Jamuna Mummy said.

Raja chimed in. "Come on, Jamuna Mummy."

Ganga Da said to Nilu, "Jamuna here was apparently a great

fan of the twist before she married me." He stood and began to do the twist in front of her. "Here, Jamuna," he said. Jamuna Mummy's eyes shifted from Nilu to her husband. Then she slowly stood, tucked the end of her dhoti into her waistband, and began to dance, jiggling her hips, her arms swinging and her elbows jutting — her face contorted to match the movements of her body.

Sleeping Dogs Can Lie

RAJA DIDN'T REVEAL Nilu's identity to Ganga Da that day, but he did two weeks later. When he informed Nilu, she held her breath. "How did he react? What did he say?" They were sitting on a hillock at the western edge of the neighborhood, an area not yet crowded with houses. Legend had it that until a few years ago, when this area was just being settled, foxes howled and barked here at night.

"He said nothing."

"But he must have said something!"

"Nothing at first. Later he came in while I was studying in my room and said that I shouldn't tell Jamuna Mummy because she might have memories of Kaki that could trigger things for her."

"Is that all?"

"Well," Raja hesitated. "He said something about his sin, that it had come back to haunt him, or something like that."

With her finger Nilu began to doodle on a patch of dust. "I'm sure he wishes that we two hadn't come together."

"Now where did you get that idea, mitini? Really, Ganga Da isn't bad. He's stupid, old-fashioned in his ideas of loyalty. That's why he's remained devoted to Jamuna Mummy, that's why he thinks criticizing our raja-maharaja is bad for the country."

"So you think he's stupid because he did not abandon Jamuna Mummy? You have a very soft heart."

"I just don't understand him sometimes. It's like everything around him is changing, but he wants to remain stuck in a previous century."

"Do you think loyalty cares which century it's in? If I were to go crazy tomorrow, like Jamuna Mummy, you wouldn't remain loyal to me?"

He put his arm around her, squeezed her. Then he nosed her neck and, moving his mouth up, bit her gently on the cheek. Aware of a small boy playing with a bicycle tire nearby, she turned her face away. "Ganga Da liked you, I could tell," he said.

"Do you always fight with him?"

"Not always, but sometimes he doesn't leave me alone."

She took his hand. "Tell me what it is you are feeling."

He thought for a while, then said, "Something is missing in my life."

They stung her, his words, even though Nilu knew that he meant his mother, not her. She wanted him to say that something had been missing until she came along, and now his life was complete. But that was foolish.

As though realizing the effect of his statement, Raja put his head on her shoulder and said, "But now you are with me. Now everything—"

She put her finger on his lips and said, "Shhh."

I'll tell him later, Nilu kept telling herself, at a more appropriate time. I'll tell him later that the man whom Raja now considered his father had used forged documents to snatch him away from Kaki. But as she began to spend more time with Raja, in and out of school and at his home, and as she became aware of the tension between Ganga Da and Raja, she couldn't bring herself to divulge this secret. She could easily see Raja going home and giving Ganga Da a piece of his mind for what he'd done to Kaki. As far as Raja knew, the servant woman who'd initially raised him had surrendered him to Ganga Da—surrendered him for his own good because she knew that he'd get a better life in Lainchour. If Nilu told Raja the truth, she could forever rupture this family, and she had no interest in doing so.

One day, however, she couldn't resist asking him whether he had any desire to see Kaki.

He appeared startled by her question, as though he'd never considered it before. He ruminated on it for a few moments, then said, "What good would that do?"

"Well, at least you'll make her happy. So happy that she probably won't stop crying."

"She might not want to let me go."

Nilu considered it. "No, she's not that selfish. She'd understand that you have your own life by now."

Raja turned thoughtful, then slowly shook his head. "Sleeping dogs can lie," he said in English.

She was too quick to correct him. "You mean, Let sleeping dogs lie."

"Yes, yes." He continued after a moment. "Nilu, I can't even recall her face. What is the point in my visiting her? It'll only inflame old wounds. Let it just go."

She didn't fully understand his reasoning. She'd thought he'd want to visit Kaki, embrace her, thank her for saving him from a life of destitution. After all, he could have ended up in a cold, uncaring orphanage with no one to love him. At the same time, what he felt was what he felt, and it was foolish to expect him to fit a mold, to think what she wanted him to think. She couldn't begin to fathom what it was like not to know the identity of the woman who gave birth to you, and although it surprised her when Raja expressed fidelity to a woman who'd discarded him in the park, where he could have died if Bokey Ba hadn't woken to his cries and if Kaki hadn't fed him milk, she decided she wasn't going to judge him. Maybe sometime in the future he could be persuaded to pay Kaki a visit.

Every day, happy after spending time with Raja, Nilu abruptly turned sober once she reached home and had to face Kaki. Half-blind, Kaki would be fumbling around the kitchen. Every day Nilu thought about telling her, "Kaki, guess who I spent time with today?" But she couldn't even hint at knowing something about Raja, couldn't inflict such cruelty. One time, however, her own emotions overwhelmed her, and after spending the afternoon with Raja, she went to Kaki and put her arms around her from behind.

"Nilu Nani, what's wrong?" Kaki asked. With her arthritic fingers she patted Nilu's cheeks, felt the dampness there, and asked, "What's wrong, my daughter? Did something happen? Did someone say anything?"

Nilu shook her head and thrust her face against Kaki's shoulder.

"Everything will be all right, dear," Kaki said. "God will make everything all right for you."

Nilu lifted her face. She couldn't help but ask, "Kaki, do you still think about Raja? Do you still miss him?"

At the mention of Raja's name, Kaki became alert. "Why? Have you seen Raja?"

With great self-control Nilu said, "No, just asking. I haven't heard you mention his name in a long while."

Kaki's face sagged again. "Not a single day goes by when I don't wonder what he's doing now. I wonder what he looks like. He must have grown tall. He was tall for his age even then. Who can tell me what he is like? Who can tell me whether he even remembers me?"

"Kaki, he grew up on your lap. He must have turned out really well. You ought to be happy with that thought."

"Do you think he misses me?"

"How can he not? You are his mother, aren't you?"

A tiny flicker of a smile appeared on her lips. "He must be a really handsome boy. He was always so good-looking. Did I tell you, nani, when he was about three years old and used to follow me around at Rani Pokhari, people used to come up to me and jokingly ask whether they could take him home, so good-looking he was. At that time I used to laugh. I was tickled that people wanted to take him away from me."

"Look at the sky," Raja said, sitting with Nilu at the mound at the edge of the neighborhood, where they liked to meet. The sun was setting behind the giant hill of Nagarjun to the west, painting the entire sky kaleidoscopic pink and red and blue and orange and purple. "Ganja colors," he said. The first time he'd likened the evening sky to ganja, she'd prodded him, forcing him to admit that yes, he did smoke pot every now and then. He'd asked her whether she'd smoked, and she'd shaken her head, and the next day after school he brought, in a small tin container that he'd lifted from Jamuna Mummy's dresser, what looked like dried leaves. He held one to Nilu's nose, and she inhaled the pungent smell. "It's good, isn't it?" he said, and the assured manner with which he ground the leaves on his palm with his thumb told her that he smoked this stuff regularly. After pulverizing the leaves, he poured the dust onto a piece of paper. Then he took out a cigarette and emptied it of its tobacco. Expertly, he began to slide the ganja dust into the hollow cigarette.

She watched his manuevers with a mixture of fascination and, yes, distaste; his smoking pot reminded her of Muwa's drug habit. But she also knew that Muwa, with her pills and her cocaine and her occasional needles, was a full-fledged addict. This, on the other hand, was only youthful experimentation—she hoped. So, when Raja held out the smoke, she accepted it. He lit it for her. She took a deep drag and coughed, and he encouraged her, and she took drag after drag, and for a while nothing happened. Then the air turned lighter and syrupy at the same time, and things slowed down so much that she could hear the shrill whistle and cries of a boy all the way down the field below, and he seemed to be shouting for her. Then she began to laugh because the pores of Raja's nose appeared as big as craters.

"What? What?" Raja asked, merely smiling, not laughing crazily like her because he was accustomed to ganja. He offered the cigarette to Nilu again, and, hysterical because the craters on his nose undulated as he spoke, she buried her face in his shoulder, leaving a wet imprint of her lips on his sleeve. He kept saying "What? What?" as he finished the cigarette. Darkness had begun to fall, and he spoke about life in his soft, unhurried voice: how you thought life was under your control, but it had other things in store for you. Occasionally a silky laugh escaped Nilu's mouth because he was so serious, but gradually his words mesmerized her.

"I want to live in a different age," he said. "I want to live during the days of the Ranas."

"Why?" she asked. "Why do you want to live during the days of the Ranas?"

"I like old times," he said. "All those palaces, all those servants bowing down to you."

Nilu laughed and said that maybe what he really wanted was the dozens of concubines that the Ranas had.

He squeezed her tighter. "No, it's not that. I want to experience what it was like to live in your grand palaces as the citizens around you walked about in tattered clothes. What it must have felt like. Did it really feel good? How good? How good it must have felt to sleep in your luxurious bed at night when more than half of your country slept on hard floors, with their roofs leaking." Raja's eyes were staring into the distance, as though he were already living those times.

The question came to Nilu like an apparition appearing out of fog: why is Raja talking about those despots of those bygone days? *Despots.* Her mind swirled around the word for a while, unable to relinquish it, so delicious it was.

"What must it have been like," Raja said, "to have the power to punish common citizens who didn't bow their heads as you walked by, to command your soldiers to flog them until they cried out for mercy? How good it must have felt" — Raja's words entered Nilu's bloodstream, vibrated in her bones — "to force your own soldiers to pay you levies out of their pathetic salaries. I want to experience all of that, Nilu," Raja said.

"No, you don't," she said.

"Yes, I do," he said. "I want another life, not the one I have. I want to be born differently."

"You are perfect the way you are," she said, but something was getting caught in her throat, and she couldn't tell whether she was about to cry or had already started crying.

"This ganja is spinning my head," he said.

"No, it's not," she said. And now she was indeed crying. "Don't say that, Raja."

He turned to her and wiped her tears from her eyes. "Don't cry, Nilu." She looked at him and in his pupils she saw a woman, wearing a tattered dhoti, walking on pavement close to a body of water. Your mother, your mother, she cried, but only her mind, not her voice, spoke those words. The woman stopped, looked around, and allowed herself to be swallowed by the water. Stop her! Something in Nilu panicked, but then she noticed that Raja's lips were soft and innocent and kissable, and because they were kissable she leaned over and kissed them. He closed his eyes, making the woman disappear from Nilu's mind, and he kissed her back, and such sweetness passed through the front of her chest, straight into her heart.

Muwa found out, eventually, through acquaintances and distant relatives who'd seen Nilu around the Jagadamba School, that she'd switched schools and that she'd been seeing Raja. "That servant boy," Muwa said. "That nathey. You are interested in him? Thukka!" Nilu spun out of Muwa's room.

A short while later, Sumit came to Nilu's door and said, "Nilu, your mother is very upset. Why are you so bent on giving her such headaches? Don't you have any feelings for her?" Nilu was sitting on her bed, and he entered the room and sat on the bed too, making it creak. Both he and Muwa had been drinking, and now his breath assaulted her. "Don't you have any feelings for me?" he asked, smiling.

"Do you mind not sitting on my bed?" she said.

"Why? We get tired too, don't we? Or do you think we don't get tired at all?"

She chose to ignore him and picked up the Charles Dickens novel she was reading.

He moved a bit closer to her, and probably would have reached out and touched her, either on her hair or on her cheek — so many times in the past he'd come close, and she'd moved away before he could do anything — when Muwa appeared at the door. In her right hand was a cigarette, one of the 555s she liked to smoke, and she said, "So, all this time you hid everything from me. Why didn't one of the sisters inform me? Why wasn't I sent a notice? Hiding in some local school! With that Kaki's boy!"

Nilu kept on reading.

"Nilu, answer your mother, please," Sumit said.

Nilu stood and stepped toward the door, but Muwa wouldn't let her pass. "Show him some respect," Muwa commanded. "Who do you think you are? He's been coming to this house for a long time now, and you still treat him like he's a stranger. You hurt him, that's what he tells me. He cares so much about you. Nilu this, Nilu that."

"Muwa, let me go."

"Where are you going?" Muwa shouted, then coughed.

"Downstairs."

"Why? To talk to Kaki? Does she know you've been seeing that Raja?"

"She doesn't need to."

"Why not? He's her boy, isn't he? What—you think you have more of a right over him now than she does? Hasn't Kaki been longing for him all these years?"

Nilu said nothing.

"I had higher expectations of you, Nilu."

"*We* had higher expectations of you," Sumit said.

Muwa fought with Nilu over Raja for a few weeks, then gave up and returned to her cocoon, now speaking even less to Nilu than she did before. It was actually Sumit who attempted to converse with Nilu, pretending he was trying to make up for Muwa's withdrawal. But by now Nilu had become an expert at ignoring him as she entered and exited the house, or when he was in Muwa's room on the rare occasion that she had to go there for something. As she headed for a combined study session with Raja for the School Leaving Certificate exam, which was coming up in a few months, she paused outside Muwa's door, hoping her mother would hear her footsteps and call her in, ask how she was doing. It didn't happen.

. . .

130

Raja bought Nilu small gifts: trinkets, a packet of beautiful Nepali writing paper, cassettes he'd recorded himself with his favorite love songs — by Boney M., Leo Sayer, Paul Anka — and love poems in both English and Nepali. At school all she had to do was step into the courtyard and he'd abandon his friends and come over. On Saturdays he rejected invitations from his male friends and waited for her at home. When she exhorted him to spend more time with his friends, who'd now begun to refer to him as Romeo and Majnu, he only smiled.

One day Raja was walking Nilu back to Nilu Nikunj from Lainchour. Darkness had already descended upon the city, and she slipped her hand into his as they passed the tree-lined avenue alongside the royal palace. Bats fluttered overhead, and at the palace gate a few soldiers stood around, chatting amiably.

Nilu had a premonition — even before Raja did what he did. His eyes became fixed on those soldiers, his expression changed, and she had to slow down because he had. Concerned, she was about to suggest that they cross the street, but it was too late. At the palace gate, Raja stopped. Then he started saluting, making guttural sounds. One of the guards, in a smart uniform and a hat with straps so tight that they squeezed the flesh under his chin, shouted, "Hey, who is that? Scat!"

But, ignoring Nilu's pleas to move on, Raja kept repeating the gesture, at times bursting into the national anthem, "Sriman Gambhir Nepali Prachanda Pratapi Bhupati," but making it sound like a cry for help rather than an ode to the crown. The soldier briskly walked toward them, grabbed Raja by the ear, and dragged him to the guard station by the iron gate, which opened onto the long driveway to the palace. Panicked, Nilu followed, unable to speak. The thought quickly crossed her mind that Raja was touched in the head like his adoptive mother. At the guard station, the soldier slapped Raja a few times, asking him who he was, asking Nilu who she was, asking her who he was, demanding to know whether they knew what they were doing, asking them whether they were college agitators from Ascol College, asking Nilu whether she was a whore and what she was doing with a boy this late at night, then laughing along with another guard who never left the guard station but watched the commotion with a smirk. Raja stood there, massaging his cheek where the soldier had slapped him. Finally, when the soldier stopped speaking, Raja asked him casually, "Dai, what is it like inside? Are the walls made of gold? Are the dishes studded with diamonds?"

"Shoot him!" the soldier commanded his buddy in the station, and the man lifted his gun and pointed it at Raja, a smile cracking his lips. Raja put his hands up in surrender, a comical gesture, as if he were obeying a "Hands up!" command in a movie. Then, grabbing Nilu's arm, he stepped away from the gate.

Nilu, her body hot and cold with fear, couldn't utter a word until they'd passed out of the range of the guards. She still didn't speak as they crossed the street in front of Keshar Mahal and walked past the Fohora Durbar. She didn't look at Raja's face, afraid of what she'd find there. He still had his hand on her arm, and she jerked it away. When he finally spoke, he seemed to want to apologize, but she said, "Crazy! You're crazy! He could have killed both of us."

He shook his head, then said, "I wouldn't have done it if I knew you'd get so angry."

"I don't want to speak to you." Nilu's heart was hammering in her chest and in her throat, and all she wanted to do was get away from him, so she walked even faster, almost sprinting. But he kept pace, offering apologies. "Please, please, Nilu, I had no idea you'd get so scared."

"Do you know what they are capable of?" she asked, suddenly stopping. "Haven't you heard enough stories?"

His mouth moved to speak, but nothing came out, and in disgust Nilu resumed walking. He grabbed her arm. "I'm sorry. I won't do it again."

"Let go of me!"

"Nilu, please."

Then she cried, walking more slowly. They were passing the Rum Doodle Ice Cream place near the British Council, and Raja took her arm and guided her inside. "I don't want any ice cream," she said.

"Let's just sit for a moment, okay?"

He calmly ordered some pistachio ice cream, and as she watched him eat it, with a serene expression on his face, incredibly she couldn't help but admire his nonchalance. What made him so disdainful of the power of those guards? She couldn't fathom such daring, especially in the imposing setting of the royal palace. "You are crazy," she finally said to Raja, hating the awe that had crept into her voice.

"I have really wondered," he said, licking his wooden spoon, "whether the walls inside the palace are made of gold."

"I worry about you," she said, placing her hand on his.

He scooped up some ice cream with his spoon and offered it to her, and her heart became filled with longing for him, even though he was right there in front of her. She opened her mouth and slurped the ice cream. "Nothing will happen to me," he said. "I can feel it. Nothing."

When Bhutto was hanged by the military junta and students flocked to the Pakistani embassy in protest, Raja was there, jostling with the others, his face contorted with reserved fury, acting like the college students around him even though he had yet to enter college. When the police, wielding batons, charged at the students of Ascol College, Raja, who stood out in his blue school uniform, hurled stones at them. He'd joined the college students despite Nilu's pleadings. At first she'd been hurt that he hadn't listened to her, but soon, as she watched the skirmish from the roof of the Jagadamba School, her worries for his safety pushed her hurt aside, for there was Raja, scampering and dashing and darting in and out of the Ascol College building and the dormitory, in and out of the surrounding lanes, as policemen pursued him. The police had cornered a handful of students and brought their batons down on their heads repeatedly. One officer was still chasing Raja, his baton rapidly whipping the air in front of him as though he was swatting at a gnat. Then Raja abruptly turned and stood his ground, halting the policeman. The officer raised his baton to strike Raja; then he paused and merely stared at the boy. Someone else might have thought that Raja had uttered a magic word to freeze the man in place, but Nilu knew that all he did was stand there. The policeman said something to Raja and walked away. Only after the officer was a couple of hundred yards away did Raja turn and hurry into the alley.

Later, when Raja didn't return to school, Nilu went to Ganga Da's house. "That stupid boy will get himself killed," Ganga Da said. He'd just arrived home from work and hadn't changed out of his daura suruwal. Jamuna Mummy emerged from somewhere in the house, stood in front of Nilu, and began genuflecting, muttering under her breath. Ganga Da lost patience and, shouting at her, pushed his wife into the kitchen, where he forced her to sit on the mat on the floor. "Don't get up until I come to fetch you," he warned her.

"Yes, sarkar," she replied. "Whatever you wish, your highness."

Ganga Da and Nilu went searching for Raja, she in her school uniform and he in his daura suruwal. At dusk, they combed the Ascol and Thamel area. The police had already left, and so had most of the students. The only signs of the earlier turmoil were some broken glasses at the entrance to the college and a pair of slippers someone had left behind. The two moved into the alleys of Thamel, hoping to find Raja in a tea shop with what Ganga Da constantly referred to as rabble-rousers. But for two hours they searched with no result, and as they were heading home, a boy wearing a school uniform came hurtling toward them. Nilu recognized him as one of the boys in Raja's circle. "Someone saw Raja being shoved into a police van, near Thamel chowk," the boy said breathlessly.

"Do you know where they've taken him?"

"I heard some of them have been taken to the Hanuman Dhoka police station."

As they conversed, darkness began to enclose them.

"I'm going to Hanuman Dhoka," Ganga Da said.

When Nilu said that she would accompany him, he told her she needed to go home, as Muwa would be worried about her. For a while now Ganga Da had been aware, through Raja, of Muwa's drinking, but he chose to pretend that he didn't know.

"I'm going with you," she insisted, and stepped toward the curb to hail a taxi.

But at the Hanuman Dhoka station, the police wouldn't let them in to see whether Raja had been brought there. "It's too late," the inspector in charge said. "Come tomorrow."

"But at least tell us whether he's in here," Ganga Da said, "so that we won't go looking for him anywhere else."

A few other parents who were looking for their sons made similar pleas, but Inspector Sharma shook his head. "When it comes to controlling your offspring, you folks allow them to run rampant on the streets, and then, when they are inhaling the air of our jail, you begin shedding your tears. Isn't it dangerous for our police brothers to go out on the streets, being hit by stones and everything? Go home, and come tomorrow morning."

Ganga Da studied another inspector who was in the room, recognized him as someone he'd met a long time ago, and went to talk to him. The second inspector finally persuaded Inspector Sharma to send a constable in to verify the names of those who'd been arrested. The constable returned and said that a schoolboy named Raja was indeed there.

"Your son is a Jagadamba School student?" the second inspector asked Ganga Da.

"Yes."

Inspector Sharma laughed. "What has happened to this country? Now even school students are going to start rioting?"

The next morning Nilu went to Hanuman Dhoka by herself, and Inspector Sharma recognized her and said, "Bahini, why are you getting into politics so early? Shouldn't you be focusing on your studies now?"

"I've come here to see Raja."

"Yes, Raja. Raja — the name evokes a king, but in deeds he's like a common crook."

"Can I see him?"

"Are you his sister?"

"No. Just a friend."

"Oh, I understand," Inspector Sharma said. "A girlfriend." He seemed to slobber at the word.

"Can I go in now?"

Inspector Sharma briefly met her gaze, then jerked his head to indicate she could go in. A constable accompanied her. Raja was holed up in a room with at least a dozen other students, all of whom were older than him. When he saw Nilu, he came to the bars. "You shouldn't have come," he said gently. "I'd have phoned you as soon as I got out."

The others in the cell were listening to their conversation, but Nilu and Raja had no choice but to let them. "I was worried," she said. "Have you eaten anything?"

"Someone passed around a loaf of Krishnapauroti. Uncut. And we all shared."

She dug into her bag and brought out a packet of arrowroot biscuits, which she handed to him through the bars. He opened it and, after stuffing a couple of biscuits into his mouth, passed the packet to the others. The college students behind him were whispering "girlfriend" and "chawnk" as they cast furtive glances at Raja and Nilu, so Raja turned to them again and said loudly, "Eh, why don't you all keep it down for a while? Can't two people talk?" And incredibly, even though Raja was a mere high school student, the college students stopped whispering. Raja turned to her. "And how is my mitini?"

A snippet of a whisper — "He called her mitini" — was stifled by the others in the cell.

"I didn't sleep a wink last night," she said.

"Neither did I."

"That's because you were in jail!"

"I kept remembering you on the roof of Jagadamba, watching me. But I couldn't come to you."

"Raja, you rushed down despite my pleading."

"I couldn't control myself," he said.

"What difference does it make to you," she asked, "what they do in Pakistan?"

He searched her eyes. "Don't say that. You have to fight against injustices in this world."

"Why? Where is it written that we must, especially if some of these things don't concern us?"

"It's not written anywhere."

"Raja, seriously," she pleaded, not liking the stridency of her voice. "Please don't do this."

He looked down and shook his head, kept shaking it for a while, then said, "This thing is getting bigger. People are in an uproar about what happened at Ascol yesterday."

"How long are they going to keep you here, Raja?"

Instead of answering her, he moved his mouth closer through the bars. Thinking that he was about to whisper something important, she leaned forward, but instead he brushed his lips against hers. Right then, Ganga Da appeared.

For the longest moment Ganga Da stood and shook his head at Raja. He was in his daura suruwal, just like last evening, but now on his way to the Nepal Rashtra Bank. Finally he spoke. "Happy? This must be a glorious day for you? It's indeed a proud moment for a father to visit his son who is in jail for breaking and shattering property belonging to the government and to other people, for acting like a vagrant raised on the streets."

He didn't mean it, of course, the street reference; and Nilu saw that he wanted to take it back even as the words escaped his mouth, but it was too late. Raja said, "Everyone knows I was raised on the streets."

"Don't twist my words!" Ganga Da said. "I didn't raise you to be a goonda and a lafanga, like the rest of these people here."

"Ganga Da." Nilu's voice cautioned him.

The college students gathered around Raja and challenged Ganga Da to repeat what he said. One of them said loudly, "Raja, is your father a mandalay? A government stooge?"

Before Ganga Da could respond, Inspector Sharma appeared. "What's all the ruckus about?" he said. "It isn't enough for you guys to be in jail? Do I have to throw piss-water on you to shut you up?"

The thought of being doused in piss elicited laughter from the students, and momentarily, the tension was diffused. Ganga Da accompanied Inspector Sharma to the office. Nilu and Raja once again huddled together, in a corner, the bars of the cell between them. He asked her if she was going to school, and she said that she really didn't want to, but the police probably wouldn't allow her to stay much longer. "I'm worried about your meals," she said. "I thought Ganga Da was going to bring you dal-bhat from home, but he's dressed for work. Maybe I'll go home and bring you something to eat."

"Someone's family will be bringing food to one of us here, and we'll all share. That's how it is in here."

"Oh, now you've become an expert on the etiquette of jail?"

With his index finger, he stroked the top of her hand. "Do you want to go see a movie after I get out of here?"

"Raja, you're thinking about a movie now?"

"That video parlor in Makhan is playing *Love Story*."

"Ryan O'Neal?"

"'Love means never having to say you're sorry.'"

"It's a sappy story," Nilu said. "I've read the book. Besides, I've begun to hate those video parlors. They're so crowded and uncomfortable."

Over the past year, every alley in inner Kathmandu seemed to boast a video parlor, where bootlegged, grainy copies of Hindi- and English-language movies, some pornographic, were shown for a fee. Nilu and Raja had been to a couple of them, where old men with dentures sat shoulder to shoulder with boisterous boys, and young brides with gold jewelry sparkling and tinkling on their wrists jostled for space with grandmothers suffering from arthritis. Their second time at a video parlor, for a showing of *Butch Cassidy and the Sundance Kid,* the room was so crammed that Nilu felt she was being smothered and had to leave, just as Paul Newman and Robert Redford entered the bordello.

"You don't want to go?" Raja asked.

"I'll go if you want to."

"I don't want to go if you don't want to."

As they were going back and forth like this, Inspector Sharma returned, opened the door to the cell, and beckoned to Raja. "You! Come with me."

All the chatter in the cell stopped.

"Why?" Raja asked.

"Just come."

"Where are you taking him?" the others asked.

"Do I have to explain my every move to you?" Inspector Sharma asked. "I have something special for you," he told Raja.

Immediately Nilu wondered whether they were taking Raja to an isolation cell. She'd read that the police often tortured political prisoners to extract information from them. And Raja was a political prisoner now, wasn't he? She looked toward the hallway for Ganga Da, but there was no sign of him.

When Raja didn't move, Inspector Sharma said, "Are you going to come quietly, or do I have to drag you out of there?"

"Don't go, Raja," the college students advised. "What can he do if you don't go?"

"Mujiharu," Inspector Sharma snarled. "You want to incite him more? Are you playing games with me?"

Inspector Sharma was a short, pudgy man but had a menacing voice, and his threat worked: the room went silent. Raja left the cell and accompanied Inspector Sharma. Nilu followed.

The inspector said nothing as they entered his office, where Ganga Da was seated.

"I should have him sign a confession," Inspector Sharma said.

"He'll sign whatever is necessary," Ganga Da said.

"What confession?" Raja said.

Inspector Sharma touched Raja's chin with his baton. "He's still a bachcha, a kid. Look. He doesn't yet know how to wash his arsehole properly, and yet he's out on the streets, shouting obscenities against the king." Before Raja could respond, Inspector Sharma said, "Forget it. You can take him home now."

Outside the police station, Ganga Da said to Raja and Nilu, "Go straight to school now, you two. Who knows what else could happen today? There are agitators everywhere. Okay, Raja? Can you promise me that you won't get involved with any of this nonsense? Please?"

Raja looked at him mockingly. He gave a Nazi salute and said, "Heil Hitler!"

Ganga Da scowled and, saying that he was already late, briskly walked away.

"You have to respect him a bit, Raja," Nilu chided him.

They lingered in the Durbar Square area, making their way down Pie Alley. At Chi and Pie they sat for an hour, eating chocolate and lemon meringue and drinking coffee, listening to Mick Jagger on the restaurant's cassette player. Then, arm in arm, they ambled toward Freak Street, Nilu resting her head on Raja's shoulder as they walked, drawing stares from other pedestrians.

In Freak Street dreadlocked hippies with long beards and baggy corduroys hung about, looking stoned and happy. A heavy smell of ganja and hash permeated the air. A multicolored van sat outside a shop, and a girl in a long, flowing frock, a cigarette in her hand, was arguing with a Nepali shopkeeper, probably unhappy about a business deal. From the second floor of a house, the steady, rhythmic beat of reggae sounded, lending the argument below an almost sensual tone. Nearby, a black man in a crewcut chatted with a saffron-robed sadhu, explaining to him that he was an American marine. The sadhu, fingering his dirty beard, nodded.

Nilu and Raja strolled in and out of shops, Nilu fingering T-shirts with Buddha's curvaceous eyes embroidered on them, Raja inspecting chillums and bongs and hookahs. They ventured into alleys strewn with condoms and cigarette butts; escaped a hippie with a runny nose who followed them, asking for "a few rupees"; drank coffee at Eat at Joe's, then made their way back up again, veering toward New Road, where they climbed to the Bangalore Coffee House, located on the second floor. They shared a masala dosa, exclaiming how hot and spicy it was, then walked to the American library, where they spent the next two hours browsing, reading *Newsweek* and *Reader's Digest,* watching each other across the table. When they headed home, it was already three o'clock, and Nilu hailed a taxi because she didn't want to walk past Ascol College or the Dairy. She instructed the driver to take the route of Chhetrapati, then approach Samakhusi from the Ring Road. "This is too much," Raja kept saying. "You are throwing your money away on the taxi driver. We could have walked home in half an hour, and I promise I wouldn't have done anything."

"Like the Hitler promise you made to Ganga Da."

The taxi stopped just a few yards from the lane that led to Raja's house. "Go and have a quiet day at home, okay?" she told him.

"And madam is not going to go there with me?" he asked, pointing in the direction of his house.

"Not today," she said. "I need to go home and rest."

"Yes, madam," Raja said, then saluted her and went toward his house.

When Nilu reached home, she called Ganga Da's house to check to see that Raja hadn't gone back out to the street. He hadn't. "What are you doing?" she asked. He was reading a Hardy Boys novel.

Soon after Nilu and Raja sat for their S.L.C. exams, the city exploded. Students were hauled around the city in pushcarts, a garland of shoes around their necks, their faces blackened. The Royal Nepal Airlines office in New Road, right across the street from the parade ground where the Rana autocrats had gathered their soldiers for pompous and useless ceremonies a century ago, became a focal point of public discontent. Cars were torched, and further up the road the buildings of the government newspapers were set on fire. Raja, incredibly, stayed away from the tumult, thanks in large part to Nilu's vigilance. At school, she kept a close eye on him, making sure to meet him during recess and tiffin breaks so he wouldn't slip out and join his college friends. After school she walked home with him, saw him off at the gate. She could see that it was hard for him. Whenever they walked by a tea shop that reverberated with the sound of the BBC radio, he paused, straining to hear the nasal voice of the reporter detailing the scuffles and arrests across the city, until Nilu pulled him by the arm and dragged him away.

"Why are you so afraid for me?" Raja asked her once. "What could possibly happen to me?" They were sitting on the ground in a corner of the alley leading to Raja's house, hidden partially from pedestrians by a large bush, although if people stopped and listened they could hear murmurs and detect the young lovers, in their blue uniforms, through the leaves. The lane was not well traveled, except just before and after school, when groups of students walked the path with their backpacks.

"You could get a bullet in your chest."

"It's not going to happen."

"If not that, then you could be crippled for life."

"Not in my destiny."

"You can't predict the future."

"Once you know your past, then you know your future too."

"But you don't know your past."

"I know that my mother didn't want me."

"You don't know that."

He laughed. "Nilu, if my mother wanted me, I'd be with her right now."

"She could have wanted you but still have been forced to give you up."

He shook his head. "Then she didn't want me badly enough."

There was truth in that statement, Nilu knew, so she didn't press the matter. A short while later she said, "Raja, please, for my sake, don't get involved in any of this."

"But Nilu, I have nothing to lose," he said.

After a moment she said, "You could lose me."

"Really?"

"Really. I can't take it anymore."

He pressed his finger gently against her lips, and that softened her feelings, although she did note that Raja didn't promise her anything.

Still, Nilu kept up her vigilance until King B unexpectedly announced a referendum, allowing people to vote to continue with the Panchayat system or open the government to other political parties.

"He's calling for his own demise," people said. But their pronouncement turned out to be false. The election came and went the next summer, and the Pancheys remained in power. "See?" Ganga Da said to Raja one afternoon. The three of them were sitting in Ganga Da's living room. Jamuna Mummy was sleeping on a blanket on the floor of the kitchen, another blanket covering her entire body, like a shrouded corpse. "The people have decided. They don't want change."

"This election was rigged."

"That's what losers always say."

"Let it go, Raja," Nilu said. "I'm so tired of hearing about the elections." By now she'd begun to feel quite comfortable in Raja's house, mostly because Ganga Da had been so affectionate and accepting toward her. He'd begun to call her chhori, and he indeed treated her as though she were his daughter.

"You are arguing against life itself," she told Raja once. "Ganga Da, Pancheys, the king. They are mere symbols of something deeper."

He shrugged, which to her suggested that even if he did agree, it didn't matter, because he had no other choice but to fight. As though to demonstrate this point, a few days later Raja got into a meaningless scuffle at a disco. That evening Raja and Nilu had gone to the Foot Tapper in Tangal, where Nilu was meeting Prateema and a couple of other friends. Prateema had had to concoct an elaborate lie to tell her parents in order to come, so she was giddily nervous as she danced. The problem began when a boy their age, wearing a hat, started dancing very close to her, and though Nilu and another friend tried to block his way, the boy managed to slide past them and thrust his hips at Prateema. The boy appeared impossibly drunk and was likely harmless; Nilu was about to appeal for help to the boy's friends, who were sitting in a corner, when Raja grabbed the boy's collar and sent him sprawling across the floor. Four or five of the drunken boy's friends swiftly surrounded Raja, pushing and shoving him. Nilu tried to intervene, but a girl stood in her way and challenged her, saying, "What? You also looking for trouble?" Nilu tried to slide past her to Raja, but the girl, who was bigger, wouldn't let her. Raja, meanwhile, wouldn't back down. He'd have received a sound thrashing but for the muscular bouncer, a former Gorkha soldier, who lifted all of them like rabbits and threw them out the door. Nilu hailed a taxi and quickly shoved Raja into it.

Shortcut Bajé

AFTER PASSING the S.L.C. exams (Nilu in first division, Raja in second), the two began attending Shanker Dev Campus. Often they were together, rarely relinquishing each other's company to join their other friends, who were not too many. Raja had a group of friends who sat around admiring him for his bravado, but he didn't hesitate to abandon them when he saw Nilu walking through the campus gates. Nilu in general kept to herself, preferring Raja's company to that of her women classmates, who seemed to enjoy gossip and talking about fashion more than anything else.

The entire city, it seemed to Nilu sometimes, knew about her and Raja. It wasn't surprising, of course, because many people saw them together, before and after class, walking the length of Baghbazar, strolling through the neighborhood of Lainchour. But she couldn't help but feel annoyed when even her distant relatives, when they ran into her, asked her if she was on the verge of getting married. Classmates at Shanker Dev also teased them about being invited to the wedding feast. But Nilu and Raja were in no hurry. They didn't talk about getting married — it never came up.

One day after returning from Shanker Dev, where she was already in her third year, Nilu stood on her balcony, watching Ramkrishan dig up a patch of garden with a hoe, when Sumit sneaked up from behind and put his arm around her. Startled, she attempted to throw his arm away, but he tightened his grasp — he was stronger than she'd thought — and thrust his face close to hers. "How are you, Nilu Nani?" he asked. His breath gave off the strong minty smell of the pan masala he'd been chewing. "How are you, my chhori?" he hissed. It was a long-suppressed craving in him, she recognized, to call her his daughter. He'd rehearsed this moment every time he'd spied her on her balcony, every time he'd seen her return from school, first from St. Augustine's, then from the Jagadamba School, and now from college. Where was Muwa? In her room, Nilu was sure, deep in a coma, and today Sumit had probably fed her an extra pill or two to ensure that she'd remain in her dark world until he accomplished his task. Yes, he had planned it, he'd waited for this day when she'd forget to lock her room, so he could just slip in. Poor bastard — all the time he'd been with Muwa, he'd been plotting to seduce her daughter. When he and Muwa had popped pills, when they'd dragged on cigarettes laced with magic to transport them to other worlds, when Muwa had spoken to him about a memory of her own childhood — at all these moments, Sumit had fantasized about touching Muwa's daughter, to sleep with her, if he could, in her bed, with Muwa close by. A pathetic little creature he was, and Nilu was going to play with him.

"I am fine, Daddy," she said, with a seductive smile, making her voice sweet and husky.

"Are you okay, chhori?" he said, suspiciously. He'd obviously not expected it to go this easily.

"Yes, I'm fine, Daddy," she said, bringing her mouth close to his. Very quickly, she moved her mouth to the left and clamped down on his ear, hard, her teeth crunching his cartilage. Sumit yowled and jerked away from her, leaving a fraction of his ear in her mouth, a tiny morsel. She tasted blood before she spat it to the floor.

Standing a few feet away from her, his left hand covering his ear, he was trying not to shout. "Badmash!" he said to her. "Just wait, I'll get you one day." Wincing with pain, he removed his handkerchief from his pocket with this other hand, and used it to cover his ear. In the garden below, Ramkrishan remained oblivious to what was happening on the balcony just a few feet above him, but Sumit's last words made the old servant glance up sharply and ask Nilu if everything was all right.

Nilu went into her room, picked up her purse, and left. Downstairs Kaki was sitting cross-legged on the veranda floor, combing her hair. Hearing Nilu's footsteps, she asked, "Where are you going, Nilu Nani?"

The taste of Sumit's ear was still fresh on her tongue. "I'll be going away, Kaki. If Muwa wakes up and asks after me, tell her that I'll return in a few days."

"Where are you going?" Kaki cried.

"I don't know."

Ramkrishan came to the veranda and, leaning on his hoe, asked, "What happened up there, Nilu Nani? I thought I heard an argument. Was it that man?" In Sumit's absence, both Kaki and Ramkrishan referred to him as "that man."

"Something like that. Listen, Ramkrishan Dai, I'm going away for a while. Take care of Muwa."

Sumit came bursting through from inside the house, his palm covering his ear, and without looking at anyone, hurried down to the yard and out the gate.

They watched his departure.

"Nani, a young girl like you," Kaki said. "Where are you going to go? Where will you stay?"

Nilu went to Kaki, embraced her, and said, "I'll find a place."

She left home without really knowing where she would go, except she was certain that she wasn't going to return to Nilu Nikunj to spend the night. She had to get away. More than Sumit, it was Muwa she couldn't look at anymore. She couldn't even look at Ramkrishan and Kaki, because every time she saw their faces, she began to feel sorry for herself. They were not her parents, but here they were, the two people in the world who worried about her, who wanted her to be happy, who cared what she ate and what she drank, who wished that she was safe and protected. Yet they were mere servants, with fewer rights than other people. Even in a court of law that was supposed to protect their rights, they'd be trounced. Ganga Da knew this very well; that's why Kaki had lost her battle before it even commenced.

Nilu found herself meandering toward Lainchour, a path with which she was very familiar. This had been the route of her first liberation from Nilu Nikunj, the road she'd taken when she'd gone to search for Raja. But today she didn't want to go to Ganga Da's house, where Raja would be expecting her. She'd have to call Raja from somewhere and tell him she wasn't coming.

She took a left at Keshar Mahal and moved toward Thamel. For a while she just wandered around the tourist district. She went into a couple of bookstores, drank tea on the narrow balcony of a restaurant, then wandered around some more. In front of the Kathmandu Guest House, she paused, then walked in.

She called Raja from a room in the Kathmandu Guest House.

"Where are you?" he complained. "I've been waiting for you for more than two hours now." He typically whined like this when she was late to meet him or when for some reason they couldn't see each other on a particular day. They had become so attached over the past three years that she didn't know what she'd do if for some reason they were to be separated. A couple of times when they'd talked about it, Raja had shaken his head and refused to even contemplate the possibility. "I would simply die, Nilu," he'd said. "I don't even want to think about it." She felt the same way, but she sensed that his attachment to her was much deeper — needier, and it emanated from a place deep inside him. Her presence in his life had turned him into a happier young man — this much she knew and took pride in. He had become a bit softer than before, more likely to laugh than to brood.

She told him where she was and that she planned to stay the night there. Maybe more nights, she added.

After some silence, he said, "Really?"

"Yes, Raja, really."

"Do you need a friend?"

"You?" she asked.

"Yes."

"You — I'll take you anytime."

"Okay, I'm coming over."

It was only a fifteen-minute walk from his house to the Kathmandu Guest House, and he arrived just as she stepped out of the shower, her towel wrapped around her. Before now, they'd petted each other in alleys, he'd sucked her breasts in his house in Lainchour, and she'd given him a hand job. But they hadn't gone farther. One time, in Lainchour, with Ganga Da and Jamuna Mummy away at Manakamana, they had come very close: Raja's pants were down to his knees and she had taken off her T-shirt and her panties, but just as he readied himself to enter her, she moved away from him and said, "Raja, no, let's wait." He hadn't argued with her, just held her tight.

But tonight was going to be different. Even without her telling him what had happened, he could sense that they had come to a crossroads. "Mitini," he said, and she came to him, dropping the towel on the way. He'd never seen her completely naked before. He stroked her breasts, felt them stiffen against his fingers, and said, "Now?"

She shook her head. "Later."

That evening they ate at the hotel, in the garden, listening to a German tourist sing Grateful Dead songs as he strummed his guitar. Listening to the words of "Sugar Magnolia," Raja looked at Nilu and she looked at him, each trying to guess what the other was thinking. She hadn't yet told him about biting Sumit's ear because she didn't want to remind herself of that awful taste. But Raja seemed to understand what she was feeling, her sadness, her sense that they were about to do something important — without her having to say anything.

After dinner they stayed in the garden until the mosquitoes began to bite, then they went out and strolled on the streets. In this tourist district they felt as though they too were foreigners, unencumbered by the weight of living in the city, the weight of their own families. A cool breeze meandered through the lanes and alleys of Thamel. They went into the Up and Down bar and danced to the entire soundtrack of *Saturday Night Fever*, laughing and doing exaggerated versions of John Travolta's disco moves.

Back at the hotel, the bed was a bit small, but it hardly mattered because they were snuggled in each other's arms.

"Raja," she said. "Have you ever bitten anyone's ear?"

He laughed into her bosom. "I've fantasized about it. Why?"

"It tastes delicious."

"Delicious like how? Does it taste like a goat's ear, burned over the fire?"

"Not that good, but it is kind of salty. I can just imagine how great it'd taste, how hot and flaming, if you sprinkled on some khursani."

"Nilu."

"What?"

"Are you a man-eating woman?"

She bared her teeth and growled, then lightly bit into his arm. "I'm going to eat you, Raja. I'm going to devour you, from head to toe. I am Kali, and I love human blood, and human flesh."

"Can we do this tomorrow, this eating-drinking business?" he said. "Don't we have another important activity to perform?"

"Do we?"

"Yes," he said, and kissed her. His mustache tickled her, making her laugh. Slowly, they unbuttoned each other's clothes. The moon had cast a white glow into the room.

"Do you have a condom?" she whispered.

"I've come well prepared," he said, and reached to the floor to find his pants pocket.

"Is it going to hurt?"

"I don't know," he said.

That night they lost their virginity.

The taxi stopped at the Guheswori Temple. Nilu watched Raja as she paid the taxi driver and they got out, but his expression was relaxed, as though nothing was amiss, as though only one road led away from the Kathmandu Guest House, and it always ended up here at this popular goddess's temple next to the Bagmati River. The last time they'd visited this area was at the start of their first year at Shanker Dev Campus, when the entire class had come for a picnic in the hills between the temples of Guheswori and Pashupatinath.

They climbed the steps into the Guheswori Temple, but midway up, Nilu veered right, into a doorway to a house. Inside it was pitch-dark, and the two held hands as they groped their way up the stairs. Nilu led him. "Where have you brought me, mitini?" Raja asked, laughing. At the top, where a miniature window cast some light, a woman was standing, and she peered at the two of them.

"Is bajé in?" Nilu asked. The woman said that bajé was taking a nap. Should she wake him? "Yes, please do," said Nilu. The woman disappeared inside.

Raja looked at Nilu. He seemed to be in some kind of a blissful state. He stroked her chin, then leaned over and kissed her on the lips. She gently pushed his face away, in fear that the woman would reappear.

"You know what's going to happen, my dear?" Nilu asked.

He grabbed her arm and placed it on his heart. "I think I do. Do you feel my heartbeat?"

The old man appeared. He wore a thick pair of glasses whose bridge was held together with tape. His eyes appeared large behind them; he had a stubble of a beard, and some white hairs stuck out of his ears. He peered at Nilu, then said, "I don't think I recognize you."

"We haven't met before, bajé," Nilu said. "But you need to do something for us." She leaned over and whispered into the old man's ear.

"Do your parents know, nani?"

Nilu reached into her purse and took out five ten-rupee bills, which she waved in front of the man, then stuffed them into the pocket of his waistcoat. "You do a good job, bajé, and I'll give you more, all right?"

"How did you know about me, nani?"

"Everyone in the city knows about you, bajé. Aren't you known as Shortcut Bajé?"

Shortcut Bajé laughed. The woman was glaring at him, and he hastily reached into his pocket and took out the money, which he then handed over to her. "Let me get some things ready, okay?" he said, then disappeared with the woman.

Raja was gazing at Nilu. "How did you become so bold? Where did you learn this courage?"

"I have nothing to lose anymore, do I? Except you."

The priest came down shortly, having changed into a clean white dhoti, which showed his thin arms, and bearing a tray of rice grains, colored powders, and other religious knickknacks, including glass bangles, a necklace, and vermilion powder for Nilu's forehead.

He led them to the temple, where he asked them to descend a short flight of steps into the shrine of Gueswori, ask for the goddess's blessing, and come back out. They did so, and on the way back up, Nilu said to Raja, "Are you going to back out now, Raja? Are you going to flee?"

He whispered into her ear, "If I'm fleeing, I'm taking you along."

At the top of the stairs, surrounded by chattering monkeys, Shortcut Bajé was waiting to unite them in matrimony.

Thamel Days

They found a flat the day after their wedding. The ceremony, true to Shortcut Bajé's reputation, was short, with the priest chanting a few key mantras, sprinkling on the bride and the groom holy water from the nearby Bagmati, placing small morsels of sweets on their tongues, and making them circle the temple a few times. Raja was half tittering, half weeping. Toward the end, when the priest had them face the shrine and chant hymns that solidified their marriage for multiple lives to come, Raja grew solemn, which made Nilu giggly.

On the way back to the hotel, she leaned against him in the taxi and said, "How does it feel, hubby?" She kissed him on the cheek, which made the taxi driver frown through the rearview mirror.

"So what now?" Raja asked as the taxi sped toward the hotel.

"Well, we're married," Nilu said. "What do newly married couples do?"

"Go on a honeymoon."

"Where do you want to go?"

"Let's go to Nagarkot. Great mountain views there, I've heard."

"You can even see Mount Everest from there," the taxi driver chipped in.

Raja and Nilu looked at each other. "Dai," they asked him. "Can you take us there?"

"Now?"

"Yes, when else?"

In Nagarkot early the next morning, as they sat on the balcony of their small hotel, watching the rising sun paint the sky and the mountains a glowing, shimmering red, they soaked in the realization that their new life together had already started and that they didn't need to return to their respective houses. The giddiness from yesterday's ceremony — Shortcut Bajé, the monkeys and their babies that circled them as they were wed, the taxi driver who, even as he disapproved of their kisses in his vehicle, was thrilled to be driving them up the winding road to the hilly resort — had given way to a sobriety. They felt that they had aged five years overnight. On the way back down to the city they were quiet, and by the time the taxi driver dropped them off at the Kathmandu Guest House, they knew they had to find a home of their own.

The next morning they came upon it, their home, near the corner by Amrit Science College, a flat whose TO LET sign had been turned into TOILET by someone's paintbrush. They could have searched for a better place: the house was old and crumbling and their flat was just a small room. But they liked the Thamel area, and the rent was reasonable, a mere two hundred rupees per month. By the evening they'd moved in, and the landlady's daughter-in-law, Bhairavi, came to chat with them. She was a sweet woman, interested in the fact that they'd married yesterday but had no possessions to furnish their flat. When she learned that Raja's home was right next door in Lainchour and Nilu's close by in Jamal, she put her hand to her mouth. "Did you two elope?" she asked.

Nilu and Raja smiled at each other. "You could say that," Raja said. "Although we're the kind of elopers unafraid of getting caught."

"To tell you the truth," Bhairavi said, "my mother-in-law is a bit suspicious of you. She is wondering if you are even married, but this room has been without a tenant for so long, she didn't want to let this opportunity pass."

With Bhairavi they formed an immediate bond. Her husband had a slight limp in his right leg. A gunshot wound, they learned that first day, that he'd acquired during the riots in 1979, the year Raja had been jailed in Hanuman Dhoka. Manmohan Dai had gone looking for a neighbor's child and caught a bullet in his leg. He showed Raja and Nilu the scar, and Nilu could tell that it sparked something in Raja, for his expression turned dark, and he said, loudly, pointing in the direction of the palace, which was only a block away, "That man is directly responsible."

With Raja's tryst with the palace guards still raw in her memory, Nilu couldn't help but imagine his voice traveling over the treetops, over the backpacking tourists of Thamel chowk, with their foreign-printed maps, over the grand library of Keshar Mahal, its ancient books gathering dust as its lethargic caretakers sunned themselves in its elaborate garden, and finally into the ears of the men protecting the palace. Nilu could just picture the guards shouting, "Who is that?" then strapping rifles to their shoulders and checking their guns for bullets. While shouting incomprehensible words, they'd rush toward Thamel, their boots thundering on the pavement; after shoving aside grandmothers, who carried baskets of offerings, and low-level officers on their way to work, at last the guards would break down this house's front door with the butt of their rifles and rumble up the stairs, their barrels pointed at Raja.

Raja ran his finger over the man's scar, which was shaped like a crescent moon. "While the bullet struck you," Raja said, now in a low, slightly shaky voice, "our king was probably sipping his wine and playing billiards and smoothing his mustache, and his wife was adjusting her bouffant hairdo for a party."

But Manmohan Dai displayed no outrage, no sense of injustice about what had happened to him. He merely smiled at Raja and said, "That's the way it is." Then he changed the subject, asking about their marriage. Raja appeared mildly taken aback by Manmohan Dai's easy acceptance of the fact that he'd been marred for life. Because of Nilu's frequent exhortations, Raja had mostly kept away from student groups at Shanker Dev, although Nilu could tell that at times he wanted to get out on the streets and protest whatever the crowd was protesting. He read the newspapers and seethed. He listened to the radio news intently as though he'd find answers to life's questions there.

He and Ganga Da carried on low-voiced debates about what was good for the country, and for the most part Raja scoffed at Ganga Da's views. But these days the debates, although intense, also tended to end abruptly, with both father and son seemingly recognizing the futility, the impossibility of reaching agreement. Raja would turn away and begin fiddling with the radio, or say to his father, "How long are you going to blather on about the same thing?" And with Manmohan Dai, Raja's disappointment with his acceptance of the status quo didn't last long, and soon he began to talk to him about other topics. He noticed, as Nilu did, how amorous Bhairavi and Manmohan Dai were toward each other. Like young lovers, Bhairavi and her husband frequently exchanged affectionate glances, always speaking about each other in endearing terms.

"This is our world, Raja," Nilu said that first day, after they returned to their single-room flat. One corner served as kitchen, and their toilet, located in the courtyard, was shared by families living in the surrounding houses. Nilu embraced Raja, rested her head on his chest, and wrapped her arms around him. "The larger world is outside. But this small world is the one that'll nurture us." He teased her about her poetry, then kissed her and said, "Haven't you heard what our great poet Devkota said?" Waving his hands in the air, addressing the window as if he were speaking to the bicyclists, motorists, and pedestrians in the street, Raja launched into a dramatic rendering of Devkota's famous lines:

> *A pouch filled with gold*
> *is like the dirt on your palm —*
> *what is the use of wealth?*
> *Eat greens and nettles*
> *with a heart full of bliss —*
> *now that's true happiness.*

"We'll certainly have more to eat than greens and nettles," Nilu said. "How about some mutton tonight to celebrate our new flat?" They bought half a kilo of goat meat from the nearby butcher shop. As they didn't have a stove, or pots or pans or dishes, they borrowed a pressure cooker from Bhairavi, who also gave them an old stove to use, and they sat on their haunches in the kitchen corner and watched the cooker hiss and whistle. The anticipation of their new life together, the mild anxiety over the looming confrontation with their families, had made them hungry, and they attacked the meat—it had turned a bit spongy—with gusto, their fingers scraping the inside of the cooker as they scooped up the gravy. They licked their fingers and their palms and loudly sucked the bones for the marrow. Overstuffed, numbed with food, Raja burped, and Nilu scolded him, then let out a burp herself; they had to hold their stomachs as they rolled with laughter on the bare floor. That night the two crawled into a narrow sleeping bag that Bhairavi had thrown into their room as they were eating. Squeezed tight against each other, their stomachs so bloated they could barely move without groaning, they became drowsy and abruptly fell into a deep sleep.

It only took a few days for Ganga Da to find out where they were living. One early morning he came knocking. When bleary-eyed Raja opened the door, Ganga Da stood on the threshold, staring at him. "What have you two done?"

Nilu had barely managed to put her jeans on and was sitting on the bedding.

"Am I going to get an answer?" Ganga Da asked.

"How did you know we were living here?" Raja asked, as though this was more puzzling than what he and Nilu had done.

"What does it matter?" Ganga Da said, red-faced, almost shouting. "People know me in this area. They know you, Raja. Our house is merely a block away. People have seen you in Thamel, they've seen you go in and out of this flat." He paused. "At first I didn't believe it. But it is true. I was never against your union, but I have also never been so disappointed with you both. Why did you have to do everything so secretively, as though I was your enemy?"

"It has nothing to do with you, Ganga Da," Raja said.

"Then why behave like this? Why live together like this without the benefit of marriage? Do you know what people are saying?"

Raja glanced at Nilu. "We did marry. In the Guheswori Temple. Maybe you need to fire your sources."

Ganga Da appeared speechless, then shook his head. "That's not what people are saying. They're saying you two are living together without the benefit of a marriage. Your Muwa," he addressed Nilu, "thinks that I have a hand in all of this, that I've somehow incited you two."

"Ganga Da, will you please at least come in and sit down?" Nilu said.

Ganga Da stepped in and looked around, then sighed heavily.

"I'll arrange for some tea," Nilu said.

He snapped at her. "Tea is the last thing I'm worried about. Why couldn't you two have come to me? How could you take such a momentous decision into your own hands like this, so casually? You've slapped me — that's what I feel like this morning. Look at this." He pointed to the bare flat. "You have to come and live in this unbearable place while down the road a perfectly fine house is sitting empty. And why did you decide not to let anyone know? First, I get Raja's call from the hotel — hotel! Whoever thinks of seeking shelter in a hotel when both of you have your own houses to go to? Then I hear from others that you've shacked up together in a flat."

"Well, what's done is done," Raja said. "Now your shouting and screaming isn't going to solve anything."

Ganga Da, looking at him in disbelief, appeared ready to strike him. Then his shoulders drooped. "Your Jamuna Mummy has gotten worse since you left the house."

"I can't let Jamuna Mummy's moods dictate my life," Raja said. "Otherwise, my life too would be, you know?" He drew circles near his head with his finger.

"Raja!" Nilu scolded him.

"You see how he talks to me?" Ganga Da said.

Bhairavi appeared with a glass of tea. She must have heard Ganga Da shouting. Ganga Da looked slightly embarrassed, and he took the tea like a docile cat. After Bhairavi left, he said that he was obliged to let Muwa know the situation. He moped around for a while, then trudged down the stairs.

Over the next few days a small part of Nilu remained anxious that Muwa would barge into the flat, create a scene, and try to humiliate Raja. She frequently glanced out the window to see if her mother was on her way. But Muwa didn't come, and eventually Nilu felt both relief and disappointment; for her mother the news of her daughter's wedding didn't occasion a visit, even in anger. Attuned to Nilu's mood, Raja consoled her. "She'll come, just give her some time."

Instead of visiting, Muwa somehow got hold of the phone number at Bhairavi's drawing room below and called one morning for Nilu. "You're living in a real nice joint, I hear," Muwa said, her voice raspy and wavering. "A real palace."

"It's enough for us," Nilu said quietly. She could hear Muwa take a drag from her cigarette.

"Who would have thought that you, Nilu, of all people would turn out like this. I had higher hopes for you. Did you know what my aunt—"

"Muwa, I have more important things to do than listen to what your aunt thinks of me."

"What important things? What could you possibly have to do?"

"I have to go to my school. I've started teaching."

"Oh," Muwa said. "You've become very independent—is that what you're trying to tell me?"

Nilu decided to ignore that question. She wondered if Sumit was in the room. "How is Kaki?" she finally asked.

"She's been pestering me about where you've gone. She won't leave me alone, saying I should bring you home."

"Tell her I'll come for a visit soon."

"When?" After a moment Muwa said, more gently, "You left without a word."

But Nilu wasn't deceived by the trace of sorrow in her voice. "I'll talk to you later," she said, and hung up.

On her way out she peeked into Bhairavi's kitchen. Bhairavi was cooking the morning meal. "Everything all right?" she asked Nilu.

Nilu nodded, though tears were filling her eyes.

Bhairavi wiped her hands on her dhoti and came over. "She'll come around, don't worry. They always do." She paused. "Why don't you eat here this morning? You won't have time to cook before school."

Nilu looked at her watch. Indeed, it was eight o'clock. The school bus came at eight-thirty, and she had yet to set the rice to boil. "I don't want to burden you."

Bhairavi slapped her on the wrist. "If I hear you say that again, I won't speak to you. How is the teaching going?"

It had only been a week since Nilu had started teaching at Arniko Academy. The job had come to her unexpectedly. Prateema taught math there. When Nilu had called her, it was not to inquire after a job but to inform Prateema about the new turn her life had taken. The two friends had chatted for a while, and Prateema had asked Nilu whether she would continue living off Muwa's largesse. A job for a history and English teacher had opened up at her school, Prateema said, and if Nilu hustled, there was a good chance she'd get it.

And within days, Nilu was in the classroom, teaching seventh and eight graders how to write an essay or explaining British colonialism, which, Raja told her wryly, was inexplicable.

In the mornings, Raja grabbed her by the waist, knowing full well that she didn't have time for it, that she'd miss the school bus if he continued to unwrap her dhoti and loosen her petticoat. But there was excitement in pressing against time like this, in jerking the curtain shut and tumbling into bed, in allowing themselves to kiss and fondle and seduce and arouse and satisfy, in sweating and panting and rubbing their bodies together. Afterward, Nilu felt giddy as she rushed to finish grading her students' homework or tests, then take a quick bath in the courtyard tap, cook rice and dal as she got dressed and applied lipstick, with her eyes on the clock all the time. Some days she only had a minute or two remaining as she raced to the bus stop, with Raja at her heels. Several times the van filled with noisy children pulled away just as they breathlessly turned the corner. Raja then accompanied Nilu to school on the city bus, which was often packed, and they had to stand, clutching the straps hanging from the ceiling, as the vehicle lurched and screeched. On especially crowded days, male passengers pressed against Nilu, their eyes innocently observing the scenery outside. Nilu reprimanded them, and they disengaged with a smirk; some acted offended by what she was suggesting. Raja scowled, threatened to break their jaws if they didn't move. On days when the bus wasn't full, Raja and Nilu got into a silly game of mocking other passengers, perhaps a somber-looking man with an overly self-important nose, or a woman asleep in her seat, with spit dribbling down her chin.

Outside Arniko Academy, Raja would hold her hand, and if she was not vigilant, pull her to him and plant a kiss as her students walked by and chanted, "Good morning, miss." She'd push him away, tell him he'd better be home when she got there in the evening. She'd say this half chidingly, because at the end of the day he was usually there, waiting for her.

The two went for long walks in the neighborhood. They stopped at shops to finger cotton bags crocheted with the image of the white Himalaya. They admired the brass and copper statues of Shuvatara, Manjushree, and Saraswati, while the shopkeepers looked on with disdain because Nepalis inspected and bargained, but rarely bought. If the shopkeepers mistook them for Indians and talked to them in Hindi, Raja and Nilu went along with it, debating the merits of the item in question in exaggerated Indian accents; then, just as the shopkeeper thought they'd finally purchase something, they switched to Nepali, often with a question unrelated to the merchandise, such as

"Brother, do you have any children?" or "Dai, for how long have you been running this shop?" For the rest of the evening, they recalled the astonished face of the shopkeeper as they traversed the crooked alleys and lanes of the city. On the way back home the shopkeepers would look at them sternly, or, if the day's sales had gone quite well, with smiles.

Sometimes in their walks they ventured as far as the Swayambhunath Temple to the west and climbed the hundreds of steps, which left them breathless. Under Buddha's beautiful eyes on the white stupa, they spun the prayer wheels and circled the base, chanting *om mani padme hum* because that's what some of the other devotees were chanting. From the top, surrounded by monkeys, they'd watch the city. Boy-monks in saffron robes would stand a few feet away, their arms crossed at their chests, gazing longingly at Nilu. These young monks, mindful of doctrines on the impermanence of desire, only watched, but the bands of young men on the street corners teased, heckled, and badgered. Nilu would ignore them, muttering "Idiots" under her breath. "They can only bully in groups," she'd tell Raja, who'd become agitated, ready to fight. When the boys made vulgar gestures or remarked on Nilu's breasts, Raja would break away from her and confront them. Once, Raja received a black eye; another time, a split lip. Nilu warned him that if he wanted to act like a Hindi movie hero, he should find himself another heroine. He did gradually learn to turn a deaf ear to these taunts and jeers on their evening strolls, though he'd be seething inside.

On Friday nights Raja coaxed Nilu to the Third Eye or K.C.'s Restaurant, and they joined other regulars, often tourists, to drink beer or chaang or tongba and snack on juicy kotheys and momos. They reveled in the names of these eating places, which felt foreign on even their tongues: Astha Mangalam, Nankha Dhing, Tso Ngon Restaurant. But their favorite was Utse, right near Thamel chowk, where they spent long hours. Nilu, who got drunk easily, would nurse a gin and tonic all evening, while Raja would guzzle beers and make broad gestures as he debated and pontificated. Because he hadn't attended a convent school like Nilu's, Raja's English was sometimes garbled, off-key, but that didn't prevent him from jabbering away, especially to the two Englishmen, Nick and Roger, with whom they'd become friends. Raja had become a bit more talkative in recent years, Nilu had noticed — a sign that he was happier, she concluded, that he no longer suppressed his emotions.

Nilu often worried about how much they'd have to pay at the end of the evening, since Raja was often magnanimous ordering chop sueys and drinks for the whole table; frequently his long arm shot out to hail the waiter for more beer, more momos. At home Nilu complained that Raja acted as if he owned the restaurant, and he laughed and said he was rich in heart, wasn't he? She didn't want to ruin his good mood, so she'd say, "But you don't have to pay for everyone at the table, don't you see? People like Nick and Roger get paid in English pounds. That restaurant bill is nothing to them."

But Raja disapproved of such talk. "They're our friends," he'd say. "And they're guests in our country."

At times the four of them — she and Raja, Nick and Roger — got into spirited discussions, especially when Raja felt that Nick and Roger were criticizing Nepal. When either Englishman commented on the corrupt bureaucrats, Raja would agree, then raise a finger and proclaim that some of the trouble was natural in a poor, third-world country. "You come from a position of luxury," he told the Englishmen. "You sit in your leather chairs in your spick-and-span offices. You weren't born here, you didn't grow up here, you haven't lived our poverty." If they dared to debate this point, he told them that if they thought Nepal and Nepalis were hopeless, they should pack their bags and return to good old England.

Nick and Roger would laugh, ridicule what they called Raja's "snot-filled patriotism," then light up a hashish-filled cigarette, which they appeared to smoke all the time when not at work. Raja would take a hit or two and hand the cigarette back to the Englishmen, who took deep drags and, while exhaling, would proclaim that smoking ganja and hashish was the only cure for the ills of Nepal. "That's what your own ash-smeared, dreadlocked sadhus discovered after years of penance, don't you know, Raja?"

Raja and Nilu would leave the restaurant and, clasping each other, meander back to their flat, along the way greeting people they knew, people loitering outside bars and discotheques, Nepalis and foreigners alike. In each other's arms, Nilu and Raja would hum under their breath, smile at people, marvel at the sky brimming with stars in the cold night air, and make their way through the main chowk, then into an alley where someone would shout their names, and they'd briefly stop to chat before heading home. Lying in their bed, they'd talk, Raja still fuming about something Nick or Roger had said, until Nilu would lean over and place her lips on his to hush him.

Many in the neighborhood had the impression that Raja and Nilu were not married, and rumors circulated that Nilu, a spoiled girl from a rich family, had seduced Raja. Those who'd heard of Muwa and her young lover, Sumit, claimed it was hardly surprising that Nilu had turned out this way. Like mother, like daughter, they said. A morally loose, lascivious woman — Nilu could hear them thinking as their eyes, critical, jeering, settled on her. Even the grocers and the tailors and the butchers of Thamel with whom the couple had become friendly seemed to mock her when they encountered her alone. When she went to these shops by herself, the men's eyes settled on her breasts; their fingers lingered on her palm when they gave back her change.

One day a pharmacist, after placing a couple of samples of analgesic tablets on the counter for Nilu's perusal, had leaned forward, his elbows on the glass, palms cupping his chin, and asked her whether she had watched any movies in video parlors lately. He was a middle-aged man, thin, with graying hair; he had a horde of noisy children and an exasperated-looking wife who lived above the shop. Nilu absent-mindedly shook her head as she debated which brand to pick for Raja, who'd suddenly taken to bed with a fever. The pharmacist continued: a number of fun videos were floating around. "Maj-jako videoharu," he said. Pleasurable. Something about his voice, how he emphasized the word, made her look at him sharply. His eyes were turning glassy, and excitement had made his nostrils flare ever so slightly.

"What, maj-ja . . . ?" she'd said, tightening her face. "Don't you know how to speak?"

"Just asking," the pharmacist said. "I thought you might like . . ."

Nilu spun out of the shop and went all the way to Pakanajol to another pharmacy, fighting a wave of nausea. He was inviting her to accompany him to watch a porn movie. Although over the years most video parlors had closed after government crackdowns, a few still operated on the sly. Nilu had chanced upon one of these while visiting a colleague's house in Ganabahal the other day. The colleague had complained that her landlord had begun to show blue movies, and that she was afraid her son, only twelve, had also begun to slip next door to the parlor.

Maj-jako. The pharmacist's word dug deep into her, and she thought of telling Raja, but it'd only aggravate him, and when she was off at school, he might decide to pay the pharmacist a visit. So she didn't. The man's lecherous eyes haunted her for days, making her feel defiled. She'd seen it happen over and over, to herself, to friends in college who dared to dress in a tight shirt or let their hair loose around their shoulders. Forget about the young men their own age, those who whistled, burst into songs, and suggested an outing, the eve teasers, as they were called — these were predictable, and in a way, easy to shrug off unless the transgression was blatant, such as when they sidled up to press against a young woman in a public bus. The more disturbing ones were the middle-aged men, those with overworked wives and well-loved children at home. Smoking and chewing betel nuts, these men loitered outside tea shops and made lurid comments to young women and barely pubescent girls. When she walked the neighborhood without Raja, Nilu felt these men's stares, and she knew that they'd interpret eye contact from her as a come-on.

Let them imagine whatever they want, Nilu thought, and every day her defiance grew — against these men and the whole idea of domesticity that gave them the upper hand while their long-suffering wives wrung huge piles of wet clothes in the yard and chased their children to make them swallow another mouthful of rice. Whenever Nilu saw such women, in her mind she'd address them: I'm not one of you, and if my Raja turns out to be like your husband, I'll leave him.

But Raja wasn't like that, had never been like those men. He didn't know how to cook, but when Nilu became overwhelmed with grading and preparing for the annual exams, he went to the market to buy vegetables and meat and spent the morning in their corner kitchen in their one-room flat, asking her for instructions as he rinsed the rice and salted the spinach. They laughed at the lumpy rice, joked that Raja could be the head chef in the city's fancy-dancy hotels, Soaltee Oberoi or Hotel de l'Annapurna. "Goat à la burnt," Raja announced as he presented to Nilu a plate of mutton charred to the bones. She waved her curry-dipped index finger in the air. "Ladies and gentlemen, let me announce the debut of our new dish, Cauliflower in a Hurtful Sauce."

Some days Raja suggested ordering something from a nearby restaurant. "I'm just not in the mood to cook, mitini," he'd say, but if she began to pump the stove, he would stop her. "Relax. I don't want you to slog either. I can go to a restaurant and get something."

If she answered that they'd better begin to think of saving money, he'd give her an impish smile. "You can't live life worrying about tomorrow. You have to trust God in these matters." He impersonated the deep-throated growl of the actor Dharmendra and said in Hindi, his upper lip curled in a snarl, "When God provides, Nilu, he tears open the roof to provide."

Her hand on her chin, Nilu observed the ceiling and said that a couple of cracks had appeared there, but no provisions had tumbled down yet. Perhaps Raja's God was a God of slow motion?

But she worried. A year and a half had already gone by since they'd moved to Thamel, and although both had passed their bachelor's in commerce exam a few months ago, Raja hadn't shown any motivation for looking for a job. "Something will happen," he said whenever Nilu raised the topic.

"How about you make it happen?" she said once, but she didn't pursue it further, thinking that she too didn't want him to work as a clerk in a dark and depressing government office or as an assistant to a Marwari businessman in New Road—the kind of jobs their classmates seemed to be landing. He's meant for something better, she convinced herself.

Usually in the morning Nilu graded student papers, and Raja watched her. One morning, Led Zeppelin's "Stairway to Heaven" cranked into the air from a new tourist shop across the street.

"So loud," Nilu said.

Raja sat down beside her. She kept on marking the student notebooks. He put his palm on her back. "You used to like Led Zeppelin before," he said. "This was our song when they played it in Village Café, remember?"

"Those Led Zeppelin days are over, friend," she told him, jabbing his nose with the eraser end of her pencil. "You need to get a job so we can start thinking about a child."

"Hmmm. You're already thinking about a child?"

"I'm not. Others are. Ganga Da is. The other day he was hinting that the one thing that would make him forget our transgressions was if we gave him a grandchild." She decided to tease Raja. "Also, people don't think we're actually married at all. Having a child will make us more legitimate, won't it, Raja?" She looked at him coyly. "Won't you respect me more, then? Won't I be a good housewife, then?"

"You're my sexy housewife," he said, feeling for her breasts, nuzzling his head against her shoulders. "I want to fuck my sexy housewife." Soon they were rolling on the floor, giggling and moaning, and fumbling with each other's clothes. "I'm going to be late," Nilu whispered, and he whispered back that her students would love her for this. "For what?" she asked as he positioned himself.

And, as he entered her, he cried, "For this!"

Afterward, it was another mad dash to the bus stop, with Nilu's hair and sari-end flying; Raja laughed and struggled with a broken slipper as he followed right behind her. They spotted the bus, jam-packed with raucous children, in the Thamel-Samakhusi intersection, and they cried, "Wait! Wait!" But the bus driver didn't hear them and revved the engine, leaving them coughing and sputtering in a cloud of dark smoke.

Sometimes Nilu was too pressed for time to give in to Raja's advances, and she pushed him away. "One of these days your Jamuna Mummy is going to come here and haul me out by my hair and spit at me for seducing her son."

"And your Muwa is going to send her goons here to break my arms and legs and poke my eyes out."

It was their standard repartee.

"I feel like another cup of tea," Raja said, stretching.

"Then make some."

"Why don't we just order from downstairs?"

She looked at him in exasperation. "Why order when we can make some right here? How will we ever save money this way? We have water, we have milk and sugar, and we have tea. What's stopping you?"

"I'm feeling too lazy."

"I'd make you some but I have to finish this. Otherwise Principal Gurung will get mad."

He sat there on his haunches, clasping his knees with his arms. "Why don't I finish those for you?" he asked.

"No, no," she said. "The last time you did it, you gave everyone nearly perfect marks. How will those kids ever learn if you don't point out their mistakes?"

"They'll become bums like me?"

She tapped his nose with her pencil. "You're still my favorite bum, though, my favorite student."

"And you're my favorite teacher," he said, wrapping his arms around her and closing his eyes. He adopted a schoolchild's voice. "Miss, miss, my pee-pee is getting bigger. What should I do?"

She shooed him away. "Let go of me. I have too much to do. I have to finish marking these, then cook the rice."

But he had pressed her to the floor, and his hardness pushed against her. He kissed her rapidly on the face. "Mmmmm," he said. "My favorite sexy miss."

Now aroused, she whispered into his ear, "Your pee-pee has indeed gotten big. Should we do something about it?"

"Please, miss, you need to take care of my pee-pee, miss." He was grinding against her and massaging her breasts. She kissed him, enjoying the smoothness of his lips, now that his mustache was gone. She hadn't complained about his mustache, but he'd sensed that she wasn't too fond of it and shaved it off the day before. He was considerate of her in this way, thinking of small things to make her happy. A few weeks before, when it had rained all day, he'd come to the bus stop with her small lady's umbrella, which barely covered him. Even huddled tight, they got soaked as they walked home.

A Job for Raja

R AJA FINALLY FOUND a job at an advertising agency through a friend, close to a year after he finished his bachelor's in commerce, but he didn't survive more than three weeks. "I just can't sit still at a desk," he said. "My boss doesn't let me design an ad or do anything creative. I get bored answering phones and filing papers." Nilu wanted to tell him that he needed to give the job some time, perhaps a year or so, before he'd be assigned more responsibilities, that this was his first job. But when she pictured him fidgeting in his chair, drumming the desk with a pencil, responding to rude, dismissive clients, she felt that he had a point. Still, she was about to ask him to stick with the job for another week or two when he said, "That's it. I'll submit my rajinama at the end of the week." The way he said *rajinama,* she had a feeling that this decision was empowering to him; it was a way to tell the world that he was unwilling to live by its rules. But she did nothing more than embrace him and say, "Something better will come along. I'd also have gone crazy if I had a job like that."

Raja checked the job listings in *Gorkhapatra* and *The Rising Nepal,* speculating on the pros and cons of the advertised positions. But either he failed to submit his application or neglected to follow up. Nonetheless, one day he received a letter inviting him to an interview at a well-known Japanese car dealership. Raja borrowed a

170

suit and a tie from Nick, the only man they knew who matched his height. Looking like a young executive, Raja hailed a taxi to go to Maharajgunj. Nilu waved goodbye from the window. She thought Raja looked handsome in the British tweed jacket and pants. The prospect of this job, assistant manager of sales, with a monthly salary of nearly eight hundred rupees, had excited both of them; when Nilu adjusted his tie, he said, "It's a good company, Nilu. It has long-term prospects."

That day at Arniko Academy she remained anxious about Raja's performance during the interview and whether he managed to convey his eagerness for the job. At the ad agency, he'd apparently not only felt bored but also appeared to lack interest in the place throughout the weeks he'd worked there. Nilu had discovered this information when, at the market, she'd run into the ad agency's manager. "Most of the time I found him doodling at his desk," the manager said. "He didn't even pick up the phone half the time. Still, we thought he'd gradually come around, but then he himself decided to quit." When Nilu heard this, hopelessness engulfed her, and she had to fight it off. All Raja had to do was to try, she thought. True, she couldn't expect him to stay at a low-level job for long, as several of their peers were unhappily doing because the competition for better positions was so high. But Raja had thrown away a good opportunity with the advertising company. What went through his head when he sat there at his desk and doodled? She could only suspect that his thoughts took him back to his mother — the woman who had betrayed him yet somehow wouldn't leave him alone. This made Nilu's disappointment evaporate a bit and increased her fondness for Raja. Poor Raja. He suffered, and she was the only one who alleviated some of his sadness.

Yet the car dealership was a growing company with diverse areas of business; its factories produced noodles, powdered milk, and shoes at different locations in Nepal. If Raja performed well, there'd be opportunities for advancement. Perhaps he'd rise to the rank of senior manager, with a separate office, his own staff. He'd be chauffeured to his office in the company car while he read some important document on the way. He'd call her from his desk and say that he was going to be late that evening, so perhaps they could just meet in a restaurant for dinner? She'd say that since he now sold Japanese cars, perhaps they should eat at the Japanese restaurant Kushi Fuji in Durbar Marg, with its large glass windows affording a pleasant view of the people and the traffic on the street below?

These fleeting fantasies made Nilu shake her head: she was turning into a regular Kathmandu wife, imagining promotions for her husband and the creature comforts of middle-class existence. The very things that she'd rebelled against, she thought, when she decided to write that Jonathan Swift parody no matter what the consequences, when she'd left Nilu Nikunj and checked in to the Kathmandu Guest House, when she'd dragged Raja to the Gueswori Temple and married him.

When Nilu reached the flat in the evening, Raja was at the window. She stood in the doorway, watching him. He turned to her and told her he didn't think he'd get the job. No matter, she said as she walked in. She began changing into the lighter dhoti she wore around the house. She talked about her day at Arniko Academy as she dressed, as she put the kettle on for tea. Raja continued looking out the window. The kettle whistled. Nilu poured the tea into two steel glasses and carried them to him. Raja accepted the tea gratefully. She sat next to him and they both looked out. Across the street stood a vegetable shop, where shawled women were haggling with the shopkeeper. A boy on a bicycle darted by, both hands dangling by his side instead of clasping the handle.

Close to twenty people had shown up for the interview, Raja said. One man had an M.B.A. degree from America; another boasted five years' experience at the Tata car factory in the Indian city of Lucknow. "I thought they'd invited me and maybe a couple of others," he said, hiding his dejection behind long slurps of tea.

"Obviously they saw something in you to ask you for an interview," she said. "You have to remain positive."

To lift his mood that evening, Nilu took Raja out for dinner with Nick and Roger, who, when told about the interview, offered their sympathies and said that these big businesses in third-world countries were corrupt to the core anyway. The interviews were fake, Nick and Roger declared, and a senior manager's relative most likely already had the job. "This is Nepal, for God's sake!" Roger guzzled his beer, then, wiping his lips with the back of his hand, and looked pointedly at Raja.

Raja pretended to be offended and, impersonating his own typical tirades, launched into a mock speech that defended the virtues of his country against "you khaireys, you imperialists, you colonialists with your funny rotten potato smell and your drinking-beer-instead-of-water habits, your awful-looking freckles." Then Nick produced his "Doobie Brother," a delicious Afghan, he said, and they passed around the ganja-filled cigarette. Since they'd moved to Thamel, Nilu hadn't smoked ganja, but today she took several drags, to keep Raja company. The world soon became soft and spacious, and the friends ordered plates of chicken chili and ate ravenously.

Nilu watched Raja, whose face, when there was a lull in the conversation, looked sad, and she reached to stroke his cheeks. He turned to her and told her she was his loving wife, that he loved her and he wouldn't know what to do without her. "You won't leave me, will you, ever, for being such a loser?" Raja cried then, sobbed on Nilu's shoulder, and Nick and Roger laughed, thinking that he was faking it, but it turned out he wasn't; all three of them, Nick and Roger and Nilu, especially Nilu, were amazed at this display of emotion. They looked at one another to confirm that he was indeed crying, and even as they watched him, in soft-hearted fascination, they expected he would lift his head and grin. But he kept weeping on Nilu's shoulder.

Ganga Da visited now and then, still resentful, after two years, of how the couple had ignored their families' feelings and gotten married on the sly. "Why couldn't you have waited a bit? Maybe allowed

Muwa to come around?" he asked. "Wouldn't everyone have been happy then? Now look at what has happened, Nilu. Your mother seems to have completely severed her ties."

Somehow Ganga Da had decided that the new couple needed Muwa's blessing—surprising thoughts from a man whose own mother, once Jamuna Mummy's madness was exposed, suggested that he abandon his new wife. By now Ganga Da knew well enough about Muwa's drug habit, her muddled brain, her lover; still he insisted that Raja and Nilu ought to have waited. He had envisioned a grand wedding for them, he lamented, with a sumptuous feast, a brightly dressed band playing music all night. He would have invited everyone he knew, even long-forgotten friends and colleagues. "Besides," he said to Raja, "that's what your Jamuna Mummy wanted. That's what she tells me in her saner moments. Do you know how many times I've had to take her to the hospital since you left the house? Four times already. Her brain is half fried from electroconvulsive therapy. Your wedding would have given her a morsel of happiness. Now she's cursing Kaki again, saying that Kaki stole her boy. She thinks Kaki has imprisoned you in the Nakkhu Jail. These days she sits on the kitchen floor, spreads all the spoons and the forks and the ladles around her, then chants gibberish so you'll be released from your shackles there."

Nilu and Raja had also come to know by now that Ganga Da was building a house elsewhere in the city, although he'd not been forthcoming about it. The money, Raja surmised, came from what Ganga Da had inherited from his mother.

Raja sat by the window, wearing a wistful smile and watching the activities on the street. "Old man," Nilu declared him, like the boodhas in the city who, their thick dirty shawls wrapped around them, haunted their own windows all day long, observing meticulously the happenings on the street below. "And you're only twenty-two," she said as she fastened the folds of her sari with a safety pin.

He said that the details of the world outside might reveal to him how the world really worked. "Look at that woman," he said, urging Nilu to come to the window, even though her bus would be arriving within minutes at the corner (he no longer accompanied her to the stop). When she bent to watch, all she saw was a middle-aged woman standing in the street, her finger on her chin, lost in thought or perhaps figuring out what to do next.

"What's there to see?" Nilu said. "She's just on the verge of a decision."

Raja nodded. "Don't you find that incredible? That woman is out there, in the middle of a busy street, exposing her thoughts to the public. You can almost hear them, can't you?" Raja also put his finger on his chin, and imagined the woman's thoughts: "I should have bought those radishes at one rupee a kilo. Should I go back? But that'd be admitting defeat with the vendor. Then again, my husband likes radishes so much. If I cook those radishes, he'll be in a good mood all day, and maybe he'll take me to see that film I've been wanting to see for so long, the one with Rajesh Khanna as the jolly chef. On the other hand, why should I always have to be the one to put him in a good mood? Why can't he put me in a good mood for a change? Just the other day, when I was complaining to him about his mother, how she always manages to make me feel small, he brushed aside my concerns as though they were petty grievances. But I shouldn't think like this about my husband. He's my husband. I should feed him well." Incredibly, the woman was still standing in the same position, seemingly frozen in time, as if corroborating Raja's version of how her mind worked.

"You're going to end up like Jamuna Mummy, in an asylum soon," Nilu told Raja. "Why don't you try going for morning walks? It'll clear your mind. You'll meet people and talk to them instead of letting your mind rot like this."

He stretched, then said that he'd become too lazy for walks but that he'd do it if she kept him company. She usually had her students' homework to look at in the morning. But for Raja's sake she started getting up earlier, around five o'clock while it was still dark outside, and lit a candle, instead of turning on the switch, in a corner of the room where she reviewed her students' work. Raja got up at around six, and they both went down to the courtyard to use the bathroom and to brush their teeth and gargle and wash their faces at the tap, before heading out.

During these walks they saw the city waking up. Street dogs stretched and yawned amid garbage piles. A few elderly men in jogging suits were walking unnaturally fast, their arms swinging wildly. They said, "Good morning," to Nilu and Raja, and after a few days when Nilu and Raja saw them approach, with their funny strides, they exchanged glances with each other and mouthed "Good morning" before presenting their public faces to the men and shouting their greetings. All winter long they walked. Some days the streets were shrouded in a heavy fog; once, in Chhetrapati, it thickened so densely that they couldn't see each other. When Raja stopped to pee against a wall and Nilu waited a few yards away, out of nowhere a swirl of thundercloud-like fog encased them, completely obscuring their vision.

"Are you there?" Nilu asked.

As he zipped up his trousers, Raja said, "I'm here." Then, to tease her, he did not respond again.

"Raja!" she cried out.

"I'm here," he said, then circled her, judging his distance from her voice.

"Where?" she said, swinging her arms. Her heart hammered in her chest, and she remained petrified until he wrapped his arms around her from behind.

Gradually, Raja began to show less interest in these hikes. At first, he insisted on returning after only fifteen or twenty minutes. Soon, he was reluctant to leave his bed. "I'm just not in the mood, mitini," he said. "You go. It'll be good for you." When she told him that she'd gone only because of him, he smiled lazily. All day he stayed in the house, sometimes writing poems, sometimes reading. Every other week he visited the city's libraries, all on one day — the morning at the Indian Library in New Road, then the one in Tahachal run by expatriate American women, and finally the British Council Library in Kantipath. The books he brought home ranged widely:

thrillers by Robert Ludlum and John le Carré, biographies of Jawaharlal Nehru and Golda Meir, history books about South America. He'd gotten into the habit of reading three or four books simultaneously, so that when Nilu reached home he'd be describing the plot of an espionage story in one breath and in another, what Nehru said to Chou En-lai when the Chinese premier visited New Delhi.

Raja's obsession with Jung Bahadur Rana — the architect of Nepal's Rana dynasty, the fearsome prime minister who grabbed power in the mid-1800s — came out of nowhere. "You know how Jungey inserted himself into the political machine of his time?" Raja asked. But he did not wait for Nilu's answer. "By jumping into a river — that's how crazy our country is. Picture this: The year is 1842. Loony Crown Prince S is traipsing over the Trishuli Bridge. An officer on a horse coming the other way doesn't recognize him, doesn't dismount and do his two hundred genuflections, so Prince S orders that he be thrown off the bridge. The officer, in tears, says that the only person who could live after such a leap would be Jungey, who was already becoming known for his crazy feats. So, Jungey appears, and lo and behold, he jumps off the bridge on his horse. And survives. This solidifies his reputation as a daredevil, which makes people afraid of him, which allows him to engineer the Kot massacre a few years later. The rest, as they say, is history."

For weeks on end, Raja kept saying Jungey this and Jungey that. "Doesn't Jungey look like Danny Denzongpa?" he asked as he admired an image of Jung Bahadur in a coffee-table book. This portrait (it was hard to tell whether it was a photo or a painting) showed the man in full regalia: the elaborate silver-jeweled costume, with a long gown that spilled to the floor. His right hand, clasping the top of a chair, displayed huge glittering rings. But his thin, ruthless-looking face and piercing eyes formed the most remarkable features of the portrait.

"Poor Danny Denzongpa," Nilu said. "Why are you comparing our famous Nepali actor to Jungey?"

"Well, a handsome face is a handsome face," Raja said.

Then, somewhere, Raja happened to glimpse a photograph of

Jung Bahadur wearing a sombrero, and a few days later, when Nilu returned home in the evening, there was Raja, wearing a hat with a brim so wide that it touched the sides of the window where he stood. "Where did you get it?" she asked.

"At the cap shop in Indrachowk. How does it look?"

"It looks . . . silly," she said. "But it suits you. What's the occasion?" She wanted to ask how much it cost, but she didn't.

"No occasion." He told her that Jungey wore a sombrero when a foreign delegation visited Nepal. Holding his hat's brim, he did a short jiggle, singing, "Sombrero, sombrero."

She cautioned him against disturbing Bhairavi's mother-in-law, whose room was directly below. "What? Your life's aspiration is to turn into a bloody dictator now?"

Raja unsheathed an imaginary sword and slashed the air in front of him.

Nilu drew the curtains and began to change her clothes, but as soon as she'd discarded her work sari, he grabbed her and pressed himself against her. "Jungey needs some love."

"Raja," she said wearily. "Not now, please."

"But Jungey is tired from plotting conspiracies and thwarting conspiracies, from accusing his brother of being weak, and from eliminating his enemies one by one."

"Jungey is hard," Nilu said, feeling his penis strain against her crotch, becoming aroused even though she was mildly irritated.

"Jungey loves wifey."

"Is quick relief all that Jungey wants? Or does Jungey actually want a long, elaborate dance?"

"With the youngest, most lissome of his wives, wifey number seven, Jungey can imagine a quickie."

And they tumbled into bed, careful not to rock it too much, lest ceiling dust powder Bhairavi's mother downstairs. Raja kept his sombrero on as he peeled away his clothes, and Nilu kept referring to him as Jungey, which appeared to excite him.

Afterward, she dozed in his arms as he spoke softly, close to her ear, "When Jungey went on his England tour, he charmed the British, especially the women. Are you listening, Nilu?" he said.

"Hmmm?"

"Jungey paid a hundred and fifty thousand pounds to sleep with London's well-known prostitute Laura Bell."

"And how do you know this, my friend?" Nilu asked drowsily. "Are you Jungey's soul, reincarnated in this life as Raja?"

Gently, he disengaged himself and went to the window, slid aside the curtain. Children's cries from their evening games penetrated the air. "When I visited Paris," he said, adopting a low, gruff voice, "I was so impressed with a ballerina's performance that I presented to her on the spot the diamond bracelet I had on." Nilu couldn't see his face under the huge hat; he could have been a stranger. It sent a chill down her spine. "In Paris," Raja continued in the same gravelly voice, "I gifted thousands of francs to a ballet troupe." He paused. "Back home I turned the king into an imbecile, kept him locked in the palace."

"Raja, stop."

He did, but he hesitated to look at her; when he did, his face was serious. Darkness had begun to fall, and the room was getting dim, hiding the contours of his face. When he came toward her, she became afraid. But he took off his hat and said, "It's only me, Nilu."

She grabbed him by the back of his head and pulled him toward her chest, where he buried his nose between her breasts and stayed there, breathing.

Raja donned his sombrero for a few days, until rumors circulated around Thamel that he was becoming touched in the head, like his mother. "Handighopté!" some people called him, likening him to a homeless madman who roamed the streets of Kathmandu in the late 1960s. The man was famous for his hat, which was completely black with dirt; often he'd walk into the middle of traffic, gesticulating. Soon after Raja found out who Handighopté was, he lost interest in Jungey, and the sombrero was slipped under the bed, to gather dust.

To stay close to Raja, after dinner Nilu would read the same books he did. When her eyes began to shut during these evening sessions, Raja prodded her with the eraser of his pencil. "Sleeping Beauty, utha! Awake, and behold the wonders of this world." She smiled sheepishly and opened her eyes wide to look at the book Raja was holding: an English translation of a Hindi novel. The book was mildly interesting ("The plot is simply fabulous," Raja declared), but after a paragraph or two, the letters began to blur. Her body was humming with fatigue. Lately she'd had to substitute for a teacher who had fallen ill with tuberculosis, and all day long she ran from one class to another, with only brief breaks for tea, then hurried home to cook dinner.

Because he was so engrossed in his reading, Raja often forgot to prepare dinner. "Oh!" he'd say when Nilu asked him why the vegetables hadn't been cut and rinsed. She'd suppress her disappointment, for he'd look so beautiful, a lock of hair falling on his forehead, as he sat by the window in the dusk. So she'd change into her house dhoti, pump the stove and put water to boil for tea, then sit on her haunches on the floor and slice the vegetables. When she needed some ginger or garlic, Raja didn't mind fetching it from the store, but he'd take the book with him and read it as he descended the stairs and all the way to the shop. Sometimes he brought home a packet of salt instead of turmeric, and scratched his head when she pointed out his mistake.

"With the amount of reading you do," she told him, "you'd make a better teacher than I do."

"Is that why you have a teaching job and I don't?" he answered back.

One evening when she came home, the door was locked from the outside. With her key she opened it and went in. None of Raja's books were lying around. Was he at one of the libraries this late? She contemplated starting dinner, but without him in the house, she didn't feel motivated. She sat by the window, waiting for Raja, wondering whether they'd go out to eat at the new thukpa place in the main square of Thamel, or, once he arrived, whether she'd muster the energy to prepare dinner. She fell asleep for a few minutes and woke with a jolt. An ambulance raced past on the street below. She glanced at her watch: six o'clock. She decided to head out to look for Raja.

She first tried the Kanchanjanga Café, where Nick and Roger now spent their evenings. It had been weeks since she and Raja had seen them, so he could have sought out their company today. But they were not at Kanchanjanga. Reluctant to return to the empty flat, Nilu began to check the restaurants and bars in Thamel, even though some of them, she knew, were not places Raja visited. She drifted in and out of them, greeting some of the managers and waiters, ignoring the pointed stares of men who sat on bar stools. Music sounded all around her: Bob Dylan, the Eagles. When one shopkeeper tried to entice her, in Hindi, to buy his masks, she remembered those times when she and Raja spoke in exaggerated Hindi to fool the shopkeepers into thinking they were Indian.

She found him at the edge of Thamel, a block away from Chhetrapati, in a dingy Japanese restaurant, with dirty tatami mats and broken bamboo curtains. He was sitting in a corner. Judging from his half-closed eyes and the pungent smell in the air, she knew he'd been smoking hash. A bottle of beer, half empty, sat in front of him. If he was surprised to see her, he didn't show it. "Come, come, my wife, the love of my life," he said loudly as he spotted her. The other guests, a European couple, glanced at them.

"How did you find this place?" Nilu asked.

He put his arm around her. "I just wanted to get away from the hullabaloo there." He pointed in the direction of Thamel.

"And here I was, thinking that all you did was read at home."

He poured a glass of beer for her, and although she didn't feel like drinking, she took a sip for his sake.

"All that reading is rotting my brain," he said. Then he added, in a low voice, his cheeks sagging, that he had been reading a Leon

Uris novel when suddenly everything got dark and he felt that he would suffocate. He felt that he was going mad. "Can you believe it? All those years my crazy mother raised me I never felt like this, and then, when I move away from her, I too start to begin to feel as if I'm going crazy."

Nilu wanted to console him but couldn't think of what to say, so she merely squeezed his hand. He leaned over and kissed her on the lips, ignoring the scowl on the face of the Nepali restaurant owner, who stood at the counter. Nilu returned his kiss with fervor. Then she said, "But smoking hash will make it even worse, will make you even more anxious."

"Today I needed something to calm this tumult inside," he said.

She pressed his head against her shoulder, making soothing sounds. With her palm on his temple, she could feel a muscle twitch.

"You're disappointed in me, aren't you, Nilu?" he asked. "I've let you down."

"Stop saying such things," she said. "Disappointed by what?"

His face was close to her breasts, and for a moment she felt as if he were her child; his voice vibrated through her. "I can't seem to do anything. I don't have a job, can't seem to find one or hold on to one. What is wrong with me?"

"There's nothing wrong with you, sweetie. Why do you think that way?"

"It's not only me, Nilu; you also think so. I see it in your eyes."

"You are imagining things."

The stereo in the restaurant was playing the Cat Stevens song about a hardheaded woman. "I sense her presence when I'm alone," he said. "Right here inside me." He pointed to his chest, not at his heart but at his sternum. "As if she's been living inside me all this time. I feel her in my body."

It didn't surprise Nilu, his awareness of his mother. Children can sense the presence of their mother, no matter how far apart they are, how distant in time, she thought. It made her queasy, this notion, as if it had a direct bearing on her life. A picture traveled through her mind: a young child, a boy, roaming the streets, pursuing her, following her every move, pausing when she paused, looking away when she observed him, disappearing when she approached him. He was a serious-looking boy, and his face was one she knew well, but when she reached out to touch him, he disappeared, only to reemerge at another point, another juncture, as if he was playing hide-and-seek.

Muwa Visits Maitreya

IMPENDING FATHERHOOD galvanized Raja. As the delivery date drew near, he sprung into action, leaving the house at sunrise to search for jobs. A look of controlled desperation had entered his eyes. The idea of Raja's swallowing his pride and knocking on doors for jobs, for the sake of their baby, endeared him to Nilu.

Ganga Da wanted to take Raja to some people he knew who'd be able to help with a job, but Raja didn't want to be obligated to anyone, especially Ganga Da. Whenever Ganga Da asked his son to accompany him to the home of a bureaucrat who could pull some strings, Raja made excuses. Ganga Da, still mildly resentful because the couple continued to live in Thamel although rooms were available in the Lainchour house, was further hurt when Raja hemmed and hawed instead of accepting his father's offer to help him.

"What is the matter with you?" Ganga Da said one morning. "Why are you so intent on being a murkha?" Nilu knew he didn't mean to yell, but he did, and Nilu, sensing an argument looming, shut the window.

"Don't call me a murkha," Raja said. "I am not a child anymore."

"You are merely twenty-three," Ganga Da said.

"So what?" Raja said. "I no longer live under your tutelage."

Ganga Da's eyes moistened, and Nilu thought, Here we go again. "Yes, yes," Ganga Da said. "I keep forgetting, dimwit that I am. You've become a big man now. Thulo manchhe. You don't need a guardian, you don't need a father."

Raja picked up a book and began to read. Ganga Da looked helplessly at Nilu, who, ignoring her own irritation toward him, said, "Ganga Da, maybe some other day. Maybe Raja is not in the mood today."

"All right," Ganga Da said. "You two have your own life now. What can I do?"

He slunk down the stairs like a bedraggled cat.

Nilu went to the bed and pushed Raja's book away. "Just be a little nice to him, okay? Even if you don't do as he says."

"What is the matter with him these days? One word, and his eyes begin to tear."

"He's suffering too, Raja."

"He was never like this while I was growing up."

"Age is also catching up with him, isn't it? So just be a bit kind."

"And who'll be kind to me, Nilu mitini?" Raja said, his hand reaching for her breast.

During her pregnancy, their lovemaking seemed to become even more pleasurable. All Raja had to do was touch her, on the neck, on her thighs, and she'd become engulfed with desire. She'd grab Raja and whisper in his ears as she unbuckled his pants. Her extended belly seemed to adjust itself easily to the curves of his body.

But today, perhaps because of the tiff with Ganga Da, Nilu wasn't aroused, so when Raja clasped her hand and placed it on his hardening penis over his trousers and said, "Who will take care of my sensitive needs?" she lightly slapped his penis and left the bed to open the window.

"Have you no shame?" she said, with a stern face. "This early you're making improper advances on a woman who is nine months pregnant?"

His penis strained in his trousers. "All right, then," he said, standing. "If you want me to roam the streets with my giant lando for the whole world to see, that's what I'll do." And with that he abruptly left the room and went down the stairs, which shocked Nilu. She shouted his name, then rushed to the window, and there he was, swaggering as he walked away. Luckily, Bhairavi's whole family had gone on an outing, so they were spared this mortifying display. But Nilu couldn't help but smile at the thought of Raja facing prospective employers with a bulge in his pants.

That evening he returned home jubilant: he'd secured a job at a well-known bookstore. He told Nilu that he'd walked into Fishtail Books in Thamel chowk late that afternoon, looking for a second-hand book by the spiritualist Krishnamurti, and began to chat with the owner, a certain Shakya-ji, who, over the course of the conversation, became quite impressed with Raja's knowledge of books. Nilu had no reason to doubt this, but she was a bit skeptical when Raja told her that the man had offered Raja a job on the spot, without his asking for it. Most likely Raja had in fact approached Shakya-ji for a position in the bookstore, just as he'd pitched himself to numerous businesses across the city for the past few weeks. His salary, Raja admitted, wasn't much — a mere five hundred rupees a month, three hundred rupees less than what Nilu made at school. But they didn't dwell on the difference between their salaries. A job is a job, they both thought silently, and this one was in a bookstore, a "repository of knowledge," Raja declared. She was about to concur when he added, laughing, "For tourists."

"Are you suggesting, my dear hubby, that somehow the knowledge purveyed to tourists is less worthy than the higher forms of knowledge that we natives have access to? Didn't you yourself go there to find Krishnamurti?"

"That I did," Raja said. "But Krishnamurti is different. The tourist knowledge I'm referring to is . . . well, fabricated knowledge."

"You better toss away that thinking if you want to survive in that place," Nilu said, her palm stroking her belly. The baby's kicks and punches had increased over the past week.

"All right," Raja said. "I'll stop making such distinctions. All knowledge is knowledge. Or rather, all knowledge is fabricated. But, my dear mitini, if all knowledge is fabricated, then what is the truth? How will we ever know the truth?" He held his temples in mock exasperation.

Nilu conked him on the head and said, "All right, Mr. Krishna-murti-in-the-making. You want to know the truth?" She took his hand and placed it on her tummy. "Here is the truth. Feel it. The truth will come out any day now, then wail and demand that we wipe the goo on its butt."

Nilu was sitting on the bed. Raja knelt in front of her and rubbed her belly. "How I love this truth," he said and closed his eyes.

Within a few days he'd read all the tourist guides to Nepal and could talk to his customers with authority about places he'd never visited. "This fascinating hike takes you north of Pokhara to the Gurung settlements of Ghachok," he recited as he massaged Nilu's lower back, which ached more as the big day neared. She lay on her side on the bed, while he knelt on the floor to reach her back easily. She placed one hand protectively on her stomach in case Raja kneaded her back a bit too strongly and toppled her. "Please remember that some Nepali men think Western women want nothing other than to fornicate," Raja continued, in an exaggerated version of the tourist guidebooks' cautionary advice to women travelers. "So, in order not to incite them, wear a sari when you go trekking."

They'd begun to refer to the baby as their "Third Person." When Raja told her how he'd cursed an arrogant tourist who'd shouted at him in a thick French accent because Raja hadn't been able to grasp the kind of book the customer wanted, Nilu shushed him. "You can't use such language in front of our Third Person," she said, and Raja had dutifully bit his tongue, grabbed his ears, and performed sit-ups as penance.

"Sorry, Third Person," he repeated each time he sat up.

Late into the night they talked about their baby. "What do you think our Third Person will grow up to be like?" Nilu asked. Because their flat was a bit removed from the tourist hotels, it tended to be fairly quiet at night. Occasionally a motorcycle thundered by, but there were no shouts from drunken revelers or bursts of foreign language in the middle of the night.

"He'll grow up to be like me," Raja declared nonchalantly. Somehow over the past few weeks they had concluded that the baby was a boy. Nilu had told Raja that she'd always felt it was a boy, and Raja concurred, saying that a boy was what he saw when he imagined his child.

"Where will he go to school?" Nilu asked worriedly. When Raja said that the Jagadamba School would be the most convenient, Nilu made a face.

He laughed. "Why turn up your nose? It was good enough for me, and you too. Remember how you kept saying how much happier you were there than at St. Augustine's?"

"That's because you were with me at Jagadamba."

"Now you're changing your story. There were things going on at St. Augustine's that you didn't like."

"True," she said, lightly massaging her belly. "But the education was pretty good. You saw how quickly I got a teaching job at Arniko."

"Well, he'll go to Arniko then."

Nilu made a face again. "No, I want him to attend a better school, then go to America or England to study."

"What if he turns out to be the nonstudying kind, or even a nincompoop? Like me?"

"You're not a nincompoop," she said. "Nincompoops don't love to read. They don't get jobs in bookstores."

He snuggled close to her. "Are nincompoops allowed to be happy? We're happy, aren't we, Nilu?"

"Yes, we are," she said. "I was getting worried about you, but now you've also found a job you like."

With satisfaction about Raja's employment and some nervous anticipation about the approaching birth of their child, those nights Nilu and Raja felt a happiness that was exuberant, expansive, seeping into the nooks and crannies of their small flat and radiating into the streets, into Thamel chowk, which pulsated with travelers and peddlers, with music as varied as Bob Dylan's nasal "Just

Like a Woman" and the Nepali folk song "Resham-firiri," with the sounds of flute and saxophone and electric guitar. That happiness embraced everyone.

A few days later they rushed to the hospital, where soon enough they were startled by the piercing, demanding cry of their newborn son.

Not too long after Maitreya was born, Muwa visited the new parents in Thamel. Nilu was in the process of trying to feed the baby. Leaning against the wall near the door, she held him in her lap. Raja was on the bed, watching anxiously, for Maitreya had problems latching on to his mother's nipples. Nilu was trying to direct her son's mouth to her breast when she saw Muwa at the door. Nilu returned her attention to her son.

It was Raja who darted to the door and ushered in his mother-in-law, the woman who had until now refused to recognize him as her daughter's husband. Muwa had seen the adult Raja only once before, soon after Nilu and Raja got married, at the Kamaladi Ganesh Temple. That morning, Nilu and Raja had been circling the temple during their morning walk when they came face to face with Muwa, who was on her way out of the shrine. "Oh," said Muwa, her gaze falling upon the young man whom she'd last seen as a boy in her house. Raja, naturally, didn't recognize her, but, judging from the discomfort on Nilu's face, he immediately understood who she was. "Everything all right?" Muwa asked, and didn't wait for an answer as she put on her slippers and walked away.

Today Muwa gave Raja a curt nod, then looked for a place to sit. Raja gestured toward the chair by the window, the place where he, until a few weeks ago, sat in the afternoons and watched the world go by. But Muwa ignored him and went to the bed against the wall. There she sat, forcing Raja to take the chair. Nilu hadn't bothered to meet her mother's eyes, and for a while the room became encased in silence, which Raja broke by declaring that he was going to make tea. Nilu nearly choked because Raja's tea typically looked gray and

189

tasted too sugary. Even during late pregnancy and right after Maitreya was born, Nilu herself had gotten up to put the kettle on. Now Muwa would get a taste of her undesirable son-in-law's tea.

Unsmiling, her eyes fixed on the baby in her daughter's lap, Muwa said, "No need for tea. I came to see the bachcha." Not "my grandson," but "the kid." Muwa didn't even bother asking what name they'd chosen for the baby, the name that would be formalized at his initiation ceremony in a few months.

"You didn't have to come," Nilu said.

"That's not for you to decide," Muwa said. She smelled minty; obviously she'd taken care of her breath before she came. But she looked worse than before: more lines on her face, slightly swollen cheeks, eyes retreating deeper into their sockets.

In the silence that ensued, Raja was the one who seemed the most nervous — as if Muwa's impressions of the couple, of their flat, of their baby, with his puckered lips, mattered a great deal to him. Had fatherhood suddenly made Raja promote Muwa to the important role of grandmother, to the category of someone whose opinions mattered, despite the fact that she had ignored him and Nilu for so long? But this reaction was not unusual for Raja. Of the three mothers in his life, the one who shunned him was the one he pined for.

Nilu felt annoyed with him. Don't act silly, she wanted to tell him. Don't kowtow to Muwa.

Muwa kept her eyes focused on her daughter and the baby, then finally said, "I meant to come earlier, but Sumit . . ." She caught herself in time, cleared her throat, and said, "Everything all right? Your health is fine?"

Ah, Sumit. So he was still around. Nilu stated curtly, "There's nothing wrong with my health."

Outside someone belched out "Mehbooba Mehbooba" from the hit film *Sholay*, and nervously Raja began to whistle the tune, then stopped abruptly, embarrassed. Muwa was looking around the room, at the rotten wooden ceiling beams, the fist-sized hole right above the bed, the stove in the corner. Her disdain was obvious, and when her gaze stopped at Nilu, she seemed to be saying, What person in her right mind would want to leave a house like Nilu Nikunj to come live here?

Nilu met her gaze and hit back with her own unspoken retort: This is better than what you ever provided me.

"What name have you thought of for him?" Muwa finally asked.

"Maitreya," Nilu said.

Muwa took a deep breath. "Hmmm. It's not a name I've heard before."

"We like it."

Muwa nodded slowly. "That's what's important."

"Muwa should go there and look at him," Raja said. The distance from the bed to the wall, where Nilu sat, wasn't more than a few feet, but Muwa made no attempt to traverse it. If Muwa had expected Nilu to stand and hand the baby over to her, Nilu thought, she had another idea coming. But Muwa didn't signal such a desire, and the three of them remained quiet. Maitreya had finally latched on to his mother's nipple and was sucking gently, his eyes shut.

"So, how much is the rent here?" Muwa asked.

"It's adequate for us," Nilu said.

"Have you taken some time off from the school right now? What is the name of your school again?"

"Yes, for a few days."

"And you?" She addressed Raja. "You've found a job?"

"I work in a bookstore."

"Bookstore?" Her face indicated clearly what she thought of bookstores.

"Right here in Thamel. I'm the assistant manager."

Nilu wondered if part of Raja's nervousness reflected his desire to prove to his mother-in-law that he was a capable provider. After all, for close to two years Raja had remained idle.

Nilu couldn't tell whether Raja's job title impressed Muwa, but her mother did say, "Well, I imagine jobs are hard to come by these days."

"It's a good job, Muwa," Raja said, then mentioned some of the

191

books popular with tourists and described some of his recent experiences and what Shakya-ji was like. His talkativeness grated on Nilu's nerves, but Muwa, perhaps to compensate for how she'd treated Raja throughout his life, feigned interest. After Raja finished speaking, there was an uncomfortable silence.

Muwa finally broke it. "Well, you know there's plenty of room in Nilu Nikunj. You don't have to . . ." Muwa's eyes surveyed the room. "Also, the servants are still there, so you won't need to be with the baby twenty-four . . ." But making the offer had become too much for her, or she'd become afraid that they'd actually accept it, so she abruptly stood. "I should be going home now. Sumit will wonder what I'm up to."

Muwa's visit didn't affect Nilu so much, for she was convinced that it was only out of some vague maternal duty that Muwa had come. "She didn't even hold our Third Person, her own grandson," she said to Raja.

But Raja was silent, and when he spoke, he said, "At least she took the first step of coming here. She'll just need some time to come around, that's all. The Third Person's birth has done it, I can feel it."

"She came here only because she felt obligated — and even this obligation must be a leftover from her past life. Just this much leftover." She pinched her thumb and forefinger together to indicate how much.

"You're being too harsh."

Nilu was folding some pieces of cloth, cut from her old dresses, to use as Maitreya's diapers. "How come you are a big Muwa supporter all of a sudden?"

"Nilu, you can't always dredge up the past to apportion blame."

"But it's not only the past. Wasn't she laughing when you mentioned your job today? Did you not notice it? Did she even look at her own grandson properly?"

"That's just her personality, and as her daughter you should know this quite well. She's getting old. I think she misses you."

Nilu looked at him in wonder. "Are you then tempted by her invitation to live in Nilu Nikunj?"

"No, no," he said, a bit too quickly, averting her eyes. "It was just a passing thought. I wasn't thinking about us. Rather, about him." He gestured toward the bed, where the baby, bundled up in an old shawl, was napping. He added, "There are moments I feel discouraged when I look around this flat. Look at us! What kind of life am I making you live? It has taken me months to find a job, and even I am not confident that I can hold it. God forbid if I end up losing this one!"

A knot had formed on Nilu's forehead. "I didn't know you were like this," she said. "I didn't know you would be willing to sell your dignity for . . . for Muwa's bribe. That's what she was trying to do—buy our affections by offering a life of comfort, and you have become seduced by it." She picked up Maitreya from the bed, and she left the room. Soon Raja heard her steps on the staircase.

When she didn't return in the next half-hour, he decided to go fetch her. He went downstairs, then emerged onto the street. He roamed the neighborhood, worried that Nilu was walking the streets with young Maitreya in her arms. Who knew what kind of illnesses a newborn could catch, exposed to the outside elements? She'd never walked out on him like this before, and he cursed himself for failing to appreciate the depth of her sensitivity toward Muwa's indifference. What was he thinking? He really didn't want to live with Muwa and her lover; he didn't feel any urge to be close to Kaki; but he had been strangely attracted to the idea of Maitreya playing in the same yard where he, Raja, had played, albeit briefly, as a child, except that his son would be a master, not a servant.

He walked all the way to Thamel chowk, almost to Fishtail Books, which he was supposed to open shortly. Shakya-ji lived right above the bookstore, but he had told Raja that he hated it when he had to open the shop in the morning. For good reason: Shakya-ji smoked ganja late into the night, often with the American and European girls he befriended in his bookstore. At around noon he awoke and ambled down to the shop, where he took an hour to drink a cup of tea and read the newspaper before heading up again to shower and eat, and perhaps smoke another joint, before he emerged in the late afternoon or the evening, when he usually let Raja go.

Raja had only half an hour to eat and arrive at the bookstore. He didn't want to displease Shakya-ji by opening the store late, so he returned to the flat, thinking he'd just munch on a piece or two of bread and go to work.

Nilu was in their kitchen, joined by Bhairavi. Maitreya was asleep on the bed.

"Where did you go?" Raja asked. "I was getting worried."

"I was downstairs, at Bhairavi's place."

"Why didn't you tell me?" Raja said. "I walked all the way to Thamel chowk looking for you."

"Oh, such love," Bhairavi said.

"Serves you right," Nilu told Raja. "Who asked you to support Muwa over me?"

"I was just giving her the benefit of the doubt, that's all. I have no intention of going to live in Nilu Nikunj."

"Big fight this morning?" Bhairavi asked.

Nilu told her what had happened.

"How can a grandmother's heart be like that?" Bhairavi exclaimed. "When I have my grandchildren, I'll smother them with love."

Her seven-year-old son came bounding up the stairs. He was obsessed with becoming a doctor when he grew up, an ambition that made his parents awfully proud. Now he came running to Raja, a plastic stethoscope around his neck, and asked if he could listen to Raja's heart. Raja lay down on the rug, lifted up his shirt, and allowed the boy to apply the stethoscope to his chest.

After Bhairavi and her son left, Raja embraced Nilu and extracted a promise from her that she'd never leave him stranded like that. He couldn't fight back the lump in his throat, and his voice broke as he said, "I don't know what I'd do if you left me, Nilu."

She stroked his face. "I'll never leave you, sweetie."

• • •

When Maitreya was two years old, Nilu and Raja moved to Chabel. The shift came about unexpectedly. As old and crumbling as their flat was in Thamel, they were happy there. They liked the landlady's family and had become such good friends with Bhairavi that they didn't want to think about living far from her. But whenever Ganga Da came to visit, he complained (he'd turned into such a complainer over the years) about their living conditions. He pointed out flaws in the flat: a new crack by the window; the electric wires danger-ously close — an arm's reach! — to the window; the ramshackle, un-hygienic outhouse in the courtyard. "An outhouse in the middle of the city?" he exclaimed. "And that too in an area where Westerners flock? Why can't your dear landlady build a modern indoor bath-room, with a commode and a flush and everything, like the rest of civilization?"

Raja and Nilu tried to hush him, fearing that the landlady would hear. Raja told Ganga Da that he and Nilu had no problem with the toilet in the courtyard. "It's exhilarating, actually," Raja said. "We get to smell fresh air as we conduct our morning business."

"Yes, yes, keep joking," Ganga Da said. "You're going to let my grandson grow up in this hovel?" He was moving his right leg rap-idly and twirling his thumbs on his lap. Nowadays he was forced to rush Jamuna Mummy to the mental hospital every few weeks, where she'd get electroconvulsive therapy. He complained that he was get-ting tired of handling Jamuna Mummy all by himself. Before, while Raja lived with them, she'd sober up when Raja scolded her, but these days nothing seemed to pacify her. She had become physically aggressive and frequently assaulted Ganga Da. The young muscu-lar man Ganga Da had hired to help him control Jamuna Mummy had quit after a few days, saying that the job was beyond him. The medications that the doctors at the hospital had prescribed for her sometimes worked, but at other moments they were useless. Often Jamuna Mummy would simply refuse to take them. During one of her hospital stays the nurses had caught her exposing her breasts to two other patients, who were also in the process of undressing.

A few weeks after Maitreya's birth, Raja and Nilu had taken

him to Jamuna Mummy in the hospital, where in a general ward crowded with patients she was sleeping in a narrow bed under a photograph of Mahatma Gandhi. The hospital conditions had improved somewhat, but not a great deal, since that first time Ganga Da had brought his wife here, right after Kaki escaped to Nilu Nikunj with six-year-old Raja. The floor was cleaner, and the nurses regularly took the patients out to the yard for fresh air and exercise. But cots still served as beds, and patients slept in such close proximity that they had to climb over their neighbors to go to the nurses' room or to visit the bathroom. The wilder patients were chained to corner poles or to heavy chairs.

Jamuna Mummy stared at the ceiling, unresponsive to Ganga Da's exhortations. Just yesterday she'd received her electric shocks, they had learned.

"Your nati is here," Ganga Da said to Jamuna Mummy. "Won't you take a look at him? Look at his cute face, look at that nose. He looks just like Raja."

Actually Maitreya's face was a replica of Nilu's: the same dimpled cheeks, the same small chin. But Ganga Da was trying hard to get Jamuna Mummy interested, and he wasn't successful. It wasn't until Raja leaned over her and said, "Jamuna Mummy, won't you speak to me? I've come to see you after such a long time, and I've brought someone along with me," that her eyes flickered and she turned her head slowly to look at him. She uttered a bunch of words no one understood.

Nilu held Maitreya up and said, "Jamuna Mummy, look!"

This time she did look and said, "Eh, where did this little goat come from? Like a goat he is, isn't he? He's going to grow a beard like a goat, he's going to drop small round pellets like a goat, he's going to go *mhhhaaaa mhhhaaa* like a goat."

"Het!" Raja said. "You can't call my child a goat. Maybe you yourself are a goat."

"Don't say that, Raja," Jamuna Mummy said. "Don't hurt your mother's feelings like that." Then she began to gently scold Raja for a number of incoherent reasons. "Don't do such things, don't bring a goat to my bed" were the last words they heard as they left her bedside.

Nilu sometimes wondered how long it would be before Ganga Da himself lost his grasp on reality. Physically something was happening to him. His abrupt hand gestures, his incessantly jiggling legs, the stubble that remained unshaved on his chin, his cloudy eyes—all these pointed to a man about to break down. When she'd expressed her concern to Raja, he'd dismissed it, saying that all his life he'd seen Ganga Da take care of Jamuna Mummy, and the man was used to it. "He's just getting a bit older, Nilu," Raja said. "He's aging faster because dealing with a crazy wife is finally taking its toll." Once again, she was struck by how casual, how dismissive he was about anything to do with his parents. It was as if nothing about them could require his intervention, or even his thought or worry.

"Ganga Da, we're not going to move in with you, if that's what you're after," Raja said one day, after Ganga Da pointed out more faults in their flat. "You already have your hands full with Jamuna Mummy, and we simply can't subject Maitreya to her unpredictable behavior."

"Who said I want you to move in with me?" Ganga Da said. "I gave up on that a long time ago. I have something else in mind. Now hear me fully before you say no." He told them that he'd completed building the new house last year, a small, one-story house in Chabel that was now rented to a family. But his tenants were moving because the husband was being posted to Birgunj. Nothing would make Ganga Da happier than to have Nilu and Raja take possession of the house. He'd rather let his family live there than have it occupied by more strangers. "It doesn't make sense that I have a house in Lainchour," Ganga Da said, "and I have a house in Chabel, but my son and my daughter-in-law and my grandchild are living in a crummy flat where they have to make a mad dash to the yard if they have a diarrhea."

"But Ganga Da," Nilu said, "we don't want to deprive you of your rent. God knows you need all the extra income for Jamuna Mummy's treatment."

Ganga Da sighed. "There you go again. Jamuna Mummy will always be Jamuna Mummy. But here you are, young parents, Raja just trying to build his career. The only thing I'm trying to do is give you two a boost, that's all."

"We'll pay you rent," Raja said.

"What?" Ganga Da looked aghast.

"We'll pay you rent. That's the only way we can stay in your house."

"See?" Ganga Da said to Nilu. "See how he treats me? Your house, he says. Is it not your house? Don't you have any right to my property? No, I can't accept rent from you."

The father and the son began quarreling, and before their exchange became heated, Nilu intervened. "Ganga Da, why don't we come up with a compromise? We will pay you rent, but if you wish you can put that money in the bank, in Maitreya's name."

Ganga Da pinched Nilu's cheek. "My chhori. That's a brilliant idea. Why didn't I think of it before?" Addressing Raja, he said, "Why didn't you think of it before, eh, lamfu? You go around pretending you're very smart, but you're as complete an idiot as I ever saw." And he also pinched Raja's cheek. Then he leaned over and kissed baby Maitreya's forehead, and left.

"I really don't feel like leaving this flat," Raja said. "Everything is perfect for us here. My work is close by. Our landlady is so nice to us. Chabel is too far, don't you think, Nilu? Maybe you shouldn't have said yes so easily. You should have left Ganga Da to me. I'd have handled him."

"Now look who's talking, the man who wanted to move to Nilu Nikunj at the first enticement. I know how you feel, Raja, but I could no longer stand that look on Ganga Da's face. He's been so unhappy lately, and I feel like we're rejecting him at every turn. I don't want to leave this flat either—poor Bhairavi, she's going to be crushed—but it's true that the house is falling apart, and it'll be nice for Maitreya to have his own green lawn to play on as he grows up."

When they told Bhairavi, she was indeed saddened, pleaded with them not to leave, said she'd speak on their behalf to her mother-in-law for a reduced rent. Nilu embraced her, wiped her tears from her cheeks, and said that it was not as if they were moving to a different town. Chabel was only a bus ride or two away from Thamel, and they'd visit each other often. "You have to see Maitreya grow up," Nilu said. "You are the only aunt he has."

On the day of their move, Ganga Da rented a truck and helped them shuttle their sparse belongings to Chabel, where the house had already been furnished with brand-new furniture — a sofa, a dining room set, a large bed. A priest appeared out of nowhere, chanted a few mantras for an auspicious occupancy of the house, dabbed tikas on their foreheads, pocketed the thirty rupees Ganga Da gave him, and vanished. A big grin was plastered on Ganga Da's face, like that of a father welcoming a new bride and groom into his house.

If Raja and Nilu had any misgivings about moving to Chabel, they were washed away when, within days, Raja found a new job as an assistant editor at Nepal Yatra, a travel publishing company based in Gaushala, within walking distance of their new house. Like the house, the job too was unexpected, for he had no writing or editing experience. An old friend, Amit, who was the financial manager of Nepal Yatra, had come to Fishtail Books one day, and as they talked Raja had casually said that it took him forty minutes to get to the bookstore from Chabel. Amit spoke of an opening at Nepal Yatra, which published two travel magazines, and suggested that Raja's knowledge of books and tourists might just be what they needed.

"But I don't have any writing experience, yaar," Raja said, "especially in English."

Amit laughed. "Which world are you living in? In Nepal you don't need writing experience to be a journalist. Look around you. Every ignoramus is a writer or a journalist now. There are a couple of boarding school types who work for our magazine. They'll edit your work and help you write; don't worry."

"But you'll get better candidates for the position than me, I'm sure."

Amit winked. "Leave that up to me."

Raja had suspected that Amit was boasting, and he was shocked when, after an interview, the editor called to offer him the position. The salary was only slightly better than what Raja made at the bookstore, but an editorial job, with opportunities to move up, was certainly better than managing a bookstore. He could also walk to work, instead of taking two buses, or the more expensive three-wheeler, to reach Thamel. "We did the right thing by moving to Chabel," he said to Nilu. "Otherwise I'd not have complained to Amit, and he'd not have mentioned Nepal Yatra."

"Oh, is that how life works?" Nilu said in a teasing voice. She found it amusing how serious Raja had become since Maitreya entered their lives. A slight crease now seemed permanently etched on his forehead — he'd become a worrier. She couldn't help but contrast him with the Raja of the past, who had hurled stones at the police in front of Ascol College, drunk heavily with Nick and Roger in Utse, and gotten into fights with young men who teased Nilu. Once in a while he got a bit excited about some news in the papers, but in general he seemed to lose interest in political developments in Nepal. "This place will never change," he said to Nilu. "What's the point? Might as well make the best of what we have." Now it was all work and family and bouncing Maitreya on his lap and reading to him at bedtime. He rarely joined his magazine colleagues after work at Nanglo or in bars in Thamel. His hair was cut shorter, and he'd had a couple of nice-looking suits tailored at Putalisadak. Every morning he went to his office wearing a suit over a shirt that he himself ironed, even though his colleagues at work dressed quite casually. "Important to look professional," he informed Nilu. "People take you seriously then."

Holding Maitreya, who was straining to grasp his father's bright red tie, Nilu patted Raja lightly on the cheek and said, "Does this mean we have to take you seriously too, no matter what a buffoon you might turn out to be?" She handed Maitreya to the servant woman they'd hired recently, as Nilu too had to get ready for her day of teaching school.

"You better take me seriously," Raja said, tickling Maitreya's face with the end of his tie. "Otherwise" — he adopted his growling, snarling Hindi movie villain voice — "*Nilu bachchi, hum tumareh muhn me ek hazaar peda ghoosadenge,* I will hold you upside down by your legs and smack you on your bottom."

Rajá's job involved visiting Kathmandu's upscale hotels and restaurants, writing about a new wing at a four-star hotel, or describing the special blend of Nepali and Thai cuisine at a popular restaurant. Occasionally he had to travel to Chitwan or Pokhara for the inauguration of a new resort or a jungle lodge, and although he enjoyed these trips, he missed Nilu and Maitreya and couldn't wait to return home. Upon arrival, the first thing he did was pick up Maitreya and twirl him high in the air. With Nilu he shared stories of his trips, the interesting people he met. "I think they'll make me an associate editor quite soon," he said. "The boss is very pleased with my work. I'm gaining a reputation as a hard worker." His eyes traveled to his son, who was stumbling back and forth in the living room, throwing a plastic ball and chasing it. "We have to provide him the best life he can get. We'll send him to the best colleges, we'll make sure that he has everything he needs. We must never let him feel that he lacks anything, Nilu."

"You didn't lack anything either when you grew up, did you?" Nilu asked. Then, realizing how insensitive she sounded, corrected herself. "Well, yes, during those early years with Kaki. But you don't remember most of it. Ganga Da and Jamuna Mummy never let you feel a lack, did they?"

"That's not what I'm talking about. I'm talking about the love of your real mother and father, which nothing in the world can replace."

"But you mentioned the best colleges for Maitreya, which has little to do with parental love."

"You," he said, smiling. "You are adept at twisting my words. What I mean is simply this: our son should never feel a want in his life."

But she knew that underneath his words was a longing for his mother that time hadn't erased. He wasn't going to let Maitreya be contaminated by his own life as an orphan who took his first bumbling steps in the streets, who clung to the dhoti of a woman selling corn on the hot sidewalks of Ratna Park, who was sneered at by the woman in whose house he'd lived as a servant's boy, who had finally been raised by a man who'd stolen him so that his mad, tortured wife would get at least an ounce of happiness. Raja wanted none of that for his son.

Fever

THE COUNTRY WAS in an uproar. Hubbub and hullabaloo — that's what this country is made of, the poet Bhupi Sherchan had written. But this was a different kind of noise. Part of the commotion traveled all the way from Europe: the sound of the destruction of the Berlin Wall. Things are happening, everyone said. The air turned sharp, pungent, and when people breathed, their lungs felt invigorated. We can do it too, they said to one another as they walked the streets of the city. For centuries we've been ruled — like dogs. Who is he? someone shouted belligerently, pointing toward the wide street of Durbar Marg, with its ice cream shops and bakeries and pizza joints and travel agencies and boutiques culminating in the towering structure of the royal palace. "It always looked ugly," someone said of the building. "Made by Indians, wasn't it?" Others nodded. "Even our palaces are designed by outsiders," they said. "What do we have to call our own?"

Something was definitely in the air, and Nilu could sense Raja's controlled excitement. Every morning, over his tea, he read the newspapers carefully. "They've declared February 18 the official day of the uprising," he said to Nilu, who was making some toast for Maitreya. He sounded too casual, she thought, as he slurped his tea.

"Mmmm?" Nilu said. She was thinking about her own classes,

what she was going to teach that day. "Don't get your hopes up," she said. "This is 1990. Even twenty years from now, in 2010, nothing will have changed. Mark my words."

Maitreya was in the next room, doing his homework. He'd stayed up late the night before, watching *The Little Mermaid* on video. "What's not going to change, Ma?" he shouted.

"Nothing," she said. "Finish your homework. The bus will be here soon."

"Hopes up?" Raja said. "What do I care about this third-class country's third-class problems?" He was clearly trying hard to feign a lack of interest.

She switched off the gas, and turned and smiled at him. "It's an okay country. It's not the best, but we're living in it, and it's serving us all right. What's your problem with it?"

"Oh, you're challenging me now, are you?" he said. "It's a horrible country," he said, "and it's all your fault."

"It's a beautiful country," she said. "The Himalaya, Gautama Buddha, Kumari the Living Goddess, no British colonialism, the only Hindu kingdom in the world. What more do you want? Every morning you ought to be touching my feet, thanking me for giving you this country, but here you are, always complaining."

Raja lunged at her, and, clasping her in his arms, tackled her to the cold floor of the kitchen, where he began to plant fervent kisses on her face, repeating, "Is this what you want? Is this what your beautiful country wants?"

Maitreya emerged from the next room and asked quietly what they were doing. He was so serious that Raja and Nilu had to let go of each other and suppress their laughter. "Don't fool around like that," Maitreya said. "I'm trying to finish my homework." Their son was very serious that way. Maitreya — with his large eyes and dark circles under them, his unsmiling face, his thoughtful, considered responses.

Throughout the winter-spring months of Falgun and Chaitya, people kept taking to the streets, demanding changes. Raja too joined them, although he tried to hide it from Nilu, and even from his colleagues. He began to slip away from the office in the middle of the day, after making excuses about the hotel owner that he had to interview in Durbar Marg or the new Mongolian restaurant he had to review in Lazimpat. And since no lack of protesters took to the streets in those days, he had no problem finding them, merging with them as he loosened his tie and raised his fist in the air. His expression was one of exhilaration, a breaking free of something — a knot — inside him.

Had it not been for an errand she had to run for Arniko Academy, Nilu wouldn't have known about Raja's afternoon adventures. But that day an awards ceremony had been scheduled at school, and the teacher in charge had become violently ill. As the hour of the prize ceremony drew near, the principal discovered that the specially engraved trophies and medals hadn't been picked up from the shop, and Nilu was dispatched to get them.

In New Road, as she emerged from the shop, holding the seven trophies and the twenty-four medals in her arms and hoping to hail a taxi, she observed a small procession heading in her direction from the Basantapur area. The procession wasn't very big, but it was substantial enough to stop traffic, and car and tempo drivers sighed wearily at this delay. She spotted an empty taxi some distance away, but because of the press of people, she couldn't make her way to it. Her arms were killing her — she'd forgotten to ask the blacksmith in the shop for a bag — but if she was to reenter the shop, she'd have to fight the throng of pedestrians who'd congregated in the doorway, waiting for the procession to pass.

She was wondering what to do when she spotted Raja among the protesters, who were now about fifty yards away. He'd taken off his tie and rolled up his sleeves, and he was punching the air above him with his fist. It's not Raja, she thought. But it was. Her arms stopped aching, and the noise around her seemed to recede. Then, as he came near, she felt an instinct to run away. But it was silly, not only because she hadn't done anything wrong but because she couldn't budge — that's how crowded the street had become. Then she wanted to turn her face so he wouldn't see her as he passed, but she couldn't take her eyes off him: there he was, swaggering, as he did early in their Thamel days.

He marched at the edge of the procession, getting closer. If he glanced in her direction, what would she do? What if she panicked, and the trophies and medals went clattering to the street? The protesters might very well trample and kick them. What would Raja say? And what would she say? Or would they just avert their eyes, like strangers? What would they say when they reached home in the evening? Would they gaze into each other's eyes to see who'd be the first one to cave in, to buckle, to admit a certain wrongdoing? But she'd done nothing wrong! Nilu had nothing to hide. The trophies she'd picked up, with their engraved student names — Raksha Budhathoki, Milan Karki, Samyukta Shrestha, Harsha Jha, Saleena Moktan, Leeza Sharma, Komal Tuladhar — and the medals with no names — she had a reason for holding them in her numbing arms. She was here for an official purpose. But Raja?

He passed so close that she could see the sweat glistening on his cheek, the small indented scar on his jaw from an old wound he didn't remember. She saw him, then, at that moment, as the child he might have been in Ratna Park, peering at the faces of women who could be his mother, circling to see if one would recognize him and embrace him. She saw him sitting dejectly under a stone umbrella at the end of the day, as the sun began to set behind the Nagarjun hill, listening to Kaki call him from across the street as she packed her corn-grilling paraphernalia, thinking that he'd join her in a moment, thinking that his mother could still appear, perhaps approach him from the very bushes where she'd left him. And when that didn't happen, Nilu saw his expression transforming, gradually, from one of hopelessness to one of anger, a fury that made him want to lash out at the world and the grave injustice it had inflicted on him.

· · ·

Nilu didn't mention to Raja that she'd seen him in New Road. Even during the prize ceremony, held on the lawn of Arniko Academy with the big peepul tree providing partial shade, she had the strong feeling that Raja had betrayed her. The thought tired her, and she began to develop a headache. Then Principal Thapa announced her name, asking her to come forward and present a trophy to the winner of the debate competition, which she'd overseen. It took Nilu a moment to register what he was saying, but then slowly she made her way to the podium, where she declared Samyukta Shrestha the winner; her tongue turned thick when she uttered the student's name, so it came out garbled. A few students tittered, and Principal Thapa gave Nilu a sharp look. To Samyukta she gave a weary smile, then, before the student had returned to her seat, quickly walked back to her own chair. Prateema, who was sitting next to her, asked, "Are you okay?" and Nilu nodded, saying that it was the sun.

At home that evening she was quieter than usual, and when Raja remarked upon it, she said that it was the heat. "It was so hot this afternoon, wasn't it?" she said.

He and Maitreya were playing snakes and ladders. Without looking up, Raja said, "I didn't notice. I was inside most of the day, then briefly I went to New Road to that new restaurant."

"What restaurant?"

"There's a new one, you don't know."

What's the name, she was going to ask, but didn't. What did it matter? He was hiding his afternoon forays with the protest gang because he was afraid that she'd object to it, as she did during their early days as a couple. He was afraid that she'd criticize him for forgetting that he was a family man now, the father of a five-year-old son, an office worker with a job that had its share of pleasures: He rode a business motorcycle to interview hotel owners in luxury penthouse offices, where together they sipped port wine in small decorative glasses. He hobnobbed with restaurant owners who had deep roots in the city's tourism industry; sporting ponytails and closely trimmed beards, they spoke of the days when only one hotel existed in Kathmandu—the Royal Hotel, run by the itinerant Russian dancer and hunter Boris Lissanevich, who allowed mountain climbers to sleep on his lawns and whose apple-red face and ready smile ushered in the Nepali hospitality industry. "Hospitality industry," Raja would say, and Nilu would experience a mild shock. The words didn't seem right coming from his lips, his face, his body. For her, the phrase conjured up an image of hospitals: the smell of disinfectant and the singsongy voices of nurses wearing white, starched uniforms. As a strange backdrop to this picture, she also saw industrial machines spewing black smoke.

Nilu thought up explanations for her husband's behavior. Most likely Raja stepped into the street now and then to clear his head of the hospitality industry and to regain something of his youth, his original self. She herself didn't believe that anything would come of the ripples of rebellion that were coursing through the country, and, confirming her theory, the government clamped down heavily—dissidents and their leaders were thrown in jail or placed under house arrest. She could see the disappointment on Raja's face as he read the morning papers, which clearly suggested that the push for political change was coming to naught. Nilu felt sorry for Raja, who obviously had high expectations. She could hear him thinking, This time it's going to burst wide open.

One night in bed, with Maitreya sleeping between them, Raja said, as though it might be news to her, "People are mocking and ridiculing the king. They're saying *Birey chor desh chhod*. I've never heard anything like it."

"Do you hear these things in the office?" she asked. The memory of watching him in the New Road procession flashed in her mind occasionally, though sometimes she wondered whether she'd dreamt it.

"No, sometimes the processions pass by our street. Then all of us go to the window to look."

Her hand, against Maitreya's exposed belly under the blanket, could feel the rise and fall of his breath. His skin was warm; something crept up her throat swiftly. She swallowed. When she spoke, her voice was thick. "Do you ever feel like joining them, Raja? Like before? Do you still have that urge?"

He didn't meet her eyes. "I wonder what it'd be like. I mean, nothing like this has happened before. Doctors and teachers swarming the streets, people openly calling Queen A a whore."

"Shhh," Nilu said, her finger to her lips. "Don't use that word in front of our son."

"It's not me," he whispered. "It's the people on the street who are saying that about the queen."

"Did the queen sleep with men for money?" she said dismissively. "Do your people on the street have proof of that?"

Raja smiled. "Why does it bother you so?" he said. "It's just an expression. Like a metaphor. They don't really mean that she's a . . . someone who does that for a living."

"If they don't mean it, they shouldn't say it," Nilu replied, now whispering loudly. "Criticizing her for what she's done to the country is one thing, but to call her that is another."

"Okay, baba," he said. "I'll let the masses know this when I see them next time."

"And when will that be?" she said sarcastically, but Raja was gazing at Maitreya, thinking about something else, and so she said, a bit more quietly, "You forgot what people said about me when we first moved to Thamel, when they thought that we weren't married?"

He looked up at her. "I know, mitini. I myself haven't said that about any woman, you know that."

His conciliatory voice dissolved her annoyance, and she stroked his face. "I know, sweetie." Then, as she turned off the light, she said, "Be careful when you go for interviews on your motorcycle, Raja. I worry that you'll get caught in a riot."

After a moment of silence in the dark, he spoke. "I'm careful. You also be careful."

As Nilu was struggling to teach her eighth graders the difference between a gerund and a verb participle, the Arniko Academy's peon appeared at her classroom door to tell her she had a phone call.

"Who is it from?" she asked the peon, the chalk between her fingers. On the blackboard she'd just written "He was swimming in a pond" and "Swimming is good exercise."

"I don't know, miss."

"You didn't ask who it was?"

"I forgot, miss."

Telling her students she'd be back in a second, she hurried to the staff room, her heart pounding. Shots must have been fired — a radio-television type of voice announced this in her mind. In the staff room, as she picked up the phone, she remembered that Raja was scheduled to be in Kakani that day, to talk to a relative of the owner of Nepal Yatra. But this fact made her more anxious. Was the Kakani trip a ruse? This morning Raja had complained that the relative was a bit of a kook who came up with grandiose ideas that never saw completion — this time, a harebrained scheme to open a massive resort at the top of a mountain. But Raja had to go along for the sake of his boss, who'd asked him to do this as a personal favor. "I really don't want to go," Raja had said the night before to Nilu. "The man is so annoying. He just doesn't stop talking. My mood will be off the whole day, listening to his drivel."

Would Raja have lied about this? She took a deep breath before she said hello.

It was the assistant principal of Maitreya's school, saying that her son was running a fever. Could she pick him up to take him to a doctor? Her first reaction was tremendous relief — nothing had happened to Raja — then irritation. Maitreya's school had a history of calling parents to take their children home because of minor health complaints. Besides, Maitreya had been fine when he'd left for the bus stop this morning. Nilu had to administer a test to the seventh grade during the next period, and finding a last-minute substitute was a hassle; all the teachers were busy with their own classes. She really didn't want to rush to Maitreya's school if her son was simply coming down with a cold, something that could wait until evening.

The assistant principal was insistent that she come.

After putting down the phone, Nilu returned to her class, gave her students a writing assignment to last the rest of the period, and went to the principal's office. Principal Thapa, as she'd expected, was unhappy about her request to leave, which rankled Nilu, so she repeated her request, making it sound more like a declaration. Principal Thapa had replaced Principal Gurung last year. Formerly the head of a boarding school in India, he quickly established himself as a bit of an authoritarian. Although happy with her teaching, Principal Thapa hadn't liked Nilu's occasional open disagreements with his decisions, which he interpreted as insubordination. During one of his dreaded staff meetings, he'd declared his intention to expel two students who'd incited their classmates to boycott their classes. The "culprits," as Principal Thapa called them, had expressed displeasure that the school hadn't shut down during a religious holiday. Nilu had come to the students' defense, saying that the punishment was too harsh for a minor rebellion. Eventually, Principal Thapa had backed down and delivered only a written warning to the students. The other teachers, who'd not spoken a word during the heated exchange between Principal Thapa and Nilu, later told her she was brave to stand up to him. "It's not a question of being brave or cowardly," Nilu said. "It's a question of fairness. He can't do anything he pleases. These boys are young, they're learning, aren't they? What will they learn if you snuff their spirit?"

She didn't tell them of her own travails at St. Augustine's, how Sister O'Malley had battled Mother Mann on Nilu's behalf. Nilu and Sister O'Malley had run into each other in the city a few times after Nilu left St. Augustine's, and they'd stood in the middle of the street, holding hands. Sister O'Malley had aged, but her eyes were still fiery, and every time she saw Nilu, she laughed as she recalled the Jonathan Swift essay. "Every time we have a new girl with some life in her, some zest, I think of you." Three months ago, Sister O'Malley had passed away while traveling on a train to South India, en route to a retreat.

It turned out that Prateema was in Principal Thapa's office at that time, and fearing an argument, she intervened and said that she'd be happy to administer the test for Nilu.

"But how will you do it, Prateema Miss?" Principal Thapa said loudly. "Don't you have your own test to administer?"

Prateema said that since her classroom was side by side with Nilu's, it wouldn't be a problem to supervise both sets of students.

Principal Thapa retorted that it would create opportunities for students to cheat.

Instead of dealing with this argument, Nilu had half a mind to simply call back Maitreya's assistant principal, tell him she couldn't come, and that they'd have to take care of Maitreya until she could get there. But she wondered if by now her son too would be expecting her. "Sir, my son is sick," she said to Principal Thapa. "Please."

Principal Thapa stared at her, then dismissively waved his hand, which Nilu took to mean she could go.

About noon she left her school and caught a tempo to Maitreya's school, which was in Maitidevi. On the way she wished that his school was big enough to have an infirmary, where someone with some medical knowledge could dispense common pills and drugs for the children, as St. Augustine's had. But surely the assistant principal had given Maitreya a Citamol or something? Maybe the fever had come down already, and she wondered if she should stop somewhere and call Raja to find out if he'd returned from Kakani, and if he had, whether he could pick up Maitreya and take him home so Nilu could supervise her exam.

She was pondering this when the tempo came to a complete stop in Baghbazar. Ahead, all the vehicles had come to a standstill. When Nilu asked the driver what had happened, he said that he'd heard talks of a julus that afternoon; he didn't know what it was for or against. "There are so many of them these days," he said despondently, "and it's our work and livelihood that suffer." He turned off the engine and rested a leg on the dashboard. As Nilu grew anxious, the tempo driver droned on. "These people have their own agenda, always — this isn't right, that isn't right. But the people who suffer are us, the poor, who not only have to survive in the city but also have to send money back home."

Nilu could barely concentrate on what he was saying. A few minutes had already gone by, and the traffic didn't show signs of budging. In the distance she could hear the shouting of slogans, but she couldn't make out the words. As she contemplated whether she should get out and walk — even the sidewalk was jam-packed now — the driver continued. "Look, sister. I'm not saying that there are no injustices in this country and that people shouldn't raise their voices. But there's a limit. These people only care that they be heard, and they block the streets for hours on end, and who suffers? Now half of my day's income is gone, but at the end of the day I still have to pay a fixed amount to this tempo's owner. When will I ever earn anything?"

The driver appeared ready to launch into another monologue when Nilu said, "I'll get off here and walk."

The sidewalk was so crammed with pedestrians and onlookers that she had to push through; her annoyance mounted with each person who blocked her path. At Putalisadak she saw a large group of people, waving flags and chanting slogans. Then she noticed that the crowd stretched all the way to the Dillibazar incline, where she was headed.

By the time she reached Maitreya's school she was drenched in sweat and vexed because on her way, several men, taking advantage of their anonymity in a crowd, had groped her. A feeling of helplessness had already come over her.

Maitreya was lying on the sofa in the principal's office, in his blue shirt and blue half-pants. No one else was around. She sat beside him and felt his forehead — it was burning. Her palm moved to his cheek, his neck. His entire body was hot. Very hot. She stepped into the corridor and shouted the name of the assistant principal, who came running. "I gave him a Citamol," he said. "His fever should be coming down."

"It's not," she said, unable to speak properly. "I'll take him to the hospital."

With a grunt, she picked up her son. The assistant principal offered to help, but all she said was "Quickly" and, panting, took him down to the yard. She could hear the children reciting in their classrooms. One group erupted in laughter.

She shouted at the guard to fetch her a taxi, but he said that the traffic had come to a complete halt; it would be impossible for her to get anywhere. Nilu set Maitreya down on the lawn, asked the assistant principal to quickly administer cold compresses to her son's forehead, and stepped out of the gate. The mass of people had now reached the school's gate. But these people were not members of the march she'd seen earlier; they were pedestrians who'd been pushed back into the school's lane because the main street had been overtaken by the marchers. All the side streets and alleys of Maitidevi were crammed.

Nilu stepped back into the school building and returned to her son, who now had a wet handkerchief on his forehead. His chest swelled and subsided fitfully with each breath. Nilu called his name a few times, but his eyes remained closed. She noted that his eyelids had a bluish tinge. The assistant principal was saying that the medicine and the cold presses ought to be working soon, but Nilu, unable to mask the hysteria in her voice, cried out for the principal. The man looked down from the second floor and shouted at the gatekeeper to run to the pharmacy down the street and fetch the compounder. A few bubbles of froth had appeared at the corners of Maitreya's lips.

Before he'd boarded the bus this morning, Nilu had demanded a kiss from him, and he'd given her only a quick peck on the cheek, since he was a bit peeved at her for making a fuss about his hair. "Can I get a smile?" she asked, and he'd stretched the corners of his mouth, offering just a perfunctory grin. But knowing his sweet nature, she was certain that by the evening he'd have forgiven her and would be her affectionate son once more.

Fifteen minutes passed. The chanting outside grew louder. She heard someone say that the police and the marchers had reached a standoff. Glass shattered somewhere close by. But the guard didn't return. Maitreya's head was on Nilu's lap. She kept dipping the hanky in a bucket of water, wringing it, and pressing it on her son's forehead, watching the water trickle down his temples. A bead or two streamed to the corner of Maitreya's eyes.

Part III

A Woman Grieving

F ROM THE MOMENT she got up in the morning to when she went to bed, Nilu felt a weight clamped to her chest; sometimes it moved up and down or migrated to the top of her head, making her vision cloudy, and she felt disoriented. When she told Raja about these experiences, he waved his hand dismissively. "That's all you talk about these days. Don't you have anything else to say? I'm so sick and tired of hearing about how your world has gone dark. Fed up! I can't listen to it anymore."

That's how he'd become over the past few weeks — quick to anger, callous about Nilu's feelings one moment, then apologetic and weepy the next. In sharp contrast to their gloom, the newspapers were filled with celebratory headlines. No one had expected King B to cave in so readily. He'd retreated! He'd given up! Well, not exactly, some pointed out. He was still the king, although only ceremonially, like the British crown. Did you forget the sacrifice we had to go through? A few hundred killed in the process, gunned down by the police and the army. But the losses suffered by those who risked themselves as protesters were accompanied by several tragic accidental deaths: a boy in Biratnagar was trampled to death by a herd of cows barreling away from agitators who in turn were escaping the police; a diphtheria-stricken girl with a swollen neck had passed away in Bir Hospital when all the doctors left their posts to join a burgeoning rally.

Someone — Nilu didn't remember who, because everything had turned blurry and weepy — suggested that Nilu and Raja petition the government to declare their son a martyr. This advice was given during the grieving period, well after Maitreya's small bony body had turned to ash on the filthy banks of the Bagmati River. Martyr. "Had it not been for that julus, nothing would have happened to Maitreya," the man who suggested it continued, softly, patiently, as one would talk to dumbfounded parents who were, understandably, incapable of clear thinking. "Maybe that's what God had in mind, to sacrifice this poor boy for the good of us all."

His words reminded Nilu of one of the Christian prophets — Abraham? — who had been willing to sacrifice his son like a lamb, to please his God.

"Every single person who died in the past few months is a martyr," said one of Raja's colleagues, emphatically, angrily.

Nilu nodded; Raja nodded. But what would the label *martyr* do? How would it change anything? But she was too weak to raise this question, didn't want to ask it. She looked at Raja, who, head lowered, was staring at his lap.

After the mourning period, Raja started going to his office early, soon after dawn, and returning late at night, sometimes with alcohol on his breath, although he was never heavily drunk. Nilu knew that he joined his colleagues at a bar in Baneswor, but she didn't pester him about it, and he didn't offer excuses as to why he was late. She could imagine him at the bar, his tie loosened as he took slow, steady sips of whiskey on the rocks while listening to the conversations of his colleagues and laughing occasionally at a joke or a witty observation. And his mind wandered — to what? To her? To Maitreya? Then he'd refocus, observing the faces at the table. They'd turn their attention to him now and then, ask him a question or two, and he'd respond, perhaps relate an anecdote about a wealthy hotel owner he'd interviewed, how opulent her home was. After an hour or two he'd find that he was no longer smiling at their jokes and, downing his drink, he'd slowly stand and say, "Bedtime for me, my friends."

In the taxi on the way home he thought about their dead son, Nilu knew that. She couldn't be sure whether he also wondered about her and what was happening between the two of them, how they could no longer talk. But surely he pondered how their son's death had come about, his role in it. Yes, Raja's role — that's how Raja thought of it; that's how she too had begun to think of it within days of their son's funeral. At times she would look at him and think, This is all your doing. The thought startled her, and she'd argue with herself and try to suppress it, but it would return when she watched Raja's drooping face as he drank his morning glass of tea. *You and your stupid protests.* But in another part of her mind she acknowledged that he wasn't even in the city when the events that led to the tragedy were set in motion.

When Raja discovered her gaze on him, something — denial, anger, perhaps even self-loathing — flashed in his eyes, and he withdrew further. One morning as the two were drinking tea, Nilu complained that Principal Thapa had instituted a new policy that only added to the headaches of the teachers. Without warning Raja slammed his palm on the table and said, "Criticize, criticize, that's all you do. As if you yourself are perfect." He stood, ready to leave, but he didn't go; he merely looked away, toward the window.

"I was only talking, Raja. You don't say anything anymore."

He faced her. "To say something I have to feel like saying it. But I don't feel like it anymore. Especially with you . . ."

She began to weep, quietly, but it had nothing to do with what Raja said. It was a reaction to how dark and gloomy the mornings had become, how tough the days.

One evening during dinner — in a burst of energy after school, she'd made some rotis, Raja's favorite — she said, "Sometimes I think that had you not gone to Kakani, things would have been different." She hadn't planned on saying this; until the moment she heard her own voice saying the words, she hadn't consciously formed the idea. She knew full well that Raja hadn't wanted to go to Kakani. But she was convinced that, had he been in the city, he'd probably have joined the march, the very crowd that had prevented her from taking her son to the hospital. In fact, as Maitreya's body had gone cold in her arms, a picture had flashed through her mind: Raja in the horde outside, his arms lifted. What if Raja had indeed participated in that march? Every time she thought of this, Nilu closed her eyes.

But Raja had indeed been in Kakani, bored out of his mind by the incessant chatter of his boss's relative, who was going to build a "world-class" resort, one with an auditorium, a luxurious garden for evening receptions, an Olympic-size swimming pool, and a terrace jutting from a cliff for an even closer view of the white Ganesh Himal.

"And what will support the terrace if it's going to extend so much in the air?" Raja had asked.

The man had paused for dramatic effect and said, "Plexiglas."

Now Raja stopped chewing and looked at Nilu. "Will you ever stop? Why are you always after me?"

His tone surprised her, for she hadn't thought she was accusing him. "I meant to say I might have been able to call you, and . . . you could have picked up the Third Person sooner, before the crowd blocked the way."

"Third Person?"

"Sorry, I didn't mean to call him that. It just slipped out."

He leaned forward on the table, rested his head on his palm, and said, "You want to talk about what ifs? Do you? I could accuse you of having been the one with him, and you didn't even try to find another way to rush him to the hospital. Instead of waiting for the damn taxi, I'd have carried my son in my arms and leapt through the crowd, kicking the people out of the way if I had to."

She laughed derisively. "Yes, correct. They'd have recognized you for the great man you are. They'd have thought you were Jung Bahadur Rana himself, the daredevil, leaping across the gorge to save your son. They'd have genuflected. They'd have said, 'Finally here's our savior.'"

Sometimes he came home after she'd already gone to bed, at eleven or midnight, and he'd quietly let himself in and stand in the doorway while she lay on the bed in the dark, holding her breath. What she expected of him, she didn't know. He'd seem not to move for a minute or two, as though orienting himself, taking stock of his surroundings. She sensed that he was contemplating what it would be like not to be faced with this anymore: the small lamp she left on for him in the living room, the dark bedroom where she was sleeping, waiting.

He'd stand before sitting on the sofa, which creaked. Then there'd be silence again. When finally he'd come to bed, he'd have visited the bathroom to brush his teeth, and the smell of alcohol would be replaced by mint. He'd gently put his hand on Nilu's arm as though he was about to wake her to give her some important but devastating news, and her heart would tremble, and she'd come close to putting her hands over her ears and saying, "I don't want to hear it. Keep it to yourself." But he'd just stroke her arm for a moment or two, then turn to the other side and go to sleep.

At night his body jerked and thrashed like a child's, and he cried out for his mother, not Kaki, not Jamuna Mummy, but the one who'd abandoned him. "Ama!" he'd wail, then mutter something incoherent, his eyebrows twitching under the lamp she'd turned on.

Once Raja came home and grabbed Nilu and kissed her passionately. His cheeks were moist. She unbuttoned his pants and stroked him, trying to make him hard. He massaged her breasts as though he was kneading dough. When her strokes didn't work, she took him in her mouth and felt him harden, slowly. He was grunting, his eyes closed, giving it all he had. She slid her mouth away and slipped her body up, adjusted herself so he'd be able to penetrate her, but within minutes he went limp. "It's pointless," he said, and put his clothes back on and left the room. When she checked on him later, she found him reading a book, but he wasn't concentrating; he didn't flip the page even after several minutes. Nilu sat on the sofa, waiting for him to speak, but he didn't. Only when she stood up to return to the bedroom did he say, "Looks like I might go to Delhi for a few days. There's been an invitation to a conference. The boss wants me to go."

"You should go."

"Yes, that's what I'm thinking."

"It'll be good for your career."

"Yes."

"It'll help you become the chief editor."

"Hmm."

After the funeral people had said, "Your heart will remain sad, but slowly everything will turn out all right. You have to trust time to take care of this. Slowly, slowly, your days will become brighter. Remember, your son's soul up there in heaven would also want you to move on with your lives. Remember that."

Two days after Raja returned from the conference in Delhi, he told Nilu that it would be better if he lived by himself somewhere.

"Did something happen in Delhi?" she asked.

"No."

"Then why now? What will it solve?"

"I didn't say it'll solve anything. Did I? Did you hear me say that?"

"Then why?"

He shrugged, sighed.

"What are you thinking, Raja? Are you thinking about us separating?"

He looked at her glumly, reached out and tucked a strand of her hair behind her ear. "Lately everything has just become impossible. Maybe, if we lived apart for a while . . ."

She didn't disagree with him; still, when he proposed it, it felt like rejection. "What happens if it leads to a permanent separation?"

From the way he stared at her, it became apparent to her that he hadn't really considered that possibility. In a way, it gave her hope, for it meant that he did envision their coming back together. But in another way it rankled, for it signaled that his urge to move away was impulsive and childish, that he hadn't taken into account the possibility that they'd remain separated forever. "It won't," he finally said.

"Raja, we might become more estranged."

"Didn't I say it won't?" he said, quickly, dismissively, making her flinch. "Why can't you think a bit positively about this? Why do you always have to be negative?"

He moved to a flat in Dillibazar. She packed two suitcases with his clothes and bed sheets, and they arranged for a truck so he could also transfer a couple of plastic chairs, a small lamp, and a large bookshelf, which two boys Amit had sent from the office carried to the truck.

After Raja was gone, Nilu sat on the living room couch, listening to the traffic in the distance, near the Chabel market, thinking that soon there'd be a rap on the door and he'd be there, saying, "You really didn't think I'd leave you, did you, mitini?"

He called her later that night. He asked her how she was doing and she said fine. "Are you in your flat now?" she asked. He said yes; he was calling from a shop below as the flat didn't have a phone. Only then did she note the background noises: voices talking, a bicycle bell, a machine whirring, someone's name being shouted. Come home, she wanted to say, but she didn't. He told her he'd talk to her soon and hung up.

For a couple of days he called daily, either from the same shop or from his office in Nepal Yatra if he was working late. He'd ask her how she was doing and she'd say she was doing fine. Then the gaps between the calls got longer. He had given her the downstairs shop's number so she could also phone him. Once, she did dial it, but she put down the phone as soon as a gravelly voice, presumably the shopkeeper's, said, "Hello?"

• • •

Ganga Da came knocking early one Saturday morning. After Raja left, Nilu had let the servant woman go, so she herself served Ganga Da tea and sat next to him, asked him how he was, how often he visited Jamuna Mummy at the hospital.

"Forget about me and Jamuna," Ganga Da said, getting emotional. "She's going to die in that purgatory any day now, and she's going to drag me into her hell with her. But you and Raja—you have your whole lives ahead of you. Yes, Maitreya passed away well before his time, but we've mourned for him. Now I have to be aggrieved over you and Raja? What's wrong with you, Nilu? What's wrong with that idiot?"

"Nothing, Ganga Da. It's just for a short time."

"Then how long are you going to allow yourself to bleed like this?"

She had no answer for him. She didn't want to bother explaining to him the darkness that constricted her head, drained away the everyday colors from her world.

"How long, Nilu?" He appeared unable to speak. The weight of events in the past years—Raja's dismissal of Ganga Da's wish for a traditional wedding, Maitreya's death, and, always, Jamuna Mummy's steadily declining condition—had taken their toll on him. He looked increasingly haggard and worn-out. He'd lost weight, and blotches marked his skin. For long after Maitreya's death, he blamed the "hoodlums of democracy" for snuffing his grandson's life. He didn't accuse Raja, didn't point a finger, but the stiffness with which he stood when he was around Raja indicated that he did consider his son's foolhardiness, his deluded thinking, partly to blame for the tragedy. But his resentment didn't last long, and one day, a couple of weeks into the grieving period, he broke down and embraced Raja, crying, "What happened, Raja? How could something like this happen?"

Lately, he'd been preoccupied with putting Jamuna Mummy in a private mental clinic; a couple had recently sprouted in the capital. In the government hospital where she was treated now, patients still roamed the hallways unsupervised, and the nurses neglected to give them their daily pills. The few times Nilu had been to visit Jamuna Mummy there, she'd had to cover her nose with her sari — so strong was the stench floating through the building. In contrast, the new private clinics had clean, well-lit rooms and nurses trained in counseling. But these clinics were also outrageously expensive. Their fees would leave Ganga Da bankrupt. And though Ganga Da had indeed saved the money that he'd collected as rent from Nilu and Raja over the years, he'd recently given it away to charity in his dead grandson's name.

But these days Nilu was getting tired of Ganga Da's constant complaints.

Sensing her displeasure, he placed his hand on hers and said gently, "Try, okay? You can't just let your life slide by like this."

She nodded. "I'll try, Ganga Da."

"Shall I talk to Raja? Ask him to return here?"

"Give him a few days, then I'll talk to him."

"You will?"

"Yes."

"Promise?"

She nodded.

But she didn't. Days drifted by, and Raja still lived in Dillibazar, and she still didn't turn on the lights when she got home in the evening. In the meantime, Ganga Da had visited Raja, Nilu was sure, to persuade him to go home. She could picture Raja telling Ganga Da the same thing she did, that right now it was good for both of them to live apart, that he would return home. In time.

She thought about leaving the city, packing some clothes in a suitcase and taking off. She could just go someplace else, perhaps Pokhara, where the scenery — the lake, the close mountains — could give her some solace. With her résumé detailing her years of experience at Arniko Academy, she ought to be able to find a teaching position. Private boarding schools were cropping up in Pokhara, she'd heard, so an English teacher would probably be in demand. It also wouldn't matter if the salary was less than what she made now — she had no one but herself to provide for.

But when she mentioned this casually to Prateema at school one day, she received a sound scolding. "You're going to give up so easily?" Prateema said. "What's wrong with you, Nilu? You've been such a strong person all your life, and suddenly you're just going to surrender?"

"Who says I'm surrendering?" Nilu said, slightly peeved. "All I'm saying is that maybe living in another city for some time will help me become more . . . balanced." She almost said "mentally balanced," but the phrase evoked Jamuna Mummy, so she caught herself.

About a month after Raja moved to Dillibazar, Nilu was in Bhotahiti, about to step into a stationery shop, when she saw Maitreya in the crowd some distance away. There was no mistake about it — the same blue shirt speckled with tiny white fish, his favorite; the same dark black hair, which covered his ears, fell over his eyes; the same intense expression. He was gazing up at the cricket bats strung outside a sports store. Her heart in her throat, Nilu stared at him. She strode toward the store, his name ready on her lips. Then, for a split second a group of college girls blocked her view, and when they moved away, Maitreya had vanished. She looked up and down the crowded street, glimpsed his shirt about two hundred yards away, weaving in and out of the mass of people in Asan. She ran after him, but when she reached the crossroads, he was gone.

Neglecting her shopping, she wandered aimlessly through the city, berating herself for being so mired in grief over her son that she was beginning to see him in open daylight. Her dreams about Maitreya were so frightening that she woke up yelling. Earlier, when Raja was still with her, he'd turn on the light and ask what the matter was, and she'd cling to him, shaking.

Darkness had fallen, and she found herself in Thamel, in front of the house where Maitreya was born. The second-floor flat where they'd lived was cloaked in darkness, and the streetlamp threw light on the same old TOILET sign next to the window. Was the flat unoccupied still, after all these years? The dark made it hard to see clearly;

still, she could tell that the crumbling house hadn't been renovated. All the time Nilu and Raja had lived there, Bhairavi's mother-in-law kept mentioning how bit by bit she was going to modernize the house, use Chinese bricks to change the façade, install a bathroom on each floor.

Sounds of dinner preparations came from the first floor. The wall prevented Nilu from viewing the kitchen window, where she imagined Bhairavi was cooking, wiping her hands on her dhoti between stirring, whipping, tossing, and mixing whatever she was conjuring for her family. Bhairavi loved to cook and was constantly making new dishes that she'd then bring up to Raja and Nilu: korma, momos, biryani, stuffed okra, samosas, chana masala. "Happy stomachs make for happy families," she used to say. Right now an aroma of fried fish pierced the air. For a moment, Nilu savored the smell, pondered whether she should walk in and knock on the door. But she wasn't sure she'd have enough to say. She hadn't spoken to Bhairavi for ages now, not since Bhairavi came to offer her condolences.

Nilu caught a fume-spewing Vikram tempo to Chabel. At home she sat in the living room in the dark, her hands between her knees, looking at the floor. Soon the chants started, a small echo in the back of her mind, of people shouting slogans. The words were indistinct, low-key; someone was encouraging others to do something, to perform a momentous deed, change the course of history. She hated these voices, their muted insistence, their sanctimony.

The phone rang, startling her, dissolving the chants. It was most likely Ganga Da, so she let it ring. Then she wondered if it was Raja. She hadn't heard from him in close to three weeks now. Perhaps he needed to talk to her, perhaps he had begun to miss her. Come home, sweetie, she'd tell him. She had to tell him that she'd seen Maitreya in Bhotahiti today. In the dark she fumbled toward the phone. Her voice was hoarse as she said hello.

"Nilu?" It was Muwa.

A wave of irritation coursed through Nilu, and she put down the phone. What did Muwa want? She'd been calling over the past few weeks. The first time, Nilu had talked with her briefly, sensing all the while that Muwa wanted to ask her something, a request, a favor, but before she could do so, Nilu had hung up. Since then Muwa had been phoning every few days, and every time Nilu had heard her voice, she'd hung up.

Soon after Maitreya died, Nilu dreamt of Muwa's charred face as she burned during her funeral on the banks of the Bagmati River. Nilu woke up from the dream deeply satisfied, then chagrined that such an awful image — the cremation of her own mother — would give her pleasure. The last time she'd seen her mother was when Muwa had visited briefly to offer her condolences after Maitreya died. While Maitreya was alive, Muwa had seen her grandson only a handful of times. Once they met outside a tailor's shop where Maitreya, in nursery school then, was being fitted for his uniform. After the tailor took his measurements (Maitreya squirmed with laughter when the tailor's hands touched his armpits) and gave him a lollipop, mother and son emerged from the shop, and there was Muwa, clinging to Sumit — yes, almost dragged by her lover's arm — her eyes glazed, a contorted smile on her lips. She was wearing a sari Nilu recognized from her childhood days — so old that the colors were beginning to fade. Why was she wearing it when she had so many new saris to choose from? Because she was drugged out of her mind, that's why; the shoes she wore were garishly new, a loathsome pink color.

Muwa, barely coherent, exclaimed that she couldn't believe how much Maitreya had grown, while he sucked on his lollipop and turned his face away in shyness. He had no idea who the woman was. One of Muwa's front teeth was missing; her hair looked different, darker, richer, but slightly askew — she was wearing a wig. Had she gone bald? She appeared giddy, both in mind and body, ready to crumple to the ground if she weren't holding on to Sumit, who had aged too, with graying hair at his temples and new lines on his face. The sight of the two, together even after all these years, nauseated Nilu. Sumit was grinning and looking at Nilu with that all-too-familiar gleam in his eyes, and she felt demeaned again, as she had when she was sixteen and he first moved into the house. Nilu offered an excuse about being late for something and made her escape, dragging Maitreya, who was slightly intrigued by Muwa's questions about whether he recognized her or not. "Bring him home to see me," Muwa had called out as Nilu and Maitreya walked away.

The phone rang again.

Nilu moved to the window. Her neighbors directly across the lane, a family that had moved to the neighborhood only recently, were seated at their dining room table. The son, who was about Maitreya's age, was standing on the chair and gesturing dramatically, perhaps rehearsing for a performance. His younger sister gazed up at him, and his father, a man with a bulging stomach who always spoke to Nilu outside his gate in the morning, was smiling, nodding, occasionally saying something Nilu couldn't hear. Although Nilu couldn't see the mother, she knew the woman was there, probably also encouraging her son. The boy finished his performance, and the family clapped. The father embraced his son, his face beaming. Then he saw Nilu and folded his hands in namaste. Nilu nodded curtly and closed her curtain.

The way her neighbors — not just the family across the lane but others in the surrounding houses — gazed at her from their roofs and balconies and windows, it was clear that they sensed something had gone wrong with her marriage after her son's death. One neighbor, a nice woman two houses down, someone who'd even looked after Maitreya a few times, had asked Nilu, on the day Raja had taken some belongings away in the truck, whether everything was all right. "Everything is indeed all right," Nilu had said, and from then on only curtly smiled at the woman when she saw her. Her heart had closed to everyone around her. No wonder Raja too had moved.

Tonight would be typical of the other endless nights since Maitreya died: either Nilu would fall asleep soon after she returned home from work, only to wake up a few hours later, or she would be terrified by a dream at some point in the night, then unable to return to sleep again. She'd become used to these patterns, and even though she felt tired most of the day as she taught, she'd stopped fighting her sleeplessness. These days, especially in the afternoon, she'd resorted to assigning exercises to the students because she didn't have the strength to stand in front of the blackboard and lecture. As the students bent over their work, she'd doze off in the chair, waking when she heard the students giggle. Before, she used to devise new ways to get the students interested in the material she taught. To prepare them for the annual citywide spelling contest, she'd found jingles that would help them with problem words: Write *I* before *E* except after *C*, or when sounded like *A*, as in *neighbor* and *weigh*. The jingles were still on display on the classroom wall. A teacher last year had received a written reprimand for napping in the classroom, and Principal Thapa had delivered a stern lecture in the staff room, saying that parents didn't pay an exorbitant amount of money for their children to be taught by sleeping instructors. The accused teacher, a man close to retirement, had sat next to Nilu, shamefaced, and Nilu had pitied him.

Nilu wondered if one of these days a student would report her behavior to Principal Thapa, or if he himself would walk by her classroom and find her dozing. Although the principal had gone out of his way to be nice to Nilu since Maitreya's death, he wouldn't hesitate to put her on notice. But, Nilu thought wearily, it didn't matter—her heart was no longer in teaching. She had started moving through her class periods perfunctorily, her mind barely registering what knowledge she was imparting to the students. She couldn't conjure up the exact words she wanted, and kept saying "that thing" instead. Frequently, she had to ask them to repeat their questions. Every few days she remembered her role and tried to perk up, imbue her voice with a false enthusiasm, as she talked about history and English: how the Rana rulers built Victorian-style palaces while the public walked around in tatters or how to concoct compound and complex sentences. But the façade wouldn't last, for soon her voice would lose its energy, and a fog would envelop her mind. The students noticed her distractedness, and they whispered, or shot paper balls across the room, or made unnecessary visits to the bathroom.

Nilu's stomach was beginning to cramp, and she knew that it was hunger, so she decided to force herself to eat. In the kitchen she checked the refrigerator and found a box of Bengali sweets that Prateema had thrust into her hands a few weeks ago. She could possibly prepare rice and dal, but the thought of cooking only for herself so late at night amplified her sense of loneliness, so she settled on the sweets.

Sitting on the living room sofa with the lights on, she began to eat. At first, her throat tight, she could take only small bites. She started with the barfis, which, to her surprise, still tasted good. Soon, she began to sample the varieties of sweets in the box: laddoos, chamchams, kalakand. Her nibbles gave way to mouthfuls, and in no time she was devouring the sweets as if they were a meal. Over the next few hours her stomach would punish her for this indulgence, but for now all that mattered was the sweetness on her tongue.

In the morning when she went to the veranda to water her plants, she saw Maitreya, kneeling by the tap in the yard in his blue shirt, cupping his palm to drink the water trickling down. Something clambered up rapidly through her spine, and instinct told her to return inside, shut the door, and crawl back into bed, wake up again to a different morning. Then he was gone.

Fear remained with her as she went to Arniko Academy that day. In Bhotahiti the other day she'd wanted to run after the boy, grab him if that was possible, ask him questions about where he was, whether he was happy there, whether when he died he'd been in pain or if he'd just drifted off to sleep, whether he missed her. But today she found herself asking further questions about his appearing to her. Why was he coming to her? What did he want? Was he going to do this for the rest of her life? It frightened her, the notion of her son's ghost haunting her without her being able to shake him off.

Perhaps because of the fear, which kept her alert, Nilu found herself more energetic than usual and taught her students reasonably well that day. Then, in her last class, she turned after writing something on the blackboard, and she saw him, briefly, sitting in the back of the room, chin on hand, looking at her.

233

In the staff room, as she collected her things to go home, Prateema said, "Your face looks kind of ashen, Nilu. Are you not feeling well?"

She said she was fine. She only needed to go home and lie down.

"Let me take you to my home for dinner today," Prateema said. "That way you won't have to worry. You can just lie down on my bed."

"No, no, I don't want to give you any trouble."

"What trouble? Nonsense."

Nilu gave in. Besides, the prospect of encountering Maitreya again was making her sick.

Prateema lived in New Road, in an impressive seven-story building her grandfather had started constructing when he first came to the country in the late 1940s. The Ganguly family occupied the top two floors, and the bottom five floors were leased out to various businesses. Prateema had married, divorced, and then returned to her parents, who, even though the street had become impossibly crowded and noisy, had continued to reside in their ancestral home for sentimental reasons. Apart from summarily dismissing her previous husband as "a very bad man," Prateema didn't say much about why her marriage had collapsed. She didn't have any children.

It was nice to be high up in busy New Road, watching the traffic and the bustle below, for it took Nilu's mind off Maitreya. "When my grandfather built the first floor of this house," Prateema said, "hardly any cars used to ply through here, only pedestrians and bicycles. The street was partially paved with asphalt, for Prime Minister Juddha Shumshere Rana wanted half of it left as gravel, for his horses. When my father was growing up, he used to hang out in Bhugol Park right there"—she pointed to the west—"shelling peanuts, watching cinemagoers in Jana Sewa Hall. He told me that those days you could even see the snowy mountains to the north from Bhugol Park. Imagine that! Try seeing past your nose in New Road now, with this smog and this crowd. My grandfather didn't mind how this road rapidly filled with banks and airline offices and newspaper stands, how the noise level increased year by year. What aggravated him was the hippies, who began arriving in Nepal in the late 1960s, with their long, matted hair and their colorful vans; they passed through New Road on their way to Freak Street. I can still hear him complaining about them. 'Filthy foreigners,' he called them. 'They're going to destroy our culture,' he said. 'Their loud music and their uncouth ways.'

"I remember one time I was sitting at the window—I must have been six or seven—when I saw a couple of hippies, a man and a woman. And they were kissing each other in traffic as they crossed the street. It was a deep, penetrating kiss, and they walked very slowly. My grandfather came up behind me and slammed the window shut. I remember the fury in his eyes. When I think about it now, it's strange that he hurled some of the same labels at them that were hurled against him as a foreigner in Nepal throughout his life, especially when he first began to set up his business. Dhoti, he was called. Thieving Indian, with his conniving ways. But he was never deterred, and he was the most patriotic Nepali I ever knew. He didn't like it when my grandmother spoke Bengali to her children at home. 'Speak Nepali!' he used to exhort them. 'You're Nepalis now.'"

Even after Nilu and Prateema went inside and shut the door to the balcony, the clamor from below didn't taper off. Once in a while, a loud honk from a car would startle Nilu. "I still can't believe you can sleep with this kind of racket," Nilu said to Prateema, who responded that the only nights she didn't sleep well were during those years when she was married to her ex-husband.

"What happened in that marriage, Prateema? Are you ever going to tell me about it?"

Prateema shook her head, her face sour. "I should have followed my instinct about my sweet Nepali language tutor. Remember him? I was so much in love with him, but then I decided to listen to my parents. Big mistake."

Sensing that Prateema didn't really want to talk about her ex-husband, Nilu changed the topic to their school days. The servant brought their dinner to the room, and as they ate, they recalled incidents from St. Augustine's. After dinner they lay in bed, feeling full

235

and lazy, and that's when Nilu told Prateema about seeing Maitreya, in the market, in the yard.

Prateema put her hand to her mouth.

"I could be imagining things," Nilu said, "but today was the third time. I don't know what's happening. I don't know what he wants from me."

"Do you think it's Maitreya's ghost?"

"Don't say that, Prateema. That's what I find scary. I don't believe in such things, but there's no doubt in my mind what I saw. I'm just hoping that somehow my depression has made me hallucinate."

"I completely believe in such things, baba," Prateema said, and she told Nilu about the ghost of her aunt, which used to haunt her grandfather in Bengal before he migrated to Nepal.

"As it is, I am frightened, and you want to scare me more?"

"What's there to be frightened of?" Prateema said. "He's your son. But why is he coming to meet you? That's what's interesting. And that's what we need to find out."

"I don't want to find out anything," Nilu said, playing with a long strand of thread that had come loose from the bed sheet. "My son is gone. There's nothing in this world that'll alter that fact."

"Nilu, you have to stop thinking like that. They say that death is just a continuation of our reality, that it's not different, that we should embrace death, instead of becoming afraid of it."

"I should be going home," Nilu said, and stood, arranging her hair at the mirror.

"Listen," Prateema said. "I want to take you to meet someone."

"Who?"

"Someone who is very wise, who might be able to help you navigate this difficult period in your life."

Nilu laughed. "Prateema, who are you talking about? A psychiatrist? I just need time; I'll learn how to live with this on my own. Raja is also trying to do the same, I know."

"It's not a psychiatrist. It's a person with a great deal of knowledge."

It finally dawned on Nilu whom Prateema was talking about. She'd heard Prateema mention, in reverent terms, a soothsayer type of person, but Nilu had never paid it much attention, dismissed it as the preoccupation of a divorced woman. "Are you talking about your janne manchhe?"

"Yes, everyone calls him Lama-ji."

"How can he help me?"

"Lama-ji knows many things about this world and beyond, things you and I don't." She paused. "He's helped me understand things about my own life, especially about that man I was married to."

Nilu put her shoes on. "I'm in no mood to meet any Lama-ji Fama-ji, Prateema. This is a temporary thing. It'll go away. I just have to try harder. That's what Raja said."

"Lama-ji can also shed some light on Raja, I'm sure."

"Uffho!" Nilu said, exasperated. "Let's talk about this some other time. You're giving me a headache."

Downstairs, as she saw Nilu off, Prateema pinched her friend's cheek. "Nilu, when am I going to see a smile on the face of my best friend, huh? Every day I see you like this and my heart breaks."

Nilu walked toward the New Road Gate. All the taxis hurtling by had passengers, so she moved toward Putalisadak, where she might find one unoccupied. As she crossed the parade ground of Tundikhel, she saw Maitreya again, this time playing football with other kids his age. Dusk had already fallen in the city, and the figures chasing the ball were blurry, but it was her son, in possession of the ball, pointing his arm and shouting.

Lama-ji

YOUR SON IS UNHAPPY," Lama-ji said. He was dressed in an old suit, the shoulders and elbows of which shone, and he even had a tie around his neck. He had a broad face covered with indentations like tiny craters. He was also big boned, so that he dwarfed Nilu and Prateema as they sat in a small room in Bouddha.

Nilu still wasn't sure why she'd come. She had a hard time believing that this man, who didn't know her, would be able to tell her anything about Maitreya. But Maitreya hadn't stopped coming to her, and every time he did, she felt like crying. When Prateema told her that she'd called Lama-ji in advance and told him they were coming, Nilu had said no, she wasn't going. But Prateema had been persuasive. "If you don't like what he says, just ignore him. Okay?"

Lama-ji's phone, which sat on the floor next to him, kept ringing throughout their consultation, and he answered it each time, granting appointments, dispensing medical advice, issuing instructions regarding a construction job. Next to him stood tiny statues and framed images of deities, along with half a dozen head-clearing incense sticks embedded in a bruised apple.

First, Lama-ji asked for Maitreya's photo, which, it turned out, Prateema had conveniently brought along in her bag. It showed Maitreya standing with one leg on a soccer ball, his hand on his hip, his somber eyes looking at the camera. Nilu remembered giving the photo to Prateema some time ago. Lama-ji took the picture and put

238

it on the floor amid the gods and goddesses and began sprinkling it with red power from a box. He threw a few kernels of rice onto the floor in front of him, studied them, and said that Maitreya was unhappy.

"Saying unhappy is not enough, Lama-ji," Prateema said. "You have to say what he's unhappy about."

Smiling, Lama-ji said something to the effect that Maitreya was trapped in the netherworld, a state of transition between this life and the next one he was going to inhabit. He mentioned a word that sounded like "bardo," but Nilu couldn't be sure. "But he is unhappy with you," he said, looking at Nilu.

"Why?" Prateema asked.

This time instead of divining from his rice, Lama-ji closed his eyes in meditation. He sharply drew in his breath, then opened his eyes and said, "I can't be sure."

"Then what good is your insight, Lama-ji?" Prateema said, exasperated. "People like us come to you so you can give us answers, not confuse us with I-don't-knows."

"I'm not a god," Lama-ji said tersely. "Sometimes these spirits are not that forthcoming. Looks like your son was quite sad while he was alive too, correct? Even when he was small, he had an old man's way about him."

Nilu was a bit startled by this revelation, for that's exactly what she herself had thought of Maitreya. The boy had been such a devoted, affectionate son that during the exam season, when Nilu became overwhelmed with marking student papers, he always offered to help. "You're too young, chora," she said to him, but he wouldn't leave her side until she told him that she couldn't concentrate well with him sitting so close and observing her every move.

"Then I'll make some tea for you," he said, and he went to the gas stove, turned it on, and put some water on to boil. Then Nilu couldn't concentrate because she was worried he'd burn or scald himself, and she had to abandon her work and go into the kitchen to take over. One time when she was sick with pneumonia, he'd refused to go to school and stayed with her all day, applying cold compresses to her forehead, running to the pharmacy down the road to purchase aspirin and cough syrup, and washing the dishes while Nilu slept in the afternoon; he did all this because the servant hadn't returned from a visit to her home village. At that time Raja was in Chitwan National Park on an assignment for Nepal Yatra, and she had no one else to take care of her. Seeing her son worried about her and doing all the household chores, she nearly picked up the phone to call Ganga Da so he could come over to help. But Ganga Da had his own worries: Jamuna Mummy's mental hospital had been vandalized, traumatizing the patients, so he had to go there every day to be by his wife's side. Nilu had even contemplated calling Muwa, but then she couldn't stand the thought of being in the same room with her, smelling her booze-breath, hearing her braying voice, watching her face break into a smile to reveal her missing teeth, her overdone makeup, her wig. She didn't want to subject her son to Muwa's influence, so she never made the call. Maitreya refused to go to school even after Raja arrived home three days later. So, for his sake, Nilu had to mask her chest pains with smiles until he finally agreed to return to classes.

Lama-ji's characterization of Maitreya as possessing an old man's ways reminded Nilu of what his teachers said about him. Maitreya was so quiet and composed in class that they had wondered if everything was all right at home. "It just seems abnormal for a kid to be so disciplined, so calm about everything, when everyone around him is so intent on bedlam," one teacher had said. Maitreya displayed a brooding quality that the teacher didn't think was healthy, so she had suggested that Nilu and Raja take him to a psychiatrist to have him examined. At that time they'd squelched their anger at the teacher because Maitreya loved all his instructors, especially this one. This teacher, however, did plant a seed in Nilu, and she began to worry, observing her son to discern any signs of mental imbalance. Maitreya had large, expressive eyes, and although he loved sports, especially soccer, he preferred to stay at home and talk to his parents rather than go out with his friends to play, which was a bit odd for a boy his age. He liked to read, and spent hours on the sofa after school with his head in a book, pondering aloud why certain characters acted a certain way, which reminded Nilu of Raja's bookishness and tendency to philosophize during his jobless days in Thamel. Perhaps this serious, questioning quality was what had caused his teacher to worry.

"My son wasn't sad," Nilu said. "But he acted quite old for his age."

"He was a gentleman," Lama-ji said.

This characterization nearly brought tears to Nilu's eyes. Among his friends in the neighborhood, Maitreya was the peacemaker, often stepping in to break up quarrels and fights. He brought home sick and injured animals — a rabbit with a gaping wound on its back; a kitten weak from malnourishment — and nurtured them until they got better.

Lama-ji's eyes were fixed on Nilu's now, and eventually he said, "It's a difficult time for you. There's a man, someone who's also suffering. But you two were connected in some past life, so you have to go through each other." Lama-ji was rambling, and Nilu was losing interest. The phone rang, and Lama-ji picked it up and launched into an animated description of designs for a shrine, in a house that he was apparently having built. Nilu signaled to Prateema that they should leave.

Prateema raised her hand and said loudly, "What to do about her son, Lama-ji?"

Lama-ji produced a rudraksha bead from somewhere in his pocket, circled it in front of the deities while carrying on with his construction talk, then handed it to Nilu. "Keep this on your person," he told her. "It'll help you, in the long term."

Nilu slipped the bead into her bag as both she and Prateema stood. Prateema placed a twenty-rupee note in front of Lama-ji, but he barely looked at it as he bid them goodbye.

Outside, Prateema apologized. "He is building his first house, so he's quite preoccupied these days."

They walked to Chabel, where Prateema caught a taxi to New Road. As Nilu entered her house, she thought about what Lama-ji had said about Raja—she was sure it was Raja: who else did she have?—that they were connected in a past life. That's what Nilu too used to think when she followed him from St. Augustine's to the Jagadamba School. But now their connection forged in this life, let alone a past one, was turning out to be tenuous. "You have to go through each other," Lama-ji had said. What a concept! Go through each other. And come out all bruised and battered on the other side? She shook her head. She should have known better than to be persuaded to visit someone like Lama-ji. These charlatans were adept at playing with people's minds.

A Visit to Muwa

As if Maitreya's visits weren't enough, Muwa also kept phoning Nilu. One day she even came to the house, shouting Nilu's name as she banged on the door. "Come on, I know you're in. Open the door! I need to talk to you." Then, in a slightly lower voice, "Something has come up, chhori. I need your help."

Inside, Nilu held her breath. Was Muwa in some kind of trouble? She fought the urge to open the door. Muwa never needed Nilu before; she didn't need her now.

Muwa had visited the Chabel house twice, once after Maitreya died and once before that, while Maitreya was alive. That first time Nilu had come home to find Muwa sitting inside on the sofa with Maitreya, who had returned from school about an hour before Nilu did and let himself in with his key. Nilu was struck by how comfortable her five-year-old boy was with his grandmother, whom he didn't know. They were facing each other, and he was reading to her; she listened to him with her head cocked. There was a yellow pallor to Muwa's skin. Her jaw had gone slightly crooked, as though she had just had some dental work performed. Add to that her jet-black wig and her dark mascara, and she looked ghoulish.

When he saw Nilu, Maitreya said excitedly, "Muwa, grandmother, has come for a visit. Had you known she was coming?"

Of course Nilu hadn't, and she attempted a smile at Muwa.

"Nilu, it has been a long time."

Nilu couldn't speak. She nodded, then turned to her son and smiled. "How was school, son?"

For the next few moments Nilu focused on Maitreya, and Muwa watched them interact. "What a beautiful boy," Muwa said, distracting Maitreya, who then turned to her and asked her why she didn't come to visit more often. There was a knock on the door, and Nilu hoped that it was Raja, arriving home from the office earlier than usual. But it was Maitreya's friend, wanting him to come out and play soccer. Maitreya looked at his grandmother, who asked him whether he enjoyed playing that sport, and Maitreya nodded. "Then you should go," Muwa told him. "I need to talk to your mother anyway."

After Maitreya reluctantly left, Nilu felt obligated to ask Muwa whether she wanted tea, and Muwa fished out a small bottle from her bag, opened the cap, and said, "Just give me half a glass of water." Slowly Nilu went to the kitchen and brought her some water. Muwa poured her whiskey or rum or whatever it was into the glass, then took a sip and closed her eyes.

"Still the same, eh, Muwa?" Nilu asked.

"At this age I can't change my habits."

"So, what made you remember us? Remember me, I should say? Your grandson you don't even know."

"You haven't given me the opportunity."

"Who has stopped you from coming here?"

"I haven't been invited."

"You're my mother. You need an invitation?"

"Nilu, I haven't come here to squabble with you."

"Then what have you come here for?"

Muwa downed the contents of her glass, then handed it to Nilu, signaling that she wanted more. After Nilu brought her more water, she refilled her glass, took a sip, and said, "I need for you to lend me some money."

"Me lending money to you? Whatever happened to all the money you had?"

"That money is still there, but I can't use it right now. That's why I have come to you."

Nilu shook her head in confusion. "I don't know what you're saying, Muwa. You ought to have at least a few lakhs in the bank, if not more. What happened to all that money?"

"It's still there, I tell you," Muwa said.

"Then use it. Why come to me? You know how much Raja and I make."

"I'm just talking about a few thousand rupees, Nilu. It's become really difficult for me."

"How much?"

"About ten."

"What do you need it for?"

"Some expenses have come up. I can't reveal everything to you."

"Sumit still with you?"

Muwa nodded. She pulled a cigarette from her bag and lit it, her hand trembling. She took a deep drag and said, "He takes care of me."

"I don't have ten thousand. The maximum I can give you right now is four."

"I've come to you after so many years. Don't disappoint me like this, Nilu."

"And you wouldn't have come here, had you not needed money," Nilu replied.

She went into her bedroom, pulled open the drawer where she kept some cash, counted out five thousand rupees, and took the money back to Muwa. "Here," she said. "Now you can leave. I don't want Maitreya seeing you smoke."

"I'll snuff it out when he comes in," she said. She put the money in her bag, then asked about Raja, where he worked now. But when Nilu began answering, Muwa dug into her bag, looking for something, which turned out to be a pill; she popped it into her mouth, then washed it down with her drink. Soon she stood and said she'd better be going; otherwise Sumit would wonder where she had gone.

Nilu saw her to the door and asked, "And what does he do these days? Doesn't he ever work?"

Muwa took her time putting on her sandal. "He used to work, but it's been hard for him. His mother died a couple of years ago. He's been heartbroken since then."

Maitreya was playing soccer in the yard. He shouted, "Grandma, I'll come to visit you in your house."

"Yes, yes," Muwa said, then held out her palm as if blessing him. She faltered on the steps and would have tumbled, had Nilu not caught her. Muwa grinned, revealing her yellowed teeth and gums. "I nearly broke my hip some time ago," she muttered. At the gate she told Nilu, "Sometimes you can come and visit me, can't you? We live in the same city, but you treat me like a stranger."

"Okay, I'll come," Nilu said.

Later during dinner she told Raja about Muwa's visit.

"That's really odd," he said. "I wonder if she and Sumit have depleted her bank account."

"But how can they spend lakhs and lakhs of money so swiftly? I don't understand. Unless he's swindling her."

Raja swallowed, then said, "I should have told you this before, but I didn't because I thought you'd be upset. I saw them together at the casino about a year ago." Raja had gone to the casino at Hotel Everest to write a special feature for his magazine; there, he'd seen Muwa and Sumit, who were too drunk to notice him. As Raja interviewed the manager and workers and some players, he kept an eye on them. They were gambling quite heavily, from what he could gather. One of the waiters told him that the two were regulars and over the months had lost a lot of money. "But they keep coming back, the waiter informed me," Raja said.

Maitreya was quietly listening to their conversation, but Nilu didn't care that he was learning these things about his grandmother. She hadn't spoken to him a great deal about Muwa and once had even told him that Muwa wasn't much of a mother. Apparently Maitreya had pondered that for days, for one day he suddenly asked her whether she wished she had had a different mother. Taken aback,

Nilu hadn't known how to respond. Hesitantly, she'd said that she wouldn't go that far, for a mother was a mother, a notion she herself didn't find convincing. "Muwa could have been a better mother had she tried, that's all I'm saying."

After mulling over her answer, Maitreya asked, "But no one is perfect, isn't that right? Isn't that what you told me?"

She smoothed his hair and said, "Of course you're right. Maybe I expect too much of her." She had wondered, then, if she was judging Muwa a bit harshly, but she knew she wasn't when she recalled her days at Nilu Nikunj before she went searching for Raja in Lainchour. No, she could not accept Muwa back into her life again, no matter what Maitreya thought. He was too young to understand; give him a few years. She just had to make sure she avoided speaking about Muwa to him.

On second thought, the news of Muwa and Sumit's frequenting the casinos didn't surprise Nilu. It seemed like a natural extension of their debauchery. What was surprising was how quickly Muwa had managed to deplete her money. As far as Nilu knew, the sale of the travel agency after her father's death had brought Muwa lakhs of rupees, along with the prime property of Nilu Nikunj and several plots of land, as well as investments in factories around the country. Just the bank account itself, and the interest it accrued, would have been enough to support a lavish lifestyle, including pandering to Sumit's whims. If Muwa needed to pester Nilu for a few thousand rupees, then where had all that money gone?

That night Nilu stayed awake for a long time, remembering her childhood—the big, empty house, Sumit's lecherous eyes, Muwa's lack of interest in what was happening at St. Augustine's. Next to her lay her son. Maitreya had his own bed in the corner, but he preferred to sleep with his parents, and excepting those nights when Raja and Nilu felt amorous, they let the boy slide in between them. Tonight, as usual, Maitreya's face was buried deep in the pillow, his favorite way to sleep. Many times in the night Nilu would gently push him so his nose would get some air, but within minutes he'd be back in the same position again. Next to Maitreya was Raja, who used his hands as a pillow when he slept, his knees pulled high up, close to his belly.

Maitreya would end up not getting a single paisa of the property that Nilu's father had accumulated—this thought struck her that night. She hated it. When she gave birth to Maitreya, it had briefly occurred to her that her son, if Muwa allowed, could inherit a significant amount of money. It was pure and simple greed, albeit only for Maitreya, not for herself. But after Muwa visited them in Thamel to see her newborn grandson, Nilu had vowed that she'd have nothing to do with Muwa's money. And now, hearing that Muwa was squandering her wealth playing flush and kitty and roulette and whatever else they played in the casinos, that old thought returned to her. Hadn't it crossed Muwa's mind that family properties were passed down from one generation to the next? Idiot—Nilu chastised herself. She herself was making a decent income; so was Raja. Maitreya was attending a good school. They had enough to eat, to buy decent clothes, to indulge themselves at restaurants now and then. Why was she grasping for something that would not make her and her family happy? What was it that Raja theatrically used to recite to his imaginary street audience in Thamel, those famous lines from Devkota? Yes: "Eat greens and nettles / with a heart full of bliss—/ now that's true happiness."

Repeating those words like a mantra, Nilu had tried to make herself sleep that night. Eat greens and nettles, now that's true happiness.

Nilu's phone didn't stop ringing. She unplugged it, then reconnected it because she didn't want to miss Raja's call if he wanted to talk. Then, one day when she answered the phone and Muwa said, "Nilu, please, don't put down the phone," she didn't have the heart to cut her off.

"What do you want?"

Muwa was weeping. "Was I such a bad mother to you? Am I so bad that you can't even speak a word to me?" A wave of emotion washed through Nilu; then she reminded herself that even as she said those things, Muwa tripped over her words. How much of this was simply the alcohol talking?

Still, she didn't hang up, and asked, "Why have you been calling me so much? What is the matter?" Her anger toward Muwa had lasted only for an instant; now she felt resignation, apathy, numbness.

"I need to see you, talk to you."

"Speak."

"No, in person. I can't do it over the phone."

"You can come over this afternoon."

"Nilu, I can't. I sprained my ankle yesterday. It's hurting badly. Yesterday I was even considering going to the hospital to make sure it's not broken. It's swollen, and I can hardly walk."

Nilu felt sorry for her. "Where's . . . he?"

A pause. Something was amiss. "He's not here. Can you come this afternoon, Nilu?"

Nilu said that she'd be there at three.

At the opening of the alley leading to Nilu Nikunj, Kancha, now old and wizened, still sat inside his soda shop. Nilu was just going to pass by him, but he peered at her from the side window and said, "Looks like Nilu Nani. Am I right?"

Nilu nodded and asked how he was doing. He said his bones were getting creakier. He was so sad to hear about her son's death. "Coming to visit your mother?" he asked.

She nodded.

"I don't know what's happening in that house in there," he said, pointing toward Nilu Nikunj. He leaned closer. "I don't see Sumit around these days. Has he left?"

"I haven't been here in ages, Kancha Dai, so how would I know?"

Kancha looked sad. "What kind of a mother and daughter are you two? Living in the same city but not visiting each other. *Tch, tch.*"

Nilu bid him goodbye and moved on. The last time she was here was when she'd secretly brought baby Maitreya to meet Kaki. Since then, she had deliberately avoided this area, often taking streets that bypassed Jamal, or, if she had to come to this vicinity to go to a bank or a bookstore, walking on the other side of the street so that she would not even pass close to the soda shop where Kancha could spot her. Years ago, within days of Muwa's visiting Nilu and Raja in Thamel to see their newborn, Nilu was walking past Nilu Nikunj on the other side of the street when she spotted Kaki, tapping her cane on the ground by her feet, in the process of exiting the alley near Kancha's shop. Kancha said something to Kaki, and briefly, Kaki turned toward him and answered. But their voices were smothered by the sounds of traffic before they could reach Nilu, who hid as best she could behind a lamppost. She watched Kaki emerge onto the sidewalk, where she sniffed the air, it seemed, to orient herself to her surroundings. Then Kaki turned to her left and began walking, tap-tapping the cane. Her progress was slow, and she was jostled and bumped by other pedestrians. Nilu knew she should have cut through the traffic to reach Kaki and aid her in finding her destination. But talking to Kaki would mean listening to her lamentations about Raja. By then Kaki knew that the two had married, but because Nilu hadn't been to Nilu Nikunj, she had no way of gauging how Kaki felt about their being together; and she had to wonder why Nilu hadn't brought Raja to see her. Kaki would also expect her to ask after Muwa, which Nilu had no desire to do; she still had a sour taste in her mouth after Muwa's visit. Besides — and this prevented Nilu more than anything from approaching Kaki — she seemed to be on a mission. Despite her slow progress, there was determination in the way she trudged along, undeterred by the shoves from other pedestrians.

Later Nilu would learn, from Ramkrishan, that that day Kaki had gone to visit her son and his wife, after nearly two decades, and had returned disappointed. "Was she expecting something from her son?" Nilu had asked Ramkrishan, whom she'd run into in the vegetable market of Asan, where he was inspecting a long white radish, holding it in his slightly trembling hands. His back was a little bit hunched, but when he haggled with the farmer, his voice was as firm as ever.

Nilu stood next to him, watching him for a moment before she called his name. He turned, squinted, exclaimed in pleasure, and threw the radish back into the basket, which prompted the farmer to raise his hand in exasperation. Ramkrishan asked how Nilu was, and the baby. When Nilu inquired after Kaki, saying that she'd seen her braving the crowd the other day, Ramkrishan shook his head, and his eyes began to tear up. "All she thinks of is Raja. There's nothing else in her mind." After her visit to her son's house, Ramkrishan told Nilu, Kaki had said nothing to him for a few days. One day Ramkrishan casually asked her whether she'd managed to see her son. Kaki didn't respond, and Ramkrishan was thinking that it'd probably be another day or two before Kaki would speak to him when she said, "My grandson is a fine boy, but I feel nothing for him, do you hear me, Ramkrishan Dai? He called me grandma, but there is nothing in my heart that I can offer him. And you know why? Because every day, whatever love I have in here" — she jabbed a wrinkled, knotted finger at her chest — "I save it for Raja, in case he comes back to me."

Now it was Nilu who, standing amid the swarm of the market, fought back tears. "I don't know, Ramkrishan Dai. I've asked Raja many times, but his heart is not in it. I'll ask him again, but after all these years, I think he's hesitant to reopen an old wound."

On the way to Thamel, however, an idea came to Nilu. At home she didn't tell Raja that she'd run into Ramkrishan or what he had said about Kaki. She hadn't told Raja about watching Kaki negotiate the sidewalk traffic the other day. It was useless with him — her pleading with him to go see Kaki had fallen on deaf ears, and she no longer wanted to push him toward it. There will come a time, she told herself, when Raja might feel a prick of conscience, and he'll go to Kaki of his own free will — but he couldn't wait forever. Kaki's health had continued to deteriorate.

The next Saturday, the day before Nilu went back to teaching after maternity leave, she carried baby Maitreya with her to Jamal. He was only a few months old, and she'd slipped a cowboy hat on his round head to ward off the winter chill. He was wearing a pair of blue corduroy overalls, and he smiled and gurgled at her, threads of saliva hanging down his chin. Raja, already at the bookstore, didn't know that she'd taken Maitreya out.

At Nilu Nikunj's gate Nilu hesitated. She had no desire to see Muwa, nor to expose Maitreya to an inadequate grandmother, but she would have to take that risk if she was to see Kaki. Gently, she lowered the latch and slipped in. Crossing the yard, she glanced at Muwa's bedroom balcony. But her curtains were drawn, just as they had been when Nilu was growing up. From the veranda she peeked in and presently saw Ramkrishan Dai inside, moving toward the kitchen. She knocked on the door, softly, and he turned and came to open it. She put her finger to her lips and whispered to him that she had come to see Kaki. Ramkrishan's face lit up at the sight of Maitreya, who had fallen asleep. She passed Maitreya to Ramkrishan and went to the kitchen. Kaki was curled up in a corner. Close up, her face was a landscape of deep wrinkles. Her body too seemed to have shrunk to half its former size. Nilu called her, but Kaki seemed to be in another land. A thread of drool snaked its way out of the side of her mouth. "Kaki!" Nilu whispered loudly. Kaki groaned, then, appearing to sense that someone was calling her, tried to sit up. Stroking her forehead, Nilu said, "It's me, Nilu. I've brought someone with me I think you'd be pleased to meet."

"Who?" Kaki said, almost querulously. Her face became alert, and she sat up. "Raja?" Kaki cried, a sound like that of a bird in the wilderness.

Ramkrishan passed Maitreya to Nilu. "It's not Raja," Nilu said. "It's his little son, Maitreya."

Kaki's face fell, and Nilu regretted not having announced right away whom she'd brought.

"Raja hoina?" Kaki asked, looking defeated.

Nilu took Kaki's gnarled and leathery fingers and placed them on Maitreya's forehead. "He has Raja's face, Kaki. Feel him carefully." Slowly Kaki began to explore the baby's face, as soft whimpers escaped her mouth.

· · ·

At the gate to her childhood home Nilu paused. Vines and creepers had strangled its façade. The house looked smaller, more weathered than what she remembered from a few years ago. She found the gate unlocked, and went in. The yard was littered with newspapers and empty Ruslan vodka bottles. The garden was overgrown, with wilted and dying flowers and tall weeds. Had Ramkrishan given up on it? On the veranda the chairs were toppled, most likely by the recent storm. She nearly stepped in what looked like a pool of oil. She wondered if Ramkrishan had taken ill. He must have been feeling lonely since Kaki's death.

When, long ago, she watched Kaki's quivering fingers explore Maitreya's face, Nilu had known that she would not live for long. Kaki was breathing heavily as she ran her palm over baby Maitreya's head. She had barely any flesh left on her bones. But more than anything, Nilu knew, her spirit was giving way. Maitreya's presence might have revived it for a short while, but then Kaki clearly wanted her Raja, and no one else could replace him. It was the faithful Ramkrishan who came knocking at the Thamel flat to deliver the news one morning as Nilu was getting ready to go to Arniko Academy. Raja had already left to open the bookstore, and Maitreya had just woken up and was being entertained by the servant girl. "She passed away peacefully," Ramkrishan told her, "in the middle of the night." Nilu wanted to go see Kaki, but Ramkrishan said that her son had already taken her to the ghat for her cremation. All day at school, Nilu's mind dwelt on the woman who'd nurtured Raja when no one else would, not even the old man who'd found him in the bushes of Tundikhel. She wondered how Raja would react when she delivered the news of Kaki's death, though she already knew that it would not sadden him, not make him pause. If anything, it might remind him again of the loss of his real mother. So, in the evening when she reached home, she told him nothing. When he commented on how quiet she was, she said that the teaching that day had tired her, and she turned her attention to Maitreya.

The next morning she left the house a bit early and went all the way to the Swayambhunath Temple, where, with the help of a priest, she lit a hundred thousand wicker lamps in Kaki's memory.

"She's one of your own children, Lord Buddha," Nilu prayed, as she watched the flames flicker in the wind. "She embodied your teaching of compassion — she gave herself completely to raise an orphan boy. Yet she died thirsting for his love. Please grant her peace."

Nilu pushed the button for the bell, but nothing sounded. She pushed it again, then knocked, at first gently, then louder. Soon footsteps sounded on the stairs, and after a moment Muwa opened the door. She wasn't wearing her wig, and Nilu saw that she was virtually bald, with only small tufts of hair remaining on her scalp; she looked like a cancer patient, which shocked Nilu. She inhaled sharply to detect the familiar smell of alcohol, but the air was fresh. Had Muwa given up drinking? Nilu refused to believe it.

Inside, the house was as disheveled as the yard and the garden. Two towels lay in the hallway that led to the kitchen. Nilu waited for Ramkrishan to come, but he didn't. "Let's go to my room," Muwa said, and walked up the stairs, holding the railing. She was limping a bit, which meant that she hadn't lied about her ankle. Nilu followed. Upstairs too, in the open hallway that overlooked the front door below, she spotted dirt, blotches on the floor where a drink had been spilled, and curls of dust. "Where is Ramkrishan Dai?" she finally asked Muwa.

"He died a couple of months ago."

"He died?" Nilu froze. She wished Muwa had prepared her for this. She had expected, she realized with sadness, that Ramkrishan would be part of the household forever; during this visit in particular she had hoped his presence to cushion herself against Muwa.

"He died during the night," Muwa said, pushing open the door to her room. "In the evening he'd brought me a glass of warm milk before he went to sleep. Then in the morning I kept calling and he didn't come, and when I went to check on him in the shack he wasn't breathing." Muwa sounded slightly piqued, as though she had expected Ramkrishan to warn her in advance about his death.

Muwa's room was dark and reeked of cigarette smoke, as usual. Cobwebs hung from the ceiling corners. All the chairs were piled high with unwashed clothes, which gave off a disagreeable smell. There was no place to sit except on Muwa's bed, and the sheets there looked unwashed, so Nilu remained standing.

"Who took his body to the funeral?"

Muwa sat on her bed, wincing as she adjusted her leg. She lit a cigarette and took a sip from a glass by her bedside table. "He had a nephew somewhere in the city. I found his number and called them. At first he wanted me to take care of Ramkrishan's funeral. He said that his uncle devoted his life to me, and that was the least I could do. Can you believe it? I don't know where these servant people get their nerve these days. It's all because of the politicians, especially these communists. They're always inciting them to ask for their rights. Now, where would I go arranging for his corpse to be burned? So I told the nephew no. 'If you don't come to fetch your uncle's corpse, he's going to rot in this house.'"

"Well, did you at least give him some money?"

Muwa eyed Nilu. "And where would I get money? Do I have a steady supply of it? I gave his nephew about five thousand, that's all. I can't live my life just handing people money left and right."

"I don't understand," Nilu said. "Where has all your money gone?" Then she recalled what Muwa had said about Sumit over the phone. "Where is Sumit? Is he not with you anymore?"

"He is!" Muwa snapped. "Where would he go, poor man. He's just gone away for a few days." The ash on her cigarette end was growing longer, and then it dropped. But Muwa was looking at Nilu, her eyes cloudy and drunk.

"Why have you let the house get to this state? Didn't you hire anyone after Ramkrishan Dai died?"

Muwa lay back on the bed, took a deep drag, blew out the smoke, and closed her eyes.

"Muwa? Why did you call me here if you are just going to lie down there? I'll go."

"Don't go, Nilu," Muwa said. "Can't you just stay here with me, for a few minutes?"

Reluctantly, Nilu sat next to her. Muwa opened her eyes and took Nilu's hand. "I've made some mistakes." The cigarette in her fingers had burnt itself out. "I've lost everything."

The news didn't surprise Nilu. "It's your money," she said. "You can do whatever you want with it. Gambling?"

Muwa nodded. "I don't even remember how I got into it. Sumit loves to play flush and kitty, and suddenly we were going every day."

"All of our . . . your property in the villages is gone?"

"Yes, everything is gone, except for this house." She looked pleadingly at her daughter. "Nilu, don't get angry with me, okay? I really don't know what happened."

"Why should I get angry?" Nilu said. "You've always been like this. It's not a surprise to me." She paused. "Why did you call me here?"

"I want to transfer this house to Sumit's name."

Nilu stared at her mother, then gave a short laugh. "Then do it. Why ask me?"

"You're my daughter," Muwa said. "I haven't kept anything for you to inherit, and I thought, this is the house where you grew up. Maybe you're attached to it, maybe I need to ask your permission first."

"My son is dead, and you think I would be worried about this stupid house?" Nilu said, unable to mask her contempt. "Give it to whoever you like. I don't need anything from you."

Raja's Flat

S HE BEGAN TO HEAR Maitreya's voice inside the house. "Ma, do you think it will rain today?" he said from a corner of the room. As she read on the sofa, he whispered into her ear, "Will you read to me, Ma?" It was as if he was teasing her, even provoking her.

One Saturday morning she was peeking through the curtains at the neighbor's house, where the son was once again performing for the family, when she heard a rustling sound behind her. She closed her eyes and prayed. But the sound continued, and when she turned to look, a boy's shadow flitted across the wall and went into the bedroom. "Maitreya!" she shouted, as though scolding her son. She strode to the bedroom, and of course there was no one there. "Stop this!" she said to the air. Then, realizing how ridiculous she sounded, she grabbed her bag, and not caring that she was dressed in her house dhoti, left the place.

She emerged onto the main street of Chabel, not knowing where she was going. A minibus hurtled toward her from Bouddha, the conductor leaning out of the back door, yelling, "La, la, Baneswor, Dillibazar, Ratna Park, la, la, la." Instinctively she raised her hand, the bus screeched to a halt, and she was inside. She had to find Raja. She had to talk to him, tell him what was happening to her. Was she losing her mind? Was that why he had left her?

As the minibus lurched forward, she held the rubber strap hanging from the ceiling. Bodies pressed against her. A couple of hands, men's, lingered briefly on her thigh. These men hadn't changed, the buses were as rickety as ever, and hundreds of girls and women were still being pawed, across the country, every day like this. But she had changed. It didn't matter to her anymore what these men did, the discomfort she felt on her thighs, her crotch, her bottom. Gone were the days of becoming offended, feeling dirty and violated when she was touched and fondled, or when young men in the streets hurled lewd remarks.

The bus dumped her in Dillibazar, and she quickly maneuvered through the dense crowd of this neighborhood and approached the building where she knew he lived. It was a nondescript three-story building—its yellow paint peeling off in spots, a satellite dish dutifully perched on the roof—becoming dwarfed by tall buildings, some still under construction. He doesn't get enough sunshine, she thought. But then, she herself kept her own curtains closed most of the time.

She hesitated at the gate. Other people lived here, and she didn't want them watching her from their windows when the gate clanked open. You are his wife, not his lover, so you don't need to be secretive, she told herself. But this self-assurance also gave her pause. It'd been close to three months since Raja had left—what was their status now? She remembered when they first got married and moved to Thamel, they'd mocked their newly married state. "Hey, hubby," she'd teased him. "Hubba, bubba!" He'd called her dulahi and demanded, as he stood from the chair where he'd been sitting, that she touch his feet like a demure, husband-fearing bride. She knelt before him, suggesting she was indeed going to place her head on his feet to receive his blessing, then quickly clasped his ankles and yanked them toward her, making him fall. His back struck the chair, which slammed against the window. Swooning in pain he hopped around the room, and, terrified, she followed him, attempting to lift his shirt to check for a bruise. He was laughing and wailing at the same time, and she saw that a horizontal welt had appeared on his lower back.

"It hurts?" she asked.

"Of course it does. Why did you do it?"

When she protested that he'd started the whole thing with his ridiculous touch-my-feet business, with a stern face he said, "Bad wifey. Now, even though I'm in pain, I'll have to fuck you. You give me no choice." And he'd begun to slowly take off his clothes in the manner of a reluctant striptease, and she kept watching him with laughing eyes until he was down to his underwear.

"Raja, the window is open," she said, but he merely glanced at it with a pained expression and flung his underwear away. The neighbors across the street had a clear view, so Nilu rushed to the window and closed it.

"What do you say, wifey? Some love or no love?" He was completely naked now, his arms by his side, his penis limp but in the process of rising, his face twisted in pain, part real, part exaggerated.

She went to him, put her hand on his penis, and said, "Who needs more love, this little man or you?"

Later, she had him lie on his stomach and rubbed some Amrutanjan on his back, blowing on the peeled skin as she did so, and he murmured to himself and said, "Mmmm, delicious."

The latch on the gate to Raja's building did clang loudly, and figures did appear at the windows, but Nilu strode in, looking straight ahead. The second floor, that's where she recalled Raja saying he lived. She ought to have phoned him before visiting, so he wouldn't be surprised, as he certainly would be now. She also remembered that he had never invited her over. At no point in their phone conversations, which had been dwindling anyway, had he suggested that she come to see where he lived. This in itself should have warned her to turn back. Nilu was on alien territory. Even more alien than how Lainchour had seemed when she had tracked down Raja in Birey Dai's shop. That time at least she had been propelled by fond memories of their childhood together in Nilu Nikunj. Today the air was heavy with death and estrangement and hurt.

But, despite everything, Raja was the only one with whom she could discuss Maitreya, so she climbed the staircase and knocked at the first door she came upon on the second floor. She heard a bit of a scrambling inside, some fervent whispers, before Raja's voice floated out, tentatively, querulously. "Who's there?"

Nilu stopped breathing, stood still. Raja asked again who it was, this time louder, more demanding, and she felt compelled to respond, "It's me. Nilu."

From the floor above, a middle-aged woman descended the stairs, arms crossed at her chest to effect a casual demeanor. Once she reached Nilu, she looked her up and down, then continued down the stairs, her slippers slapping. Raja's door opened, only a few inches, and he peered out. He was wearing his undershirt, and tufts of chest hair poked out. "Nilu?" he said. "What a surprise." He gave her a nervous smile.

"I was passing through." She lied. "And I thought—"

"One minute, okay?" he said. "I'll be right out." He shut the door and she was left standing; she could hear the footsteps of the middle-aged woman beginning to ascend the stairs. From inside Raja's door rose the high-pitched voice of a woman, a young woman: "Now?" A hand clamped over a mouth—Nilu could almost visualize it—then voices muffled, panicky, and once again silence.

The door opened, and Raja slipped out, shutting it behind him. He wore a shirt now, a bright red-and-white one that Nilu remembered purchasing for him the day she received a bonus from the school, a year before Maitreya died. "Let's go out," Raja said, taking her by the arm and leading her downstairs.

Nilu allowed herself to be led down, through the yard, out of the gate, and into the dusty alley, where Raja said, "I was inside all day, cramped, suffocated. That's why I wanted to come out." She nodded. The middle-aged woman was now on the roof, leaning against the balustrade, looking toward the horizon. "Shall we walk around to get some fresh air?" he asked, and she nodded, again, unable to think coherently.

As soon as they entered the main thoroughfare of Dillibazar they were assaulted by the loud honks of trucks and fumes from passing taxis and old chug-along vehicles. They moved quickly, almost frantically, as they turned right toward Gyaneswor. Apart from a few mutterings about the crowd and the black smoke, they didn't say anything substantial—how could they, walking so fast, weaving through pedestrians? The crowd only seemed to thicken as they moved, and because of some construction up ahead, the little walking space on the street had completely vanished. Occasionally a three-wheeler or a motorcycle darted closely past Nilu, almost touching her because she was closer to the street. Finally irritation made her ask, "Where are we going, Raja?"

"Maybe the street opens up a bit farther down," he said, but she simply stopped walking and shook her head, kept shaking it. If she cried, she was going to make a fool of herself in public.

"Well, what do you want to do?" he asked, resentfully. "It's not my fault that there's no breathing space here."

"I shouldn't have come," she said, looking straight ahead.

"That's not what I mean," he said. "You came—that's good. I was just thinking about you this morning."

She didn't believe him. She didn't trust him, couldn't anymore. It occurred to her—with such force that she nearly stumbled—that the woman inside his flat was someone he'd either met in Delhi or who'd accompanied him there. His reason for wanting to move out after returning from that trip was more than a rift with his wife—he'd actually found someone else. The power of this realization made the world go completely dark for a split second, before she could see again—the people swarming like flies, the heat rising off the asphalt, the *ding-ding-ding* of construction, the dust swirling and smothering the air.

"Let's just find a place to sit. Right here—how about this?" In front of them was a grungy-looking restaurant, with a stained curtain partly open to reveal chairs and tables inside. The proprietor, who had a huge belly, sat on a platform next to the door, where pakoras and other fritters simmered in a vat filled with thick oil. It didn't matter how sickening the place was; she wanted to sit, exchange some words, then head home. Get it over with.

"Here?" Raja pointed toward the proprietor, who was watching them.

"Yes," she said, then parted the curtain and walked into the eatery, which was empty. He followed her.

A young boy in blue shorts and a vest came to take their order. "Two cups of tea," Raja told him, and after the boy left, he looked at Nilu defiantly, suggesting that since they had escaped the prying eyes of his slipper-slapping neighbor and the deafening noise outside, he could handle what she was going to say. But when she said nothing, merely met his eyes and looked away, his demeanor softened and he said, "I still can't believe that you came to see me here."

"Should I not have?" she asked.

"What kind of a question is that?"

"I'm just asking."

"Of course you should have."

The young boy slapped two glasses of tea on their table. He asked them whether they wanted snacks, and they both shook their head. They watched the boy as he went back to the proprietor, and through the gap in the curtain, they saw him kneel and begin washing dishes in a bucket of water.

"That boy is Maitreya's age," she said in an accusatory tone.

Raja observed the boy, took a sip of his tea, and made a face. "How are you, Nilu? We haven't talked in a long time."

"Well, looks like you've been keeping yourself busy," she said.

Oh, stop acting like a spurned wife now, she chided herself. Let him have ten women in his room if he wants. He can go cavorting with them in the gardens of Godavari. He can give them all fancy necklaces and rings. He can present them with red-red-roses, whose smell they'll inhale, and they'll ooh and aah and gaze at him lovingly. He was still a handsome man, notwithstanding how gaunt he'd become recently. The soft, scraggly beard on his chin made him even more desirable. It should be no surprise that women were falling for him.

"It's not what you think," he said with a sigh.

"What?"

"What you saw in the flat."

She laughed, a little too loudly. "What did I see in the flat? You didn't even open the door."

He splayed his palms and looked at them. "She's Amit's niece. You know, Amit from Nepal Yatra. She comes to visit me every now and then. Sometimes she wants help with her English vocabulary."

"*You're* teaching her English?"

He appeared hurt. "I do write for an English magazine, and I'm pretty good, even though I didn't go to a boarding school, like some people."

"I shouldn't have come without a warning," she said. "Should've have given you time to . . . prepare yourself."

"It's nothing like that, I'm telling you," he said, quite loudly. He quickly flared with anger toward her; absence hadn't changed that. Did he act this way with that woman in his flat too? Did he speak sharply to her?

"Then what is it like?" she said. "Did you meet her in Delhi?"

"No, I didn't meet her there. But she was also in Delhi."

"Ah."

"Amit had taken her there at his own expense, for sightseeing." He seemed to have reconsidered why he'd need to explain anything to her, for he said, "Look, seeing you after so long, I don't want to spend time here talking about Jaya, who is just a friend, nothing more, nothing less."

"A young woman spending the day in the flat of a married man. I mean, you and I are still husband and wife, aren't we? Or has that changed?"

He began to rub his temples.

"Or has that changed?"

"It hasn't changed," he said, not looking at her.

"At least you can meet my eyes when you say it."

But he didn't, and to her that was proof that he had moved on. "I see."

He snapped his head up. "Well, it has changed somewhat, hasn't it? Otherwise we wouldn't be living separately, Nilu."

"It was not my idea."

They were aware of the boy, who had drifted in at some point and was standing in the corner, watching them.

"But you drove me —" He stopped himself. "Look, I would have gone mad had I still been in the Chabel house. And, given how we're behaving today, I think we need some more time apart."

She didn't like how she felt — jealous, which made her sarcastic — but her ears were still ringing with that woman's querulous voice. Nilu had come to talk about how she was seeing the ghost of Maitreya, thinking that Raja would commiserate with her, hold her hand, offer suggestions. But here they were, bickering and wrangling.

The waiter boy was still standing, observing them with his large eyes, but strangely, his presence wasn't bothersome or intrusive. He's my witness — this thought floated through Nilu's mind. Raja combed his hair with his fingers. The silence grew, and deepened, and she looked down at her hands, and he looked at a stained poster on the wall, of Krishna playing his flute, his sixteen hundred maids frolicking in the background. Outside, the traffic rumbled; then it was the clouds that rumbled; and it began to rain. The proprietor called the boy in a loving voice. She wondered if the young woman — what had he said her name was? Jayanti? Jaya? — was waiting for him in the flat. If she was, he didn't show signs of impatience.

"Nilu," Raja said quietly. "Trust me, please. There's nothing between me and Jaya. These past few months have been really hard for me, being away from you."

"Do you know something?" It came out before she could stop herself. "The reason I came to visit you was because I've started seeing Maitreya. In person. In the market, in the yard."

He gazed at her quietly. Finally he said, "I don't know what to do. It's been a year since Maitreya passed away, and every day it seems to get worse for you. Now this —"

Nilu stood and said, "Go back to your hussy right now — that's what's bothering you, isn't it? That I dragged you away from her, from whatever you two were doing in that room?"

He didn't stop her, even though it was pouring outside and she didn't have an umbrella. She walked out into the drenching rain, holding her bag above her head as she headed toward Chabel. The rain made it hard to see whether the cars passing by were taxis or private, so she kept moving, completely soaked.

A Young Man in the City

S HIVA CAME INTO Nilu's life as someone whose sole purpose might be to pay back Raja for the hurt he'd caused. Even as she went searching for Shiva's apartment across the city, even before the two began to keep each other company, Nilu knew that their association was going to be short-lived. There were moments when she thought of Shiva as a slightly younger, less suave version of Raja; at other times in the maternal feelings he evoked in her she recognized textures of emotions she'd have felt toward her son, had he been alive.

Shiva had appeared one day at Arniko Academy, looking for a job, and Principal Thapa had yelled at him, saying that the young man had heard wrong, that the school's lab assistant position had already been filled. It was the principal's yelling, and not the fact that there were no jobs, that Shiva had found offensive, as he told Prateema in the staff room, where she took him, out of pity, after the confrontation. He was wearing a pair of black pants and a blue shirt that had some dirt encrusted at the collar. He had a slim face, with big eyes. He was wearing sandals. The humiliating encounter had brought a defiant look to his face.

As he sipped his tea, Nilu told him that she'd talk to Principal Thapa on his behalf, and she asked him to come back the following day. She didn't know why she said that, and she regretted her words immediately. "Don't feel so despondent," she added. Speaking like

266

this released something inside her. She felt protective toward him, and he looked at her sharply, alerted by something in her tone.

"I'm not despondent," he said. "I'm just amazed at how people can be so heartless. He began to yell at me as soon as I asked him about the job." Nilu noticed that his hands shook a bit as he held the cup. He asked her what her name was, and she told him, mildly surprised that it didn't feel odd to be conversing with this stranger in the staff room where teachers entered and exited all day, coming in between their classes for a cup of tea or just to relax or to mull over what they would cook for dinner that night or to read the newspaper and chuckle at the myriad strange happenings in the city and the world.

The bell rang for a change of classes, and suddenly a babble of voices and noises surrounded the two of them. Nilu repeated that Shiva should return tomorrow and that now she had to teach, and he nodded. But when she left the school premises that day, she found him outside the gate, his hand behind his back, studying the street.

"Don't you have a house to go to?" she asked.

He smiled wanly.

"Walk me to the bus stop," she said, and he obeyed like a devoted younger brother. Since moving to Chabel, she'd been taking the city bus to and from work, as the school bus didn't reach her neighborhood.

On the way to the stop, she and Shiva didn't say much, but he waited patiently with her until her bus came. "Okay, go home now, and come tomorrow," she told him as she stepped into the crowded vehicle.

Maitreya was at the front of the bus, facing her. She averted her gaze. What do you want? she asked him in her mind. Why don't you leave me alone? Her heart was pounding, and perspiration broke out on her forehead. Slowly she turned to look: he was still there, sandwiched between two men, their sweaty bodies squeezing him between them. But he didn't appear uncomfortable, and he continued to stare at her, making her anxious, then afraid. With a great mental effort she challenged him from across the bus: what do you want? But he continued to observe her, steadily, until she couldn't bear it any longer and got off at the next stop. She didn't think it could come to this—becoming fearful of her own son. But all the way home she remained tense, wondering whether he'd appear by her side, accuse her of something, demand something from her that she couldn't give. Her hand instinctively dipped into her bag and fingered the rudraksha that Lama-ji had given her. At home, without changing her clothes, she crashed on the sofa.

Loud music sounded, right next to her window. It had the screech of heavy metal. She'd seen him, the neighbor boy, at this window, with a gleaming cassette player, probably a new gift from his parents or perhaps a relative. Apparently everyone doted on him. And here he was, trying to get her attention, she was sure, for he'd seen her go into her house and only then had he increased the volume. She went into her bedroom to get away from the noise, but there too the music thumped loudly. Finally, she opened her bedroom window a bit and waved at him. He waved back, grinning, then swayed his head to the music. She gestured to him to turn down the volume, but he kept smiling and closed his eyes. She shut the window and pulled a pillow over her head, muting the noise.

On the way to Arniko Academy on the bus she kept an eye out for Maitreya the next day, but he wasn't around. Throughout the bus ride she remained alert, expecting to be jolted by Maitreya's sudden appearance, or by his whisper close to her ear, asking her if she could make him some alubada, the potato patties that were his favorite snack. She was so tense by the time she entered the school premises that she had to hurry to the bathroom and close herself in a stall for a few minutes before she could go to the staff room.

During recess, she wondered what would happen if Maitreya were to visit Raja, how he'd react, whether that would cause a rift between him and that woman of his. Over the past few days, just recalling the woman's voice had hurt her ears, given her headaches, made her miserable. After her visit to Raja's flat that day she had gathered all the photos of him, and of her and Raja together, hanging on the walls of the house, and put them away in a box. The one in the bedroom she didn't put away because it also had Maitreya.

Lost in thoughts of Raja, and Maitreya, she'd forgotten about Shiva until she heard Principal Thapa's voice, instructing the peon. She briefly hesitated to intervene, then, fortifying herself, went to his office. For the next half-hour Nilu argued with Principal Thapa, told him that she knew the lab assistant's position hadn't been filled. The principal said that he'd already promised the job to a qualified person he knew, and Nilu answered that it was unethical for him to hand the job to someone without conducting proper interviews. They went back and forth like this until Nilu said, "Sir, this is the kind of matter the school board might not take lightly."

The mention of the school board alerted Principal Thapa. Just two months ago the school board had reprimanded him for keeping at home a secondhand Apple computer that the board had approved for the staff room. It was too soon for the board to hear about another instance of improper conduct, especially if his chosen lab assistant didn't have a background in science. "Nilu Miss," Principal Thapa said, then took off his glasses and began to polish them vigorously. "Small things like this don't need to be taken to the board. Okay, I'll talk to him. No guarantees, though, and that you should note."

As she made her way to her classroom, Nilu felt mildly jubilant, as though she had scored a victory against Principal Thapa as well as the world at large. See what I can do? she said to herself. To everyone. To Raja.

But Shiva didn't show up. Nilu waited for him for nearly twenty minutes at the end of the day, as the children and staff and teachers of Arniko Academy streamed past her. When the school was empty, Nilu went to the guard and asked him whether Shiva had come by that day.

The guard shook his head. "Yesterday, he and I spoke for a few minutes before he went in to talk with the principal saheb. I discovered we were from the same area in Gorkha. That's why I let him in. Had I known the principal saheb would yell at him like that . . ."

"Do you know where he lives?"

The guard thought for a moment. "Wait. I think he said he lives behind a hotel in Kalimati. Oh yes, Hotel Gandhi."

She said goodbye to the guard and headed home. But as she neared the bus stop, she was repelled by the prospect of going to her empty house, sitting alone on the sofa and staring into a corner, possibly getting frightened by the ghost of her own son. Without wanting to, she found herself picturing Raja with that young woman. She saw them, drinking tea, standing shoulder to shoulder by the window, watching the activity on the street below, listening to the faint sound of jazz from the stereo, jazz because Raja had given up on rock 'n' roll after Maitreya was born, finding it too discordant and noisy. Raja would turn to the woman, who'd smile at him, her lips very close to his mouth, and then they'd —

Nilu hailed a taxi and gave the driver her destination.

Kalimati was a hubbub of activity in the evening. The vegetable market was in full swing, and the depot was filling with buses that had arrived at the city after long-distance journeys from Pokhara, Birgunj, and Biratnagar. She hadn't come to this part of town in months because it was far from Chabel, nearly at the opposite end of the valley.

She moved up and down the street once, craning her neck to look at the signs. But she couldn't locate Hotel Gandhi. Then she took the road that ended with a fork toward Tahachal on the left and Basantapur on the right. Somehow she felt uncomfortable asking anyone about where the hotel was, conscious that people would think she was staying there. She mocked her own feelings of insecurity about this. Who cared what anyone thought, really? Then she happened to glance into an alley, and there it was, a sign saying Hotel Gandhi. It was affixed to an old house that adjoined other houses in the alley. She hadn't expected anything as crummy-looking as this, and now she was unsure about what to do. For a few minutes she waited at the opening of the alley. The marketplace around her hummed with shoppers buying vegetables and fish and meat. Bicycle bells tinkled and cars honked incessantly. Her school guard had said that Shiva lived behind Hotel Gandhi. But since the hotel was not in a free-standing building, there was nothing behind it. She wondered if she ought to turn back, but then she realized she'd already come this far, she'd argued for Shiva with Principal Thapa, and it seemed like a waste to not go this extra step.

She had to stoop a bit to enter the door of Hotel Gandhi, and as soon as she was inside she was bombarded by a smell, half food, half something rotten. She resisted the urge to pinch her nose, as there were people in the little room where she now found herself. Behind a small desk sat a man, reading something, and he smiled at her as she entered. In the corner was a dumpy woman cooking momos in a large pot. Two men sat on benches alongside the wall, waiting for the food. Was this a momo shop? "Sit down, sit down," the man said. She asked him whether this was Hotel Gandhi. Yes, it was, the man said. Did she want momos?

"Oh, this is a restaurant? I am actually looking for a hotel called Gandhi, you know, the night-sleeping kind."

"The hotel is upstairs," the man said. "Do you need a room?"

The men on the bench looked at her expectantly. So did the woman, before she removed the lid from the large vat in which the momos were being cooked. "It'll be another minute or two," she told the men.

"No, no," Nilu said to the man. Now, with two men and the cook watching her, she felt foolish telling them what she was looking for. "I'm looking for someone who lives nearby, behind Hotel Gandhi I was told, but I don't know where to look."

"Come with me," the man said, and stood.

He turned and began to climb the stairs next to him.

"No, no, you misunderstood," Nilu said with urgency. "He's not staying at the hotel. He's renting a room somewhere nearby."

"I understood what you are saying. From a window up there I can show you the houses nearby and tell you which ones are rented out."

She glanced at the cook, who encouraged her with a nod. Nilu followed the man. The stairs were narrow and wooden, and she wondered what kind of people stayed in a hotel like this, what the nightly rate was. On the second floor, there were two rooms; the doors were closed.

"Do you have guests in the hotel?" she asked.

The man nodded. "All the time. It's a good location, with the bus station so nearby. If you have friends . . ." Then he looked her up and down and probably realized that she and her ilk might not stay at his hotel. He beckoned her to a small window on the second-floor landing. Standing next to him, she could smell his wife's momos on him. "See, that house over there has two rooms rented out," he said, pointing. "And that one over there has one."

"How do I get there?"

"You have to go around to the main street, and enter through another alley."

"But it's right there," she complained. "Isn't there a way through the back of your hotel?"

The man shook his head, then looked her up and down. His body was quite close to hers, and his wife was downstairs. At once she said, "No problem. I'll find my way."

Out on the street, she entered the small alley he'd mentioned, and she was in a courtyard, from where she could see the back of Hotel Gandhi, even hear the low murmur of the stove. She stepped into the first house that the hotel owner had pointed out. Once again she had to climb some stairs to reach the second floor. A man was leaning on the railings that overlooked the courtyard, and he glanced at her questioningly. She told him she was looking for a man named Shiva, from Gorkha. The man pointed to the opposite side of the courtyard, told her that someone from Gorkha lived on the fifth floor. Nilu couldn't believe how difficult this search was turning out to be. She was already beginning to feel tired. Right now it appeared as if she would not find him. And it was quite possible that he was not home — a young man like him, he could be out with friends, or gone somewhere to eat dinner. A pink hue had spread across the sky; within minutes it could turn dark, and here she was, quite far from home, looking for a man she hardly knew, based on the words of a guard who could have gotten it all wrong. But the house was just a few dozen yards away, and she felt she had no choice but to plod ahead.

Nilu made her way to the house and climbed the stairs, this time to the third floor. Then she saw him, through a window on the narrow balcony that ran alongside the building. He was at another window in his room, sitting on its ledge, head leaning against the wall, looking out to the north of the city. He cut a glum profile, and for a brief moment she watched him. Finally she called his name, "Shiva!"

Startled, he turned to her. "Didi?" he said. He stood and desperately tried to hide something, and once he straightened up, he looked like an animal that had been frightened out of its wits.

"What a pleasure," he said, but didn't come to the door.

"I have come to deliver some good news," she said. "Aren't you going to let me in?"

Embarrassed, he opened the door. Immediately she was assaulted by a strong stench of alcohol. She saw, on the windowsill, what he'd been trying to hide: a bottle of Khukri rum, which lay exposed because the newspaper he'd placed over it had slid down. She looked at him. His eyes were glassy, and he wore a silly, sheepish grin.

"You've been drinking?"

"No, no," he said. Then his eyes traveled to the exposed bottle, and he said, "Just a peg or two. I was getting bored. Please come in, please."

"Maybe I shouldn't," she said. A gust of wind blew her hair, and she tamed it with her fingers.

"Please, didi," he said, and scrambled to empty a chair — his only chair — of its magazines and clothes. The floor was littered with books. Two of them lay open near the floor by his bed.

Nilu sat down primly, even more unsure about the wisdom of this visit. The drinking, naturally, disgusted her.

Shiva stood before her, like a child awaiting instructions. He was frazzled, clearly, for his hand kept smoothing his hair.

"I came to give you some good news."

"Didi, I'll make some tea, okay?" He rushed to a corner stove, where a few pots and pans lay about. She thought of rejecting this tea, but she also wanted to see what he would do, how he would make it, so she remained quiet. He rinsed a pot in the sink, filled it with water, and set it to boil on a portable gas stove. He sat on his haunches, watching the water, seemingly afraid to face her. She felt herself melting. Poor guy. He looked terribly depressed and lonely.

She went to the window, which commanded a broad view of the city because Shiva's flat was so high. The Swayambhunath Temple could be seen in the distance, rising above the city's hazy smoke. Everywhere she looked there were houses. When she and Raja took long walks in the city before Maitreya's birth, they'd ventured into this area, she now remembered. But in those years most of this area was open fields or farmland. She squinted toward Chabel, but it was too far away for her to discern anything familiar. "It's a nice view from here," she said. Her eyes fell on the bottle of rum on the sill, and she picked it up to examine it. Three Xs were marked on the label, letters that also could signify, she noted with bemusement, blue movies. "I've never understood what the charm of this thing is," she said. She rotated the bottle in her hand; the glass glinted in the sunlight. She opened the cap and brought her nose close to the opening. The smell hit her nostrils quickly, then traveled down her throat. She took a deep breath, then closing her eyes, she put the bottle to her lips, took a swig. The rum burned the inside of her mouth, and when she forced herself to swallow it, it sizzled down her gullet. She turned toward Shiva, who was watching her.

"Didi?" he asked, in astonishment.

"What? You thought I couldn't drink? Watch me." And Nilu took another gulp, this one bigger because the first one had already dilated her throat.

"Drink from a glass, please," he said, and brought her one.

But she didn't take the glass from him. Warmth was already welling up in her chest, spreading down to her belly. Her head swam. It had been ages since she'd drunk alcohol. Probably the last time was in Thamel, with Raja. Are you going to turn out to be like your mother now? a part of her mind asked. But she knew that wouldn't happen. It was just a momentary impulse, ignited by something, mostly by the images of Raja and the woman in his flat. She moved a bit closer to Shiva, and, handing him the bottle, said, "Now it's your turn. Drink."

"Didi, you have surprised me a great deal today. I didn't expect you to . . ."

"More drinking, less talking." She was on the verge of giggling — she had to control herself. This frivolity was reminiscent of her days in Thamel with Raja.

Shiva also took a swig, then wiped his mouth with the back of his arm, like a bandit. Nilu laughed at him.

"What? What?" he asked, smiling. He had let his hair go long, going down past his earlobes, which, again, reminded her of Raja's hair when they lived in Thamel.

She took the bottle from him and swallowed another mouthful. The alcohol now tasted sweet. "Do you stay cooped up in your room like this all day, drinking?"

"Sometimes," he said. "Sometimes I'm not in the mood to do anything. Nothing seems to matter anymore. Even reading I find boring."

"Why? What's wrong?" she asked. She stifled an urge to put her arm around him. He aroused something in her, an impulse to protect him. He had that face.

"I just feel so disillusioned sometimes."

"Come, sit here," she said, and she set the bottle down on the floor and sat on his bed, as though this were her room, and patted the spot next to her. "Tell me what's wrong, babu," she said.

He came and sat next to her, his body not touching hers. Good boy, she thought, in her increasing drunkenness.

"I don't know, didi. Sometimes I just feel like giving up and not even going out of my room, not opening the door or my curtains, not getting out of bed in the morning, just sleeping and sleeping until, until . . ."

Hesitantly, she tousled the hair on the back of his head. Her hand moved down to the back of his neck, and briefly she squeezed him there. Then, conscious that her hand was on a virtual stranger, she withdrew it to her lap. The water he'd set for tea had been boiling for some time, but neither he nor she got up to turn off the gas.

His face had slipped into a sad look, which returned whenever there was a lull in the conversation.

"Who is in your family?" she asked.

"A brother and a sister-in-law. My father passed away recently."

"Is your brother also in the city?"

"I don't want to talk about him right now," he said. "Didi, have you eaten?"

She shook her head.

"Will you eat with me today?"

"Here?"

"No, we'll go to my regular restaurant nearby."

"Well, shouldn't you be saving money by cooking at home?"

"Sometimes I get disheartened just cooking for myself."

"Well, you have no reason to be lonely now," she said, then paused for dramatic effect. "The principal wants you to return for an interview."

"Really? After his yelling yesterday, I thought he'd never give me that job. That's why I didn't come today."

"Well, I talked to him, persuaded him." Nilu was disappointed by Shiva's reaction, which was not as enthusiastic as she'd hoped. She'd expected his face to light up, for him to thank her profusely, but none of that happened. "So, you have to come by tomorrow to talk to him."

"Okay," he said. "Shall we go out to eat?"

She glanced out the window. It was already dark outside, and she was far from home. She'd have to take a taxi on the way back, as most of the buses and tempos would have stopped running by now. But who was waiting for her at home? No one, except shadows of her dead son. "All right, let's go," she said.

Her mind was still swimming from the rum, and she took his

arm as they left the courtyard and emerged onto the main street. The eatery was quite close, and as soon as she entered it Nilu realized that it served mostly out-of-towners, or bus drivers and conductors who plied the highway out of Kathmandu. She was the only woman in the bhojanalaya, and the men stared at her as she entered, still holding Shiva's arm, but it didn't bother her. "Sit here?" Shiva said, pointing to a corner, and she nodded.

When the meal was placed before Nilu — steaming rice, chicken floating in gravy, delicious-smelling dal, two other vegetables, and some achar — she discovered she was ravenous. "This is the best bhojanalaya in the Kalimati area," he said. "It's famous."

The food was very good, and soon she found herself immersed in sucking the marrow of a bone or chewing on spicy potato achar. He ate more slowly, staring into the distance at times so that she'd ask him, "What are you thinking?" He shook his head at her. After they were done eating, he directed her to the tap in the corner, where she washed her hands and gargled to rinse out the remnants of the food. She wiped her fingers and mouth with a grungy towel hanging on the wall and was surprised that she didn't blanch.

After dinner they strolled through the Kalimati area for a while. She had slipped her arm into his, and he seemed to think there was nothing unusual about it. She wondered what would happen if Raja, in the unlikely event that he'd come to Kalimati, would chance upon them. Would he get angry? Upset? Then she thought of Maitreya, and for a brief moment she let go of Shiva's arm. Dwelling on Maitreya distressed her, made this small bit of happiness she was experiencing with Shiva seem fraudulent, inappropriate. But — and she was startled by this renegade thought — her dead son didn't have a right to pass judgment on his mother.

After strolling for a while, the two headed back to Shiva's flat. A woman with a baby stood on a landing and smiled at them as they went up; Shiva didn't even notice her. In this city, Nilu thought, there's always a woman poised on a landing or a staircase, prying into other people's lives. Inside his flat, she said, "I should be going home. It's getting very late."

"Do you have to go now, didi?" he said. "I feel like you just got here."

"Okay, I'll stay for a minute or two more. But you also need to get a good night's sleep so you're fresh for your interview tomorrow."

Shiva poured himself another drink. He also offered her more, but Nilu declined. Her mouth felt acrid now, and her mind was slowing down. Propping a pillow behind her head, she lay on the bed; her legs extended beyond its edge because it was small. Holding the drink in his hand, he sat next to her. "The principal must already have chosen someone for the job. He just said okay to you to make you happy. These people are all alike, I know it."

"Don't think so negatively."

"Negative? Didi, you can't even trust your own family these days, your own blood." He downed his drink, grimaced, then set down the glass.

He lay down next to her and rested his head on her shoulder, before she could say anything, before she could tell him no, that that's not what she came here for. But she realized that he wasn't going to try any hanky-panky, that he was merely tired, and sad, and incredibly, she leaned over and kissed him on the temple. He turned his face toward her, like a child. After a while he said, as though he were talking to himself, "This city. It makes me sick. So many people, so many cars, so much money, and all of the people wrapped up in their own worlds. I feel like screaming sometimes. If I stay here one more day, I'll begin to unravel, go insane. I won't survive. All I want to do is stay in my room and drink." There was an undertone of something in his voice, a mild aggression, a rejection of this world.

"Why don't you go back home if you don't like it here?" she asked.

"I don't want to bore you with my long-suffering story."

"You won't bore me."

"I can tell you only if you stay with me tonight."

"Are you blackmailing me?"

"Okay, if you say blackmail, then it's blackmail." He smiled at her.

She looked at her watch. It was already ten o'clock. Where had all the time gone? She didn't look forward to making her way down to the street, then trying to find a taxi in the dark, then traveling through the poorly lit streets. But then, she couldn't stay here, could she? Could she? She pictured Raja learning that she'd spent the night in Shiva's bed, and she felt the urge to get up immediately. Several excuses floated through her head as to why she was here in Kali-mati in the first place. Then the voice of the woman in Raja's flat sounded in her ears, like an echo that had been hounding her for days. No one really cared where she was, what she ate and where she slept. Shiva was right. The city would carry on of its own accord; it wasn't going to stop to ruminate and lament over her life, nor over this poor boy here.

"Okay, I'll stay," she said.

Absurd

NILU AWOKE, STARTLED, to the blaring noise of traffic. The sun had already come in through the window of Shiva's room. The unfamiliarity of her surroundings gave her a jolt. What had she done? The rum bottle was on the windowsill, now empty. The entire room reeked of alcohol. Her chest and stomach felt sticky from sweat. Her temples were throbbing, and she knew that a headache was coming.

Had she and Shiva . . . ? But no, nothing had happened. They had talked late into the night; he had drunk some more; and then, she remembered now, he had fallen asleep in her arms. It had been close to two o'clock when she'd at last fallen asleep, her mind occupied with images from Shiva's life. His story was not an entirely unfamiliar one: an aging father; an older brother whose loyalty to his father and his brother begins to shift once he gets married; a beautiful but conniving and manipulative sister-in-law who slowly begins to dominate the house. Shiva's brother and sister-in-law had not bothered to hide the sounds of their lovemaking in the family's small house in Gorkha, and that's the act, Shiva claimed, that killed their old father, who had stopped speaking, more out of shame than any illness, the last few weeks before his death. After their father's funeral, Shiva's brother, egged on by his wife, had intensified his bullying of Shiva, so one morning he'd quietly packed his bags and come to Kathmandu. He drifted from job to job, most of the time finding it easier to lie in bed all day, drinking. When he went without work for a long time, a kind of panic would grip him, and he'd have visions of wasting away in his flat as life went on around him: no one to look after him, and no one to knock on his door. That's when he renewed his efforts to search for a job, and that's how he'd ended up in Nilu's school.

His face was turned away from Nilu, his mouth slightly open as he slept, and he had pulled up his legs. Affection toward him welled up inside her. She glanced at her watch. It was nearly eight o'clock. She wouldn't have time to go home, wash up, change her clothes, and head to Arniko. She could call in sick, but then today was Shiva's interview with Principal Thapa and she needed to be there so Shiva wouldn't be summarily dismissed.

She sat up in bed and stretched. Where was the bathroom? She knew it was somewhere in the building, but where? She stood and went to the mirror attached to the wall. Her hair was a jumble, and her eyes puffy. Absurd, she thought, as she took stock of the unkempt room, the sun lifting the haze outside to reveal a landscape dotted with houses, the cries of children somewhere close to the building, Shiva sleeping soundly in his bed.

She had to go to the bathroom. She opened the latch on the door and peeked out. Seeing no one, she went down the balcony. There were two more doors on the floor, but they looked like rooms. She went down one more floor. The woman with the baby was standing outside, watching her descend. There we go again, Nilu thought. "Are you looking for the bathroom?" the woman asked. Nilu nodded. "It's right at the end of this balcony." Nilu hurried in and shut the door. It was filthy, with feces encrusted on the commode and a pool of murky liquid on the floor.

Holding her breath she finished her business, then washed her face quickly in the sink, wiped it clumsily with her handkerchief, and stepped out. Seeing the expression on Nilu's face, the woman with the baby said, "I have given up on telling these people to clean the toilet. No matter how much I tell them, these young men don't listen. Each one of them needs a wife to take care of him." Then, smiling coyly at Nilu she asked, "And who are you to that young man? I don't even know his name because he never stops to talk to me."

"I'm his sister."

"Really? Then how come I've never seen you around here before?"

Nilu felt like playing with the woman a bit. "I eloped with a truck driver when Shiva was very young, but finally I've returned. And I'm going to live with him."

The woman's face paled. "Eloped?"

"Yes. Now that I'm going to live with Shiva, you and I can be friends."

"Yes, why not?" But clearly the woman now didn't want anything to do with her.

Nilu returned to Shiva's flat, took the comb from her bag, fixed her hair at the mirror, and rearranged the folds of her sari. Shiva was still sound asleep, so she went to him and put her hand on his shoulder and said softly, "Don't forget to come to the school for your interview. Around eleven or twelve, okay?"

He opened his eyes briefly, said, "What?"

She repeated her reminder, and nodding, he went back to sleep again.

Shiva didn't show up. By the time the afternoon recess rolled around, the tenderness that Nilu had felt toward him last night had evaporated. What was his problem? During recess she went to the gate and asked the guard whether he'd seen Shiva, but the man said he hadn't. As she went back in, her eyes met those of Principal Thapa, who was leaning against the wall outside his door.

"So where's that young man of yours?" Principal Thapa asked her. "Do you think this is some kind of a game, Nilu Miss? One day you are in my office, ready to eat me alive, and then when I tell you to bring him for an interview, he's not here? What do I owe him that I need to keep holding the job for him? More accurately, what do I owe you?"

"Nothing," she told him. "You owe me nothing. You can give the job to your own person."

"I'd rather give it to my own person than to your person," he said, and walked away.

When Nilu went to the bus station, Shiva was standing there, waiting for her, and she pretended that she didn't see him and boarded her bus. He jumped on after her, but the bus was crowded, and two or three people were squeezed between them, so he couldn't get close to her. Once or twice he attempted to lean forward to speak to her, but he was either pushed back or chastised by other passengers. When she got off at Chabel, he too got off and followed her, apologizing, saying that he simply had slept until the afternoon. Just before she turned the corner to her house, she stopped and confronted him. But when she spoke, none of the anger remained, and she said, matter-of-factly, "That job is already gone. I don't understand you. Why didn't you come? It's not about me, it's not for me, it's for you."

He hung his head in shame, and she kept speaking, then gave up and invited him for tea and snacks before he headed home. He followed her like a chastised and sobered child. Once they reached her house, she thrust her index finger in front of his face and sternly said, "Why do you make it so hard for yourself?"

He said that sometimes he wished the ground beneath him would simply melt and he would be sucked in and that would be the end of that.

"Stop saying such things. You are young, and you have much to look forward to in your life. Don't give in to these momentary feelings of hopelessness."

She let him sit on the sofa, handed him a magazine, and went to the kitchen to make some food for him. She had some onions, which she chopped, dipped in batter, and plopped into a frying pan, to make pakodas. She also made some yogurt lassi and took the tray of food to the living room. He had made himself comfortable on the sofa, his legs stretched out, his hand supporting his head as he read the magazine. He ate the pakodas with gusto, praised her cooking, drank the lassi and burped, and gave her an embarrassed smile. "Eat more," she told him, but he said that he had eaten late that day and so his stomach was full.

Shiva stayed with her until darkness fell, then, gradually sadness descended on his face like a shadow, and he said that he ought to be going. Nilu told him that if he wished, he could stay at her place, sleep on the sofa, as it would be hard for him to find transportation back to Kalimati at this hour. "Here, I'll fetch you a blanket and a pillow," she said, and once again he complied. She checked on him during the night and discovered that his blanket had slid onto the floor. She picked it up and put it over him, and in a state of semisleep, he muttered something; whether it was "Dai" or "Didi," she couldn't tell.

Nilu imagined Raja visiting her to find Shiva's head on her lap while she read to him. She would not crack her door only a bit, as Raja had done, and deny him the pleasure of meeting Shiva. She would not hem and haw about who the young man on her sofa was, as Raja had done concerning his young woman. "He's my boy," she'd say to Raja. "Mero keta," she'd repeat, and leave him to deduce what exactly that meant. She imagined him telling her not to be so silly, and she'd respond, "I'm over Maitreya now."

Nilu was aghast at herself for wanting to use Shiva as an instrument of revenge. Her emotions were spiraling out of control. She was fully aware that with Shiva she experienced a cravenness that was more maternal than anything. She anticipated his arrival at her house each evening, cognizant of the watchful eyes of her neighbors. The boy's mother across the way refused to look at Nilu when they happened to meet in the lane; the boy hurried inside when he saw her coming. She could see her neighbors' minds churning: a supposedly grieving mother, abandoned by her husband, is entertaining a young man at home. Some grief.

Those days when Shiva didn't come, Nilu went searching for him in Kalimati. She'd find him in his room, sitting by the window, drinking, in the same position she'd found him when she first went to his flat. He'd be wearing the same blue shirt, the same gray pants, his head would lean against the wall at the same angle, and he'd be drinking the same Khukri rum. The picture was so similar that she experienced a momentary confusion, as though she'd been thrust back in time to relive that earlier occasion. "Shiva?" she'd call, just as she had the first time, and he'd appear startled again, but now — and that's how things had changed — he'd make no attempt to hide his drink. He didn't say, "What a pleasure," as he had the first time.

She'd make snacks for him when he came over: spicy chickpeas, fries, and even alubada. Nilu didn't tell Shiva that alubada were Maitreya's favorite, that her son could eat dozens and dozens of them at a single sitting, and then complain of a bellyache; that she made these potato patties for him even when he was sick just so that he would get some food into his stomach. She watched Shiva carefully as he bit into a patty, to see if he expressed the same kind of delight that Maitreya had, and then she immediately was struck by how foolish she had become.

"What a strange thing," Shiva said, when he learned how Maitreya had died. "When everyone else was hailing an event as a great moment for our country, your life turned upside down." She noted that he said "everyone else was hailing," not what he himself thought. He never talked politics, anyway, which she found to be a relief. She forced herself not to think about her son while she was with Shiva. Maitreya no longer came to her, but she sensed her son's eyes on her, sad as always, but sometimes, she imagined, also a bit critical. She hadn't divulged much to Shiva about Raja. Shiva did know that she and Raja were estranged, but somehow he'd gotten the impression that Raja lived abroad.

Nilu tried not to offer Shiva any drinks when he came to visit her, and most days she was successful — he seemed fairly content to lounge around in her house. But some days he became so fidgety that she had to pull out the quarter-bottle of Khukri rum from her cupboard and pour him a drink or two. She couldn't believe, given that she'd resented her mother's drinking all her life, that she was pouring drinks for Shiva. But it's not the same, she told herself: Muwa is my mother; I don't have a blood attachment to Shiva.

One of these days I'll convince him to quit, she thought, then inwardly mocked her stupidity. But even if she did allow him to drink, she put away the bottle quickly and usually suggested that they go for a walk.

It was during one of these walks that she thought of heading to Raja's neighborhood. The idea came to her suddenly, as they were standing in front of the Chabel Ganesh Temple, where she had steered Shiva after they left the house under the watchful eyes of the neighbors, who had congregated on their rooftops to take the evening air. Let them talk, Nilu thought, let them disapprove. Let them die with disapproval etched on their forehead.

At Chabel Ganesh, as she stood, eyes closed, in front of the shrine, it occurred to her that she wanted Raja to see Shiva. What for? a part of her mind queried. What good would that do? But Raja needed to know that she . . . was capable of looking after her own needs. Her own needs? She couldn't believe her own rationalizations.

She steered Shiva toward Dillibazar. He was like a child, really, she thought, someone who had been thrust into a world that had hurt him and confused him. She slipped her hand into his, and only then she realized that people she knew could walk by and see her like this; they'd talk about her for days. Ganga Da would hear of it, if he hadn't already, and he'd probably make a phone call or visit, asking what was going on, who was the young man she was being seen with. "Why have you given up on Raja?" he'd ask, as he'd asked a thousand times before. "Why have you two given up on your marriage like this? What is the point of remaining married if you're each going to go your own way?" In anger, he'd then suggest that they get a divorce, which wasn't, of course, what he really wanted. But he'd say it only to startle her into the realization that divorce was a real possibility unless she and Raja mended their ways. But Ganga Da was old-fashioned. He assumed that Nilu and Raja were nice people, who didn't ruin themselves through divorce, whose basic goodness would throw them back into each other's arms. This same steadfastness had made him bristle at his mother's suggestion that he get rid of his crazy wife, that had made him love and care for Jamuna Mummy, even though living with her, and shuttling her between the mental hospital and home, had turned him into a frazzled, irritable man by age fifty.

Dillibazar was a bit far away, but it was nice to breathe in the evening air instead of taking the bus, as Nilu had done the last time she'd visited Raja. She wasn't sure what was going to happen, but she hoped that somehow Raja would spot her with Shiva. She didn't know what else to expect. What would happen if Raja were to become riled up and challenge Shiva, as he used to do to street hoodlums during their Thamel days? Somehow she couldn't picture Raja behaving like that now. Maitreya's death had defeated him, and now he too was merely surviving, trying to eke out whatever small pleasures the day doled out to him. Seeing things this way made Nilu feel for Raja, but it didn't prevent her from thinking this: he has to see me with Shiva.

They walked down the hill that led to Kalopul, which resembled a shantytown now, with shacks and huts cropping up under the black bridge alongside the thin river. They kept moving, turned left in the direction of Dillibazar. "Where are we going?" Shiva asked, and Nilu said that it was merely an evening walk. She recalled the long strolls with Raja, who, because he read so much, was more of a historian than she was, even though history was one of the two subjects she taught at Arniko. He used to give her minilessons as they traversed the city. The neighborhood they passed in Kalopul, she remembered him saying, was where Dharmabhakta Mathema, the wrestler who'd plotted to kill Juddha Shumshere Rana, had been hanged from a tree. When they visited Chobar, he reminded her of the story, one she knew but still enjoyed hearing him recite, about the gash on the side of the mountain: the bodhisattva Manjushree had sliced the mountain there to drain the water from the valley, thereby giving birth to the Kathmandu Valley. It was Raja who told her that barely more than a couple of decades ago, Tribhuvan

Airport used to be a cow pasture; before Indian pilots landed their small aircraft, they had to radio in to request that the animals be shooed away. At this airport King T had landed when he returned from his exile in India, after the Rana autocracy was toppled. King T—emerging from the door of the airplane, clad in daura suruwal and the national cap, waving at the thousands of jubilant faces that welcomed him—this photo was forever etched in every Nepali's mind. "The benevolent king returns home," Raja had intoned, "after setting his people free."

But it was the story of King T's escape from the clutches of the Ranas, who had kept him captive in the palace, that had really excited Raja. "Listen, Nilu, this sounds like a clip from a thriller. One early morning the king's entourage leaves the royal palace for a picnic, with the king and his sons insisting that they drive. As they pass the Indian embassy, all the cars glide into the embassy's gate. Chaos. Bedlam. The Ranas are furious, frothing at the mouth. They can't believe the king has sought shelter with the Indians. They slam the poor infant Prince G, King T's middle son who'd been left behind, onto the throne, declare him the king. The Indians orchestrate the royal refugees' escape to India; the anti-Rana Nepali Congress begins attacking Nepal from the south, capturing cities, and makes inroads into the hill towns. Eventually, Mohan Shumshere Jung Bahadur Rana has no choice but to give in. The rest, as you know, is history."

"What happens after that, Raja?" Nilu had asked coyly. "Tell me please, sweetie, I'm dying to hear it. It's so enchanting, like a fairy tale."

"But no happily ever after there, mitini," Raja said, with a dramatic sigh. "Out of the hands of the Ranas, into the hands of the Shah kings."

Shiva had no such story to tell Nilu.

He had fallen silent as they approached Raja's block in Dillibazar. And abruptly, in Raja's lane, what Nilu had desired came to pass. Raja stood on the roof of his building, enjoying the evening air,

and he now was staring at Nilu, clearly incredulous that she had appeared near his gate, with another man. Next to Raja was a young
woman with long, dense black hair, the woman in his room, Nilu
was sure, none other than who she thought it would be. "Nilu?"
Raja shouted.

Nilu had no choice but to stop. "How are you?" she shouted back
to Raja.

"What brings you here?"

The young woman was looking at them, then looking away, then
looking back again.

"We are just taking a walk," Nilu said. She didn't know why, instead of standing there like a fool, she simply didn't move on.

"You came for a walk from Chabel to Dillibazar?"

Between the gate and the roof, the distance was about twenty-
five or thirty feet, but somehow Nilu was able to read their facial expressions with surprising clarity, a trick of her own mind, she was
sure, to amplify her embarrassment. What had led her to start out
on this incredibly foolish venture? What must Raja be thinking of
her now? And what would Shiva think when he found out who Raja
was, for clearly he hadn't yet, as he was standing there patiently, a
half-smile plastered on his face, waiting for the niceties to end.

"Yes" was all she could say to Raja's query.

"Is everything all right?" Raja asked.

She nodded.

Raja turned to his woman and said something Nilu couldn't hear.
To Nilu he shouted, "Wait, I'll be right down," and disappeared. The
woman stayed on the roof, her arms crossed at her chest, looking
fidgety. Raja appeared on the stairs, where the middle-aged woman
with the smacking slippers had miraculously materialized. She
asked Raja something, and Raja responded and hurried down.

"Who is he?" Shiva asked as Raja approached them.

"Someone I know very well," Nilu said, sounding mysterious,
thinking that she could probably still escape without Shiva's discovering Raja's identity.

The latch was lifted, the gate swung open, and there was Raja, flesh and blood. He joined his palms in namaste to Shiva, then addressed Nilu. "You can imagine my shock at seeing you here, so far from Chabel."

"Well, I don't know how we ended up here. Isn't it strange?"

"And who's your friend?" Raja asked.

"This is Shiva," she said. She could have sunk into the earth.

Shiva shook hands with Raja, who didn't mention his name. But even if he had, Nilu didn't think it would register with Shiva, who might have heard her mention Raja by name only once.

"And who's your friend up there?" Nilu asked, tilting her head slightly toward the roof.

"You know who she is," Raja said. He seemed emboldened by the fact that now Nilu too had someone; he no longer had to feel defensive. "I told you about her." He called out her name, Jaya, and asked her to come down. Then Raja addressed them. "Well, since you two walked so far today, your feet must be aching. Why don't you come inside and have tea? I don't have a big flat to boast of, but it's enough for us to sit around and chat."

Nilu had begun to say no when Shiva said, "Actually, I was just about to say to Nilu Didi here that we ought to stop somewhere for tea."

Everything was moving too quickly — did Nilu imagine that glint in Raja's eyes when he heard Shiva call her didi? — and Nilu felt her mind go blank. Jaya appeared at the gate, looking anxious; perhaps she had expected an altercation between the estranged husband and wife by now?

"Let's go in," Raja said, ushering Shiva and Nilu in, while Jaya looked on in disbelief. "We're all going to have tea." He put his hand on Shiva's shoulder. "Shiva Bhai," he said, emphasizing the *bhai* for her benefit, Nilu was sure. Don't tell me Raja is going to have fun with this, she thought. What have I gotten myself into? Nilu was reminded of the way she and Raja, at his prompting, used to poke fun at passengers in the city buses. As Maitreya grew up, Raja had enlisted their otherwise serious son to play pranks on Nilu. One time they hid the final exams of her students that she was supposed to grade for the following morning. In panic Nilu ransacked the flat for the stack of papers. Raja and Maitreya, who was four and a half years old then, looked on, with concerned expressions. Nilu phoned the guard at school and asked him to check the staff room for her exams, all the while eyeing her son, whose solemn face was getting strangely distorted. Then Maitreya could hold it no longer and he burst into tears, declaring to his mother that he'd never pull a trick on her like that again. Raja stood on his toes and pulled the exams out of the top of the cupboard. But so unhappy had Maitreya been with his participation in this practical joke that he'd remained upset for hours — that was the kind of boy he was.

Surely Raja wasn't going to try anything tricky now, Nilu thought, as they climbed the staircase. But the slipper-slapping woman was standing right outside Raja's door, obviously waiting to get a closer look at the entourage. Outside the door Raja introduced her as some aunty, his landlady, without bothering to tell her who Shiva and Nilu were, although Nilu was certain the woman knew who she was. The woman remained outside the flat, staring at them, even after Raja shut his door behind him.

Nilu had imagined Raja's flat as an unkempt, messy affair, much like Shiva's room, but it was neat and tidy, with not a speck of dust anywhere. The sofa had clean covers; small statues of Ganesh and Krishna gleamed on the side tables. When they lived together, Raja was notorious for leaving his clothes lying around, which even young Maitreya found exasperating.

Obviously, Jaya had been taking care of him. The younger woman's incursion into Raja's territory was deeper than Nilu had assumed, deeper than Raja himself had let on when they met in the restaurant a few weeks ago.

Jaya was hiding behind Raja as they stood in the room. Shiva said that it was a nice-looking flat, asked Raja how much rent he was paying. Raja said that it wasn't exactly cheap, and the two drifted close and began conversing about renting in the city, which left Nilu and Jaya awkwardly by themselves. Jaya threw a furtive glance at Nilu, who gave her a wan smile and asked, "So, what do you do?"

Jaya took two steps toward her and said, "Didi, I attend a local music school. I am studying music."

Nilu nodded. She had nothing more to say to the girl. She wished Raja and Shiva would stop talking so she'd not feel compelled to engage her in conversation, but Raja and Shiva, talking with animation about the profusion of houses in the city, had now moved to the window, and so she and Jaya were even more by themselves.

"What kind of music?"

"I play the sitar." She paused. "Didi, I . . ."

Afraid of what was coming next, Nilu said, "You must be very good."

"I'm okay. I play in the hotels around here. I also sing."

"Really? Then you must be excellent."

Jaya smiled shyly.

How old was this girl? Did Raja say she was twenty-five or thirty? He never gave a clear answer. She couldn't be more than twenty-one, or at the most, twenty-two.

"I can play for you, didi, if you want."

Nilu was thinking of a response that would quash this idea. She was getting annoyed with how the girl addressed her as didi. Was she deliberately acting naive? But then, Shiva also called her sister, and what exactly was Nilu's relationship with him? Raja had obviously been listening to the women's conversation, for he turned to them and said, "Yes, yes, you should play. You should hear her, Nilu. She's really good. When famous Indian classical singers come to play here, Jaya gets to accompany them onstage."

"Maybe some other day," Nilu said.

"What's wrong with today?" Raja said, and he slapped Shiva on the back. "What's wrong with today, eh, Shiva Bhai? You tell her." The gleam in his eyes made him look almost manic. But Nilu noted, with satisfaction, that the sorrow on his face showed when he thought no one was looking. In the downward curve of his mouth, the sag of his jaw.

"Didi, what do you say?" Shiva asked. "Shall we stay for a while?"

"Yes, what about it, didi?" Raja asked emphatically.

Nilu resented how much enjoyment Raja was getting out of the situation. But, tired of being the naysayer, she said okay.

"I'll make tea, then," Jaya said, and she went into the kitchen. The apartment had two rooms: one the kitchen, and the other the fairly large bedroom, half of which functioned as a living room. The bed was made, the windows covered with clean, pretty curtains.

Raja sat on the bed, and Nilu and Shiva on the sofa, facing him. After a moment, Raja began to ask Shiva questions. Where was he from? How many in his family? What was he doing in the city? As the conversation flowed without Raja's revealing his identity, Shiva seemed to become impressed by Raja's friendliness, for he smiled more. He listened to Raja attentively. Nilu didn't say much but rather watched Raja, who every now and then returned her look.

Jaya returned, bearing a tray of tea and biscuits, which the men consumed quickly, their lips moving as they chewed and talked. Jaya sat scrunched on a corner of the bed, well distanced from Raja, and let her toes trace a pattern on the rug. Occasionally she stole a glance at Nilu, who felt as if she was playing the role of the jilted, troubled wife in a bad movie. But that's not how it is, she told herself forcefully. Since she didn't know where she and Raja stood with each other, there was nothing wrong with what was happening. Then she couldn't help but be amused at her own anxious attempts to render as normal what was ultimately absurd: the husband, his lover, the wife, and her friend all coming together for some chia and biscuits and music, sung by the husband's lover — and all of this in a country where even widows and abandoned wives dared not express any longing for men. It increasingly felt like a scene out of an awful movie. Any moment now, she thought, something terrible is going to happen: a fistfight is going to erupt between Raja and Shiva, Jaya is going to shed her silly inhibitions and lunge for Nilu's hair, to drag her out of the flat. Or, less melodramatically, Jaya is going to insinuate, through words and gestures and facial expressions, that Nilu is threatening her territory, that if Nilu thinks that Jaya is a young filly who's going to take it all lying down, she is mistaken.

Of course none of that happened. After they finished tea, which was delicious, much better than Nilu knew how to make it, Jaya picked up the sitar that had been leaning against the wall next to the bed. (Did she keep the sitar here? Was she living here? What about her family? Would they allow this kind of indiscretion—let her live with a married man so openly?) Then Jaya asked Raja, "What shall I play?"

"Well, I don't know if these two can listen to the twang-twang of your hardcore classical music. Why don't you play something lighter, something they might know?"

"But I play the classical ones better than the others, you know that."

"You might bore them is all that I'm saying."

Jaya considered what to do and then settled on a popular Hindi song. She had a very sweet voice, making nice modulations as she sang, and it was hard not to fall into a kind of a trance listening to her. Nilu watched her face: pretty, with tender lips and innocent eyes, luxuriant dark hair. A girl who'd just barely stepped into womanhood. Nilu watched Raja. His hair was graying on the sides, and he had gathered a few more thin lines on his cheeks than Nilu remembered, but he was as handsome as before. It wasn't surprising that Jaya had fallen for him. Nilu herself had pursued Raja all the way to the Jagadamba School when she was a teenager, propelled by the tug of her heart. Why was it a surprise that Jaya was in love with him too? He treated women well when he wanted to. He liked to laugh, and although their son's death had stifled that laughter, he hadn't completely lost his mischievous streak. There was no reason why a young, talented woman like Jaya wouldn't want to spend time with him, especially if the alternative was to content herself with the half-grown, emotionally stunted, uncouth men her age who populated the city. Take Shiva, for example. Although he was sweeter than most men she'd encountered, he'd yet to come fully into his own. This became evident when he got that lost look on his face. Nilu tried to imagine Jaya and Shiva together, which seemed the more logical union, given how close they were in age, but she couldn't. Jaya, as young as she was, wouldn't go for someone her age, Nilu was sure. It was ridiculous, sitting there listening to the melancholy tune of the sitar, to Jaya's equally moving, penetrating voice, and allowing these absurd thoughts to crowd her mind.

The music stopped, and as if on cue the doorbell rang. Raja went to the door and opened it. A boy entered, carrying a tray with a bottle of alcohol, four glasses, and some snacks in bowls. "A little celebration as we listen to Jaya's music," Raja said as he took the tray from the boy and gave him some money. At what point had Raja asked the boy to fetch the drinks, Nilu didn't know, for he'd never left the flat while the four of them were there. Did he have an arrangement with his landlady to send drinks when he entertained company? Did he have regular company? There were so many things about Raja and his new life, Nilu realized, that she didn't know.

Raja poured the drinks. Nilu was too lethargic to protest, and Shiva eyed the glasses as Raja filled them. Shiva glanced at Nilu, seemingly seeking her approval, then quickly looked away. Raja passed the drinks to everyone. Jaya smelled hers, scrunched her nose, and turned her face away. Nilu held her glass in her hand.

"Cheers," Raja said, and raised his glass. Raja's and Nilu's eyes met as the glasses clinked, and Raja seemed to be mocking her a bit, fondly, as though she had called this encounter down upon herself. I can just get up and leave if I want to, she answered back with her eyes, and took a gulp. The whiskey was hot as it went down her throat. She drank more, closing her eyes. "More?" Raja said, and without waiting for her response, refilled her glass. Shiva and Jaya were conversing about some well-known classical sitar players, and Raja, gazing into Nilu's eyes softly, asked, "So, what else is going on in your life?"

"Nothing," she said. "What's going on in yours?"

"Nothing."

Something was welling up in Nilu's chest, and it would have come out, had Shiva and Jaya not been there. And Raja too for the moment appeared to abandon his mocking attitude, for she could tell that he was also trying to say something. But eventually the only thing that came out of his mouth was "Everything all right?"

She nodded. "Everything all right with you?"

Jaya and Shiva could hear everything they said, but it didn't matter. There was no pretense that it was a private conversation between a husband and a wife. In fact, there was no conversation — it was only small talk.

Nilu's eyes were tearing up, and so that Raja wouldn't see it, she turned to Shiva and Jaya, who had moved on to discussing popular singers. Nilu could feel Raja's eyes on her, as though he was hurt that she had turned away when he was trying to express something significant to her. But it was too late now. A door had closed between the two. It was unbearable, what was happening, but she couldn't blame Raja, and yes, she would be perfectly happy blaming herself for it, but what good would come of it? To quell her own thinking, she asked Shiva and Jaya, "What are you two talking about?"

"Just some singers," Shiva said, then he stood and went to the bathroom.

"Who do you like, didi?" Jaya asked.

"I hardly listen to music anymore."

"He says that you two used to listen to rock 'n' roll when you were younger."

Nilu glanced at Raja, who was looking out the window. Shiva returned and sat down, slightly off balance.

"His favorite was . . . what is it? Leed Zaplin or something? I can't even pronounce it. I can't stand that music, didi. So loud and obnoxious. Gives me a headache."

"Well, we were all younger then."

Shiva had closed his eyes, as if trying to understand and digest images running through his mind.

"Where did you meet him?" Jaya asked Nilu.

"Oye, Shiva-ji, where are you?" Nilu asked.

Shiva opened his eyes, which were beginning to turn red.

"She wants to know where we met. Shall I tell them?" Her intention was to respect any hesitation he might have about revealing how he'd come to her school looking for a job, but her tone, as she asked him, sounded contemptuous, and he noted it, for he appeared a bit startled, wounded.

"You may, if you wish," he said. "I have no problem with it."

Something about his voice annoyed her. "It doesn't matter," she told Jaya.

Raja was watching both their faces intently.

For a while there was silence; then Nilu said that they'd better leave. Shiva didn't move. He gulped the drink he had in his hand, then poured himself another one. "Let's go, Shiva," Nilu said, standing.

"Let me finish this."

She remained standing. Raja asked her to sit down, but she didn't want Shiva to get drunk in front of Raja, so she shook her head. She wished Jaya the best of luck with her music, then went and stood by the door. Her chest felt constricted, as though she was being squeezed into a tight place. Shiva was taking his time finishing his drink, and by the time he stood, slightly tottering, she was already outside Raja's door. When Shiva did emerge she quietly walked in front of him and went down the stairs.

Nilu didn't speak to him as they left Dillibazar. Night had fallen, and of course they were already tired from their earlier walk. The logical course would be to catch a bus, and so they headed toward the corner.

"Did I do something wrong?" Shiva asked.

"No, nothing."

"Then why are you mad at me, didi?"

"I'm not mad at you."

In silence they waited for the bus. Was he assuming that he was going with her to Chabel? Tonight she didn't want him there; she wanted to be by herself, thinking about Raja, about what was going to happen to the two of them, whether she had lost him forever to Jaya or to whoever might come along next — whether there was still something left between them that could be rekindled, then handled with care.

She remembered how Raja had wept for days after burning Maitreya's body on the ghat of the Pashupatinath Temple. On the other hand, she, instead of crying, had sunk deeper into depression, day by day. Then the gloom had transformed itself into a weight that sat on her chest, her head, until it discolored her world. Instead of mourning with Raja, she'd allowed her own grief to overshadow his; surely that was why he'd turned away from her. She had known Raja for how long now? More than two decades, since those days when they played together in the yard of Nilu Nikunj, as Kaki watched over them; when as teenagers they laughed and chased each other into the barely passable alleys and lanes of Lainchour, when they sat on the hilltop looking over Samakhusi, with the Swayambhunath Temple in the distance, as darkness fell and fireflies began winking in the rice paddies below. She didn't want to recall those moments by herself, in the darkness of her own room. She didn't want to remember Maitreya by herself; she wanted to clasp Raja's hand and draw strength from their collective memories, before their son was born, after their son was born, after their son died. They shared a history. There was a reason Raja had come to live in Nilu Nikunj when he was barely six years old. There was a reason she'd gone looking for him when she was sixteen, a reason she'd pulled him to the Gueswori Temple for their shortcut wedding — well, the wedding was a shortcut, but the bond was long-standing.

Won't you help me, Raja? She pictured herself asking him this question. And yes, she could see him melt before her, because he was her Raja, and he loved her, and she suspected that tonight he'd wanted to say a lot more than he could. She had to give him another chance, and he had to give her another too.

The minibus to Chabel arrived. The boy-conductor leaned out the back door and, thumping the bus's side, shouted, "La, la, la, Chabel, Chabel, Chabel. Chabel-Bouddha, la, Bouddha-Chabel."

She waved at the bus, then glanced at Shiva's face. He was looking at her expectantly, waiting for her to ask him to come along.

"Chabel?" the boy-conductor asked her as the bus halted.

She nodded. Turning to Shiva, she said, "You go home now, okay, Shiva?" And she boarded the bus. He stood there, gazing at her as her bus pulled away.

Book Two

Part I

A Daughter in America

Y EARS LATER, after their daughter Ranjana had left for America, Raja occasionally teased Nilu about Shiva. "So, whatever happened to that Shiva of yours, mitini?" Raja would say as they went out for their evening walks in Budhanilkantha, where they'd moved a few years after Ranjana was born.

"How would I know?" she said. "And what about your own Jaya? What did you do with her?" She knew what had happened to Jaya, but she went along with the ritual bantering, even took pleasure in it—making fun of their transgressions made both of them equally guilty, therefore equally exonerated.

"You know she got married soon after you and I got back together," Raja said, a bit sheepishly.

"I bet she's still pining for you. She probably thinks of you at night when her husband is snoring next to her."

"And what about poor Shiva, eh? You were all over him in those days, weren't you? Poor, unhappy Shiva. I wonder what he's up to now."

Nilu didn't know. Over the years she'd anticipated running into him, but every year Kathmandu's population burgeoned, making its streets narrower and more constricted. She could be out all day without seeing the face of anyone she knew, not even distant acquaintances. Nearly two decades had gone by since she'd bid a goodbye, which turned out to be final, to Shiva at that Baneswor bus stop. He could be anywhere in the city, or even out of the country, for that matter, as so many Nepalis were leaving these days. He could have gone back to Gorkha to his brother and sister-in-law. Perhaps they'd reconciled; perhaps Shiva had forgiven his brother.

How absolutely crazy it had been in Raja's flat that day—she with Shiva, Raja with Jaya, but both she and Raja yearning, as they'd admitted in the intervening years, for each other. And as if their wishes were combining forces in the air above the city, she had run into Raja in New Road two days later. By that time something had already begun to change inside her. It was subtle, but she felt it: her mind felt lighter than it had in a long time, less crowded, more spacious. She'd catch herself smiling as she lay in bed because of a sweet feeling of anticipation that reminded her of the days when she and Raja began to talk, shyly and hesitantly, in Birey Dai's shop long ago. Where was this tiny bit of happiness coming from? It didn't make sense, for Raja was still with Jaya.

Then she glimpsed Raja in an eyeglass store in New Road, trying on a pair of sunglasses. She was on her way home from a visit to Prateema, who'd taken to bed with jaundice. For a moment she simply stood outside and watched him. He was looking at himself in the mirror, trying on different styles. His eyes were slightly puffy—he mustn't be sleeping well, Nilu noted. The shop was too small for her to step into, so she called to Raja, loudly, from the sidewalk, "Who are you preening for?"

Startled, he'd turned toward her. "Nilu? What brings you here?"

She told him about Prateema's jaundice, then asked him what he was doing.

"My eyes have been hurting in the sun lately," Raja said.

"Did you see a doctor?"

"Not yet."

"You might need glasses."

"That's why I am here." He was smiling.

"No, I mean glasses prescribed by a doctor."

So, that's how it was for a while. Nilu stood outside the shop, watching him while he tried on different frames and turned to her for advice, just like the old times. She watched his face, the circles under his eyes, his sad chin. She stifled the urge to touch his cheek.

Soon he settled on a pair that she endorsed, and he took out his wallet to pay, but it turned out that he had less money than he thought he had. Typical Raja. Nilu dug into her purse for the three hundred rupees he needed. And it didn't seem unnatural, once he emerged from the shop, that they'd walk together, and he'd ask her whether they should have tea, and they'd slip into a restaurant inside a hotel next to the Juddha Shumshere statue — the very restaurant, Nilu realized, once she was inside the revolving door, where she'd written her Jonathan Swift essay. The place still looked the same, except everything had become a bit rundown: paint peeled off the wall; a dank smell hung in the air; the waiters' uniforms looked faded. She could even remember the table where she'd sat that day, and she led Raja to it. Nearby, that long-ago afternoon, a few government workers had sneaked away from an official rally, then bolted back to it out of fear of repercussions. There was no one else in the restaurant today.

At the table, Nilu and Raja looked at each other. The silence reminded Nilu of their Lainchour days, when they could spend long hours without speaking. But they were adults now, having lived apart for nearly a year, and a kernel of unease had grown between them. Still, for Nilu it felt good to be with Raja. She enjoyed just looking at his face in the brand-new sunglasses, which he hadn't taken off.

Raja broke the silence. "Why are you smiling?"

"Nothing. I was thinking you should keep a servant."

"Just for a single person, it's a bit too much."

"But surely you don't wash your own clothes?"

"A washerwoman comes to the building every week to collect the laundry."

The waiter brought their tea.

"The flat is maintained very well," she said, and watched his face carefully.

"And you know the reason."

"Maybe I don't."

"Don't act naive."

"Jaya? Is she the reason?"

He smiled. "I don't know what you're thinking."

"I don't know either. She seems like a very sweet girl. I don't blame you for liking her."

"And I don't blame you for liking Shiva."

"What I am to Shiva is not the same as what you are to Jaya."

He read the accusation in her voice. "I don't want us to sit here and blame each other, Nilu."

"I'm not blaming you, Raja," she said. "Just clarifying. I treated Shiva like a brother." Sometimes like a son, she nearly said. "Shiva is not a happy soul."

"Who is?" Raja asked.

"You look like you're happy now."

For some reason Raja looked upset. "You don't know what I'm thinking, what I'm feeling."

"What are you feeling, Raja? Why can't we talk to each other anymore?"

He averted his gaze, then reached across the table to clasp her hands. "I worry about you every day, mitini."

"Do you?"

"How you're eating, how you're sleeping. Every day."

"You never come to visit me."

"I want to. I'm afraid that you'll start on about Maitreya again, and forgive me, Nilu, but I've already grieved for my son. It has to end."

Their tea, murky brown, was getting cold. Holding hands felt good, their smiles felt good. Once more, the silence stretched. Then, out of nowhere Nilu said, "In just the past day or two I've felt a lift, a lightness." She didn't know what more to say, and he watched her face. Finally, she asked him about his work.

He had nothing new to report, except that he was getting tired of traveling and was taking on more desk assignments now. "How is Muwa?" he asked. "Have you heard from her?"

She told him about her visit to Nilu Nikunj, Muwa's squandering of the property, how she wanted to transfer the house to Sumit.

Raja shook his head. "You did well to get out of that house when you did."

"I couldn't have done it without you."

"No, I had nothing to do with it, Nilu. You did it because you're strong."

She mulled over what he said. "Well, I'm not so strong after all, given how I wasn't able to move past Maitreya for so long."

"That has changed now, hasn't it? Our son wouldn't have wanted you to grieve over him forever."

She realized the truth in what Raja was saying. Maitreya hadn't haunted her for a while now, and she had a feeling that he wasn't going to come back. She felt a sharp ache at that thought, but it soon subsided when she fixed her gaze on Raja's face.

They talked well into the evening, as customers drifted into the restaurant for dinner. Nilu and Raja ordered some finger foods, but the chicken chili and the pakodas sat cold as they held hands — he had moved to her side of the table — and leaned against each other.

They stayed together until about eight, then left the restaurant. "Shall we walk?" Raja said. She nodded.

They walked for a full hour, all the way from New Road to Chabel, where the lights were out because of load-shedding. "Do you want to come in?" Nilu asked, as though they were just exploring the initial stages of courtship.

"Just for a little while," he said. "Don't ask me to stay the night, though."

"I won't."

She was aware of someone's eyes on her as she opened the door. It was the boy next door, at his window, his face shrouded in darkness. A candle burned on a table behind him, and Nilu saw his father by the door to their room. "Don't sit in the window in the dark, son," the father said in a reprimanding tone.

Inside, as she hunted for matches, Raja grabbed hold of her and pulled her toward him. He cupped her cheeks with his palms and

309

kissed her, deeply, hungrily. Then they held each other, the darkness around them strangely calming.

As Ranjana grew up, Raja and Nilu teased each other and laughed about that period in their lives. "You wrenched me away from Jaya," he said to her.

"I did orchestrate that walk down your lane, but the rest, you're to blame for it."

Intermittently, well into their middle age, when Nilu became the principal of Arniko Academy and Raja was promoted to the position of chief editor at Nepal Yatra, when the house became quiet after Ranjana left for America, they bantered like this. And now, nearing fifty years of age, in this nice, quiet house in Budhanilkantha, one of the few places in the city where people could escape the crowd and the smog, Nilu was no longer haunted by Maitreya. Some days when Raja went to a friend's house to play chess and she was alone at home, she stood still in the kitchen, listening to the sounds around her. Or when in the garden, reading, she lifted her eyes from the page and scanned the shrubs and house, to see if she'd feel her son around her, hovering, demanding her attention. Sometimes, on the bus going into town, she simply closed her eyes to find out if he'd come to her in her mind's eye. But he didn't.

They'd all — Nilu, Raja, Ganga Da — reveled in the arrival of Ranjana, a vivacious little baby. Ganga Da especially doted on his granddaughter and saw her as a symbol of the reunion of Raja and Nilu. Ganga Da was the one who had given Ranjana her name. Rejoicing. "She's going to grow up to be something, you just watch," Ganga Da frequently said.

But Ganga Da himself wasn't able to see whether his prophecy would come true. When Ranjana was two years old, Ganga Da was hauled off to jail on charges of accepting bribery. The government alleged that he'd received ten lakh rupees in exchange for approving a loan application for the construction of a mega hotel. It happened quickly, and before Nilu and Raja could figure it out, Ganga Da was imprisoned. At first he denied the charges, saying his enemies were behind this. But on Nilu and Raja's third visit to the jail, Ganga Da broke down and admitted his guilt. He said that he was only thinking of Jamuna Mummy and how he wanted her to get into a nice private clinic where she'd be taken care of properly. "My thinking was muddled," he kept repeating. "Something was moving fast inside my mind, like a train."

"Why didn't you simply sell the Chabel house?" Raja asked, confounded. "The one where we live? That would have been more than enough to pay for Jamuna Mummy's clinic."

"Then I'd have had to ask you to leave," Ganga Da said. "I couldn't bring myself to do it."

"That's extreme foolishness!" Raja said. "We could have simply moved to another flat. It's not as if we can't afford it. As it is, we are paying you some rent."

Ganga Da hung his head in shame. "It's not that easy. I put the Chabel house in Ranjana's name last year."

Raja and Nilu stared at him. When they told him that they could worry about Ranjana later, that they'd still need to sell the house now to pay for his growing legal expenses, Ganga Da would not let them. "That property belongs to my granddaughter," he warned them. "Don't you dare touch it."

When Raja and Nilu went together to see Ganga Da, he appeared tough, even laughed and cracked jokes, but when Nilu went to him alone, he wept. "How is my Jamuna doing?"

Nilu told him that she went to see Jamuna Mummy in the mental hospital every two weeks and that she was the same as usual. She hadn't become any worse, if that was what Ganga Da was fearing.

"Did she ask about me?"

Nilu couldn't tell him that Jamuna Mummy referred to her husband as "that gadha," had told Nilu that he was in cahoots with the royal palace to have her hanged from the ceiling of the mental hospital. "He thinks I don't know," Jamuna Mummy said. "The newspeople on television tell me everything."

That was the year that the director of the mental hospital had started allowing the patients one hour of Nepal Television in the evening. Otherwise, the condition of the hospital hadn't changed from when Nilu had visited it with baby Maitreya. Now it was Ranjana she carried with her to the hospital.

Nilu had promised Ganga Da that she'd try to visit Jamuna Mummy every week, but with her teaching and taking care of Ranjana she hadn't been able to keep her commitment. Then, within a few months of Ganga Da's imprisonment, Jamuna Mummy died in the hospital. The prison officials didn't allow Ganga Da to attend his wife's funeral. The next time Nilu and Raja went to visit him, he looked so frail and malnourished that he could barely stand up behind the bars. In moments of incoherence he asked about Jamuna Mummy, what she was doing. Then, a few days later, the jail warden called Raja in his office and informed him that Ganga Da too had passed away, in his cell.

Nilu and Raja soon came to terms with Ganga Da's death, for they had Ranjana to focus on. And how fast their daughter had grown. One day she was catching the bus to kindergarten and returning home to sing them the *do re mi*'s she'd learned, and the next day Nilu had to buy her sanitary napkins because she'd suddenly bled at school.

Ranjana's birth had helped heal their marriage, Nilu felt, for their joy at their newborn daughter gradually dissolved any remnants of the pain of that one year when they'd drifted apart. Raja had missed her terribly during that time — that much had become clear to Nilu, and she also knew that his short association with Jaya had been nothing more than an attempt to nurse his wounds, to drive away his loneliness, the hurt he felt when Nilu wallowed in her own grief, excluding him.

Now when she looked back, her grief over Maitreya seemed to verge on insanity. Could she have willed his ghost into her life? That soothsayer, Lama-ji, had said that her son's spirit was unhappy about something, and over the years she had wondered, although she hadn't told Raja this, whether he'd been sad about his parents' separation. Otherwise why had he stopped coming once she and Raja reunited? The entire thing remained a mystery to her.

But so much had happened since Maitreya's death that his short life seemed deep in the past. When Nilu contemplated the mind-numbing sickness that crippled the country a few years after they'd burned their son's body, the trauma of her son's death paled by comparison. Within months of burning Jamuna Mummy's and Ganga Da's remains at the ghat, the Maoist rebels unleashed their violence. They seemed to come out of nowhere — with their old, clunky rifles and their unforgiving eyes. The countryside became awash with blood: policemen butchered, the throats of villagers cut, husbands shot in front of their wives and children.

"I don't care," Raja said, as Nilu pointed out, on the television screen, the rows of bodies strewn across a hillside. "It's kaliyuga in Nepal. It's hell. Let them butcher one another until none are left alive. I don't have faith in anything anymore." But that was not true. Of course, Raja cared. How could you not be affected when you had to take care at the vegetable market, lest the garbage bag lying in the corner explode in your face? How could you not be moved by the photo of the village teacher whose throat had been slit, his head hanging low as he remained tied to a stake? The mayhem sweeping across the country, the ineptitude and idiotic arrogance of the several governments in handling the crisis, stunned all, and although Raja tried to remain aloof from it, Nilu could tell that it was becoming hard for him. When he played with Ranjana — even until she was eight or nine Ranjana liked to play hide-and-seek inside the house, ducking behind furniture, squeezing herself into closets — he stopped abruptly in the middle of the living room, transfixed by the news of, say, how a family of innocent peasants had been gunned down by the army because they were suspected of hiding the rebels.

"Papa!" Ranjana would shout in complaint when she realized that her father was no longer searching for her, wouldn't come and lift her up and swing her around the room.

"One second," Raja would shout back. If Nilu entered the room, he'd pretend that he was still hunting for their daughter. Why Raja had to put on this mask of indifference, Nilu could only suspect: if he allowed himself to feel again, the old, tormenting emotions from Maitreya's death would return in force. It was all a question of not allowing oneself to feel too much about Nepal's rapid plunge into darkness, into a free-for-all. And, adding insult to injury, one sum- mer evening the crown prince went berserk and gunned down his family members, including his father and mother and brother and sister, inside the palace. "What a bizarre country we live in," Raja said. "Look, look." He pointed to the television, which was show- ing a younger, more handsome photo of the crown prince, now in a coma after shooting himself at the end of his killing spree. "That moron who just wiped out his entire family is now officially our king, even though he is virtually a corpse."

Nilu shook her head.

"What does this remind you of?" Raja asked. "Didn't the Ranas do this when they ruled our sorry bunch, ages ago? Kill their own fathers and sons and brothers so they could be declared Western Senior Commanding General or Southern Commanding General, or the Maharaja of Kaski and Lamjung, or whatever ridiculous title they gave themselves?"

"You remembering Jungey again?"

Yet what had happened inside the palace seemed only a natural extension of the feudal days of the Ranas, those days when a prime minister would be brutally murdered by his cousins as he got his feet massaged; when a nephew would shoot his own uncle in the head from behind, as Jungey did, in his quest for power.

Whenever people took to the streets, shouting, something still flickered in Raja's eyes, and he began to pace the room. When Ran- jana was fourteen and thousands of people jammed the lanes and alleys of Kathmandu, asking that King G relinquish his powers, Raja told Nilu, "Bewakoofs, all of them. Nothing is going to happen. They could topple this king, and in his place will emerge another hundred-headed monster."

"Like the demon Ravan, Papa," Ranjana said from the floor, where she was drawing on a piece of paper.

"That's the truth," Raja said. "Look at these people. They'll gather in the streets, shout their slogans, people will die, and another regime will be born. What changes? Nothing."

"But things are always changing, Papa," Ranjana said.

"And how do you know that?" Raja said, eyeing her suspiciously. "Do you have access to a secret that I don't? Do you have a private guru somewhere who tells you what life is like?"

"I have a private guru right here," Ranjana said, tapping her head. Then something occurred to her, and she stood up and meekly approached her parents, who were sitting on the sofa. She joined her palms in namaste and bowed her head, then said, "But what is that saying? *Mata, pita, guru, daivam*—Mother and father before even teacher and god. Don't the scriptures encourage children to touch their parents' feet at least once a day?" She knelt before her father and her hand reached for his feet.

Raja, at once realizing what she was about to do, quickly lifted his legs onto the sofa, laughing. "No, you won't. I was fooled once. I won't be fooled again."

"Darn!" Ranjana said. "I thought I had Papa this time." She went and sat by Nilu, who was watching all this from behind the pages of a novel.

"Don't blame me," Nilu said to Raja. "I didn't teach her that. You are just paranoid from something that happened more than twenty years ago."

"When you first moved to Thamel?" Ranjana asked.

"Yes, and I still have the scar to prove it," Raja said, and lifted his shirt to reveal an indentation, the size of a fingernail, on his lower back.

Nilu ran her finger over it and said. "That's it? And you call that a scar?"

"It looks as if Ma lovingly bit you there. What are you complaining about?"

"Like mother, like daughter," Raja said. "Too clever."

315

"Who do I look like more, Papa?" Ranjana said, placing her cheek alongside her mother's for comparison. "Ma or you?"

"You look like me, of course," Raja said. And she did. Ranjana had his height, the same tapered face. This made him happy.

When Ranjana first announced her intention to go to America, Raja was heartbroken. Her decision had surprised both Nilu and Raja, but Nilu said later that it wasn't as if Ranjana had gone behind their backs and sneakily applied to American colleges. They knew she was interested in going abroad, but somehow they hadn't really thought it would happen until the day she received the acceptance letter from Northwestern University.

"But there are good colleges here, aren't there?" Raja had said. "America is overrated anyway. Have you ever seen anyone from America who's happy? The future is not there, but here."

When Ranjana said that she was going there to study, not to search for happiness, Raja responded, "Studying in America is overrated too. Look at all these people who are returning with their M.B.A.'s and whatnot and still they can't find a job. At least if you study here, you'll make connections. You'll be able to—what do they call it now—yes, network."

"But Papa, I want to study anthropology, not business, and America is much better for a field like that."

Raja was about to object when Nilu butted in and said, "You have to let your daughter make some of her own decisions at some point, you know."

Unhappy as he was, Raja had relented, and before long Ranjana had flown to Chicago, where she was going to stay with Umesh as she attended Northwestern. Umesh was Raja's cousin, a distant nephew of Ganga Da. He was a chemistry professor at the University of Chicago. Initially, when Ranjana applied to colleges, Nilu and Raja had hoped that she'd get into Umesh's university and live with him and his family, at least for the first year. But the University of Chicago had rejected Ranjana; instead, she'd been admitted to

Northwestern in a northern suburb of the city. Ranjana had stayed with Umesh's family in his house in Oak Lawn for the first month, then, soon after the semester started, found an apartment near her university because she said the commute consumed a lot of her time.

Ranjana's move turned Raja into a bit of a worrywart. He fretted at night about her, and in the morning, bleary-eyed, he'd call his daughter in America, asking petulantly whether she had eaten well and whether she was getting enough rest between her studies. "You aren't lonely there, are you?" he'd ask.

One July morning, well into a year after Ranjana began her U.S. studies, Raja and Nilu were sitting in their living room when Raja mentioned that perhaps Ranjana's career choice was not a good one. "Whatever can you do with anthropology anyway? Do you know any anthropologists? I don't. I can't even pronounce the word properly. She should get on a better track, such as business, or even study to be a journalist, and those opportunities are plentiful right here."

"I don't understand where this track business is coming from," Nilu said to him. "You are beginning to sound like typical Nepali parents, worried that their children might not turn out to be doctors and engineers. You and I were never on track. In fact, we got miserably off track, remember?"

"Yes, yes," he said impatiently. "But I'm talking about a career track, not in the sense you're talking about."

"You need to let her go. I know she's young, but this is what she wants to do, and she's a levelheaded girl. You have nothing to worry about. She's so devoted to her studies that she has been taking classes all summer, when most other students go on vacation in America." In fact, Ranjana had been so busy with her studies that her communication with her parents had been irregular, unusual for a girl who had diligently written letters every two weeks during the first few months she'd been in America. These days Nilu and Raja were lucky if they received an e-mail from Ranjana once every few days. Most of these messages were perfunctory: describing how swamped she was and how she had little time for recreation, the e-mails were devoid of the trademark erudition and witty language of her letters. Lately, when Nilu or Raja called Ranjana's apartment, her roommates said that she was either in class or at the library, studying. And Ranjana would phone back a day or two later, sounding weary, saying she was calling from a phone booth somewhere on campus, using a phone card; then she'd explain that her summer classes were so intense that she barely had time to breathe. When Nilu or Raja suggested that she didn't need to work so hard, didn't need to take so many classes, Ranjana said that this big push would be over soon enough.

Their daughter sounded almost defeated. It worried Nilu that whenever they phoned, Ranjana was never at home. But Ranjana had reassured Nilu. "Don't worry about me, Ma. This will all pay off later." Ranjana was ambitious about going to graduate school, and her hard work now was bound to reap dividends when it came time to apply. She'd been getting top grades in all of her classes, Ranjana had written, and taking extra ones during the summer would allow her to complete her bachelor's degree a bit earlier. In August, Nilu thought, once Ranjana's classes were over, she could take some time off to recuperate before the next school year began. Perhaps Nilu and Raja could send her a few hundred dollars for a vacation somewhere, maybe Washington, D.C., where Ranjana had friends.

"I know she's diligent, Nilu, but in America even normal people get funny ideas," Raja said. "What if she ends up joining a hippie group there, or a cult?"

"There are no more hippies in America. You know why? They all came here in the sixties. You were one of the homegrown ones, so you should know. A Nepali hippie, smoking ganja in Thamel's restaurants or down Pie Alley."

Raja chose not to get her joke. "Yes, but those days were different. Now people don't blink when they chop someone's head off."

Nilu couldn't tell whether he was referring to the fairly recent past, when jihadists in Iraq had decapitated Nepali migrant workers, or whether he was referring to the Maoist rebels in their own country, who used to roam the hills with their enemies' severed heads in their arms. But these gruesome, outlandish images had nothing to do with their daughter's college life in America, Nilu reminded Raja.

"You always dismiss my concerns about Ranjana," he said. "I can't have a serious conversation about her with you. I'm worried."

"Come here," she said. She was sitting on the sofa, making a list of flowers she wanted to purchase at the nursery for the forthcoming growing season.

Raja sat next to her, and she set the list aside. "What has come over you?" she asked. "You know your daughter. You don't need to worry about her. She has always made good decisions, hasn't she?"

"But now she's in America, the land of the crazies." He bit his tongue soon after he uttered the word. "I shouldn't really say such a thing. May Jamuna Mummy's soul rest in peace."

"You called her crazy all the time when she was alive."

"Yes, but one shouldn't say such things about dead people."

"You've become so serious these days," Nilu said. "Relax a bit."

Raja became thoughtful. "You know, sometimes when I look at Ranjana, I don't know why but I suddenly think of my mother, my real mother, the one who gave me birth."

"The one you never saw."

"Why are you smiling?"

"I'm not."

"Yes, you are. You have that mocking smile."

"Well, it's amazing how after all these years the woman who you never saw, who abandoned you, is the one you think of more often than either Kaki or Jamuna Mummy."

"She's never left me, Nilu. I think of her at least once a day." He paused. "And lately . . ." He didn't go further.

"Lately what?"

After some coaxing, Raja told her that lately he'd been having frequent vivid dreams about his birth mother. She was skinny, with sunken eyes, roaming the streets of the city trying to feed her baby on her dry, shriveled breasts. Desperate, she left the baby by a shrub in Tundikhel and crossed over to Rani Pokhari. She struggled with the bars around the pond, her palms lacerated by their sharp points as she climbed over them.

The Singer and the Beauty

(Raja's Mother's Story)

SHE DRIFTED TO the drawing room window when she knew he'd be coming, which was in the afternoon. He rode an old Hero bicycle with rusted wheel covers. Expertly maneuvering the bike, rarely touching its bell, he slithered through the alleys of the city center, with its hordes of pedestrians. He was a singer, and he sang as he rode underneath her window.

Mohini had to be careful because her father was in his room, listening to the radio, where King M was making an announcement. The year was 1961. King M had just jailed the prime minister. The king's voice drifted into the living room, where Mohini sat by the window. In the past Father had beaten her when her eyes had lingered on the neighborhood boys. He'd brandished his cane and whacked her on the legs, saying, "You want to be a harlot? That's what you'll be — a whore!" Mother, a small woman with a broad cabbage face, sometimes asked her husband not to hit their daughter too hard, lest he injure her so badly that she'd become crippled or defaced, which would make it impossible for her to marry. But most often Mother just watched.

"We have to accomplish in years," King M said, "what other countries have taken centuries to do."

Mohini had an older brother who had quarreled with her parents and lived a few blocks away, somewhere in Indrachowk—she didn't know exactly where, and she wouldn't know because her parents had kept it a secret from her, and had warned her against visiting him. She had adored Pradip Dai all of her life, and now she missed him terribly. She couldn't visit her friends after school because her parents didn't want her to socialize. She had a couple of cousins, but they were boys, which meant that apart from polite hellos and how-are-you's, she was not allowed to speak to them.

Pradip Dai had become estranged because he'd married a girl of a lower caste, which was scandalous, unthinkable. Even when it turned out that the girl's father's business, selling various types of cooking oil, was quite lucrative, and that Pradip Dai would inherit the business because the girl had no brothers, Father didn't budge. "They're telis," he said to his wife. "It'll stain our family name forever. We can't be bought with money." Mohini sensed that Mother was attracted to the money, but didn't dare say anything because she was afraid of Father's cane, which, when he deemed it necessary, also came down on her. Mohini could see it in Mother's eyes, the greed, which slowly gave way to bitterness toward Pradip Dai and her new daughter-in-law.

King M said that he had to sack the government because it couldn't maintain law and order and it was getting too corrupt.

Mohini had talked to her sister-in-law only once. At that time Pradip Dai still lived at home, but slowly rumors had begun to spread that he and the teli's daughter had something going. Mohini herself had heard it from one of her friends, and she had even teased her brother about it. "I want to meet her, let me meet her," she'd said excitedly to her brother, who'd merely smiled, then put his index finger to his lips as Father, his thick, odorous shawl wrapped around him, appeared with his cane at the doorway to the room. Mohini learned that sometimes the girl tended her father's oil shop, but when Mohini passed by a couple of times, she saw only the oil-soaked father, or another man who could have been the uncle. Then, one afternoon as Mohini sat by the window, she suddenly became aware of a girl about her age walking back and forth on the street below. Mohini sat at the window when Father wasn't around, and today he'd gone out to meet some people; Mother, although she frowned when she saw Mohini doing what she called "revealing all your goods to the world," didn't discipline her, as her Father did, so Mohini was bolder with Mother.

Mohini stared at the girl, who, after glancing up and spotting her, hurried on, with her head lowered, then stopped at the general store some distance away. Mohini moved away from the window and flattened herself against the adjoining wall, her eyes focused on the road. A few minutes later the girl walked by again, eyeing Mohini's window. Ah, Mohini thought. She tiptoed out of her room. Mother sat on the floor of the balcony facing the inner courtyard, sifting through the rice to weed out the small stones that could chip teeth. Mohini pretended to have drifted there to enjoy the spring sun. Mother briefly glanced up and muttered something about helping with the chores. Then Mohini began inching away toward the stairs, hoping that the girl was still outside.

Mother went into the kitchen, balancing against her hip the nanglo full of rice, and Mohini bolted down the stairs. At the front door she held her breath; she scanned the street. The girl was nearing the house, her eyes still trained on the window; she didn't spot Mohini until she was a couple of feet from the door. Then her eyes widened in alarm. She quickly looked away, but Mohini asked, in a low voice, "Are you looking for Pradip Dai?"

The girl searched Mohini's face for a few seconds, then she nodded. "He told me he was going to meet me there." She vaguely pointed to her right.

"What's your name?" Mohini asked.

"Chanda."

"I'm Mohini."

"I know," the girl said shyly. "He's talked about you. Often."

"Something must have kept him," Mohini said. "I'll let him know as soon as he gets home." She wished she could talk more with Chanda, who had a smooth, gentle face. Mohini could see herself becoming Chanda's friend for life, growing old together as they fondly complained about Pradip Dai. Mohini told Chanda that she had to go back indoors. "We'll talk again," she half-whispered, and crept up the stairs. Mother had returned to the balcony, this time sifting through lentils. She glanced up at Mohini when she saw her emerge from the staircase and mumbled something Mohini couldn't hear. Sometimes Mohini suspected that if it hadn't been for Father, Mother would have been all right. Sometimes Mother talked to Mohini about a piece of jewelry, or some aspect of her childhood, that indicated that she too, in her younger years, had felt what Mohini felt — this restlessness, this strange yearning in the body, this silly impulse to show the world a part of yourself that was wild, unexpected. At times Mother laughed, as a sister might, over something Mohini said. But in the presence of Father, Mother frowned and stood sternly with her arms folded when Father berated their children.

"The whole world is mocking us," Father had said one day a few weeks ago, waving his cane at Pradip Dai, who kept his gaze lowered. "This can't go on."

Pradip Dai said, in a low but firm voice, still not looking at Father, "Chanda and I want to get married."

The silence was long.

"Married?" their father said finally. "To a teli's daughter?"

"Shame, shame," Mother said. "Our entire khalak's name will forever be tarnished." Then she said a bit more softly, "Okay, you've had your fun. Now forget about her and marry a nice girl from a suitable family."

Pradip Dai looked up, directly, into Father's eyes. "We are getting married."

Father lifted his cane to strike, but Pradip Dai calmly stepped back so that the cane struck the air between them with a *whoosh*.

"Don't expect me home anymore," Pradip Dai said, and left the house.

After Pradip Dai and Chanda got married, the neighbors indeed mocked Mohini's family. One very old woman with a bent back, so old that her face resembled cracked earth, spat on the ground whenever she saw Mohini or her parents. Father went to argue with Chanda's father, who said that he too had been against the marriage. Chanda's father wore a cap soaked in oil. The two men traded barbs. Father accused the oil man of using his daughter to marry up. Chanda's father stood in his small shop, surrounded by canisters of mustard oil, ghiu, peanut oil, soybean oil. He asked Father, "What do you have? An old, rotten house about to fall down? Do you know how much land I own? Do you have any idea how well my oil business is doing?"

"You can take your oil and massage your own balls," Father said.

"Muji!" Chanda's father beckoned to a couple of young men standing nearby, presumably his relatives or neighbors. They came over, gave Father some severe up-and-down looks, but eventually stood still and looked at the ground, cowed. Father, with his substantial belly and his cane, was formidable. He hit the ground with his cane, repeating his assertion that the old man used his daughter to marry up. The young men glanced at each other, danced on the ground as though they couldn't wait to be gone, then fled, apologizing to Chanda's father that they had an urgent appointment and stating that he ought to reconcile with Father, as they were in-laws already, whether they liked it or not.

After the young men left, a glaring match ensued between the two old men. Chanda's father, smaller in frame, oily but sinuous, stood inside his shop, ignoring customers who stopped by with their bottles for oil. Father, his cane tip resting authoritatively on the ground, stood with one hand on his hip; a cow gently nudged his behind with its nose, as if smelling something there. The cow pushed him toward the shop, and Chanda's father pointed at Father and laughed; despite himself, Father also smiled. "Even God is making fun of us," said Chanda's father, and Father grunted. Soon, he was sitting on a stool in front of the shop, a cup of tea in hand, talking in a low voice with Chanda's father about how hard it was to control your children these days, that his son had basically cut the nose of the entire family. Chanda's father expressed similar sentiments, and the two men commiserated. Their talk drifted to politics. Chanda's father said that King M made a big mistake by playing soccer in Dashrath Stadium with the prime minister. The announcement of the game late last year had caused a sensation in the city, and people had flocked to the stadium. The king and his brothers had battled the prime minister and his cabinet on the field. "A king is a king, don't you understand," Chanda's father whispered to Father.

He agreed, then added, "But this king is not a fool. Watch him. He's got something up his sleeve." And Father was right, thought Mohini, for King M had indeed moved swiftly, jailing the same prime minister barely a couple of months after the king returned from his trip to England. The king, who wore dark sunglasses all the time, was a figure of mystery to Mohini. He looked so solemn during his coronation a few years earlier.

Mohini's whole family had gone to witness the coronation, at her insistence. She was fourteen then, but wielded more power over Father than she did now, and she had pestered him for days to take her. Father, who loathed crowds, had finally relented, and on that day Mohini, Father, Mother, and Pradip Dai had gone to Tundikhel, where they'd stood with thousands, for hours, under the hot Baisakh sun, waiting for the king to arrive. The parade had been delayed because its many elephants had become gridlocked outside the Hanuman Dhoka Palace, where the crowning had taken place. Father had complained throughout, and Mohini and Mother had hushed him, afraid that others wouldn't take kindly to his voicing of discomfort on such a great day. Finally, when the procession arrived, Mohini was stunned by its opulence. Huge elephants, lavishly decorated, carried the dignitaries, including the queen of England, on a slow passage through the streets. Marching bands and cars followed. After the king sat upon the mandap, a plane flew overhead and scattered flower petals on the pavilion and the crowd.

After watching the king's coronation, Mohini experienced a special attachment to him. Sometimes when she went to the temple, she found herself praying for his well-being as well as her own. These days, when she listened to Father and the neighbors debating current events, she felt that she knew a great deal more about it than many of her friends did. She imagined discussing the workings of the state with her future husband, and in his expression she saw his growing admiration for her insight, her knowledge.

That day, the two fathers established a truce, but that didn't prevent them from disapproving of the marriage of their children.

From then on, whenever someone mentioned his son, Father said, "Don't say his name to me."

For days Mohini ached to visit Pradip Dai and Chanda. She sent a letter to Pradip Dai through a local boy, telling him about the general neighborhood where they lived, and although the boy claimed that he delivered it, she never received a response. She asked him what their home looked like, but the boy gave only a muddled answer. A couple of times she tried to gather the courage to visit the newlyweds, even anticipated confronting her parents, especially Father, her chin up, her voice unwavering as she told them that no one could prevent her from having a relationship with her brother; it was rightfully hers. But when she faced them, she ended up lowering her head and meekly going about her household chores.

One day after lunch, Father went out for the whole afternoon to a relative's place. Only Mohini and Mother were in the house. After cleaning up in the kitchen, Mother sat on the mat on the balcony, warming herself in the sun. Mohini sat next to her, and as she half-dozed, an idea came to her. In a lazy voice, she said, "Mother, shall I oil your hair?"

Mother smiled. Mohini hadn't made such an offer for a while. "How come you are thinking not of yourself but of your mother today?" she chidingly said to Mohini, then patted her head and said yes.

Mohini heated some oil and brought it out to the balcony. Seated behind her mother, she began to massage the hair, the scalp, the nape of the neck. "Ahh, that feels good," Mother said. She closed her eyes. After about five minutes, as Mohini gradually lessened the pressure of her strokes, Mother's head began to loll, and she drifted into sleep. Mohini carefully rested her mother's head on the floor, placed a blanket over her face to ward off the sun, then tiptoed downstairs. Only after she stepped into the street did she realize that she had her house clothes on, a faded, torn frock that slightly reeked of the garlic she'd chopped that morning. But she couldn't risk going back up and waking Mother, so she set off, threading through alleys to reach Indrachowk, which was only about ten minutes away. In the square, she inquired about the whereabouts of Pradip Dai's house, nervously scanning the streets for someone who might recognize her and tell her parents. Mother could have awakened by now, but Mohini could manufacture an excuse to placate her, to convince her not to tell Father.

Everywhere she asked about Pradip Dai, people shook their heads, and as the minutes went by her anxiety grew, and she began to perspire. She was about to return when she spotted, at the second-floor window of the house above her, a girl's figure, a half-turned face in the semi-dark room. "Pradip Dai!" she shouted, her cry almost hysterical. The girl leaned out the window. It was indeed Chanda, already looking more like a woman, with a fuller face, a streak of vermilion powder gracing the parting of her hair, her arms covered with bracelets.

"Recognize me?" Mohini asked.

"Mohini Bahini!" Chanda gasped. "Are you here by yourself?"

Overcome with relief and happiness, Mohini could only swallow and nod.

Chanda waved her up, and Mohini went in through the front door and bounded up the dark stairs. Chanda was waiting for her at the landing, outside her flat. She asked whether Mohini's parents knew about this visit, and when Mohini shook her head, Chanda grew concerned. "Why act so foolishly then?" Chanda asked, as she beckoned her inside.

"I wanted to see Pradip Dai, and you."

Chanda had her sit on the bed. She held Mohini's hand and gazed into her eyes. "You're only a year younger than me, do you know that?"

Mohini nodded. "Is Pradip Dai not home?"

"He's out at a friend's place. Should be coming now."

Mohini looked around. The room felt a bit damp, but it was fairly spacious, with a corner for a stove and a washing area with a tap.

"Let me make tea," Chanda said. "Unfortunately, there's nothing to eat right now, but I can make something."

Mohini said, "I should be making some tea for my new sister-in-law."

"No, no, you sit there and talk to me," Chanda said. She went to the corner and began to pump the stove. Mohini too sat on the cold floor. As the water boiled, they talked. Mohini learned that Chanda's mother had come to visit the newlyweds and that although Chanda's father hadn't come with her, he had sent some money, about a hundred rupees, a week later. Her side of the family had gradually begun to accept their marriage, Chanda said. "But your parents, they still don't like me," she said as she poured the tea into steel cups.

"They are very strict," Mohini said.

The door creaked open and Pradip Dai entered with another man. Pradip Dai exclaimed in surprise at seeing Mohini there, then asked about the health of Father and Mother in the bluff manner of inquiring after mere acquaintances. The man with him was short but had handsome features and soft, lovely eyes that lingered over Mohini's face a second too long, making her blush. The two men sat on the bed while Chanda served them tea, then she joined Mohini on the floor again, facing the men. The conversation soon turned to the cinema, and Mohini learned that Pradip Dai and Chanda had seen almost every Hindi film now playing in the theaters. *Hulchul* with Dilip Kumar and Nargis, *Chhaliya* with Raj Kapoor and Nutan, *Kalpana* with Padmini and Ashok Kumar. Mohini had been to the cinema only once, to see *Aan* in Jana Sewa Hall when she was about seven years old. Pradip Dai had taken her, secretly, when Father and Mother had gone to a relative's house in Patan for the day. They'd dashed through the lanes of Asan and Indrachowk and arrived breathless at the cinema, which was at the corner of Juddha Sadak. Pradip Dai had stolen some coins from Father's pockets, and after buying two third-class tickets, he'd purchased a bottle of guch-chey soda from the soda shop near the gate of the cinema. Inserting his left thumb into the mouth of the bottle, the soda man brought down his right fist on top of the thumb, hitting and loosening the colorful marble that had been lodged at the neck, and sent it diving down to the bottom of the bottle. He then offered the soda to Pra-dip Dai, who took a swig and passed it on to Mohini. The fizz assaulted her nose as she tilted the bottle and gulped.

It was her first time watching a film, and the whole experience enthralled her: the horses galloping on the screen, the close-ups of people's faces, the deep voices of the actors. The handsome man with the large, doelike eyes and pouty lips, who was singing a song next to a horse, was the famous Dilip Kumar, and for days Mohini couldn't get his face out of her mind. Pradip Dai's friend also had lovely eyes and smooth skin that reminded her — she realized as she inhaled sharply — of Dilip Kumar. His name was Yudhir, she learned, and sometimes he joined Pradip Dai and Chanda Bhauju when they went to the cinema. For a while the three excitedly talked about a Raj Kapoor movie they'd seen recently, in which the actor played a crook. Before Mohini knew it, Yudhir began to sing a song from the film.

His voice was intoxicating. It penetrated her, addressed the yearning she'd been feeling lately. Every now and then he closed his eyes, and the song spoke of why the heart was so afraid of love, how the journey ahead was so difficult. His voice was slightly nasal but suffused with so much emotion that she felt a lump in her throat. As if he knew how he was making her feel, Yudhir let his glance linger on Mohini a moment longer than it did on the others. Only toward the end, as he neared his final note, did she realize that she'd heard the song, a duet, before, but it hadn't caught her attention. Now Yudhir had made the song beautiful.

"Doesn't our Yudhir here have a fine, fine voice?" Pradip Dai proudly said to Mohini, and she nodded.

For a while, then, as the four sat conversing, Yudhir and Mohini sneaked glances at each other. At one point Chanda got up to go to her cupboard in the corner of the room, Pradip Dai went down to the courtyard to use the toilet, and Yudhir and Mohini were left alone, he sitting on the bed by the window and she on the floor in front of him. Words curled and twisted inside her; her throat throbbed, but she couldn't speak. He played with a ring, taking it off his finger and sliding it back again. His eyes roamed the room, then landed on her face. Sing again, she said to him in her mind, this time just for me, and, as if hearing her appeal, or simply hiding his nervousness, he began to hum a tune from an old, old Hindi movie, an emperor's lament at the loss of his queen, which led to the creation of that giant tomb, the Taj Mahal.

"I know that song," Mohini whispered, without looking at Yudhir, and he stopped singing and asked her how often she went to the movies. She murmured that her parents wouldn't allow it.

He didn't say anything after that, and soon Pradip Dai was back, and he teased them. "You two sitting here like newlyweds, blushing and whatnot. Maybe I can persuade Father and Mother to get you two married." Mohini stood and slapped Pradip Dai's arm. Realizing what time it was, hastily she said goodbye to everyone. "I don't know when I'll be able to visit again," she told Chanda, who squeezed her hands.

Down on the street she looked up at her brother's window, and there was Yudhir, following her departure with his gaze.

Her father whacked her calves with his cane, making her swoon. Every time he struck her, she let out a cry and reached down to rub her legs. Mother stood to the side, watching, arms crossed, jaw set, her eyes watery, as if she was trying hard not to cry. "No daughter of mine will leave home without my permission," Father said as he raised his cane once more. Mother muttered something, and momentarily it seemed Father was distracted, for he said, "Hainh!" to Mother, who cleared her throat and said loudly that Mohini was going to be a slut. Father looked at Mother in disbelief, as if he hadn't expected his wife to say such a thing. He looked at Mohini, who had now crumpled to the floor, tears streaming down her cheeks.

"Get up now," Father said. "Go wash your face."

The next morning she couldn't move. Mother shouted at her to come to the kitchen to make tea for her father, but every time Mohini tried to set her legs down on the floor, pain shot up her legs to her hips, then on to her back.

Mother stood in the doorway. "Did you not hear me?"

"I can't move."

Mother's eyes softened, briefly, then turned hard again. "Come to the kitchen."

A few minutes later, Mohini did manage to hobble to the kitchen, bracing herself against the walls so she wouldn't fall.

Mother had already made tea, and she quietly gestured toward the stainless steel cup; steam curled from it like smoke. "I might spill it," Mohini told Mother, who, seated in front of the hearth, was already stoking the fire and preparing to set on it a pot of lentils. Mohini bent down; pain shot through her calf, but she gritted her teeth and sat on her haunches, then reached for the cup. The metal was hot, and she jerked her hand away. Gingerly she reached for it again, this time circling her palm around it so the heat shot through her hand, up her arms, and into her chest, making her forget about the pain in her legs. She stood slowly, as if she was performing a dance. Her right palm clasped the cup as she inched her way toward Father's room, where he was sitting on the floor, his back against the bed, his broad face hidden behind the day's *Gorkhapatra*, only his thick fingers visible. When he lowered the newspaper, his gaze at her was almost devoid of expression. "Tea," she said, and her voice came out hoarse.

"Sit," Father said, and she was relieved at the offer because she couldn't stand for much longer. The tea's heat had already dissipated, and the ache and throb in her legs, the underside of her thighs, had started again and was now spreading down to her heels.

Mohini lowered her body and put the tea down in front of Father, then allowed her rump to collapse on the floor. She pulled up her knees and lowered her head onto them. Much of the anger, the burning humiliation she had felt throughout the night had simply vanished, and now all she felt was exhaustion. If Father had started talking about a piece of news — the two neighboring countries, big communist China to the north and messy, dirt-poor India to the south, exchanging razor-sharp words, threatening battle — she would have pretended interest, dragged herself closer to him, sniffed the tobacco lingering in the air from the hookah he smoked first thing in the morning, and rested her head on his lap, which she was allowed to do until she was five or six.

"Tomorrow someone is coming to see you," Father said.

She understood what he meant, and she nodded. Last evening Father had said to Mother that girls like their daughter would be brought under control only by a strong, disciplinarian husband. Then Father had left the house, saying that he was going to see some people about this right away.

"Make sure you walk properly by then," he said from behind his *Gorkhapatra*.

How badly Mohini wanted Father to look at her with amused eyes, how badly she wanted him to rub his coarse chin against her cheek and make her squirm, as he used to when she was younger. She stayed for a minute or two more, and he continued reading his newspaper, so she once again stood up, with difficulty, then returned to her room.

That afternoon, the pain in her legs lessened a bit, and she dragged herself to her window. Father had gone outside somewhere, maybe to confirm the arrangement for the next morning, when a potential groom would arrive at the house. Since last night, her heart had been numb toward Father and Mother, and if she was to enter a stranger's house tomorrow as a bride, she'd not feel any loss. I no longer care about myself — these words reverberated in her head as she looked down at the street. A ray of afternoon sun had somehow managed to squeeze into the narrow alley. Usually the sun shied away from this side of the house, which faced northeast; the other side, facing the inner courtyard, basked in sunlight. Down the street outside the grocery shop, a man stood leaning against his bicycle, talking to the shopkeeper. Something about him held her attention;

then he looked up at her, and a tremor passed through her body. I'm going to die, she thought. Did he raise his eyebrows? Did he? Was that a smile on his lips? She also attempted to smile, but it came out like a smirk.

The man said something to the shopkeeper, who leaned forward from his cushion and passed him a cigarette. After he lit it, smoke billowed up from his face. Waving goodbye to the shopkeeper, he walked his bicycle toward her, looking straight at her as though he'd already made his decision about her and nothing was going to hold him back. She became lightheaded, afraid she'd fall out of the window. Falling out of the window, into love.

He stopped, and for once she didn't care that Mother was in the next room and could possibly hear their conversation, which she knew would start any minute now. Dragging on his cigarette, blowing the smoke out, he asked her how she was, and she said she was fine and what was he doing in this neighborhood? He said something about a friend who lived nearby, but he didn't mean it to be a convincing excuse because he was smiling, his eyes boring into hers. Won't you come down for a moment, he asked, and she shook her head: she didn't want him to witness her pathetic state, hobbling and limping. Do you want to come up? she asked slyly, and he laughed and said he didn't want to get slaughtered by her parents. Mother's voice rang behind Mohini sleepily, asking whom she was talking to, and she responded that it was no one. You are no one, she whispered to him loudly. He waved his hand in the air; it's all out of control, he seemed to suggest. Sing to me, she said, her chin on her arm, which rested on the windowsill. Now? he asked. She nodded. He looked to his left and right. People were going about their business. In a low voice he sang a few lines from a song she didn't know, but of course it was about love, and the heartbreak therein. The singer had been wandering, barefoot, for exactly seven lives searching for his beloved, and now that he'd found her, he'd been spurned.

The next morning Father said that she was a lucky girl: the prospective groom had liked her photo, and now he wanted to see her. Although Father would have preferred no personal contact between the two until the day of the wedding, this boy was modern, and also too precious to pass up. "You will not betray me," Father said.

At about nine o'clock that morning, the prospective groom, his father, and his uncle came to look at Mohini. Fully decked out in a colorful sari, lipstick liberally applied to her lips, Mohini was ushered by Mother into Father's room, where the guests sat on cushions on the floor. She kept her head down, not looking at the face of the prospective groom. She sat by the door, eyes on the multicolored rug her mother had spread out this morning, her sari veil covering her face. The two fathers were talking, with the uncle chiming in occasionally, and when they began to guffaw about something, she made a show of stretching her neck, and stole a glance. The prospective groom too seemed discomfited by the ritual, for his eyes roamed restlessly. Father called Mother, who was then instructed to lift the sari veil. Mohini kept her gaze lowered. "Mohini Nani is very beautiful," the prospective groom's father said.

Mother swooped the air with her arm and said, "In the whole neighborhood she is known for her beauty."

"Just as you are known for your ugliness," Father told her, and the two fathers had a hearty laugh at Mother's expense.

Mohini glanced at the boy, whose name, she had learned, was Daya; he was now looking at her steadily, his earlier restlessness gone, his eyes boring into her. It was an aggressive look, designed to intimidate, and suddenly she became aware that he was really not a boy but a man, with definite lines to his face, a hard jaw already in battle with the world. She closed her eyes and willed Yudhir's face to come to her, and it did. This was all she needed. All she had to do was close her eyes and he'd be there, and all this nonsense, with these two old men laughing at the joke about Mother's lack of beauty, this man with his bullying eye, her soon-to-be husband, would simply fade away.

That afternoon Father came to her room and informed her that the man had approved of her and now they were moving toward an engagement and a wedding date. "Did you see the watch he was wearing?" Father asked. "Romer watch, from Switzerland. One of a kind." He paused at the doorway. "You are lucky."

Mohini sat by the window, the pain in her legs now a dull throb. Yudhir came by toward evening, ringing his bicycle bell. He passed below her window, teasing her with a faint smile as he looked straight ahead. Her eyes followed him as he rode to the shop, where he stopped. He had a brief conversation with the shopkeeper, who again handed him a cigarette. After he lit it, he looked at her, but he was too far away for her to gauge his expression. Then he hopped on his bicycle and came toward her, the cigarette dangling from his lips. When he passed by her window, he swung his arm and pitched something up, and her hand darted from her shawl to grab it. It was a crumpled piece of paper. He turned the corner in the distance and disappeared. She cast a glance behind to ensure that neither Father nor Mother had seen the exchange, then unfolded the paper. "Tomorrow, khari tree in Tundikhel, three in the afternoon," he had written. She tucked the paper into her blouse. There wasn't any way she could go, she knew; it was too risky, especially at this time, when Father and Mother, in anticipation of the impending wedding, would be watching her like hawks. Still, she felt the pressure of his note against her chest, and at one point in the night even took it out and felt the creases of the paper in the dark.

Early the next morning a servant from the groom's family delivered an invitation to the engagement ceremony. But Mohini was preoccupied about the afternoon. Since waking up this morning, she'd been filled with a sense of doom: if she didn't make it to this rendezvous with Yudhir, she'd lose him forever; then she'd be married to a man toward whom she felt nothing. Daya (what an unappealing name!) would press himself against her, day and night, making her squirm, and she'd be forced to think of Yudhir, his fingers touching her chin as his voice melted into her ears, his hand slowly rubbing her hips, then up to . . . she sharply inhaled . . . her breasts . . . oh . . . oh . . . oh, and then his hand moving down to her belly, rubbing in circles there. Her breathing turned erratic, and her mother, talking about how many guests they should plan on, saw the stupendous smile on her face and said, "Look at you. Already dreaming about becoming a bride."

Father was supposed to be out all day, meeting with a potential buyer for a small plot of land in Bhaktapur, which Father needed to sell to finance Mohini's wedding. "Don't expect me until the evening," he told Mother as he went down the stairs, tapping his cane against the wall. Mohini monitored Mother's mood. Apart from a few moments of irritation over some household matter, Mother remained happy, often praising the groom's family — what a stellar name they had in the city. "Two servants work in their house, do you know? Only the raja-maharajas live like that."

Mohini acted pleased.

A few minutes before three, Mohini wrapped a lipstick and a small handheld mirror in her handkerchief, which she then tucked into her suruwal; then, carrying a few of her schoolbooks from last year, she went to Mother. "Sarita has asked for these books right away," she said. "I need to go to her house to return them."

"What books?"

"These," she said, thrusting the books toward her. "Don't you remember? This S.L.C. guess paper for practice from Ratna Pustak Bhandar, and others. I borrowed them from her last year."

"I thought we bought those."

Mohini feigned exasperation. "Mother! You don't remember anything."

"She wants them now?"

"She'd sent her brother by this morning. Her cousin is going into ninth grade next year, and needs the books."

"Wait until the evening, after Father comes."

"Her brother was here just a moment ago. They need the books now."

"Why didn't you just hand them to him?"

"I couldn't find them at that time." She smiled shyly. "Besides, he came during the time when those men brought those . . . things for the wedding."

Her mother eyed her. "Now that you're betrothed, you shouldn't be going out. People will talk."

"I don't want to. I'd rather stay here with you and learn how to make radish pickle, so I can prepare it in my new home. But Sarita will be very angry with me." She was talking a bit too much, and she told herself to slow down. "She lives in Tangal. I'll be back within an hour."

Mohini's interest in radish pickle won Mother over, for it was Mother's special pickle; for a long time she'd wanted to teach Mohini how to make it, yet her daughter had resisted, until now. This meant that the girl had finally come around and was anticipating her new life with her husband. How could Mother then say no to a short excursion to a friend's place, to return some important books? "Father will skin you alive if you don't return in time," Mother warned.

Mohini bounded down the stairs. Betrothed! she thought. And I'm going to meet my lover.

She rolled the word *lover, premi,* on her tongue, and every time she said it Yudhir appeared before her with his shy smile, and he ran his index finger down her face and repeated, "My betrothed lover." The combination of the two words seemed to galvanize Mohini as she emerged onto Kantipath, where the sun was alarmingly bright and the movement of traffic and pedestrians disorienting. She glanced at her watch; it was already three-fifteen. He would be waiting. Holding the books to her chest, she trotted down the sidewalk, brushing past pedestrians. The old spitting lady from the neighborhood, the one with the horribly bent back, was a few yards away, stooping in front of a peanut vendor, arguing about something, probably asking for samples with no intention of buying. As she breezed past her, Mohini thwacked her on the back of the head with her books, making her tumble forward, onto the mountain of peanuts arranged on a nanglo, which scattered all over the sidewalk.

Mohini didn't break her stride as she propelled herself forward so she could lose herself in the crowd. She stuck to the walls as she went past Durbar High School, which she had attended until Father

338

decided that she needed to be primed for marriage. A quick look back, and she saw, in the far distance, a crowd in the area of the peanut vendor. Although she couldn't see much else, she pictured the poor vendor scrambling to scoop up his peanuts as he chased after young boys who grabbed them by the fistful and scurried off.

She entered Tundikhel and saw him, leaning against the khari tree on the marble platform and playing a flute. The platform was accessible by a short flight of stairs, and the tree was lush and inviting. His eyes followed her approach, and it seemed as if he was playing to greet her. Even after she sat down he didn't stop.

Finally, she said, "They're going to marry me off."

He stopped and said, "Congratulations! When is the feast?"

She was slightly hurt by the way he said it. "You have no idea —"

He reached over and touched her lips with his flute. "Let's not mention anything like that, okay? Let's just sit together, talk about sweet, sweet things."

She slid a bit closer to him on the platform, well aware that someone who knew her — a relative, her father's friend — could easily come in for an afternoon stroll, or cross the field on the way to Singha Durbar. She wondered why he had chosen such an exposed spot, right in the heart of the city, for their rendezvous, but maybe it was better here than in a secluded place. One could simply pretend to come here for the pleasure of open air. She remembered learning from her teacher at school, and from snippets she'd heard from Father, the history of this khari tree. For more than a century, Rana dictators had climbed onto its platform, dressed in full military gear, to make important announcements. The sly Jung Bahadur, who launched the Rana dynasty, stood at this very spot in the mid-1800s and turned the army against King R. It was from here that slaves were declared free nearly forty years ago. Soldiers had been summoned to this spot and dispatched to fight for the British in World War I. After the cruel earthquake of 1934, Prime Minister Juddha Shumshere Rana had stood here and in a sorrowful voice announced that relief would be provided for the suffering.

Mohini told Yudhir about the stooped lady, and he laughed.

"Where did you get the nerve to do something like this?" he said. "When I look at you, I see a scaredy-cat."

"A scaredy-cat?" she said. "You have no idea what I'm capable of."

"What are you capable of?" he asked, sliding closer to her. Now both were sitting only inches away from each other, and she could see a line of grime on the inside of his shirt collar. She pictured herself washing his shirt for him so he could wear it to work and pressing his overcoat with the coal iron that her parents would gift her as dowry. His hand inched closer to hers on the platform but didn't touch it.

"You want to see?" she said.

He continued smiling.

"Then come with me," she said, and her words, even as they left her throat, sounded as if they were coming from somewhere above her. Her eyes scanned the area and fell upon the temple of Bhadrakali a few hundred yards away. The shrine sat amid a cluster of trees and small pavilions. She touched the back of his palm with her finger, then motioned to him to follow her as she headed toward the temple. Her heart was drumming so fast that it seemed to be vibrating in her throat, making breathing difficult. She resisted the urge to look back as she traversed the field to reach the temple.

Once inside, Mohini stepped into one of the side pavilions, not knowing what she was doing. She'd come here before, in the mornings with Mother, when some regular devotees sat in the pavilion, playing harmonium and singing devotional songs. At this time of the afternoon, however, the pavilion was empty. She found herself in front of a small door, and on impulse she pushed it open and went inside. It was a small room, apparently used to store musical instruments for the singers in the morning and evening: harmonium, sitar, cymbals. Yudhir was right behind her, and she could hear his breath. "Is this your room?" he asked. She asked him to shut the door. He did, and asked her, "You think the goddess will approve?"

"If she didn't," Mohini said, "she wouldn't have left this door open for us."

She pulled him toward her. "You think I'm a scaredy-cat, huh?"

They both fell on the dusty floor. His chest pressed against her breasts, making her nipples swell, and she could feel him down there, rising, and she wanted to laugh. It was she, not he — he was too stunned to know what to do — who lifted her head a bit and planted her lips on his. Where did this boldness come from? Was she going mad? *Slut, tramp, harlot, whore* — these words passed through her mind in quick succession. Then everything, everything that had been gathering inside her burst forth, through her mouth, her breasts, her thighs, and it seemed only natural to want this man on top of her, to grab the back of his head and press him hard against her own body, to tell Father, Look, see, look what I am doing. Do you see? Right in the heart of the city. Do you believe it? Do you like? She no longer cared if someone heard their moans and sauntered by to investigate, or if Yudhir thought she was a licentious woman, which she had no way of knowing, not yet. His hands were roaming her upper body, pinching her nipples, sliding down to her crotch. His penis was hard against her, and she bucked her hips so it felt as if they were copulating, although she had no idea what copulating really felt like because she was a virgin. I'll be a virgin no more, she thought.

He didn't fuck her because voices sounded outside, discussing something about the evening, and, hearts pounding, the two scrambled to get up. They opened the door slowly. A few feet away, two men were smoking and arguing. Mohini and Yudhir sneaked outside, then casually strolled to the shrine, with smiles on their lips.

A few days later in a seedy hotel in Baghbazar, down the street from Tundikhel, they made love. The neighborhood, at the edge of the fields where jyapus grew spinach and radishes, was known for heavily made-up women standing outside their doors and making lingering eye contact with men, and married men swiftly ducking in and emerging half an hour later, with a satisfied gleam in their eyes. The shoe shop owner next to the hotel had smiled suggestively at Mohini and Yudhir as they walked up to their room. As they made love, Mohini mentally addressed Father, Do you like this, Father? Do you think my husband would like this? And in the middle of their lovemaking, she cried, from the incredible pain that was pulsing between her legs, also because she really didn't want to hurt her parents, but that's what she was doing.

Mohini bled profusely that afternoon. The bed sheets stained, and she became afraid. Yudhir spit on his handkerchief and smudged the stains as best as he could. Then he sang to her, a sad song that made her want to cry. It hurt her down there, a sharp sting every few seconds. She felt raw, bruised, and already a fullness inside her, akin to what she imagined pregnant women feel. She didn't tell Yudhir about this, but the thought occupied her even as she listened to him speak, with a cigarette smoldering between his fingers, about how he knew people in Radio Nepal who could give him a break and have his songs be broadcast nationally.

"I know I am better than a lot of other singers you hear these days." And he recited names that meant nothing to Mohini—she knew only some of the songs he mentioned. She agree that all Yudhir needed was one song broadcast on the radio, and the public would clamor to hear him day and night. He nodded, distracted, as he inhaled, then said something about how he would produce record after record, and might even go to Bombay to become a playback singer in Indian movies. "Sometimes I think I sing better than Mukesh," he said, so innocently that she had to suppress her laughter. There he was, still in his underwear, exposing his hairy thighs and claiming to be better than the most famous singer on the radio; even she, who didn't get to watch Hindi movies, knew that Mukesh was like a god. Her hand on her belly, Mohini told Yudhir that she'd never thought Mukesh was good, anyway. She meant it half in jest, but he nodded again without looking at her, dragged on his cigarette, and threw the smoke to the ceiling in a moody way. "Or maybe I should buy a few Bhagyodaya chithha tickets," he said. "Test my luck. You know how much the jackpot is now? One lakh fifty thousand rupees. I could buy all of Radio Nepal with that kind of money, and I could sing to my heart's content."

She couldn't help but smile fondly at him. The late afternoon sun had barged in through the drapeless windows, and the shouts and screams of children in the neighborhood had gotten louder. Sounds of an argument somewhere nearby — a man pleading about something, a woman insistent, softly adamant — played like background music to the pleasing lull she felt surrounding her. He stubbed his cigarette and looked into her eyes. "You're going to get married soon, aren't you?"

She nodded.

"Maybe you and I should elope together," he said. He wasn't serious, of course.

"Where?"

"Bombay."

She nodded, also not serious. "That makes perfect sense. You will start singing for Hindi movies, and I'll also get a job and raise . . ." She stopped before she mentioned the baby. The baby was more hers than his, it seemed, and there was no point in telling him about it.

"Actually, that does make sense," he said, quickly and excitedly. He sat up, crossed his legs beneath him, and leaned toward her. "Have you met this man you're getting married to?"

"Yes, he's a good-looking man."

"Really?"

"He's a man, not a boy like you," she teased.

"A good-looking man from a moneyed family, eh?" A hint of jealousy crept into his voice, which made her happy, made her want to tease him more.

"He has a manly face."

"How rich are they?"

"Very rich. They have many servants in the house, I hear, so I'll live like a queen. That's what Mother says. Also, the cutlery they use is made of pure silver." The last part she made up.

He laughed. "Only the Ranas and the Shahs and the darbaris in the palace can afford silver cutlery in this country."

"You want to bet?" she said. "I dare you to go to their house and look."

"Why don't both of us go then?"

The thought made her laugh again, the idea of she and Yudhir climbing the wall of the groom's compound and peeking into their kitchen, which she imagined as spacious and airy, with the servants on the floor, peeling, cutting, slicing vegetables and meat for dinner, two fires burning in the corner. But the thought of being trapped in a house like that made her somber.

"What's the matter?" Yudhir asked.

"I don't know what's happening," she said. "Between you and me."

He studied her face, then said, "What do you want?"

"What do I want?" She repeated it again. No one had asked her that before. "I don't want to get married right now."

He shook his head impatiently and flicked cigarette ash to the floor. "I didn't ask you what you *don't* want. I asked you what you *do* want."

She didn't know. After a while she said, "I want to spend time with you." I want to discuss important intellectual topics with you, she thought, then asked him, "So, what do you think of the Rashtriya Nirdesan Mantralaya?"

"What?"

She spoke slowly as if addressing a child, or a deaf or dumb person. "The king's National Guidance Ministry."

"What's that?"

She laughed heartily. "Don't you pay attention to what's happening in our country? Don't you care?" Then she echoed something she'd heard Father say. "It should matter to all of us what the raja-maharajas do."

Yudhir waved his hand in the air to indicate that he couldn't be bothered with that sort of thing. It disappointed her, this dismissal of what she thought he'd find impressive.

"I know you want to spend time with me," he said impatiently. "That's a given. What else do you want?" A smile spread across his face. "Do you want to marry me? Is that what you want?"

It was as if he were teasing her, and it made her sad. Also, she'd end up marrying the man Mother and Father had chosen for her — this much she knew for certain. "It's my destiny," she mumbled.

"That's bogus. Completely bogus thinking."

"Easy for you to say," Mohini said. "You're a man. Look at me. What can I do?"

"Elope to Bombay with me," he said, smiling.

"Don't joke. My mood is off now. I won't see you after I get married."

"I'm not joking," Yudhir said. He took a long drag of the cigarette and blew the smoke in her face.

She waved the smoke away and climbed out of bed. "I hate that smell," she said, and went to the window. The sun assaulted her eyes, and she quickly stepped back. Once her eyes adjusted, she again looked out. On the street below people walked, shopped, or lingered on the sidewalk, smoking and chatting. She saw two women in bright saris and ample makeup, their midriffs showing, outside the steps of the hotel, watching and smiling at men walking by. The Ghantaghar bell sounded, and with a start she realized that it was four o'clock. But the normal anxiety that clamped her stomach was absent today, and she knew that she would linger for a bit longer, perhaps for another half an hour, then head home, and even if Father was home, he wouldn't flog her because he'd be afraid of her bruises showing so close to the wedding. Her wedding. She pictured herself circling the pyre, the priest's monotonous chant ringing in her ears all morning, her husband's eyes settling upon her on the wedding night.

"How will we get to Bombay?" Mohini asked, without looking at Yudhir.

"You leave that up to me. So you've changed your mind?" He blew cigarette smoke to the ceiling, then turned his head to look at her.

"What happens if you abandon me once we get there?"

"Do I look like the type?"

Mohini faced him. "It's been only a few days since I've gotten to know you," she said, and it was true. But already she liked him so much. Even his aloofness she'd come to love: how at times he simply seemed removed from everything around him. He had the detachment of a passerby who had nothing at stake, who could witness events unfolding without bias or prejudice, allowing everything to take shape in its own time. Such a sharp contrast to her parents, who were so involved in her every move, every gesture, which was then analyzed, scrutinized, pondered, and—condemned. Her husband would be no different, she'd already deduced, by the aggression she'd seen in his eyes. From one hell to another, she thought. The word *hell* released more bitter feelings. Here was this man, luxuriously smoking a cigarette on a filthy bed in this questionable hotel in this alley where good girls from good families would rather die than venture into, and by his mere presence he was offering her something new, a door cracking open to a place where you could just linger and taste and touch and laugh without judgment. On the bed, he was now gazing at the ceiling, the cigarette butt so tiny that it was close to burning his fingers. Yudhir was apparently lost in lines of a song—he began to softly croon mournful lyrics bemoaning the cruelty of a lover, and Mohini felt like laughing because in her world it was not her lover who was cruel to her, but everyone else.

Missing

RAJA'S TALK of his mother unsettled both of them, throwing them into a pensive mood. They hadn't discussed her in years, and when they had, they'd mentioned her only in passing, usually prompted by Ranjana's pesky questions. When Ranjana was a child she was unwilling to believe that her father didn't know anything about her grandmother, and she threw tantrums when Raja told her he had been raised by two surrogate mothers. As she grew up, Ranjana expressed more interest in the grandmother she'd never known than she did in Muwa, who lived in the same city.

Yes, Muwa, incredibly, was still alive, still drinking, still living with Sumit. After Nilu Nikunj went to Sumit, the house survived in his hands only for a few years, after which it was sold to a philanthropist who wanted to set up an orphanage. Most of the money from the sale went to the repayment of Sumit's own debts, Nilu had learned. He did have enough remaining to afford a modest home in Bhainsepati, where he and Muwa now lived. Sumit hadn't kicked Muwa out onto the street, as Nilu had expected. In fact, Nilu could tell that in his own way he was fond of Muwa, made sure she ate well and took her medicine, dusted seats for her and brought her a sweater on chilly evenings in the garden, even though he did nothing to prevent her from drinking. Muwa was approaching age seventy-five, and she'd begun to stoop; every few months she had to be rushed to the hospital. Years of drinking had corroded her organs, but she still walked by herself, and still spoke, albeit in a voice so raspy that it sounded as though she had chronic laryngitis. Every day Nilu expected a call from Sumit, telling her that her mother had passed away. Every few months she went to visit Muwa. The bitterness she'd felt toward Muwa all her life was replaced by a mild contempt, alternating with unexpected surges of compassion. Perhaps it had to do with age, a sense of resignation that certain things in life, in people, remained the same. Muwa walked around the house with a cane, wrapped in a shawl, a cigarette between her fingers. Some days Nilu found her in the garden, inspecting the flowers with trembling hands.

Raja went for a stroll, and Nilu begun to think about what he had said — that his thoughts turned to his real mother when he looked at Ranjana. Nilu was filled with a sense of foreboding, as if Raja's mother, after all these years, had decided to infiltrate their lives by laying a claim to Ranjana to compensate for the claim she had forfeited — her own son. Nilu faulted Raja for having mentioned his seemingly unstable mother and Ranjana in the same breath; Ranjana was the most levelheaded daughter anyone could ask for. She had been absolutely no problem, even during her early teenage years. Now she was already nineteen. Still, she was far from home, and lately she did sound as if she was carrying a weight that was hard to balance on her delicate shoulders.

The more Nilu attempted to dismiss her anxieties, the more a sense of doom pressed upon her. She opened the window and let in some fresh air, took deep breaths to fill her lungs, to drive away the pressure settling on her forehead. And swiftly, as though it had never left, the familiar heaviness swooped down on her — the anguish that had been her life in the aftermath of Maitreya's death. Except this feeling had nothing to do with Maitreya, with whom she'd made her peace; it concerned her daughter, the pragmatic, loving Ranjana whom both Nilu and Raja knew would be a solace for their old age, someone who had already healed not only their heartbreak over Maitreya but also their marriage. All of this had vanished in an instant because of Raja's silly comment, which he had likely already forgotten along his walk, as he paused to chat with neighbors. When he returned, Nilu was going to tell him how annoyed she was. "For twenty years I haven't felt like this," she'd say to him. "And you go and say something that you yourself cannot make sense of. And here I am, broken in pieces about it."

But it wasn't Raja's fault; she knew her vexation at him was misplaced. He was merely expressing something that had been bothering him lately. She was overreacting.

Nilu went to her room and opened her big steel cupboard. She took out the metal box where she kept her daughter's letters and sifted through them to see if she could spot any cause for concern, any passage that had made her pause when she first read it. Nothing. All the letters spoke brightly about Chicago, the apartment she shared with two roommates, her classes, the university, the great body of water nearby. She mentioned that she missed Nilu's cooking, but which child living far away from home wouldn't?

Nilu rearranged the letters in the box and put it away in the cupboard. She went down to the garden and sat in a chair, waiting for her emotions to change. As the sun began to set, she heard Raja at the gate, back from his walk. He had a hint of a smile on his face, perhaps from having joked with the neighbor next door. Her speculation that what he'd said affected him less than it affected her, turned out to be true.

"How far did you go?" she asked.

"Oh, just up to the mound."

He began recounting the dog problem of Satyal-ji, their loud, guffawing neighbor, but she cut him off. "We need to call Ranjana. Urgently."

The panic in her voice startled him. "Why? What happened?"

Nilu had to look away and feel her breath in her chest before she could respond. "Something has happened to Ranjana. We need to call her."

Now it was Raja's turn to be filled with dread. "What? Did you hear something? Someone called from America?"

Her eyes fell on the flowers she'd planted and admired only yesterday — a batch of bright yellow roses that appeared to have lost their luster overnight.

"Nilu! Why are you not speaking? Something bad happened to Ranjana?"

"I don't know," she said, and stood up and went inside. It seemed she was punishing him, but for what, she didn't know.

Raja followed. "Hoina, why are you acting like this? Why are you keeping me in the dark?"

As she went to the kitchen and poured water in the kettle for tea, she controlled the shaking of her hands. She felt Raja's presence behind her, and she didn't know what to say to him.

"Tell me what happened," he asked again, this time a bit more gently.

"Let's call her," she said, turning to face him.

"Did someone tell you something?"

She shook her head and moved to the living room, where she sat on the sofa, picked up the phone, and began dialing. The number to Ranjana's apartment in Chicago, which she shared with her two roommates, came to her easily. Raja stood next to her, watching. The phone rang three times before one of the girls answered, in a drowsy voice — it was very early there. Nilu asked to speak to Ranjana. The last few times she'd called, one of the roommates would pick up the phone and tell Nilu that her Ranjana was at the library. Nilu still couldn't tell these girls' voices apart, even though one of them was a red-headed American and the other was a Japanese girl who had immigrated there when she was a child.

"Who is this?" the girl asked.

"This is Ranjana's mother, from Nepal. Is this Angela speaking?"

"Oh, hello." Her voice was suddenly alert. "Ranji isn't here."

Nilu had never liked the shortening of her daughter's name to Ranji, and now in the roommate's American accent it seemed even stranger. When Nilu had asked Ranjana why she allowed her roommates to call her that, she'd responded that it was an easier name for them, and that it really didn't matter, did it, what she was called?

"Where is she, then?" Nilu asked Angela. "She's never home when I call her."

"I need to . . ."

"Is she at the library again? What is she doing so early at the library?"

"Mrs. Basnet, I need to tell you something. Actually, it's been nearly two months now since Ranjana moved out of here."

"Moved out? To where?"

"I don't know. She's never told me."

"Two months? But that can't be true," Nilu said. "She's never mentioned anything like it, and she's been calling me." Was this roommate making a fool out of her? Was Ranjana in on the joke, instructing the girl? "Let me speak to Ranjana!"

"I swear I'm telling the truth, Mrs. Basnet." The girl was pronouncing it Bass-nyet. "She asked me not to tell you, and I went along because we all love Ranji here. But we're all worried about her."

"What do you mean worried? She asked you not to tell me? Why?"

"I have no idea. I wish I could tell you more."

"Is she still in Chicago?"

"I don't know, Mrs. Basnet. The last couple of times you called, I sent her e-mails to inform her, but I don't know whether she's still in Chicago."

Nilu's world swam. Her own voice seemed to come from a distance. "But how did it happen so suddenly? Was there a problem?"

"There wasn't any trouble with us," the roommate said. "She paid us a month's rent so we could look for a new roommate."

Raja was making hand signals, inquiring what had happened.

"But something must have happened!" Nilu said. "Otherwise why wouldn't she leave a phone number with you for us? That's not like Ranjana at all. You aren't hiding anything, are you?"

The roommate grew defensive. "I have told you everything I can. Why would I have any reason to hide anything from you?" She then said that she had to go to class and that if she learned anything more about Ranjana's whereabouts, she'd call Nilu.

Nilu stared at the phone after the roommate hung up. But Raja was bursting at the seams, so she told him what the roommate had said.

The color drained from Raja's face. "But she'd have told us if she was going to move. This doesn't sound like Ranjana. Maybe the girl is mistaken."

"She didn't sound like she was joking."

"I'm going to call Umesh and see what he knows. It's possible that she got fed up with her roommates and moved back to Umesh's house."

But Raja's conversation with Umesh soon revealed that he didn't know that Ranjana had moved elsewhere. The last time he spoke to Ranjana, Umesh told Raja, was several weeks ago when he invited her home for some Nepali food—but she couldn't come because she was busy writing papers. Unfortunately, Umesh himself was struggling to meet the deadline for a book he was writing, and thus he hadn't called Ranjana, except for one time, when he was told that Ranjana was at the library. He'd left a message, but Ranjana never called back.

Raja seemed about to cry as he spoke into the phone, "For goodness' sake, where could she have gone? This is so puzzling."

Nilu took the phone from him and spoke to Umesh. She told him that he must go to Ranjana's apartment right away and find out from her roommates what exactly had happened, especially the one named Angela, with whom Nilu had conversed earlier. The roommates were hiding something; Nilu was certain of that. "Please, Umesh Babu, this is an urgent matter."

Umesh said something about an important committee meeting he was scheduled to run that afternoon, and perhaps he could just phone Ranjana's roommate. Nilu said that she was worried sick about her daughter, and if Umesh didn't go there immediately, she wouldn't know what to think of him. As Ranjana's guardian in America, it was his responsibility to make sure that nothing happened to her. Nilu was about to add, in her anger, that he'd already failed his duties as their daughter's guardian by not keeping a close eye on her, but she only said, "Put yourself in our shoes. How would you react if she were your daughter?

Raja was making desperate hand signals, advising Nilu to calm down.

"Bhauju, you are panicking for no reason," Umesh said. "She could have found new friends to live with."

"I know my daughter," Nilu said. "She's not like that. She'd have told us."

"America is a different place, bhauju. People get busy here, so maybe she's just too swamped in her studies to call."

"For us Nepalis, this is where your own kith and kin come in handy, Umesh Babu. Busy or not busy, you'll need to go to her apartment today."

She thrust the phone toward Raja, who spoke in a more placating voice with his cousin, suggesting that Umesh go to Ranjana's apartment just to satisfy a mother's heart. Umesh said that he'd have to make a few phone calls to his colleagues to cancel his meeting and that they'd not be happy, but he now was worried about Ranjana as well. He would try to drive to Evanston by late morning to determine Ranjana's whereabouts. "Expect my call later in the day," he told Raja.

Nilu leaned her head against the sofa and closed her eyes. Ranjana had asked her roommates to deceive her parents, to give them the impression that she still lived in the apartment. Why? Why was she hiding? More important, where was she? Pictures of Ranjana's body, mangled on a Chicago sidewalk, flashed through her mind. Oh God, not again, she implored. Not again. For the past six months she and Raja had talked about visiting Ranjana. They'd really wanted to escort their daughter to Chicago when she'd left a year ago, but Ranjana had argued that the few thousand dollars spent on their airfare would be put to better use elsewhere; they were already spending a lot for her travel and living costs in America.

"We just want to make sure that you adjust to the place properly," Nilu had said, "that you face no troubles."

"But Umesh Uncle is there," Ranjana said. "And it's better you come after a few months when I can show you around. Right now I don't see the necessity. It'll just be extravagant."

And since Ranjana had always been persuasive, even in small matters, they'd finally come to see her point, especially after Umesh too assured them that he would make sure she adjusted well, that she would lack nothing as she began her studies in a new country.

After Ranjana's departure for Chicago, the house became so quiet that within weeks the two were discussing a visit to Ranjana, which became even more compelling when she moved closer to the university. Nilu and Raja pored over a map of the midwestern states, which they'd bought in a store in Thamel; they tried to determine the distance between where Umesh lived and where Ranjana's university was. Raja was of the opinion that the two places didn't look far apart on the map. "Maybe the distance between Balaju and Patan," he estimated. "Nothing that she couldn't manage if she wanted to." Nilu said that maps were deceiving that way, that they needed to trust their daughter's judgment. Every other week, particularly after a phone conversation with Ranjana, they contemplated their trip across the ocean. Raja got on the phone with a travel agent he knew, and one time even booked tickets, but Ranjana complained that they'd be visiting in the middle of the semester, when she'd be neck-deep in studies and would feel guilty because she couldn't show them around or spend much time with them.

"But we won't get in your way, we promise," Raja said with a laugh. "We'll stay with Umesh, and you can come over when you're free."

"But with you so close, I'd want to visit you all the time, don't you understand?"

"So, now you're saying Umesh's house is close to your university."

"Papa!"

Nilu intervened, telling Ranjana that they wanted to visit, but if Ranjana didn't think it was the best time, they'd wait until her summer vacation.

"Papa sometimes doesn't understand," Ranjana said.

Later Nilu had mildly chastised Raja, telling him that he had to stop treating his daughter as though she were a child. "She's all grown up now, and we have to respect her decisions."

But what had Ranjana done now? Or what had happened to her? "We should have gone to visit her last year, middle of the semester or not," she said to Raja, then realized it was only a thought that had floated across her mind, like a balloon; she hadn't actually spoken it.

The next idea that flashed through her mind Raja expressed out loud before she could. "Maybe Ranjana has been hiding something from us all this time?" Raja said. "Maybe that's why she didn't want us to visit?"

"She'd never do that," Nilu quickly said, trying to suppress this idea before it became convincing. "There has to be a simple explanation. Once she gets in touch with us, then everything will be clear, and we'll end up laughing at ourselves for being so suspicious."

But Raja wasn't listening; he appeared to be tracking a trajectory of his own mental events. Nilu called his name, and he held up his palm, witnessing something in his mind. "No, something is wrong, I can feel it."

Neither of them slept a wink, expecting the phone to ring at any minute, Umesh at the other end, or Ranjana herself, upset at her parents for overreacting, then perhaps realizing her error, offering a flurry of apologies, a perfectly logical explanation that'd turn into a source of laughter for Nilu and Raja for years to come, the kind of tales they'd tell their grandchildren: "Listen to what your mother did when she was studying in America."

At around four o'clock Raja jumped out of bed. "I'm going to phone Umesh. My head is about to explode."

"Don't call now," she urged. "It's only late afternoon in Chicago now. He's probably not back home yet. You call, he won't be there, and it'll only increase our worries. Come, I'll make some tea."

She took him by his hand, and they shuffled down the stairs without turning on the lights. His hand was clasped tightly in hers as though he were a little boy. I have to get hold of myself, Nilu thought. If I allow it, he will simply fall apart. How defeated he looks. Defeated and depleted. If something had indeed happened to Ranjana, Raja wouldn't be able to take it; he'd simply collapse. She wouldn't be able to take it either, but she had to be the stronger one. She'd let her control slip once; she couldn't allow the same to happen again.

She patted his hand in the dark as she led him down, the phrase "blind leading the blind" popping into her mind. She turned on the light in the kitchen, sat him at the table, boiled some tea, and asked if he wanted to eat toast or an egg, just as she used to ask Maitreya, ages ago. Raja looked at her as if to say, Have you lost your mind? Here I am, worried to death about my daughter, and you want me to swallow eggs? But all he said was "No," and she realized that he'd sensed the odd tone of her voice, a trace of solicitousness, of maternal concern, that had less to do with him and more to do with memories of Maitreya. Raja wouldn't tolerate it if Nilu ushered the presence of Maitreya back into their lives; he wouldn't let her fixate on the boy. "Don't pollute our love for our living, breathing daughter with a son long past dead," he'd say.

Nilu handed Raja his tea and sat at the kitchen table with her own. The two sipped in silence, their ears alert for the phone's ring. Six o'clock in the evening in Chicago now, she calculated.

"We'll go crazy waiting this way," Raja said.

The tea calmed Nilu a bit, but Raja remained pensive. Worry lines had deepened on his forehead. His eyes fell upon her and he asked, "How did you sense that something was wrong without even phoning? You were fine when I went for a walk last evening."

"A mother's instinct," she said, unwilling to divulge anything further.

But Raja was onto something. "It's that thing I said, isn't it?"

The stridency of his voice told her that she'd better handle this calmly. "What thing? It was just a misgiving I had. Soon Umesh will call, or Ranjana, and all of this will amount to nothing. Now finish your tea, and maybe we should get back to bed."

"Nilu, please, don't hide things from me," Raja said. "You don't tell me, it'll fester inside you. Look what happened with Maitreya, and how long it took us to get back together."

"I'm not hiding anything, sweetie," she said, her voice about to crack. She realized that she hadn't called him sweetie in a while, especially as Ranjana grew up, as though the word was inappropriate for an aging couple. She went to him, put her arms around him.

"It was what I said," he repeated, his voice shaking. "I put a curse on my own daughter by comparing her to my mother."

Nilu laughed, scoffing the outlandishness of his idea. She explained that his thinking was irrational. "You mentioned your mother and Ranjana yesterday evening, and Ranjana's roommate said she moved out a few weeks ago. So your curse traveled backward in time? Don't be foolish."

The sky turned lighter, and the neighbor's rooster cried.

"Too late to go back to bed?" she asked him, and he nodded. "Do you want another cup of tea?" He shook his head.

Memories of her dead son, his sad, intelligent face, were once again returning to Nilu, and she wondered whether she was losing control. What would happen to her and Raja in this old age if she never heard a peep about Ranjana? She recalled glimpsing photos on CNN—the faces of American girls, pretty and young, who went missing. And when found, they had been raped, their bodies mutilated. If Umesh couldn't locate Ranjana, would she and Raja fly to America to search for their daughter?

Of course they would, and the thought terrified Nilu: she and Raja, at their age, on the streets of Chicago, carrying the photo of Ranjana that she herself had sent to them soon after she reached there, close to a year ago. With the Sears Tower in the background, Ranjana stood with her fingers held up in a V, her hair flying in the wind, and her backpack slung over her shoulder—her favorite backpack from her school days in Kathmandu, the one she said was perfect for lugging her books around the Northwestern campus. "Have you seen her?" Nilu imagined asking pedestrians on the streets of the city. Ranjana had sent pictures of famous Chicago sites, so Nilu

357

could visualize the Navy Pier, with its festive atmosphere; the large, slowly turning Ferris wheel, which lifted passengers high up to view the skyline; Millennium Park and its glass screens, where children's astonished faces would appear; the Hindu temples, with their intricate carvings, in the suburbs.

People would brush her and Raja aside, Nilu imagined. Americans are cold-hearted people, she sometimes heard Nepalis say; Americans think only about themselves, their individual needs, nothing else. But Ranjana's letters had indicated otherwise. "My friends here are so warm and supportive, Ma," she'd written. Her classmates and her roommates, Angela and Yuko, had helped her with everything, Ranjana had told her on the phone.

"Aren't there other Nepalis at the university?" Raja had asked. "Don't you spend time with them? With them at least you'll have your own food, your own language."

Raja's exhortation had set off a small dispute between him and Nilu after he'd put down the phone. She told him that if all their daughter wanted was her own food and own language, she'd have stayed in Nepal. "What is the point of spending so much money to travel all the way to America if all you ever did was fraternize with your own countrymen? She's going there to study, not to immerse herself in Nepali culture, which she knows well by now."

"You look like you're ready to chew me up," Raja said. "All I'm suggesting is that one shouldn't forget one's culture and language, no matter where one goes."

"Who's speaking of forgetting?"

"All right, no one," Raja said. "Calm down now."

But Ranjana had deliberately shied away from gatherings organized by Nepalis because — Nilu remembered this abruptly, catching her breath — a boy had begun to make her uncomfortable. This boy, Ranjana had told Nilu over the phone one day when Raja wasn't home, appeared at every party, every gathering, and stared at her. "Don't tell this to Papa," Ranjana said. "He'll want to jump on the next plane and come over to beat up the boy. You know how Papa is." And so Nilu hadn't mentioned anything to Raja, although Ranjana's words had hovered in the back of her mind. In another conversation with Ranjana she'd asked her, after making sure that Raja was in the bathroom, whether the boy still acted the same way. Ranjana said that the boy had cornered her one day during a momo party to confess his love. He wanted to marry her, he said, and his father, a former home minister by the name of Narayan Dhakal, knew Raja and would soon speak to him about joining the two families.

Nilu had been aghast, but Ranjana had only laughed. "Don't worry, Ma. In a way that boy has made it easier for me. Now I have a very good excuse not to go to those Nepali parties. I mean, the people are nice, but mostly they just gossip, or brag about their sampatti, their SUVs, and their property back in Nepal. I've just got too much work to do anyway."

Nilu had been relieved, and she felt right about defending Ranjana when Raja had gone off on his tirade about language and culture.

Now, as their neighbors began to wake up and cough and sputter, Nilu's first impulse was to blurt out to Raja the information about the Dhakal boy. But she stopped herself. He'd jump up from the chair and call Umesh, or even call Minister Dhakal's house and demand that they contact their son in America this very minute to see if he had done anything to Ranjana, or was involved in her absence in any way. A vision flitted through Nilu's mind: the boy had harassed and pursued Ranjana until she had been forced to do his bidding, forced to move with him into his apartment. But Ranjana had never been a wilting, whimpering kind of girl. The idea that she'd wither under intimidation or psychological pressure was inconceivable.

Still, Ranjana was in a foreign environment.

The more Nilu thought about it, the more she became convinced that the Dhakal boy, the one who stared at Ranjana from across the room, who told her in a slurred voice that he was going to marry her, had something to do with this mystery. These creeps, thought Nilu. Weren't they always like this? Hadn't she seen enough of them when she was young, when she and Raja lived in Thamel? The way their beady eyes undressed her, the way their lips glistened as they made lecherous remarks.

"My daughter's disappeared." The sentence floated across her mind. *"Meri chhori harai, Ranjana harai,"* she pictured herself saying to friends and neighbors, and watching their eyes, their expressions, grow incredulous.

"What do you mean harai? Impossible! America is a big country. She's probably gone somewhere for a few days with her friends. She'll come back. They always do. The pull of parental love is too strong. Have patience. We simply can't believe that anything bad would happen to our Ranjana." And they'd go on and on about how beautiful she was, what social skills she possessed, how she was always thoughtful about everyone's needs, had kind, praising words for everyone she met. "A girl like her God will protect wherever she goes. Rest assured." And they'd offer to make calls to people they knew in America, sometimes confusing Chicago with California, assuming every Nepali in America would know other Nepalis scattered across the vast country.

We won't have to go to America, Nilu firmly told herself as she heard the sound of the water vessel being filled in the neighbor's front yard. But lack of sleep was making her mind take flight against her will, and soon she imagined trudging with Raja along Chicago's congested streets, its wide avenues, displaying Ranjana's picture, entreating people on the sidewalk for help, and walking into shops where the clerks would shout at them as if they were indigents.

Eloping

I N HETAUDA, MOHINI waited by the window in a corner of the rest house, watching the traffic and the crowd in the street below, inhaling the smoke spewed by the buses that plied this dusty town on the way to the border city of Birgunj or back to Kathmandu. They'd arrived here at three o'clock in the afternoon on the day of her wedding. Every time Mohini thought about home, fear crawled up her skin. She saw Father's face, angry and bewildered, and mentally she offered him a fervent, tormented apology: Father, I didn't mean to. I had no choice.

She didn't want to dwell on what was happening at home, but hard as she tried, she couldn't help but picture Mother waking up in the morning and discovering Mohini's absence. Mother would think that Mohini had gone down to the courtyard for a bath or to the toilet. Humming, Mother would mentally check all the things she, along with a horde of women who'd soon show up, had to do this morning before the groom's party, escorted by a loud band, arrived around nine o'clock. Even when Mohini didn't come up after half an hour, Mother didn't make much of it. She'd meant to observe the courtyard from the balcony, but each time a hundred things — flowers for the ceremony, colored cloths the priest had demanded, sweets such as laddoos and pedas — had occupied her mind.

There had been some disagreement between the two families about the most propitious time for the wedding entourage to arrive at the bride's house. The bride's priest, after consulting several religious calendars and patros, came up with eleven o'clock. But the groom's priest had configured a time of nine A.M. as the most auspicious moment as dictated by the stars and the planets. "Amateur," he'd declared the bride's priest to be, and the bride's priest, the more humble of the two, had consulted his calendars and books again and scratched his head: the nine o'clock time his colleague had deduced showed the dark shadows of Mars in ascension, and everyone knew that Mars wreaked havoc on marriages, unless its corresponding position in the birth charts of both the bride and the groom neutralized its ill effects. The bride's priest consulted the groom's chart again. Mangal was safely ensconced in the fourth house, whereas in the bride's it sat in the fifth. "Impossible," the priest muttered to himself. But he was a young priest who had been forced to take over the family's occupation because his father had died abruptly, and he couldn't imagine going up against the elderly priest from the groom's side, someone who had known his father. Still, he meekly suggested to the bride's mother that perhaps the more venerable priest had miscalculated the influence of the planets. Mother rebuked him, saying that his dead father would probably have concurred with the groom's priest. "But, but, look here," the young priest stuttered, waving the patro at Mother.

She simply shoved him aside and said, "What difference does a couple of hours make? Devote your time to more important matters than quibbling over an hour here or there." It makes all the difference, the priest thought, but he didn't say more. Still, he had managed to plant a seed of doubt in Mother's mind. Her son had shacked up with the oil man's daughter without the benefit of astrological consultation, and she was sure that the stars, had their alignment been considered, would have directed her son to a different, less scandalous life. So Mother did pass on the priest's misgivings to the middlewoman who'd initially talked to Father about the alliance. The middlewoman scolded her, said the groom's priest was sought after by royalty and aristocrats, and how dare the young priest question his judgment! The matter was settled.

In her mind, Mohini saw the women from the surrounding houses barge into the living room, asking where the bride was so they could begin to style her hair and make her pretty. Father would already be down in the courtyard with the priest, making preparations for the big event, which, Mother would realize in a panic, was only a couple of hours away. "Can you shout at Mohini to finish up quickly and come up?" she yelled at her husband below. "She needs to start getting ready."

Father nodded. He was busy instructing some neighborhood boys who were setting up chairs for the guests. He shouted in the direction of the outhouse, urging his daughter to be done immediately. Then Father turned to help a boy string some colored papers across the length of the courtyard, and upstairs Mother rummaged for some gold and silver coins she'd need later.

"Has Mohini eloped? Where is she?" one of the women said, joking, and the rest guffawed; at the sound of their clamorous voices, Mother dropped a gold coin, which rolled across the floor, then slid under the large cupboard by the door. That's when Mother knew that something was amiss: she hadn't seen or heard Mohini all morning long. Asking the women to retrieve her coin, Mother rushed down to the courtyard, perspiring. Without speaking to her husband, she made her way to the outhouse and softly called Mohini's name, so as not to attract attention. When there was no answer, she reached out and pulled the door, which swung open. The outhouse was empty.

She turned and ran back upstairs, ignoring Father, who called to her, asking why she was in such a hurry. There, one of the women was lying on the floor, her cheek flat against it, her thin arms groping for the coin under the cupboard. Mother reached Mohini's room, and out of desperation, she looked under the bed, wondering if the girl was hiding there because of wedding night jitters. She ran down again to the street, hoping that her daughter, on a whim, had sauntered to the corner shop to buy some spicy titaura. Mother looked left and right. By this time, her thumping up and down the stairs had aroused the suspicion of the women, who came to the window and asked her what the matter was. The more astute knew instantly the reason for Mother's desperate look and cried out, "She ran away, didn't she?"

A pedestrian who had stopped, attracted by the bright red cloth sign that announced AUSPICIOUS WEDDING, looked up at the women and shouted, "Who? The bride? She ran away?"

Everything exploded then. Father, who had been showing a boy how to tie the bamboo poles together for the wedding pyre, bellowed, "Who ran away?" He knew the answer before he'd completed his question. Letting go of the bamboo pole, he hurried upstairs and checked and rechecked every room, warning the women, "Don't make a fuss. Mohini has probably just stepped out. Maybe she's hiding somewhere as a practical joke."

Less than an hour remained before the groom's arrival. Mother's small yellow suitcase with a broken hinge was missing, and its contents were found dumped in a corner of her bedroom. Father opened his safe and discovered that four hundred rupees had evaporated. "Your son probably has a hand in this," he said to Mother. "Send someone to that bastard's house immediately."

He glanced at the clock: half an hour left. Still enough time to salvage this, he thought, although his mind was getting slower by the minute. If Mohini had indeed sought shelter at her brother's house, he had enough time to drag her home. I'll tie her with ropes to the wedding pyre if I have to, he promised himself; I'll gag her with a piece of the priestly cloth. "Wait, I'll go myself." He warned the women in the room, "Not a peep to anyone. She's your daughter too, not only mine. If the groom's party arrives here before I do, distract them, act normal. If my nose is cut today, yours will be too." Not all the women were persuaded by this my-family-is-your-family appeal. Some would be gleeful to witness the shaming of this family one more time, and now they pleasurably considered the likelihood that another scandal was about to strike the old man. But they did not show these feelings; their faces looked grave.

A small crowd, murmuring and gesticulating, had already collected below the AUSPICIOUS WEDDING sign. They fell silent as Father, dressed in his starchy wedding kurta suruwal, hurried in the direction of his son's house, scanning the street for the taxis that sometimes appeared on this side street. He couldn't find one, but that didn't stop him; he began jogging toward his destination. He prayed that no one from the groom's family would spot him in this state, his face flushed and frightened. Why had both his children chosen to bring such enormous pain to the family? He glanced up at the sky as if beseeching the gods, but saw only stealthy black clouds gathering. People said that a rainy-day wedding foretold great happiness for the couple; perhaps the swirling clouds did mean that his daughter was at her brother's house, simply afraid. In that case all he needed to do was coax and cajole her, use a sweet voice he vaguely remembered using when she was a child and climbed onto his lap, demanding stories.

Mohini loved — he remembered now — hearing him talk about the Giant Earthquake of 1934, which leveled the city and left thousands dead.

"Where were you, Father," Mohini asked, "when the earthquake struck?"

"I was in this room, right here," Father said. "It was a little bit past two in the afternoon. I was lying on the floor, dozing, when I heard a rumble, like something was boiling under the ground. I thought I was dreaming. But my whole body was shaking, so I sat up. You know that pomelo tree outside?"

Mohini nodded.

"It was slapping the side of the house — the whole tree swaying like a leaf. I stood, but the floor moved so much that I had to crouch. I cried for your mother, then remembered that she had gone to her parents' house." His wife had taken some leftover ghiu and chaku from the previous day's Maghe Sankrati festival to her aging parents.

"Father, were you worried about Mother?"

He had been more than worried. His in-laws' house was nearly a century old, with a roof that had already begun to crumble, and he couldn't see how it could survive any earthquake, let alone a monster this big. He could hear thunderous crashes as houses in the neighborhood collapsed. In his mind flashed a picture of his wife, buried under the rubble of his father-in-law's house. "A little," he told Mohini. "I didn't have time to think."

Even as his house rocked, he managed to stumble down the stairs, then was jettisoned into the street, where the ground moved back and forth like a sieve. All around him houses were collapsing, emitting booming sounds like cannon shots. Dust swirled, sideways and upward. Wails and cries penetrated the air. A young man crawled down the street on all fours.

Then the earth became still.

"And Mother was all right?" Mohini asked. "She didn't die?"

"Of course not, silly," he said, pinching her nose. "If she'd died, how would she be alive today to be your mother? Your mother, fortunately, had gone to the local dhara to fetch some water, so she was spared. But both her parents perished under the weight of the roof."

"Do people who die in earthquakes go to heaven?"

"Why wouldn't they? Of course they do. Besides, your grandparents were very religious people, so I'm sure they're sitting on God's lap at this very moment, just like you're sitting on mine."

"But people who kill themselves don't go to heaven."

"Where did you learn that?"

"Pradip Dai told me."

"And how does he know this? He's barely a few years older than you."

"He said people who kill themselves return to earth as ghosts and scare other people. He says that there's a ghost who lives under our stairs, a khyak, with no flesh on his body, only bones."

Father laughed. "Your Pradip Dai is nothing but trouble."

"Pradip Dai says that at night, on the Rani Pokhari pond there are women kichkanni ghosts who float on water. He says their feet are strange, with their toes facing backward, their heels in the front. They prey on single men and suck their blood. Is that true, Father?"

"Nonsense," he said.

After a few moments, Mohini asked, "Father, do you love Mother?"

Her question had embarrassed him, for men didn't confess such love unless it was in the dark, at night in bed. He certainly hadn't felt the need to proclaim his love for Mohini's mother. They were husband and wife — didn't that say it all? But that afternoon of the earthquake, after the city stopped rocking and heaving, his heart had collapsed as he'd pictured his wife's body mangled under the weight of her parents' roof.

Driven by anxiety, he'd made his way across the city to her. Many houses had simply crumpled to the ground. Survivors walked around, injured, tottering, crying out for their loved ones. He could see, from across Rani Pokhari, that the beautiful Ghantaghar clock tower no longer rose to the sky. In the distance to the south, Dharahara's piercing top was absent; the monument had broken in half. As he moved into Asan and Indrachowk, he had to skirt or climb over mounds of rubble; he occasionally glimpsed a severed arm or a head among the debris. Once he spotted a face between the bricks, eyes staring, the mouth moving as though attempting to converse.

"The Tundikhel parade ground has ruptured," he heard someone say. In the Basantapur Durbar Square, the tops of several temples had been shaved off. The Kal Bhairav statue, with his glaring dark face, had remained more or less intact, and Father prayed in front of the fierce god, briefly, before heading on to Jaisideval, where he found his wife wailing, her childhood home in ruins, the pitcher full of water she'd fetched next to her on the ground. He'd put his arm around her, the first time in public, and asked her what was wrong. She'd buried her face in his chest, cried a bit, and said that she thought both her parents were dead.

Unable to answer his daughter's question directly, he'd ended up saying, "I love everyone in this family." He'd stroked Mohini's hair and whispered, "And I'll tell you a secret. I love you the most."

He tried to recall that voice as he pushed through the vegetable-buying crowd in Asan, but he couldn't. All he could hear was a preachy, judgmental voice that now began to castigate him, telling him how pathetic he looked running around, trying to find his daughter on the day of her wedding, with the groom's party, in full regalia, probably already en route to his house. Father felt like giving up; he wanted to crawl into a corner of the marketplace and weep. But he pressed on, pushed through the multitude until he reached his son's house, the very son he had expressly forbidden to attend Mohini's wedding.

"It'll create a bad impression," he'd said with pursed lips to Pradip when his son came over with his wife a few days earlier, on their first visit to the house since they got married. "You'll have to wait until the wedding is over. Then you can visit Mohini, but only after she returns here for a few days, not at her new home."

Pradip had glanced at Chanda, disappointed. "But she's my sister. Why can't I attend her wedding?"

"I can't stop you, but as a big brother, do you want anything to go wrong during Mohini's wedding? Do you realize how hard we've worked to secure this family, this groom, especially after the two of you" — he gave a small nod toward his son's wife, her presence, her validity as a new member of his family — "after you two . . . well. I'll leave that decision up to you."

Pradip looked pained, caught in a quandary. He turned to his wife, but she had her head down, too cowed by her father-in-law to say anything. Finally Pradip said, "Well, I so badly want to attend, but not at the risk of ruining things for my sister. I will visit her in her new home, though, in a few days, and you can't stop me." He addressed Mohini, who, throughout this exchange, had been quietly leaning against the wall. "Right, bahini?"

As he neared Pradip's house, Father realized that he ought to have sensed something was wrong right then, for Mohini's face had paled when her brother mentioned visiting her at her new home. As he stood in front of his son's house, Father hesitated. Had Mohini done this out of spite? Had he been such a bad father? Had he been too strict? After all, it was not one child of his but both who had expressly defied his wishes and damaged the family name for generations to come. They had been good kids when they were young, and as a father he'd provided them with all they needed. So what went wrong?

Standing in the street, facing his son's second-floor window, Father was about to call Pradip when he became certain that Mohini wasn't inside. Fleetingly, he saw Pradip through the window, then his daughter-in-law, who, he had to admit, looked like a good, well-brought-up girl when he saw her a week ago. His son and his daughter-in-law appeared to be jostling in their room, laughing, mildly punching each other. Then Pradip turned his head and saw Father on the street, leaning against his cane, his face pale and stricken.

At first Pradip felt embarrassed at having Father witness the amorous scuffle between him and his wife; then it dawned on him that now was the time of his sister's wedding. He knew something was terribly, terribly wrong. Yudhir came to his mind, suddenly, for his friend had, Pradip thought, been acting quite strange lately, casually plying him with questions about how he would feel if someone eloped with his sister, just as he'd eloped with Chanda.

"Why? Are you planning to elope with her, muji?" Pradip had said. "If you look at my sister with a crooked eye, I'll gouge it out, break your arms, and throw you into the Bagmati River."

Yudhir had failed to catch the joke and had become defensive. "What are you saying, yaar? Your sister is like my sister, isn't she? My question was more philosophical than anything." Pradip had thought that perhaps Yudhir had developed a small crush on Mohini; no surprise there, as she was beautiful, and no harm in a minor infatuation. But now, with Father outside his window, looking as if he was going to disintegrate like a poorly constructed doll, Pradip knew, instinctively, that his sister had vanished and that Yudhir was involved.

Pradip could imagine the two of them together, seated on a bus, shoulders touching, on the steep, winding road carved out of the sides of the hills that began at the western edge of the Kathmandu Valley. Their fingers occasionally inched toward each other, hidden from other passengers. Strained but hopeful smiles lingered on their lips. Yes, Pradip could see how it would be: he knew his sister, he knew his friend, and he knew their smiles. She must not have slept all night, waiting for the *ding-dong* of the grandfather clock to announce three in the morning. That's when she'd sit up, pull out the yellow suitcase from under her bed; she'd crammed it with a few of her clothes and some knickknacks. She wouldn't bother to change her crumpled dhoti, for she didn't want to waste any time, and the rustling of the clothes could wake up Mother in the corner. With the aid of the streetlamp, which threw some light into her room, she combed and knotted her hair, then tiptoed out. Her door creaked, as it always did. She nearly tripped over something Mother had laid on the balcony right outside her room, and she stopped momentarily, holding her breath. She didn't hear any movement inside, so she quickly went down the stairs with the nimbleness of a cat.

The bus ride was hair-raising. The driver was a wildly enthusiastic fellow who sang filmi songs half the way there, and he took risks with the dangerous curves that started as soon as the bus began to climb past Thankot.

She could tell that Yudhir was nervous, perhaps more than she was. He remained quiet as their bus nearly brushed against large trucks as the driver negotiated treacherous corners. Sometimes the bus's wheel came so close to the edge of the road that Mohini could look down a distance of hundreds of feet; it made her heart rise to her throat. Tribhuvan Rajpath was the country's first highway; it allowed people to come and go from the capital without having to walk for days. Because it was the only road out of the city, everyone called it By-Road.

The bus passed through clouds, and Mohini squeezed Yudhir's hand, to reassure him. "Once we get married and return in a couple of years, after earning some money, they'll accept us," she whispered, her head nestled against his shoulder. Gone was the confidence he had on the day when he challenged her to take this trip with him. Now he looked like a little boy, afraid of the punishment coming to him at the end of the day. As the bus droned on toward the south, climbing up and down the hills, white mountains shone to the north. Twice the bus had to stop because of landslides, which laborers in ragged clothes were clearing with shovels. Only a few years old, the highway sometimes closed down because of these landslides, at times for days. During these delays, the couple watched cargo being transported up and down the hills on ropeways.

The more their journey progressed, the more Yudhir avoided Mohini's eyes, and when he did look at her, he appeared frightened. When he smiled, the expression was so tentative, so forced, that she couldn't help but rub his chin with the back of her fingers and reassure him that everything would be okay, that they were following the beats of their hearts, weren't they? But he didn't appear comforted, and strangely, his fears made her own anxieties more tolerable. "Scared?" she asked him.

His eyes were focused on the big windshield up front, which revealed rolling hills as far as the eye could see. "Just a bit worried, that's all," he said.

She knew that he lived with his uncle in the city; his parents remained back in the village. His uncle was a strict Brahmin and disapproved of his nephew's singing because most of the songs he sang were from films, which his uncle considered lewd and corrupt. His uncle wanted him to sing hymns and use his God-given talent solely for God's service, and since that wouldn't make a good career, had commanded him to pursue something else. "Sometimes I get so mad at the bastard," Yudhir had said to her in the Baghbazar hotel. "He is a good guardian, but he is stuck in the previous century. Do you know what he's like? If an untouchable person passes within five feet of him on the road, he'll head straight home to take a bath."

"I'm not an untouchable, but I am of a lower caste than you. What will he think of me?"

"Who cares what he thinks? He's not going to dictate my life for me."

As the bus wove in and out of the mountain clouds, and as the woman sitting behind them stuck her head out the window and began to retch, Mohini wondered if Yudhir too sometimes saw her with the eyes of his uncle. Then she dismissed this line of thinking and squeezed his hand.

She would have been right to wonder whether he had begun to view her differently. The moment they'd boarded the bus at five in the morning, guilt had begun to creep into Yudhir's chest, his throat; as they began their journey and the sun came up and the driver sped through the cramped roads of the hills, it had amplified until it consumed him. He was betraying a cherished belief of his uncle: caste purity. His uncle had given him more love and care than his own parents had. All right, so the man could be unreasonable and vexing, but he was still blood, and here was Yudhir, with this girl he hardly knew. She was sweet, yes, and he'd already tasted her juices, but what else did he know about her? Nothing. As her head rested on his shoulder and she murmured about plans for the future, he was already beginning to feel sick of her jasmine-scented hair oil, a smell he'd found intoxicating a few days ago. He stifled the urge to push her away and jolt her out of this stupid, stupid dream. I never promised to marry you, he told her in his mind. Already he'd begun cursing himself for this foolhardy move. Who was this girl? Nobody. He could have played with her for a while, taken her out to a movie or two, then moved on. He ought to have let her marry whomever she was about to marry, and within weeks she'd have adjusted to her husband and begun to feel happy with him. That's how things always worked. Rarely had he seen an arranged marriage, fixed by the couple's parents, fail, and rarely had he seen marriages born through silly romantic notions of love survive more than a few years. Our society, he theorized, channeling his uncle's voice, is simply not equipped to handle this thing called romantic love, even though our extravagant, melodramatic movies constantly lure us to it. For us, it's family, status, economic well-being, caste. A meeting of the minds trumps any meeting of the hearts!

Mohini fell asleep against his shoulder toward afternoon, as they began the descent to the lush vegetation of the lower hills. Beads of perspiration appeared above her upper lip, and every now and then she winced. Yudhir could sense the worries that arose in her dreams, and he felt sorry for her, for now he had begun to feel calm. He knew what he had to do, but he didn't know exactly when or how to do it. Once they began their train journey across the vast expanse of India on their way to Bombay, there would be numerous opportunities for him to simply slip way. He closed his eyes and saw himself stepping off the train onto the platform of a minor station somewhere, with the name of Sitapur or Rampur or Laxmanpur, in the searing heat of Bihar. "My throat is parched," he'd say. "Let me go find something to drink." And he'd simply go behind the small rectangular building that served as the train station and catch a rickshaw into town. He could even watch her from behind the station house: she would be at the compartment window, scanning the platform, her expression growing more anxious by the second, especially after the train whistle blew. Would she shout out his name? Would she too step off the train to find him, leaving their luggage on board? As the train jerked into motion, what thoughts would race through her head?

In the bus Yudhir closed his eyes, savoring her likely hysteria. Numerous strategies arose in his mind. As the bus stopped in the middle of nowhere and the driver stepped out for a trickle in the bushes, Yudhir knew that he could gently disengage himself from her right now and get off, in these lower hills with their numerous riverbed crossings, and hop on the next truck heading to the capital. What would she do then? She'd probably wake up about half an hour later and, not finding him next to her, at first think that he was chatting with a passenger up front. Still drowsy, she'd peel an orange, suck the juice, while her eyes roamed the interior of the bus, searching for him. When she realized he wasn't on board, she'd bolt to the front of the bus, lurching into passengers, and she'd yell at the driver that her man was missing. Negotiating a hairpin curve, the driver would say that it was impossible to turn back now.

She was softly snoring against his shoulder. The driver got back to his seat and started the bus. Yudhir would wait until Hetauda, then right after they stepped off the bus, he'd tell her that he had to find a place to urinate, badly; then he'd vanish, catch the next bus to Kathmandu, or head to the border, watch a few movies in Raxaul or Muzaffarpur, and then return after a couple of days. His uncle would be angry at him for a day or two, but so what? It was not as though he'd run away from a wedding his uncle had arranged for him! The thought made him laugh inwardly. The idiocy of this girl! What was she thinking when she decided to run away on her wedding day—of all days!—and ruin her family name forever? It was downright criminal. Her brother, Pradip, was another story; he was a man, and his transgressions would be forgotten in a year or two. But not the daughter of the house. If Yudhir had a sister who'd behaved like Mohini, he'd flog her for what she'd done. This thought made him strangely happy—the idea of this girl being beaten by a man—if not him, then her father, or perhaps her husband. He could easily see his uncle beating this girl, if she were his daughter. The idea of punishing her physically for her monumental sin Yudhir found exciting, and to his surprise, he began to harden. He closed his eyes and pictured himself slapping her around a bit, then grabbing her roughly by the hair and kissing her fiercely on the lips, then asking her to take off her blouse and show him her breasts, which he'd then fondle. He'd command her to take off her sari and stand in front of him in only her petticoat. He'd tell her to begin rubbing herself down there, gently at first, then harder and harder, until she'd moan and ask him to come close. But he'd deny her request, say that she was a dirty girl and he wouldn't touch her in a million years. He was rock hard now, next to her on the bus, and he stealthily took her hand, placed it on his crotch, and rubbed it against his penis, picturing her with her pointed, delicate tits, her face pleading with desire. Abruptly he came, and then went limp. He lifted her hand and placed it back in her lap. His thighs were sticky now, and he was slightly disgusted with himself.

He could take her all the way to Bombay, he thought, begin a semblance of their life together in that giant, pulsating city. He could try for work in the film music industry, and she could get a job somewhere — as what, though? A girl from a respectable family, she couldn't possibly do housework. Could she get a job as a secretary? But she didn't know how to type and could speak only a smattering of English. Who would give her a job in that big city where, he imagined, everybody spoke perfect English? He would be the sole breadwinner, and she would be a burden, though he could tell that she'd work hard at home, making it spick-and-span for him, cooking him delicious meals every night. His optimism about becoming a singing sensation had dampened considerably since the morning. He was no longer sure that the path to stardom in Bombay would be easy. He knew he was talented, but how many young men like him, all across India, were making the trip to Bombay right now, dreaming of breaking into the film music industry? The notion of battling hundreds of singers to reach the ears of a director or a producer tired him. He had a better chance, he thought, of winning the Bhagyodaya lottery.

"Foolhardy," he whispered to himself, and hearing his voice, she awoke and asked him where they were.

"I think Hetauda is close by. We can eat some snacks there and find a bus to Birgunj."

"I had such troubling dreams."

"They were only dreams," he said, smoothing her hair.

• • •

375

In Hetauda, they learned at the bus park that a big accident just up the road to Birgunj, near the toll station of Amlekhgunj, had obstructed traffic completely. Many Birgunj–Hetauda and Birgunj–Kathmandu buses had returned to Birgunj. "The road could be clear tonight, or tomorrow; we can't be sure," they were told. "Your best bet is to find a place to sleep here overnight, then try tomorrow. The government is sending some folks to help this evening."

And that's what they did. It was a two-story rest house in the main market, near the bus stop. Each floor had a large room with about a dozen cots, where the passengers slept. At the counter Yudhir looked at Mohini, who pulled fifteen rupees from her bag. An image of Father flashed through her mind, but she forced herself not to think about home right now.

As soon as they entered the rest house, because of anxiety or the dust in the air, Mohini began to cough viciously; Yudhir thumped her on the back, but still the coughing continued. He felt her forehead and said, "There's no fever." Her face was turning purple though, and he honestly became worried. He suggested that he go to buy some cough syrup because she seemed to have caught a cold — "a change of air and water, I'm sure" — and although she shook her head no, that he shouldn't bother, she continued to cough.

"You need some medicine," he said. "I'll be right back."

Downstairs he asked the rest-house owner where the medicine shop was.

It was less than a block away, around the corner, right next to the bus stop where they'd got off. He asked the compounder, who was seated inside on a stool, for a remedy for his wife's unrelenting cough, relishing how easily he called Mohini his wife, and how good it felt to say it. The compounder gave him the bottle, told him the dosage she needed. Yudhir stood outside the shop, holding the bottle in his hand, reading the label. Then he walked to the bus park. He asked around to see if a bus would be leaving for Kathmandu that evening. The drivers shook their heads. "Too dangerous," they said. A truck engine was revving up a few yards away. Yudhir walked toward the driver, who was a Sikh, wearing a large turban. In broken

Hindi, Yudhir asked him whether he was going to Kathmandu. The Sikh caressed his mustache and said, "Come in, come in. I could use some company."

Yudhir hopped onto the high seat of the truck. In his mind he began forming excuses for his absence that would placate his uncle when Yudhir reached home early in the morning.

Nilu's Hunch

NILU AND RAJA TOOK a taxi from Budhanilkantha to Lainchour. The traffic grew increasingly congested as they approached the city, so that by the time they reached Lazimpat, they were caught in a dense and stifling snarl, with no sign of movement. The taxi driver was talking rapidly into his mobile phone, seemingly arguing with his wife about when he was going to get home. He turned off his phone, cursed, and turned on the radio, to a program featuring a young woman who spoke quickly, in a language that was a heady mix of English and Nepali. She pronounced the Nepali words with such a westernized accent that it was hard to decipher them. The taxi driver laughed at something the radio host said.

Two weeks had passed since Nilu and Raja first learned of Ranjana's disappearance. Her roommates hadn't been able to reveal anything further to Umesh, except that Ranjana seemed to have undergone a bit of a personality shift during the spring semester. Gone was the laughing, vivacious girl, and in her place was a brooding, melancholy roommate who answered most questions in a monosyllable. Initially, Angela and Yuko had thought Ranjana was deeply homesick, and they had tried in various ways to revive her spirit, but she had shunned them. She'd declined their entreaties to join them for outings and remained shut in her room. One day she'd abruptly announced that she was moving to an apartment by herself. And even though Angela had repeatedly asked for her new address, Ranjana hadn't given it to her. Before the taxi took her away, Ranjana had asked her roommates not to tell her parents that she'd moved. "Just tell them I'm at the library, studying," she'd instructed them, "and send me an e-mail, and I'll contact them." Did the roommates know anything about a boy who'd been harassing Ranjana at Nepali gatherings? Yes, they were aware of him, knew that he was the son of a big shot in Nepal. Ranjana had complained about him. They weren't sure whether she'd had any contact with him outside of those Nepali parties. Did she have a boyfriend? They weren't aware of one. She hadn't shown any inclination toward having boyfriends. "Getting involved with others just takes too much time," she'd said. "I'm here to study."

Over the past few days Nilu and Raja had sent messages to Ranjana's Yahoo and university e-mail addresses several times, but she hadn't responded. Umesh had already made several trips to Evanston and had enlisted the help of the Nepali community there and across Chicago, asking people to be on the lookout for Ranjana, describing her as he passed her photos around. He'd even gone to the police station to file a report, but since Ranjana seemed to have left of her own volition, and since she wasn't physically or mentally handicapped and there was no suspicion of foul play, the officers couldn't register her as a missing person.

Foul play. The phrase sent a chill down Nilu's spine. Somehow she was still convinced that the Dhakal boy was involved. Could it be that Ranjana had gone into hiding to avoid him? But then, why would she ask her roommates not to tell her parents about her move? Nilu had finally told Raja about Minister Dhakal's son, and Raja hadn't become angry and upset, as she'd thought he would. Instead, he slumped deeper into his chair and said, "But boys harass girls all the time. That boy could be a badmash, but . . ." He seemed too exhausted to finish his thought, and she understood: each idea could ramify in many different directions, and the longer she or Raja obsessed about them, the more tired and weepy they became.

"Still, we should find out what the story was with that boy," Nilu said.

"How?" Raja asked.

"Maybe his parents know something."

Raja was hesitant. "You want to go to Minister Dhakal's house?"

"His son claimed to Ranjana that he knows you; does he?"

"We played a bit together when we were growing up, that's all, because Dhakal also lives in Lainchour. But how would the boy learn that Dhakal knew me unless he spoke to his father about Ranjana?"

"It's not hard to find out who is who in this city."

"What will we say to his parents when we go to them?"

"We will tell them what Ranjana said about their son. They're also parents — they'll understand our pain."

"What will we ask them to do?"

"Oooph! You're giving me a headache. If you don't want to go, I'll do it alone." With that she went to her room to change into a sari. Raja followed her, and he too got ready.

When the traffic in Lazimpat didn't show signs of budging, Nilu said, "It's not that far from here; we can walk." She thrust two hundred rupees at the taxi driver and got out. In the process she nearly got hit by a motorcyclist who was trying to squeeze through. He hurled an obscenity at her; it hit her hard, as though the man had spit on her. "Machikney," he said. Motherfucker. It baffled her, these random acts of hatred and cruelty, these vulgarities that people so easily directed at strangers but suppressed in social niceties when they needed to. The man on the motorcycle could easily be a friend's son, who, if he was visiting in Nilu's home, would be calling her aunty and respectfully mumbling ji-hajurs in every other sentence. Raja didn't hear what the motorcyclist said, for he was still getting out of the taxi. But had he heard it, what would he have done? Would he have run after the man, who, she now observed, was desperately trying to find an opening through a cluster of cars two hundred yards away. Had Raja heard the young man's word, he'd probably have stared after him, dumbfounded, as she was doing. But he wouldn't have chased after him or sought retribution, as he'd have done when he and Nilu were younger. Maitreya's death, now Ranjana's disappearance—Raja looked as if he was ready to crumple to the ground right here.

Nilu had to be strong, for him, for Ranjana. She had to inject some of her own strength into her husband. She took his arm as they began walking toward Lainchour. They passed the motorcyclist about a hundred yards farther up. Trapped, he was impatiently revving his engine. She couldn't help but cast a glance at him, and he quickly averted his eyes. Close up, you're all cowards, she thought.

"Let's go this way," she said as they reached the Hotel Ambassador.

"Straight is quicker," he said.

"I know, but I feel like going this way."

His gaze showed that he thought it odd to consider what one felt like doing when the destination was so important, but he acquiesced, and they took an alley that ran alongside the British embassy. Soon they reached the neighborhood in Lainchour where they used to roam when they'd first fallen in love, after Nilu switched schools. This inner part of Lainchour was close enough to the Jagadamba School to be convenient, but far enough from it to ensure that they'd encounter no one who knew Ganga Da or Jamuna Mummy. "Do you remember Kapur Dhara?" Nilu asked Raja, and he nodded. "Let's go that way," she said, and he threw up his hands in exasperation. She clasped his arm as if to say, Just humor me today.

This direction took them farther away from Minister Dhakal's house; they slipped into an alley that narrowed even more, allowing just enough room for a person walking from the opposite direction to pass. As teenagers they'd held hands in this very lane, their bodies pressed against each other, challenging those who looked. Their fingers entwined, their arms swinging, they'd walked this entire neighborhood.

When they reached Kapur Dhara, Raja said that he was feeling thirsty and needed a drink. He descended the short flight of stairs to a stone spout gushing with clear water. Nilu remembered it as somewhat larger than it actually was. She watched as Raja waited for a couple of women to notice him and give him room to reach the waterspout. The women were chatting away and didn't see him, but Raja didn't say anything, just stood with his arms limp by his sides. How different this Raja was from the one who'd mocked and taunted the royal palace guards, terrifying Nilu. Now, watching him in Kapur Dhara, she wanted to protect him from the harm — she had only a vague sense of what that harm might be — that the world might inflict on him. She recognized this impulse to shield him as something that she'd harbored since Raja first came to live in Nilu Nikunj and she'd discovered that he was a servant's boy who could barely read.

Raja was drinking from the spout now, his palm cupped to hold the water. He was thinking about Ranjana, she knew. A memory descended upon her: the day that she and Raja went down to this very spout to quench their thirst and ended up splashing water at each other. Why was she remembering these nostalgic moments when she ought to be focused on her daughter? It was illogical, irrational, yet she experienced vividly the laughter of those years, the water sparkling in their palms, Raja's hair wet from a recent dousing, the voices of women washing clothes nearby: "No shame!" "Whose children are these?" A middle-aged woman, her petticoat tied above her breasts to cover them, her hair in soapsuds, shouted at them, "I'm trying to bathe here, and these nakkacharas are hogging the tap." Her eyes gleamed when they fell upon Raja. "Raja? What are you doing here? And who is this girl? Have you snatched her from her parents?" Raja blushed beet-red and motioned to Nilu to get out of there.

Now they took the longer route through Samakhusi to arrive behind the Jagadamba School. The house where Raja grew up, which Raja had sold after Ganga Da's death, had been transformed: three more stories had been added, and the house had expanded sideways too, crowding the neighboring house. But they didn't pause; they went farther and stood in front of Minister Dhakal's house, which was surrounded by imposing walls. A guard asked them who they were, then disappeared inside. He returned to let them in.

• • •

The former home minister greeted them warmly, chatted with Raja about their childhood days. But he was slightly dismissive of their plight. "A young girl. First time out of the clutches of her parents. Maybe she went touring the country, driving one of those, what do you call them." He turned toward his wife, who shook her head, indicating she had no clue about what he was referring to. "You know," he continued, "those big vans with everything inside — bathroom, television, kitchen, bed. O-ho. What do you call them? R something. We saw plenty of them when we went to America two years ago." He began to describe his visit.

People still came to see the former home minister, despite his having lost his position, for "source-force," to seek his patronage, to have him pull strings on their behalf. He still knew many important people in town. So you couldn't really blame him for thinking that Raja and Nilu wanted his help in finding their daughter. Perhaps they'd heard that his son too lived in Chicago.

But when Nilu mentioned what Ranjana had said about his son, the home minister stared at her incredulously. His wife, her lips trembling, said, "Our son is not like that. How dare you!"

"I was simply wondering if you knew anything, or if your son did."

"It's best if you leave this house," the home minister's wife said, pointing her finger toward the door.

As Nilu and Raja were about to leave, the home minister spoke, in a semi-conciliatory tone. "Our son can be difficult at times, but he'd never stoop so low. Still, I'll ask him. Leave your phone number."

Two days before they were to fly to Chicago, Nilu woke at night from a terrible dream, her heart hammering in her chest. She jiggled Raja, who was sound asleep next to her, beaten by worry, exhausted from getting all the paperwork ready for their departure. Umesh had advised them that they ought to bring with them every document concerning Ranjana that they could find.

"I saw something," she said to Raja.

"What?" he said, his voice hoarse.

"She's here," Nilu said. "Ranjana is here."

Raja jerked upright in the bed, and peered into the darkness. Perhaps he too had been dreaming about their daughter. "She's here?" Then, realizing what had happened, he clasped her hand and said, "You had a bad dream. Go to sleep."

No, no, Nilu said, but apparently she said it only silently, not aloud. "I saw something," she whispered. Raja had already drifted off. She too closed her eyes again, but the images from her dream kept pressing against her eyes. It's only a dream, she reminded herself. In two days we are going to America to look for our daughter. What she saw was her mind playing last-minute tricks.

Sunlight streaming through the curtains in the morning did nothing to change the sense of foreboding left from her dream. Today she had to go to the pharmacy to get enough medicine — for her various allergies, for his diabetes — to last a month, their projected length of stay in America. Umesh had informed them that medicine was expensive in America. Raja and Nilu hadn't discussed what they'd do if, after a month, they hadn't found Ranjana. "Let's take enough for a month," Raja had said, and they'd both looked at each other, leaving the unspoken question hanging in the air: what then?

As Nilu rode the microbus into town — first she had to go to the pharmacy in Jyatha, then to Thamel to buy some Nepali paper as a gift for Umesh's family — Chicago seemed just too far away, too alien, too . . . unfruitful. Waste of time. The phrase kept repeating itself in her mind as she got off the bus at Rani Pokhari and headed toward Jyatha. She stopped at the big pharmacy where they always bought their pills. The middle-aged man behind the counter greeted her. By now, several people in the city who knew her had learned of Ranjana's disappearance. One tabloid newspaper had somehow gotten a whiff of Ranjana's disappearance and carried a report, filled with inaccuracies. The publicity had irked Nilu, for people had started gossiping and speculating. Ranjana's photo, black and white and grainy and taken when she was in eighth grade, had accompanied the article. Nilu had no idea how the tabloid managed to get that photo, for it wasn't one she'd seen before. She suspected it was taken at a friend's house. Seeing it had mildly shocked Nilu. Her daughter looked different, more subdued than she was in real life, like a timid girl who'd ventured alone to the city, seeking shelter and solace.

After the photo appeared in the newspaper, acquaintances called to offer their own theories about what might have happened. Some phoned not to sympathize but to pontificate: this is what happens when you send your children so far away. One well-wisher said that her children didn't go to America, despite having been offered outstanding scholarships from Ivy League schools, precisely because America was such a violent, unpredictable country, where gangsters were ready to slit anyone's throat for a dollar or two.

The pharmacist gave Nilu the pills she wanted and said in a solicitous tone, "Now that you are going to look for her, I'm sure she'll be found."

Nilu said she too was confident, but as she went toward Thamel, she couldn't see herself getting on an airplane to travel so far away when . . . when . . . She paused in the middle of the street and looked around. Ranjana is here — the sentence rang in her mind again. The crowd around her swelled, pressing from all sides; the street itself seemed to narrow, squeezing its occupants. The sun boiled in the sky. The voices around her sang loudly against her ears. Her head felt heavy as a stone, her legs went limp, and she crumpled to the ground.

There were people around her. An authoritative voice said, "Leave room, leave room, she needs to breathe," and a hand cradled her head. Someone sprinkled water on her face, and gradually her head cleared. It was embarrassing to be lying on the street, on the lap of an elderly man whose anxious eyes were focused on her. She sat up, said that she was okay now, that she could walk by herself. Someone thrust into her hand a bottle of water, its cap unscrewed, and she drank it gladly. She stood, swaying. "Come, come," the elderly man said, and took her to the nearest shop, where she was given a stool to sit on. Yes, it was a good idea to rest for a while here, she agreed. The shopkeeper ordered a lassi from the restaurant next door, and when it came, she drank it, grateful for these small acts of kindness. The elderly man and the shopkeeper were talking about how human and vehicular congestion in the city was likely to give even young, healthy people heart attacks, let alone people Nilu's age. The elderly man said that that's why he'd sent his college-age children to America, to Nebraska specifically, where they were studying. The shopkeeper also had a niece somewhere in America, and they compared notes. Nilu listened to them quietly, nodding occasionally to signal that she was listening. Her eyes roamed toward the pedestrians, pausing on young women of Ranjana's age. Most of them were fashionably dressed; some spoke English; all were laughing and smiling and gazing admiringly at the wares displayed outside the many gift shops.

The urgency of Nilu's presentiment that Ranjana was nearby made her heart ache; it compelled her to get up from her stool and apologize to the elderly gentleman and the shopkeeper. She explained that she had to leave; her husband was waiting for her at home. "Are you sure you're okay to go home by yourself?" the elderly man asked. "Why don't I see you to a taxi?"

"No, no," she protested. "You have done enough for me already. I'll find a taxi here, around the corner."

At Thamel chowk, instead of boarding one of the waiting taxis, she headed straight north, not knowing where she was going. If Ranjana had indeed returned, wouldn't someone have seen her by now? Kathmandu was a small city, after all, and someone, somewhere would have recognized her, surely? If she had returned, certainly she'd have flown in, and the airport was tiny enough that someone would have speculated, "Isn't that Nilu's daughter, the one who vanished in America?" Or someone would have recognized her name on the immigration or customs form. Perhaps a taxi driver would have done a double take in the rearview mirror, trying to remember where he'd seen this passenger. But even if people had recognized Ranjana, what would they have done? Gone to the police? And say what? "I just saw the girl who was reported lost in America?" Absurd. Besides, Nilu reminded herself angrily, if Ranjana through some freakish chance had ended up here in the city, she'd have come home. If something bad had happened to Ranjana and she'd been forced to return to Kathmandu, her parents would be the first people she'd seek out for comfort.

Still, every time a young woman of Ranjana's build or hair passed by, Nilu scrutinized the face carefully, as though Ranjana would have returned to the city in disguise.

When Nilu arrived at home, she was about two hours late, and Raja hovered by the gate. He told her he was worried about her, that he'd called her repeatedly on her mobile phone, but every time he got a message about network failure. "Our entire lives have turned into a big network failure." He'd attempted a joke but couldn't muster a smile. She embraced him and took him inside, and for a while they stood in the living room in each other's arms; the only sound was the ticking of the clock on the wall. Raja was not doing well, she knew. She had to be strong for him, now and throughout the trip. But the thought of travel once again troubled her. Raja must have sensed she was pondering something, for he asked her what the matter was. She shook her head. If she told him what she was thinking and feeling, the very questions that had been hounding her for the past couple of days would come flying out of his mouth: Why would Ranjana come back? If she has, why wouldn't she come home? And Nilu wouldn't have any convincing answers for him.

She had to decide fast. Raja was fiddling with the suitcases, muttering something about how the latch didn't seem to be working.

Nilu took a deep breath and asked, "What if she returns here while we are in Chicago? Have you thought of that?"

Raja stopped fidgeting with the latch. "Why would she return here without telling us?"

"I don't know. Just thinking."

He sat down on the bed, frowning. "That's the oddest thing you've said. You mean, what if she returned unannounced, after all these days?"

"It was just a thought. Don't worry about it."

He came and sat next to her. "No, something is going on. What are you thinking?"

"Nothing, really."

"Nilu."

"It's probably my mind going in all directions. But what if she's in some kind of trouble, decides to come home, and finds the house empty?"

"But if she hasn't been abducted, or, God forbid . . ." He couldn't complete the sentence. "Wouldn't she have contacted us by now if she was free to do so? I mean, if no one had harmed her, no matter what kind of trouble she was in? It makes absolutely no sense."

Nilu turned away from him, partly because he was echoing her own nagging doubts. "Nothing that's happening right now makes sense," she said.

Wrapped up in their own thoughts, they didn't say anything to each other. Raja went out to the garden to get some fresh air, then returned after a few minutes. "So, what are you suggesting?" he asked. Obviously he had been mulling over what she had said.

"I'm wondering if you should go to Chicago, and I should stay here in case she comes home. And I'll make further inquiries here." She added, as an incentive, "Maybe I'll go to Minister Dhakal again."

"You want me to go all the way to America by myself? What further inquiries?"

She couldn't tell him, not yet. "I'll wait here for a while. Then, if nothing happens, I'll join you."

He looked out of the window anxiously. "You might have a point here. If she's in trouble and returns home, one of us should be here."

She went to him and stroked his chin. "I'll be worried about you all the way to America. You're not in very good shape right now."

"I'm fine," he said. "And I won't return until I find her, I swear. Besides, Umesh is there to help me, so I won't have to search for her all by myself."

But a short while later Raja began to wonder aloud if he'd be able to do it alone, without Nilu, and she told him that he had to be strong for their daughter's sake. Raja looked baffled, unsure, and she held him, then gave him instructions, wrote down important phone numbers for him on a piece of paper, and repacked one suitcase just for him. By the time they went to bed, she was impatient for him to leave so she could have more room to move, to do whatever she needed to do without having to explain anything to anyone. A feeling of strength had come into her limbs. She was ready to turn the city upside down to find her daughter.

Part II

A Young Woman in
a Black Overcoat

EVEN IN THE HEAT of August the young woman was wearing a large black overcoat, which hung to her knees when she first appeared on Bhairavi's doorstep. She asked if a room was available, as indicated by the TO LET sign on the outside wall that a ruffian, long ago, with the insertion of an *i*, had changed into TOILET. The young woman, pretty and intelligent looking, with somewhat familiar features, had eyes that indicated she'd done some crying. Her cheeks were slightly puffy. She held her body carefully, turned and moved with a slowness that made Bhairavi wonder if she was ill. "Only you?" Bhairavi asked. Bhairavi's husband had died a few years ago, and her children had married and lived separately; she rented rooms on the first and second floors and lived on the third floor; the young woman had knocked at her third-floor door. One room had remained empty on the second floor for months now, probably because it was fairly small, with a window that overlooked the street and a ceiling marred by a large crack resembling a river delta, which oozed during the rains. Interested tenants glanced at the room and scrunched their noses. This girl too would most likely reject the room once she viewed it.

The girl nodded.

Where's your family? Bhairavi wanted to ask. Then she thought:

Who cares? I have a family, but they no longer visit me unless they want something.

But the girl said yes, even before inspecting the room completely; then she sat on the floor.

"Here, let me get you a cushion," Bhairavi said, and ran up to her room.

When she returned, the young woman was looking out the window. Bhairavi placed the cushion on the floor. "It's only noisy during the day. At night it's quiet." But she suspected that the girl's mind was on something other than the clamor that rose from the street below.

A cot lay in the corner, bereft of a mattress or bedding. In another corner stood an old pumping stove that was still functional, Bhairavi knew, because she had cranked it up a couple of months ago. She'd left it there, hoping that some poor soul might consider it an attractive feature of the room. And although the girl too, like the other tenants, barely glanced at the stove, it dawned upon Bhairavi that apart from the large black bag the young woman had brought with her, she carried nothing else. Had her parents kicked her out? Was she a refugee of some sort? The young woman's speech showed that she was well educated, and her face indicated she was from a good family, although it was very hard to tell these days. Daughters of respected families no longer hesitated to appear half-naked in dance bars and casinos.

The young woman met her gaze and asked how much the rent was.

Normally Bhairavi quoted a slightly high rate, to leave room for bargaining, but with this young woman she didn't. "Six hundred." The girl reached into her bag, took out an expensive-looking purse, and opened it. She grabbed a handful of money and began to count, separating what looked like foreign currency — dollars? — from the Nepali bills, which she then handed to Bhairavi.

Bhairavi wanted to ask her many questions: Where are you from? Why are you alone? Why do you have foreign money? But she refrained; it was none of Bhairavi's business. She no longer even knew her own children. And the strangers who occupied her rooms stayed for a few months or years and then moved on; another person's story replaced theirs. Still, the blown-away, exhausted look on the girl's face seemed to indicate that she had traveled from afar and hadn't eaten or slept well for days, and Bhairavi couldn't help but feel some concern for her.

Bhairavi did ask the young woman whether she had any bedding and when she planned on occupying the room. The young woman asked whether it would be a problem if she stayed here starting now. "That mat will be sufficient," she said, pointing to a straw mat in the corner. "And this will be my pillow," she said, gesturing toward the cushion.

Later Bhairavi brought the girl some bedding and an old blanket. Dusk was approaching, but the girl still lingered by the window, still wearing her overcoat; beads of sweat clung to her forehead. She'd scarcely moved. This one is in another world entirely, Bhairavi observed. She turned on the light, fixed the bed, then told the girl that though cooking was allowed in the room, Bhairavi expected that stale food and dirty dishes would be taken care of. "I have a fridge upstairs that you can sometimes use if you wish," Bhairavi said, surprising herself because she'd never offered this to a tenant before.

Back upstairs, as Bhairavi ate her dinner — nothing grand, leftovers from this morning, consisting of rice, dal, two pieces of chicken, and some spinach — she wondered if the girl had gone to the restaurant Bhairavi had recommended, where the food was relatively cheap, fresh, and tasty. Somehow she knew that the girl hadn't done so; judging from her pallor and her dull eyes, most likely she was a halfhearted nibbler. Bhairavi set aside a piece of chicken and some spinach, mixed them with rice from the cooker, and took the plate down.

The girl had moved from the window to the bed, where she had fallen asleep. Apparently she'd unbuttoned her overcoat before lying down, for it was now open, revealing her red shirt. The girl's stomach protruded — she was pregnant.

• • •

Bhairavi didn't sleep that night, worried about what she should do. Propriety dictated that she ask the young woman to leave: such a tenant couldn't be allowed to live in her house. Her other boarders would protest; also, Bhairavi's own reputation was at stake. Her son and daughter, now married with their own children and living elsewhere in the city, would eat her alive. "What's she to you?" they'd ask. "Why are you bent on cutting our nose among our friends and relatives?" They'd see this as another instance of their mother's harebrained approach to life, her willful disregard for simple propriety and how flouting it could lead to unpleasant consequences for the whole family. Yes, they'd feel free to insult the young woman in the second-floor room; they saw themselves as respectable people. People of culture, of class. Even Bhairavi, their own mother, they considered uncouth and, yes, stupid.

Her son had actually called her that recently, when he sensed that she wasn't going to sell this old house where they'd grown up. "Where else can we find a woman more stupid than you?" he'd yelled.

Her daughter had added, "Exactly so!"

This interchange took place in front of their own spouses, their own children, Bhairavi's grandchildren. One of them chanted, "Stupid, stupid, grandmother is stupid."

If Bhairavi allowed this girl to stay here, it would give her son and daughter one more reason to be angry with her. As it was, they were furious that she'd not caved in to their demands to sell the house, and the valuable plot that went along with it, to the businessman who was willing to pay a hefty price for it. Over the years they had become critical of everything she did. When they visited, they commented on how shoddy her dhoti looked, or what sorry-looking tenants she had in her building, the smell of which made them feel nauseated.

But of all the houses in the city, this girl had chosen Bhairavi's to seek shelter in, and there was a reason for it.

Don't be a fool, Bhairavi told herself. Don't be duped by your heart. This girl means nothing to you. Once she leaves in two days, you'll forget about her, and things will be exactly as they should be: your children will be their normal, grumbling selves, and your tenants will go back to complaining about the paucity of water in the building, the electrical outlet that doesn't work, the noise from their neighbors. But this thinking made her laugh. Why grow so quickly afraid when something a bit out of the ordinary happens? At least Bhairavi should first learn of the young woman's situation. Maybe she had no place to go. Maybe she was impregnated, then abandoned; maybe the girl came here as a last resort, after being trampled upon by the outside world. Find out her story, then decide what to do. Or, at least let the poor girl catch her breath, until she finds some other place, perhaps with a sympathetic relative or a kind friend. What better use for that stupid room, which, perhaps like the girl, had remained unwanted for so long? Bhairavi knew she could be inviting trouble by letting her heart rule on this matter, but it had been a while since she'd experienced such softness toward anyone.

The Kick

IN THE MORNING when Bhairavi went down and knocked, the girl asked her to come in. Sitting on the bed, her overcoat fully buttoned, the girl was looking out of the window. "I left you some food last night," Bhairavi said. "Did you eat it?"

The girl said that she ate it this morning; where should she wash the plate? Bhairavi said that there was a tap in the courtyard below. "But there's a faucet on my balcony upstairs if you don't want to use the courtyard tap, which the first-floor families use; their children can be quite rowdy. And rude, if you ask me. It's incredible to me how undisciplined some children are these days, and how their parents let them run wild, do what they wish, say what they want, to whomever they want to say it!" A picture appeared in Bhairavi's mind of this young woman being teased and poked and prodded by unruly children, so she said, "Yes, why don't you just come up when you need to wash, or when you need to use the fridge. This stove should work. Try it. If it doesn't, I'll loan you another one until . . ." She didn't want to say "until you buy one" to this girl — it might be too much for her. "Here, let me see right now if it works."

And Bhairavi sat on the floor and dusted the stove, then pulled out its lever and began to pump it. She worked on the stove for a while, and the girl remained silent. Questions swirled in Bhairavi's mind: Whose baby are you carrying? Are you desperate, suicidal? Is that why you've come to my house — you think this might be a good place to die?

Bhairavi got the stove to work. She found its sound soothing; it reminded her of her dead husband. They'd purchased the stove after she'd come into this house as a bride, before she gave birth to her children and was sucked into endless days of feeding them and wiping their bottoms and singing them lullabies. Whenever Bhairavi thought of her husband, tears welled up in her eyes. He'd been diagnosed with cancer soon after their children got married, and she'd tried to take care of him as best she could. But he'd lost weight within months and had turned frail and gaunt. What had saddened her the most, however, was how her children had failed to show kindness and consideration to their ailing father, the very man on whose lap they'd learned their ABCs and their two-plus-twos, the father who'd gone into debt to get them wedded. Bhairavi remembered that she'd passed on the old stove to Nilu after she and Raja started living in this flat. Bhairavi had lost touch with Nilu, especially after Nilu's young son died. Her son's death had broken her heart, poor Nilu. The last she knew, Nilu and Raja had given birth to a baby girl, but that was ages ago. Over the years Bhairavi had contemplated trying to renew contact with her old friend. But she couldn't think of anyone she could call to find out Nilu's whereabouts. They didn't have friends or acquaintances in common. After Nilu had moved to Chabel, she and Bhairavi slowly lost touch, despite Nilu's pleas that Bhairavi remain an aunt to Maitreya.

Time and again Bhairavi had pondered going to Nilu's house in Chabel, where she'd visited after Maitreya died, but for that she'd have to go all the way across the city, fighting the traffic, especially in the madhouse streets of Gaushala and Chabel. And who knew whether Nilu and Raja still lived in that house anymore? It was not like the old times, when folks stayed put in one place. These days everyone seemed to be constantly moving, to bigger or better houses, to sleeker and shinier condos. No one continued clinging to their family's old, crumbling, disintegrating house, as Bhairavi did.

But the more her children badgered her to sell the house, the more Bhairavi adamantly refused, not only because she was disgusted with their greed but also because she treasured this house: it was the one in which her husband had grown up. That courtyard was where he'd played marbles and hide-and-seek, where he'd drunk water from the tap after an afternoon of running through the streets. This house was where Bhairavi's mother-in-law, the kindest woman she'd ever known, had begun her married life. That was so long ago; the black-and-white photograph that showed the young bride in her wedding regalia, her head slightly bowed in modesty as her husband shyly inspected his fingers, seemed to belong to another era entirely. It reminded Bhairavi of the daguerreotypes that she had once seen at a museum: grainy images of kings and queens wearing their crowns and their gowns and holding their silver canes; their faces were composed and solemn.

Bhairavi glanced at the young woman, who was still wearing her ridiculous overcoat. She wouldn't be able to keep her pregnancy hidden for long, for soon her tummy would push against even that bulky outerwear. The largeness of her belly would soon be unmistakably apparent. She must be at least seven months pregnant, Bhairavi suspected. More like eight.

"Here, do you want to cook something?" Bhairavi asked the girl.

"I don't have anything to cook."

"Well, why don't you go shopping for vegetables then? The market is right around the corner."

The girl said that she might do so later in the afternoon.

Bhairavi turned off the stove and left the young woman alone. She went back upstairs and lay in bed, her mind filled with memories of her husband. After he died, the silence in the house overwhelmed her, and she began to have crying spells. Despite the grudge she held against her children, she did try to reach out to them, but they remained wrapped up in their own lives, their own children, and their cars and parties. She couldn't understand how something like this could happen: children she devoted her life to wouldn't call for weeks to see how their widowed mother was faring.

Bhairavi decided. She would not to ask the girl to leave. Even if her children chanced upon the girl and noticed that she was pregnant, Bhairavi would defend her. The girl was on the brink of something dangerous, Bhairavi felt.

In the afternoon she went down again to check on the girl. The door was shut but not locked, and she gently pushed it. The girl was lying on the bed, sleeping in her overcoat, which was unbuttoned, but she had placed the blanket on her belly. Bhairavi sat on the bed; the girl didn't wake up. Bhairavi watched her: such an innocent face, so beautiful. But her eyes were scrunched tight, as though she was battling the visions in her dreams.

With her palm Bhairavi touched the girl's forehead. It was hot. To compare, Bhairavi touched her own forehead. The difference was obvious, and it was not just heat from wearing the overcoat: the girl was running a fever. Bhairavi went up to her own flat, poured water in a bowl, found a hand towel, and brought them back down. Wetting the towel, she made a cold compress and placed it on the girl's forehead. The girl's lips were twitching. As Bhairavi applied the towel to her forehead, the blanket slid off the girl's body and fell to the floor. Bhairavi stared at her belly. Then, instinctively, she placed her hand on it, wondering if she could feel the baby. Given the bulge, there was no doubt that the baby was alive and kicking. Bhairavi tried to remember when she was pregnant with her own children, how it had felt, but it was such a long time ago that the only thing she remembered was the pain of the latter stages of pregnancy and childbirth itself; without the help of her mother-in-law and her husband, she couldn't have survived them.

Bhairavi lowered her head and put her ear to the girl's belly. It felt like the natural thing to do, to see if she could hear the baby. There was no movement. And then, suddenly, she felt a push against her ear. The baby had kicked! Bhairavi felt a thrill of excitement. It was as though the baby had sensed her presence and sent her a signal.

I'm here, I'm alive, it was saying. I'm ready to come out. Inexplicably, a wave of pleasure washed over Bhairavi. Why? She wasn't related to this young woman, and in a few months, like her other tenants, this young woman too would most likely disappear from her life. Yet this happiness reminded her of the time when she and her husband were young, before the children came along. Could a person derive such great pleasure from the unborn child of a complete stranger? What else in this world don't I know about? Bhairavi asked herself. What else is in store for me? And, strangely, this thought buoyed her.

Bhairavi covered the girl's belly with the blanket and continued to apply the compress. After about twenty minutes, the temperature came down and the girl's lips stopped twitching. Bhairavi smoothed the young woman's hair. The innocence of her face reminded her of her own children when they were younger. Her son had had great ambitions of becoming a doctor and used to run around the house with a toy stethoscope, making diagnoses and offering prescriptions. But Keshav turned out to be an average student, not up to the rigors of medical school, and had to settle for the job of an accountant at a medium-size firm, which, he complained, was filled with petty, backbiting people. And her daughter, who used to be a sweet child, offering other children her toffees and lollipops, had changed after she got married. Her husband's family was quite traditional, with strict notions of how a daughter-in-law should conduct herself. Seema was under the thumb of her mother-in-law, a severe-looking woman with eyes that narrowed in response to even small infractions; everyone in the house craved her approval. Maybe Seema thought that the kind of money she'd inherit from her mother after the sale of the house would weaken her mother-in-law's grip on her.

When Bhairavi thought along these lines, her attitude toward her children softened. Maybe she should reconsider the businessman's offer. They could split the money three ways, and that would make Keshav and Seema happy. Bhairavi could look for a small house far away, maybe near Bhaktapur or Godavari, and spend her time reading the scriptures, which had begun to interest her lately. The possibility of giving up this house in Thamel brought a lump to her throat, but perhaps it was time to let go.

The girl opened her eyes. She seemed embarrassed to find Bhairavi sitting on her bed, for she attempted to sit up, carefully shielding her belly with the blanket. "No, no," Bhairavi said. "You keep sleeping. You need to rest." She was about to add that she needed to conserve her energy for the baby, but she didn't want to spook the girl by letting on that she knew.

Bhairavi ended up cooking for both of them in her room upstairs and bringing the food down. Perhaps because her fever had come down, or because she'd not eaten well for days, the girl ate ravenously, and Bhairavi experienced an odd pleasure in catering to her, asking whether the meat was well salted, whether she wanted more dal.

The girl finished her food, let out a small belch, and then gave Bhairavi an embarrassed smile.

"It's good to see you smile," Bhairavi said. "You haven't smiled since you've come here."

"That was the best food I've eaten in days. As good as my —" A shadow came over her face.

"Go on, as good as whose?"

"Nothing," the girl said. Her hand was still unwashed, so Bhairavi brought a carafe of water and poured it for her while the girl rinsed her fingers. Bhairavi handed her a towel. The girl wiped her hands and mouth.

"I don't know much about you," Bhairavi said. "You haven't even told me your name yet."

The girl hesitated, then said, "Ranji."

The Return Home

S HE HADN'T MEANT for it to be this way. She kept saying it to
herself, to Papa, to Ma: I hadn't meant for this to happen. But it
did happen, and she ended up returning to Nepal, to bear the child
of someone whose face she had to try hard to remember.

The guilt she'd felt over her pregnancy had, just once, made her
contemplate suicide: slashing her wrist in the bathroom, overdos-
ing on sleeping pills — methods of snuffing one's own life that she'd
read or heard about. They all sounded alien to her. They won't
work, her mind had told her, and it was then that she began to experience sensations of drowning: at first in two-second flashes, then
for longer stretches, as the pregnancy progressed. She'd be sitting at
her desk in her room as Angela and Yuko watched television in the
next room; then, abruptly, she'd find herself transported — she was
immersed in water, gasping for breath, flailing; small schools of fish
darted about her; larger ones watched her as their mouths slowly
opened and closed. Even while it was happening, she knew she was
living someone else's experience.

Ranjana hadn't felt much for Amos. She'd met him at the post office
one early December day, when she'd gone to mail a letter to Papa
and Ma. She was in a hurry; her math exam would begin shortly. He
graciously allowed her to go ahead of him in line, and that's when
they began to talk. They conversed about how cold it was getting

by Lake Michigan already. He hosted an international program at a community radio station in Chicago. When he found out she was from Nepal, he said that he'd been there, "in my younger days," and backpacked at the foothills of the Annapurnas. He wore an overcoat and a nice scarf around his neck; the scarf looked so soft that she wanted to run her hands over it. Then she looked at his dark skin, the cleft in his chin, and thought that it'd be nice to stroke that face too. The thought had surprised her, for she'd barely been interested in boys here, so busy had she been with academic life. But this man, probably in his late twenties — exactly thirty years of age, she learned later — was self-assured, with a trace of laughter in his eyes that made her want to smile for no reason. She exchanged e-mail addresses with him before they departed into the freezing Chicago air.

She kept him a secret from everyone; she didn't know why. She didn't tell Angela and Yuko just because they'd get overly excited, start calling him her boyfriend. She liked him, but her thoughts didn't dwell on him when she was away from him: when she took walks in Evanston as the school closed and snow blanketed the streets and glistened on the treetops, or when she went to a little Christmas gathering at Yuko's aunt's house deep in the suburbs, or when she attended a bash organized by the Nepalis to celebrate the New Year.

Later she wondered if she had ended up sleeping with Amos because she'd been disturbed by how blacks were spoken of at the Nepali gatherings she'd attended so far.

"These kaleys," she'd heard several Nepalis say. "They are dangerous." During the New Year's party, one skinny Nepali girl had said, "I get so scared when they come near. I feel like they're going to rob me or rape me or something." Ranjana was informed that blacks were lazy and prone to violence. Yet here was Amos, more gentlemanly and intelligent than most Nepali men she'd come across so far.

What Ranjana heard from the Nepalis made her angry, and when, early in the New Year, Amos told her that he was interested in having her as a guest on a radio show focused on Nepal, she said yes. He wanted to play Nepali music, discuss the Maoist rebels and how they managed to get into the government after years of mayhem, converse about the culture in general. She told him that her knowledge of Nepali politics was minimal, and they'd better stick to the culture. "Only what you know, Ranji," he said. "I never feature experts on my show. I'm interested in real people, not talking heads."

The program had gone well, and she'd been pleased with how she'd spoken with both coherence and real feeling. A couple of people had phoned in during the half-hour, asking her about her experiences in America, wanting her to contrast it with life in Nepal.

That evening Amos took her to a Thai restaurant. He praised her performance, then invited her to his apartment for some wine. She said that she was underage, and he said that they could pretend they were drinking in Kathmandu. In his flat they ended up kissing—her first kiss. She stopped him when his hands began to roam over her breasts, but the next time, a few days later, she didn't. He was gentle with her, talked to her about her aspirations and her family as they cuddled in his apartment, and so when, after a few meetings, their kisses grew more passionate and he picked her up—he was a tall man—and carried her to his bedroom, she found her resolve weakening. She thought about Ma and Papa, briefly, but they seemed far away.

Amos made her dinner and fed her in bed, laughing as he told her stories about the eccentric guests he'd hosted on his show. He told her about the environmental activist who had received an on-air call from his wife, who accused him of cheating on her with a colleague of his. He described a local councilman who had leapt across the table at Amos because he'd been offended by the radio host's provocative questions.

"You lead an interesting life," she'd told him. "All I seem to do is study."

"Whenever you need a break from your books, come visit me."

She remembered Ma and Papa later that night and vowed to herself to consider this occasion a one-time thing; she'd not return to Amos. But she did, three or four more times, finding in his soft, measured voice a degree of relief from the loneliness of being so far from home. He was intelligent, deeply knowledgeable about many things—how the city was run, the science of the brain, the controversy over climate change. He cooked well, and his apartment was always filled with intoxicating aromas.

Spending time with him was easy; she didn't notice the days, the weeks go by—until she discovered that she was pregnant. She got angry at herself for being so foolish, for not taking more precautions; she got angry at him, for she thought that he'd somehow duped her. But he hadn't; she'd seen him put the condom on every time.

Initially she thought she'd have an abortion, for that would solve everything. Ma and Papa wouldn't get a whiff of what had happened, and she too would soon forget her lapse with Amos and refocus on her studies. But every time she picked up the phone to call Planned Parenthood, her hand trembled. She didn't understand why: she wasn't opposed to abortion. But when she put her palm on her belly, she thought she felt something remarkable there, a movement, a signal, a transfer of emotions. Every time she braced herself to make an appointment at a clinic, a voice inside her mind said, Not yet, not yet. As days turned to weeks, the impulse to end her pregnancy weakened. Guilt prevented her from telling Amos that she was pregnant, as though what was growing in her was only hers, not his.

Now Ranjana felt it was even more important to hide Amos from everyone: from Angela and Yuko, from the local Nepalis, from whom she'd distanced herself a while ago anyway, especially after that home minister's son began to harass her. Still, Amos wanted to see her more often, sent her e-mails expressing hope, saying that they had something "special going on." She evaluated her emotions then, but discovered that apart from a mild interest, she felt nothing for him, and now that another life was growing inside her, Amos seemed to recede to the back of her mind.

She stopped responding to his e-mails. Gradually, she began to skip classes, finding instead a quiet spot under a tree on campus from where she could observe the other students. It was already the middle of March, and the air was hinting at warmer days to come. She didn't yet show, but to be sure, she had begun to wear, on top of her winter jacket, an extra-large, misshapen black overcoat. She'd found it on the heavily discounted rack at the Burlington Coat Factory.

Sometimes she sat in a theater by herself, her mind hardly registering what was happening on the screen. Memories of a faraway past came to her, a past that was not hers:

She carries her baby in her arms, out on the streets, the hot sidewalk burning her soles. A small pile of rice, along with some coins, rests on a piece of cloth in front of her. She's trying to nurse the baby, but the frantic movements of his cheeks produce just a dribble of a pale creamy substance, more water than milk. Hunger has hollowed her stomach, so occasionally, after lifting her palm for a coin, she picks up a grain of rice and inserts it into her mouth. She wishes someone would simply take her baby away, so she could crawl to a corner and die. Or go to sleep right here, in the middle of the sidewalk in front of the Durbar High School, with its screaming children, with Rani Pokhari in front of her. Her eyes are drawn to the water, its glitter under the sun, the ripples raised by a breeze.

Ranjana saw more:

The mist swirls around her as she walks into the parade ground in the half-light of early morning. The baby cries as she lowers him behind a bush. She's aware that the homeless old man with the goatlike beard, the one who keeps to himself and looks away furtively when he meets a person's eyes, is sleeping under the khari tree nearby. She straightens up and, casting a last look at her baby, walks north toward the pond. When she reaches it, she finds an opening in the bars, and slips through. In her mind's ear she hears her baby crying, and for a second she considers making a mad dash back to the infant boy. But she jumps in, then thrashes her arms and legs about, in the hope that the motion will buoy her back to the pond's surface. But she is descending deeper, and water quickly fills her lungs. She keeps whipping her arms and legs, and in the last minute before her world turns completely dark, with feeble awareness, she flings out a prayer. And her prayer shoots up through the churning water, breaks the surface, and jets into the air, soaring through the sky then down toward the khari tree, where it lands on the forehead of the goat-bearded derelict, who hears a baby crying in his dreams.

The last day before spring break, Ranjana was walking back to her apartment from the university when she saw Amos coming from the other direction, on Church Street. Her first impulse was to run, for she didn't want him to even suspect that she was pregnant. But he'd already seen her, and as he approached, it struck her that he had, by this time, become an absolute stranger.

"You could have just said no," he told her, with a slight smile. "I would have left you alone. But not even answering e-mails?"

She didn't know what to say.

He waited, then said, "All right, you don't need to answer."

There was a brief, awkward silence; then Amos asked her whether she'd join him for a cup of coffee at the Starbucks nearby.

As she and Amos drank their Frappuccinos, which he bought, they indulged in small talk, punctuated by long silences. Finally with a deep breath he informed her that he was moving to a new job at a public radio station in Boston. She congratulated him, wished him the best in his career. Outside, as they said goodbye, his expression registered disappointment, but he continued to smile, told her he'd keep her updated. Clearly he hoped she'd encourage him to keep in touch, but she had nothing else to say.

By April Ranjana stopped attending classes completely, and by early May she'd moved to a tiny studio apartment in Skokie whose address she didn't divulge to anyone, not even Angela and Yuko. The apartment cost six hundred dollars a month, and she had about seven thousand dollars, money she was supposed to use toward next semester's tuition; that would help her survive for a while. "Don't tell my parents I've moved out, please!" she said to her roommates, unsmiling, as she stood in the doorway, wearing her overcoat. The temperature outside had already climbed to sixty degrees Fahrenheit. "Just tell them I'm studying somewhere." Before she left, she added, "And send me an e-mail if they call."

By this time she knew that she was going to give birth to the baby. Thoughts of abortion appeared ridiculous. Yet she also felt an urgent need to hide her baby; the world would pounce upon it if she didn't. To shield her baby, she stayed in her room most days, eating a banana here, some nuts there, ramen noodles, scrambled eggs, and Swad-brand microwave packets of alu bhaji, eggplant curry, tofu, and potatoes.

She worried about Ma and Papa, and when Angela sent her e-mails saying they had called from Nepal, she went down to the pay phone a block from her apartment, under the awning of the Chinese store. Its owner, a lady not more than four and a half feet tall, always put in a roll or two of seaweed for her, free. "Good for your health, hanh!" she said as she handed Ranjana her bag of groceries.

On the phone with her parents, Ranjana pretended that she was exhausted because she was juggling three intensive summer classes. Just tell them what's happening, a voice in the back of her mind exhorted her. They're your parents, they'll understand. But of course she said nothing of the sort. "I'm fine, Ma," she said. "Just tired, that's all. Don't worry if you don't hear from me. Once these summer classes are over, I'll be so relieved. I miss home, Ma."

In the sultry evenings of July, as she poured soy sauce onto the noodles left over from lunch, she tried hard to remember whether she had brushed her teeth that morning. When the confinement of the room became too much, she'd board the city buses and ride them all day, traveling from Skokie to Des Plaines to Northbrook. She wouldn't meet the eyes of South Asians she saw on the bus, in the streets, or outside the newspaper stands, fearing that they might be Nepalis she'd met at a party. They'd ask her what she was doing, how her classes were going; their gaze might travel to her belly, note how big she'd become. But the oversized coat was more than adequate to camouflage her pregnancy—it turned her body into one shapeless mass. If anything, she appeared to have no fashion sense,

someone who didn't know what suited her and what didn't, someone who might even be a bit absent-minded, not all together in the
mind department. And she lived up to that image. For minutes she
could look out of the bus window and see nothing; out on the street
or in her room, she'd find that she was whispering to herself.

She wondered if someone at the university — a professor, a student from one of her classes, a secretary, perhaps someone at the
international center — had noted her absence, had been troubled by
her failing grades for the spring semester. She worried that Papa
and Ma might call the university, then she dismissed that fear — they
wouldn't know whom to talk to. I should pick up the phone and call
them and let them know I am all right, she thought, but she knew
that if she did, her voice would break, and Ma would sense that
something was terribly wrong. In any case, Ma and Papa must have
sensed that something was amiss. Why wouldn't they? For days now
she hadn't gone down to the public library to use the computer, to
check her e-mail, afraid of the panicked messages from them that
she'd find.

She was sitting in her apartment, listless, her palm over her belly,
when she was seized by the idea that there was nothing for her in
America anymore. She'd already fallen off her academic track, she
didn't have any friends she could, or wanted to, talk to about her situation, and Amos, even if she wanted to see him, was somewhere
in Boston. Logic told her that it was here, in America, that she could
give birth to the baby and lead a secluded life, just she and her child,
at least for a few years before she came out of hiding. Her remaining
money would probably last her until the baby's birth, after which
she could find a job, perhaps in the Chinese grocery store owned by
the tiny, kind lady, or as a cook or a waitress in some restaurant. She
could lose herself in this country, maybe even move to another state,
another town, disappear forever, with her baby. A bit of romance
colored this scenario, she realized, and every time it ran through her
mind — she, a working mother with a child in America, hiding from
everyone — it rang false, as though she was pondering the life of a

woman she didn't know. Besides, she could not imagine doing that to Ma and Papa.

There's nothing for you here anymore, the voice inside her kept insisting. She opened her window and looked out. Outside her apartment building was a park. An old Indian couple sat on a bench near the children's playground, the man in his safari suit and a baseball cap, the woman in her sari, with a large tika on her forehead; the two watched the children swing and slide. The facial features and the dark complexion of the couple told Ranjana that they were most likely South Indians. The woman had something bundled in her lap, which she kept passing on to the man, who would fumble with it, then toss something into his mouth. Peanuts. The couple had bought some unshelled peanuts from the Chinese grocery store and carried them to the park, just as they'd do back in India. They didn't talk. The woman passed the peanuts to her husband, and they both shelled them and popped them into their mouth, as their eyes followed the antics of the children, none of whom were dark enough to be their grandchildren. Ranjana watched in fascination, tears forming in her eyes.

Ranjana was in a daze as she boarded a plane at O'Hare Airport three days later. Fellow passengers glanced at her with curiosity: her outsized overcoat and large sunglasses both disguised her and made her stand out. Over the past two nights she hadn't slept, and even on the plane, whenever she closed her eyes she pictured the disappointment on her parents' faces when they saw how big she'd become. She would break their hearts — this thought kept hounding her as she switched planes at Heathrow, as she waited overnight in the Delhi transit lounge for her connection. By the time the plane landed in Kathmandu the next morning, she was almost feverish with apprehension. Her fingers trembled as she tried to complete the immigration and customs forms, and a woman standing nearby helped her. The woman told her she looked familiar, asked her who her parents were, in the event that she knew them, and Ranjana, in disoriented anxiety, stuttered that she grew up abroad.

When she cleared customs and emerged into the open air, she expected someone to recognize her, a relative, a friend of Ma and Papa, an old classmate, but no one shouted her name, no one leapt toward her with exclamations of surprise. A taxi driver was already at her heels, asking her in English where she wanted to go, and she responded to him, in English, that she wanted to go to Thamel, to a hotel. She couldn't go home, not yet. Better find a cheap hotel first, to get her bearings. "Madam, madam, this way," the taxi driver said, shoving aside other taxi drivers who also wanted her business. She got into his taxi, which took off quickly, exiting the airport area and cruising down the Ring Road toward Gaushala.

More than a year had passed since she left Kathmandu, and nothing had changed: the same litter on the streets, the emaciated stray dogs trotting across the Ring Road, the sweaty porters bent over, carrying loads on their backs. Here she was, back home permanently but unable to instruct the taxi driver to take her home, where, under different circumstances, she'd have flung the door wide open in joy. As the taxi passed the Gaushala intersection and raced down the hill toward Ratopul, she slid further into her seat, fearing that someone on the street would spot her. Her mouth tasted acidic, and she felt nauseated. She stroked her belly.

"Which hotel, madam?" the taxi driver asked when they reached Keshar Mahal.

"Take me to a cheap one." She had lapsed into Nepali.

The driver eyed her in his rearview mirror. "I thought you were Indian."

"Take me to a hotel that's not in the main area. Something a bit secluded."

The driver turned left into a side road, then right again, and came to a halt at a building with a sign that said Swagat Hotel.

She decided, as she entered the hotel's tiny lobby, that she would continue to pretend she was a tourist, perhaps an Indian one, and speak only English. Fewer questions asked that way. A single room at the hotel cost twenty dollars a day, which wasn't much, and if she looked around, she could probably find an even cheaper one that was also livable. But she didn't have the energy or the motivation to search for another. Besides, if she wandered off into the streets, someone might recognize her.

In her room, she opened the window to breathe in some fresh air. The evening sun illuminated the houses below with an orange glare. There was a patch of ground below where a couple of boys were kicking a ball. One of them, after a particularly vigorous kick, looked up and noticed her and shouted, "Hello, missus! How are you? *Naakvari singan chakvari goo!*" The outrageousness of what he uttered — a not-so-pleasant scatological ditty she recalled from her own childhood — made her laugh. She waved at the boys, then shut her window.

Although the hotel was in an area that didn't see throngs of tourists, at night it was still noisy; shouts and hollers from late-night revelers drifted up to her room. Her sleep was fitful. She dreamt of Ma and Papa silently yelling her name from the large glass screen in Millennium Park. She was swimming in a pond; then the water became as heavy as syrup, dragging her down.

At about five she awoke, tired, and after washing her face, went for a walk. A morning mist was hovering. She wore her overcoat, and for good measure had wrapped a scarf around her head; but at this time of day, the chance of running into anyone who'd know her was slim. So she allowed herself to enjoy the sounds of a lone bicycle bell ringing in the distance and the sight of two farmers carrying spinach and radishes in their kharpan to the market, their baskets swaying as they walked. She headed toward the city center; the lack of a good night's sleep made her head hurt, though not too unpleasantly. She walked quickly into Asan, where vendors already were displaying their fresh vegetables; then she emerged into Ratna Park. She circled Rani Pokhari and stood watching the water from under the area of the Ghantaghar clock tower, inside the Tri-Chandra campus. The morning sun was glinting on the pond.

I am not that weak, Ranjana whispered to herself. No. I will survive this.

She moved down Kantipath toward Lainchour, and walked past

414

the western gates of the royal palace, where Papa had long ago mocked the palace guards and traumatized Ma. But now, following the king's ouster, the palace had been turned into a museum and a government office, and it no longer looked formidable.

She went past the Dairy, past the Jagadamba School, where Ma and Papa had fallen in love, and turned left into Thamel. Two blocks away from the Swagat Hotel, she was in the neighborhood where her parents had spent their early years of marriage, where her younger brother was born. Ma had shown her the house once, during Ranjana's early teens, and now she tried to remember where it was. It stood a little bit off by itself, she remembered, not attached to any neighboring structures, as most houses were in this area. Then, abruptly, she was facing it: an old house, with crumbling bricks and carved peacock windows, which is how she recognized it. It didn't seem that the house had been renovated at all since Ma and Papa had lived here, more than two decades ago. This was unusual — most of the city's old dwellings were being torn down and replaced with towering multistory cement buildings, which dwarfed the neighboring homes and crowded the skyline. A sign hung on the second-floor wall, a TO LET that had been revised to TOILET.

A tea shop across the street from the house was just opening its doors. Ranjana asked the shop owner if she could get a cup of tea. The woman sleepily nodded, then turned on her gas and set the water to boil. Ranjana sat on a stool outside and looked at the house. After a short time, the window on the third floor opened, and an elderly woman with gray hair appeared, rubbing her eyes. She spat out the window, then stared toward the horizon, lost in thought. The shop owner brought Ranjana her tea, and she slurped it thirstily, hoping its warmth would drive some of the cobwebs from her mind. But the more she drank, the more she felt weepy. Here she was, more than eight months pregnant, back in Kathmandu, without the knowledge of her parents, who, a mere half-hour ride to the north, must be worried sick about their daughter. Oh Papa, Oh Ma, she cried silently. I am right here, looking at your old flat in Thamel.

Sensing the girl's distress, the shopkeeper asked, "What's the matter, bahini? Anything wrong?"

Ranjana shook her head. She clasped her arms around her own shoulders, as if she were feeling cold, and asked the woman, "Do you know if anyone has taken that flat up there?"

"Oh, that? It's been empty for months now, I think. The room is small, that's why. But the rent is reasonable, from what I've heard. Why do you ask? Are you looking for a place to stay?"

"Maybe," Ranjana said, then paid for the tea and went back to her hotel.

She picked up her bag from her room and checked out downstairs at the counter. Within half an hour she was back at the old house in Thamel. She didn't know why she was doing this, for she had enough money to secure a better room elsewhere, in a newer house. But this was where Ma and Papa had spent many happy days, and she felt that she owed something to that past, even if she couldn't, in the present, reveal to them what they would surely see as a betrayal of their trust. She climbed the stairs and knocked on the door on the third floor. The woman who opened it was the one who'd appeared at the window earlier.

Looking at the woman's kindly face, Ranjana knew that this was the house where she would give birth to her baby, who, by its vigorous kicks, was letting her know that it was almost time.

A Birth

R AJA WOULD FLY Thai Airlines — good service, smooth ride, people said — to Bangkok; from there, he'd proceed to Los Angeles, where he'd board an American Airlines flight to Chicago. Umesh would be waiting for him at the airport. How long would Raja actually stay in America? Though he and Nilu had estimated one month, he knew the real answer: until we find her, or her body — this had been their silent understanding. As the moment of Raja's flight approached, Nilu had to fight back her guilt about sending Raja on what might be a fool's errand. But how could she persuade anyone, including Raja, to believe her unusual yet remarkably strong intuition about her daughter? This was the best way: with Raja in America, she'd be able to focus on her search, on following her instincts, without his questions raising doubts in her mind. And, if by some chance she was completely wrong, at least one parent would be in America to search there.

Within hours of his departure, the empty house became desolate, and Nilu wondered if she'd turned into a foolish old woman. If Ranjana is still in America, I'll slit my own throat, she thought that night, after turning off the bedroom light. Earlier that evening, to distract herself from thinking about Raja, she turned on the television, which she hadn't watched for days. The news carried the usual reports about bickering between the leading political parties, then moved on to an item about a religious group in the city. Nilu's mind began to wander, and she was about to turn off the TV when the photo of a bearded man, in the screen inset, caught her attention. He had fierce eyes and a dark beard and dark mustache that hid most of his face, but the resemblance was unmistakable. But it couldn't be, could it?

Swami Shiva, the newscaster said. Nilu slowly sat up straight. An emerging spiritual leader in the city, the newscaster called him, someone who had stepped forward and valiantly led his disciples since the death of the group's founder several years ago. In a few days Swami Shiva would be conducting a mass meditation session in Tundikhel, where spiritual and religious groups from throughout South Asia were congregating to observe silence and chant and pray for world peace. The news showed a short clip of Swami Shiva's interview: he spoke slowly, deliberately, his pink lips glistening underneath his beard. "Given the turbulence in our world today, given our own country's recent decade of bloodshed and destruction, it is essential that we learn how to harness our minds and our emotions. This mass gathering is a way to concentrate the peaceful energy that exists in all of us, and send it upward, outward, into the world, so that it touches everyone, opens their eyes in awareness, makes them realize the beauty of existence. That's how we create a world of harmony."

Had it not been for his burning, troubled eyes, Nilu might not have recognized Shiva, for he spoke differently now, more deliberately, more carefully, as though each word had consequence.

For a few minutes, Nilu stared at the screen, entranced by the images of Shiva speaking to his disciples in a serene setting, sitting lotus style, as the TV reporter commented on his rising popularity. But apart from the shock of recognizing him, Nilu felt nothing about this Shiva, this swami. Moreover, she couldn't waste energy contemplating how the Shiva she knew had turned into a guru. She had to keep her mind focused on Ranjana, and she had to find her quickly.

Where was that photo of Ranjana, taken outside the Sears Tower? She couldn't find it where she'd seen it last, so she began to ransack her cupboard. As she was sorting through an old shoebox, her fingers stumbled onto something. For a split second she didn't know what it was. Then she recognized it, Lama-ji's rudraksha, which he'd said would help protect her, bring her luck. Some luck! She was about to toss it across the room, but she restrained herself; then, inexplicably, she slipped it into her bag. She found the photo a few minutes later, in one of Raja's books that he'd been planning to take with him; obviously he'd forgotten it.

Nilu turned off the light and lay down in bed. Sleep, she commanded herself. Sleep now so that you'll have strength and clarity of mind tomorrow. But of course she slept poorly, and by four o'clock she was wired and wide-awake and ready to go.

For the next few days, she ransacked the city. She hopped on buses and taxis and microbuses and tempos. She entered and exited lanes and alleys and side roads and back streets. She went into malls and department stores and markets surging with shoppers, wove her way through traffic jams and chakka jams, ignored people she knew who saw her and called out her name, knocked on the doors of houses and apartment complexes and condos. She had tucked in her bag a photo of Ranjana, which she produced for strangers as she asked whether they'd seen anyone resembling this girl.

Most people shook their head and looked at her strangely, as though she was a madwoman. One portly man exclaimed, "Oh, yes, oh yes!" and Nilu's heart fluttered with hope, but it turned out he was excited because he'd recognized Ranjana's face from the tabloid newspaper. The man expressed sympathy for Nilu, reminded her that America was the kind of place where young girls' bodies were hacked to pieces and thrown in dumpsters, where sexual predators cruised the highways. Other people consoled her, offered her tea. Others still, touching her arm, told her that they'd keep an eye out for her daughter, and they'd let Nilu know — wouldn't she give them her phone number? — if they found her.

In New Road she paused outside Prateema's house. She missed her friend and wished she was around, just so she could talk to her. After Prateema quit teaching, she found work at an NGO focusing on literacy in remote villages. Soon thereafter she'd fallen in love with a Bengali widower from Calcutta, who was in Kathmandu to work for the United Nations. The two had met at the Yak and Yeti Hotel during a program on literacy in Nepal, and Prateema said that it was love at first sight.

"That he's a Bengali is only a coincidence, Nilu. It's a connection forged in some past life."

"Is that what your Lama-ji told you?"

"No, no. That's what I feel, and that's what Dev feels too. I do wish, though, that Lama-ji still offered consultations. But now he has turned into a full-time businessman, focusing only on real estate."

Prateema had married Dev and moved to Calcutta with him, where she reported that she was very happy. She and Nilu talked occasionally on the phone. "I have never felt so satisfied, Nilu. Who knew that I could find happiness at this age?"

Nilu stopped outside Bir Hospital, watching hundreds of people go into Tundikhel, where Swami Shiva was about to lead the mass meditation. Some, judging from the way they were swaying, how their eyes had a faraway misty look, had already entered a transcendental state. Police vans and trucks had lined the street in case of riots and mayhem, but they were respectful of the meditators and cleared the path for them.

From her vantage point outside Bir Hospital, Nilu could make out a saffron-clad figure, seated inside the amphitheater and facing the participants. She couldn't see his face, which she didn't mind; she didn't know what emotions it might stir. The mike carried Swami Shiva's voice to her. "Let us begin with a chant for universal energy. Repeat after me. Om."

As the crowd's voice rose to the sky in unison, Nilu left her spot and moved away, into Mahabouddha, then Asan. The chanting followed her for a while, but the familiar din and clamor of the

Asan vegetable market overpowered it. Intuition guided her toward Thamel.

She entered and exited hotels, including the Kathmandu Guest House, where she and Raja had found sanctuary ages ago. No nostalgia, she told herself sternly. She began knocking on doors of residences; she was inching closer to their old flat. She lifted her head to scan the windows of the houses. Most had tourist shops or eateries on the ground floor, with people living above them. A sense of urgency overcame Nilu. She showed Ranjana's photo to the shopkeepers, who shook their heads. The sun shone hard, making her sweat. Her ears buzzed from exhaustion. She stopped at a shop for a Fanta, and as she reached into her bag to pay, she spotted Lama-ji's rudraksha hiding beneath a stash of bills, keys, a lipstick, and a mirror. She fished it out and enclosed it in her fist, feeling its rough surface bite into her palm.

A boy began to follow her. At first she didn't even notice him, but when she did, she observed that he wore a school uniform: blue shirt and blue half-pants. The boy didn't look at her face; he merely tagged along two feet behind her. She turned to stare at him, and he looked away; as soon as she moved, he moved with her. She knocked at the door of a house and showed Ranjana's photo to the middle-aged woman who opened it. The woman told her that she hadn't seen Ranjana. When Nilu turned around, the boy was standing in front of her. "What are you staring at?" she asked him. "Haven't you seen a woman before?"

The boy sweetly smiled at her and said, "I know who you're looking for."

"Who? How do you know?"

He reached over and tapped the photo that Nilu clasped between her fingers.

"Have you seen her?" Nilu asked. "Around here?"

"Maybe."

"What do you mean maybe? Either you have or you haven't. Don't waste my time for no reason."

"What will you give me, old mother?"

A warm shiver rose up Nilu's spine. Her legs felt weak, and she gazed at the boy intently for a few seconds. When she spoke, she spoke slowly. "What do you want?"

"I'm craving some alubada, old mother. It's been so long. There's a restaurant right there." He pointed to a house a few yards away. Nilu could hear the blast of its stove.

He took her by the hand and led her there. The eatery was small and cramped. She asked the man standing over boiled eggs and fritters and rasgullas floating in sweet syrup to give the boy two alubada. The man handed the boy a plate with the potatoes. The place was full, so they sat on two stools outside. The boy ate hungrily, chomping his food, curling his tongue around his lips to wipe off little dabs of sauce.

"How is it?" she asked him. She could hardly speak.

"Delicious, old mother," the boy said. He finished eating, wiped his mouth with the back of his hand, and said, "Now I'm ready. And you must also be in a hurry. Come." He reached out to hold her hand. She allowed herself to be led.

The boy paused at the house where they'd lived, Bhairavi's house. "Try this one. The second floor." He gave her hand a squeeze and headed down the street.

She watched him for a while, fighting back tears. No nostalgia, she reminded herself.

Inhaling deeply, she turned her attention to the old house, their old flat.

It couldn't be. This had to be a mistake.

Miraculously, the same old sign still hung on the house, the letters visible despite a film of dust. The house, close to two decades after she'd seen it last, remained the same. Did Bhairavi's family still live here?

The tiny door creaked as she pushed it open and entered. The wooden stairs were narrow, rickety, and she was aware of the thump of her feet as she climbed. Then she heard muffled moans somewhere above, and her heart beating faster, she hurried along. The sound of the voice became more distinct; it was accompanied by murmurs, certainly a woman's; and yet another voice, a third one, mingled with the others — she couldn't figure out whether it was a man's or a woman's. She raised her hand to knock at the second-floor door, then paused. A husband and wife could be sharing a private, amorous moment. How ridiculous would she look if she interrupted them to show them the photo of her daughter.

Then the moans got louder, followed by a gasp, which Nilu recognized. She banged on the door. There was pin-drop silence inside. Nilu waited, then banged again. "Open the door!" she said. After some more silence, there were some whispers. Someone shuffled toward the door, unlatched it, and opened it a couple of inches. An eye, a forehead, and a mouth of a woman. Bhairavi.

"What do you need?" Bhairavi asked, not recognizing Nilu immediately.

Nilu thrust the photo right next up against Bhairavi's eye. "Bhairavi, my daughter is in there!"

Bhairavi opened the door a bit more, her eyes wide in amazement. "Nilu?"

"Ranjana is in here, isn't she?"

"Ranjana?"

Someone inside cried, then appeared to stifle that cry.

"My daughter. Open the door, for God's sake, Bhairavi." This time she thrust her right foot into the gap between the door and the wall, so Bhairavi couldn't shut it.

Bhairavi opened the door and let Nilu in. Ranjana sat on the floor, her legs wide apart, her face contorted in pain; now, as she saw her mother, shock and shame complicated her feelings even more. She was about to give birth; Nilu glimpsed the baby's tiny head between the hands of another woman, who was trying to coax the infant from its mother's womb. Ranjana's back was against the window; a stream of light illuminated the scene.

"Chhori?" Nilu said.

Ranjana let out a piercing cry, and the baby plopped into the midwife's open palms; "It's a girl," she announced.

Part III

Kali

Kali was a chubby girl, with a naughty streak. "Like a dark monster," said friends and relatives, who had resigned themselves to the fact that Ranjana had birthed a child without benefit of marriage and that, quite shockingly, her parents had not only accepted the baby but doted on her. As though she was the product of a legitimate union, as though this child fulfilled their aspirations as grandparents!

"What do you expect?" some said. "The grandparents themselves did a lot of shacking up, together and separately, don't you remember?" And those who didn't recall the details received accounts of the grandparents' separation after their young son died, when Raja had a sitar-playing concubine and the mother had a young, jobless lover. "It runs in the family," people said. Sometimes the talk bothered Nilu and Raja, and they thought about asking Ranjana to allow them to find a husband for her, a decent man who'd be willing to take on a three-year-old girl as his own, someone who'd cushion them from the insults and accusations that Kali's birth had precipitated.

This idea of a marriage had first been floated when Nilu brought Ranjana and the baby home from Bhairavi's house, after Raja, stunned to hear of the turn of events, arrived home from Chicago.

But Ranjana had said, "I'm fine with it if that's what you want." Then she reconsidered. "But I don't really need a man." Nilu and

Raja had exchanged looks, understanding that to press her would be wrong, at least for the moment. They didn't want to lose Ranjana again. "Besides," Nilu said to Raja in the darkness of their bedroom, "we ourselves are not ready for a son-in-law, are we? Imagine a stranger in this house, demanding our deference, our samman."

"No, I can't imagine a stranger in this house," Raja said. "I can only imagine the three of us." Then, immediately he corrected himself. "The four of us." And she thought, Yes, we have to include the baby in our conversations, in our life now.

Ranjana hadn't told them who the father was, and even after three years they didn't know what had happened with her daughter, why she'd gotten pregnant, why she'd decided to go forward with the pregnancy instead of getting an abortion in a country where it was easy and safe. And the most baffling of all: why had she decided to return to Nepal and give birth to her baby in an old house in the middle of the city, hiding from her parents?

But Ranjana's silence, the way she averted her eyes when the conversation turned to her days in America, told them that she considered that chapter closed. Judging from the darkness of the baby's skin — "as dark as coal," someone had said cruelly but accurately — and her curly hair, the father had to be an American black, "a habsi," the same person had condescendingly noted.

Nastiness followed that observation.

"Chee!!" people said. "A baby with a habsi father. Disgusting! These kaleys are the worst. Mugging, drugging, murders, riots — you name it, and these blacks are the ones behind it. I mean, if she was going to get pregnant over there, why not choose a kuirey, a white man? At least the baby would come out decent-looking. Look at this baby girl now — as dark as black smoke, as sewage water."

Kali's real name was Binita, but as she grew up, Ranjana began to call her Kali, in defiance of people's disdain for the color of her skin. "She is dark, and she ought to be proud of it," she said to Nilu and Raja.

Whenever Nilu and Raja — mostly Raja — asked about who the father was, why things had happened the way they had, Ranjana

428

clammed up. Over the years they learned not to persist, fearing that their insistence could seem like badgering and push Ranjana away, along with Kali. Yes, in that sense their daughter had changed. Ranjana had always been stubborn but had used charm to navigate difficult situations. Now, her refusal to tell this particular story seemed to reveal a peculiar hardness of heart. The look on her face was tougher, perhaps a defense against the criticisms that had been showered upon her. Her jaw had tightened, and her eyes, except when they fell upon Kali, were wary, distrustful. She didn't utter a word about Kali's father; she said little about her life in America. Not important, not relevant, her eyes told anyone else who happened to ask.

"She's aged, our daughter," Nilu said to Raja in the quiet of their bedroom.

And Raja said, "At least we found her."

Raja seemed astonished at the sequence of events: Ranjana's disappearance; his own short trip to America; Nilu's premonition about her daughter's return to the city; the dark baby girl who now ran around the house like a small tornado, demanding their attention and devotion; the scandal that had erupted, alienating some friends and relatives. Amazingly, Nilu and Raja had withstood all of it and still managed to smile at everyone, especially their granddaughter, whose demands they could not ignore, whom they showered with gifts and kisses at every opportunity, and who had become a noisy, vexing, delightful, integral part of their household.

As time went by, they stopped wondering who Kali's father was. By the time the girl turned five and started attending kindergarten, Ranjana was working for a public relations firm and taking evening courses at a nearby college. Nilu and Raja had also stopped thinking about a husband for Ranjana, a father for the girl. Their daughter hadn't shown any interest in a man, and they'd concluded that if she wasn't interested, they themselves had no reason to be. Over time people's criticisms had softened, and Nilu and Raja had once again attended gatherings among friends and relatives. Ranjana often refused to go but didn't object if they took Kali along. And unflappable Kali, it seemed, most especially loved visiting the houses of those who sneered at her dark skin, at her unknown father. If she noticed subtle mistreatment, Kali chose to ignore it. When she visited, she led children on rambunctious adventures in the yard or the neighborhood, which elicited a plethora of complaints. Once, a relative called her habsi, and somehow Kali seemed to know what that meant, for she told the relative, "Yes, I am habsi and proud of it. My mama has told me to be proud of it."

Kali got along well with Muwa, who, although bedridden and unable to speak, was still alive. The little girl delighted in using hand signs to communicate with her great-grandmother. The two developed a code, a mishmash of regular sign language and their own innovations; especially in company, they loved to carry on secret conversations. Muwa's drinking, although somewhat diminished, nonetheless continued. Her trembling fingers still groped for the bottle of vodka underneath her bed, but not when Kali was around. When her great-granddaughter visited, Muwa became energized and, with Sumit's help, got out of bed. She let Kali lead her down the stairs to the garden, where she sat in a chair and watched the girl kick a soccer ball toward a goalpost constructed of two poles; Sumit acted as goalie. Muwa's hand frequently reached to tousle Kali's hair, to stroke her cheeks; at times Nilu had to look away because a lump was rising in her throat.

If Kali ever wondered about her father, she didn't show it. In the second and third grades, the family was twice summoned to the school because Kali had beaten up a boy. Although the girl had been reluctant to divulge the reason for the fight, it became apparent that in both cases the other party had made a reference to her absent father and commented rudely about her mother. In both cases, Nilu and Raja and Ranjana suspected that the insult to the mother had provoked the scuffle. In both instances, the boy was the one who suffered — split lips, black eyes, broken fingers.

She was a boisterous girl, with thunderous footsteps. Without meaning to, she tended to break or shatter household objects — toys, cups and glasses, vases, windowpanes. She took up a lot of space — even more than her large physical size required.

Yet Kali was also a softie — she cried easily at the suffering of others, especially animals, which reminded Nilu of Maitreya. One day Kali entered the house, cradling in her palm a baby bird with a broken wing; it had fallen onto their veranda. For hours she didn't let anyone touch it, ignoring the frantic chirping of the mother bird, which had fluttered and pranced on the nearby tree. Another day she brought home, from an alley nearby, a puppy with a broken leg. The adults were forced to take it to the vet. Then, of course, the puppy had to stay with them. To suggest otherwise would have made Kali tear down the house. Nilu and Raja and Ranjana marveled at how adeptly, and with what astounding seriousness, Kali took care of the puppy. She named it Kalibhai, after herself — the dog was her brother.

Kali's softest spot was reserved for her mother; she was particularly sensitive to Ranjana's moods. Slowly Ranjana's face seemed to be shedding the grim expression it had acquired in America, and now she smiled more. But still there were days when a cloud of melancholy hung over her head. If she was thinking about her days in America, about "that man," as Nilu and Raja had come to think of Kali's father, she didn't let on. But Ranjana wasn't lost in thought or sad reveries; her behavior made it clear that she was yearning for something other than "that man." Nilu and Raja couldn't put their finger on what it was, and perhaps they never would. But her experience in America had fundamentally changed her, and she seemed to be carrying not only her own burdens but also someone else's.

Kali was so attuned to her mother that at the slightest shift in mood, she'd abandon her toys and her friends and seek out her mother's lap, where she'd talk to Ranjana in a consoling voice and caress her face.

Mother and daughter often fell asleep on the living room sofa; Kali's thick arms surrounded Ranjana, whose head lay on her daughter's lap. Watching them, Nilu thought it was hard to tell who was the child and who was the adult. Ranjana furrowed her forehead now and then, and Kali, whose left palm rested on her mother's face, stroked her eyebrows gently.

Nilu turned from the mother and the daughter and went to the window. Raja was sitting in the garden, hunched over the plastic table, writing on his laptop. Over the past couple of years Raja, in addition to his job at Nepal Yatra, had began to publish columns in newspapers and magazines. Often these pieces were highly critical of the government, of the misdeeds that went on in the ministries and secretariats.

A few months ago he'd been called into the Hanuman Dhoka police station, where a high-ranking officer had interrogated him, inquired about his party affiliation, and asked him what he meant by specific points in the offending column. Nilu hadn't known about this brief detention until Raja reached home in the evening, and initially he'd not told her anything. But during the course of the evening meal he revealed that he had "visited" Hanuman Dhoka. Nilu asked him whether he'd gone there to interview someone. Raja shook his head, and said that he'd been called in for a "friendly inquiry." Nilu immediately understood what it was all about. Over the past few months, several journalists and editors had been hauled off for questioning. But she said nothing in front of Kali, or Ranjana, who, cutting her daughter's pizza into bite-size pieces, appeared not to be paying attention to what her father was saying. In bed later, Raja told Nilu what had happened, how he'd finally been let go with a warning. Nilu lay with her hand on her chest. She clasped Raja's palm and put it on top of her heart, which was beating rapidly. "Raja, don't do anything foolish, please."

"At this age, even if I tried, I couldn't do anything foolish."

"You don't have to take on the burden of the whole country," she said. "You don't have to write about everything that's wrong. There'll always be things that are wrong. Sometimes also write about things that are right with us. After all, we have come far, haven't we?"

"Yes, we have," Raja said, sighing and leaning back against his pillow. "That's why it's important to remain alert. Otherwise . . ."

"Otherwise what?"

"Otherwise things will fall apart."

"And the center cannot hold? You've been reading Chinua Achebe lately. Or Yeats."

He laughed, then put his hand over his mouth because Kali and Ranjana were sleeping next door. "All right, my next piece will be a positive one."

And although in the next few articles Raja traced the country's achievements since the end of the Rana rule in the 1950s, criticisms still crept in. The piece he was working on now was a frontal attack on the prime minister, charging him with corruption, detailing his oversized foreign bank accounts where, Raja wrote, European companies had deposited large amounts for profitable contracts in Nepal. Nilu had stumbled upon the article only because Raja had printed out a draft of it, with his margin notes, and apparently forgotten it on the dining room table. As she read it, her body turned cold.

When she returned to the dining room table an hour later, the draft was gone. She thought of confronting Raja about it, asking him to tone it down. "What will I do, Raja, if they take you away?" she wanted to say. "What'll I do if they do something to you?" Then she realized how melodramatic she sounded, like a silly housewife in a movie, or a novel. This is what Raja wanted to do as he approached old age, this is what was important to him. It excited him, made him walk with a spring in his step. At fifty-five, he was growing his hair long, as he did during those Thamel days, and sometimes when she looked at him she saw her old Raja, commanding the streets with his long strides, planting kisses on her in front of her students, observing the people who walked below their windows and waxing poetic about them.

Now, his back to her, he was typing away furiously on his laptop.

ACKNOWLEDGMENTS

I would like to thank the following people and institutions for their support in the writing of this novel: Indiana University's College Arts and Humanities Institute, for providing me with course release to work on the initial drafts of this book; Kanak Dixit, Amar Gurung, and Sajan Subedi of Kathmandu's Madan Puraskar Library, for allowing me access to their invaluable archive of Nepali newspapers; my longtime friends Thakur Rijal and Nirjhar Sherchan, for entertaining many of my pesky questions; my editor, Anjali Singh, for making this book smarter; my agent, Eric Simonoff, for always looking after my best interest; my wife, Babita, for reading and rereading numerous drafts of the book; and my parents, for buying me a typewriter when I was fifteen so I could begin seeing myself as a writer.